/
RISING

WHEN A RIOT BECOMES THE REVOLUTION

ROSKO JAHL-BENNY

Includes
Appendices,
Footnotes, Glossary,
Turin's Rules.

You should know this and remember, I am not Ash and Meko is not Meko; these are just names. Meko knows me as Ash and I know her as Meko, but we know these are just names and will change and must. To you I will always be Ash, and this goes for everybody that I talk to you about; to you the names will remain the same. You can be whoever you want to be, even yourself, and be it always without change. Our identities have to change, and often. There are reasons for this and the reasons are very good. That's just the way it is.

CHAPTER 1

With my necker pulled up and my hood down, all black and grey, I'm just another shadow. That's good, we don't attract attention, it's a rule. I stand waiting in the shadow of a doorway. I look out, I observe.

I watch the street lamps fizz and pop. I see them fling cascades of sparks down through the clammy, damp atmosphere. In the mildly acid, saturating mist, everything corrodes. They flicker blue against the iridescent sky, or whatever it is that hangs dull above our heads and catches the perpetual light show from The City. The City that was once a capital, now just a fun park.

Across the walkway one of the lamps hums in darkness whilst it considers whether to have another go. They usually do, and it does. It grumbles into shining brightly its deathly white before fading back to blue, then flickering out again, nice try. But it still hums. Everything and everywhere hums in Urbia; there is never silence.

Doorways are usually sealed off with a grill, this one's rare. It's big enough for six or more baggers, but they must be on holiday. I have a good view, a ringside seat.

Baggers wander the streets by day and street-sleep by night. They doss down sharing something that lifts them out of this world into the fantasy of another. Then sometime after the grey night has dawned into another grey day, they splash back down into a cold, damp reality. They never last long though. Soon they get collected and taken off to Rehab and the holiday of a lifetime from where they'll never touch down again. Goodnight Vienna!

Across the street from my doorway and to the right is The Bakery. That is what I'm watching. That's why I'm waiting. That's why we are here, Meko and I. To the right of The Bakery an old steel bridge carries a long disused track towards The City. Beneath it a couple of alkies shrink back into the friendly darkness between some supporting pillars. They saw the reflected yellow light of a vehicle pan across the bridge and they feared it was coming their way. Andy patrol vehicles have yellow lights. Gradually the alkies reappear, peeking out like rats, then one of them darts into the road and tries to pick up a smoke he dropped in his panic. Bending down he loses his balance, cracks his head on the road and lies motionless, curled up like a foetus. The other sneaks out, goes through his pockets, picks up the smoke and staggers off into the blackness beneath the bridge, leaving his buddy to take his chances with any passing truck.

Light over the bridge picks out the mist as it falls in spirals. It settles on the ground, runs down walls, drips from roofs, streams from gantries, makes rivulets that course into puddles that collect, then it cascades into the sewers that echo below. You see it, feel it through to your bones and hear it all the time. It's been like it as long as we care to remember, but we don't care to. Old folk sit in bars and talk about the last dry spell. Why? Because they'll never see another. A few months ago they found a web footed rat. If nature's given up on a dry spell, you can bet it's going to be wet; that's all you need to know. If you hope for anything better, you hope in vain; that's the same with everything, and everyone.

Well, not everyone.

The walls of glass that tower above, glisten with a chaotic palette of flashing neon that echoes across the roof tops from a nearby city get-through. It decorates the sky above but not the black felt space down here. Outside my doorway the only illumination besides another perpetually spluttering street lamp, is the pale cream light that sprawls out from The Bakery window. It trips across the walkways, hops into the street and follows the rain down a gently chortling culvert. The Bakery is all that's round here, which is perfect. Brick walled alleys lead in every direction, under, round, and through the silent blocks above. In six hours or so the morning siren, keen to see a job well done, will bring out the responsible workers and then these alleyways will throb with their regulation footwear as they walk to their regulation stations in the glass walled towers above. They'll tap screens and crunch numbers until the same siren, now disillusioned, tells them it's had enough of their tapping and crunching and they might as well go home and try again tomorrow.

Suddenly a yellow pod drops through the swirling mist and not before time. It nearly hits the office blocks on all sides, cuts its retros too soon and falls the last few feet. At best, day or night, you can only just pick out the gantries where the surveillance pods dock. During the night, the grey blanket that is the sky is illuminated by the pod beams and The City light spill, so the difference here between day and night is just another grey. At night the farms used to light up the horizon, but I haven't seen that since I was a small boy, not even from a high rise.

The pod lands between The Bakery and my doorway, slithers on the wet tarmac and bounces off an old twentieth century post box that the souvenir department has painted yellow. They're yellow because too many people bumped into them when they were red. They used to be red, because they always were. What they were, was the reason they were preserved. Now they're yellow the souvenir department wonders if they're worth preserving because they don't look like they used to.

The pod spins a couple of rotations before settling uneasily. A long scratch now runs through the corp insignia, '4U' and the PR line 'Giving people what they deserve'. These are just BGbots, body guards, not full security bots but more than the average surveillance type. The wing doors lift and the bots, dressed in simulated tuxedos and black ties, begin to struggle out. The door nearest to me malfunctions and drops suddenly. It pushes the bot back into the pod who then thinks it's under attack. His auto pistols fire and the door is blown off its hinges. It cartwheels across the walkway and lands up spinning like a top under the bridge. The other bot squeaks at him and they bicker like two demented parakeets as they walk up the steps to The Bakery.

Every night our two targets call in for a bag of doughnuts and to listen to Ernie Finglestene play his antique piano while his wife shouts the orders to the kitchen above. They are high ranking execs, that's all it takes. BGbots are contracted to keep them safe, do all the stuff that real body guards are supposed to. It's a corp perk, a status symbol, but these bots are no defence and their arrogance makes it easier. All they do is let us know the execs are in the building. Bots can't eat doughnuts and don't understand music, nevertheless they rock their heads back and forth, tap their feet, smile at each other with a kind of limp gape, nodding as if they're having the time of their lives.

Then the cue I've been waiting for. The piano has stopped playing. Ernie's wife is no longer shouting orders. The killing ground is clear. I draw slowly back into the darkness of the doorway and the protection it gives. I shove in the earplugs as the targets get the message and scramble for the door. But it's too late.

The Bakery is sensibly obscured but the blinding flash bounces of every wet surface and for a millisecond everything is brilliantly illuminated like a bleached photo. A moment in time is revealed in its static brilliance like the flash of an old stills camera. The violent thump that accompanies it shakes the ground before a moment of respectful silence heralds everything crashing to earth, then the mayhem begins. Until the first scream, the opera that is the music and light show of a rapidly expanding golden ball of super heat ripping through a building, is perfection. I never get over it. It gilds its way down corridors, up stairwells, through doors and bursts out of windows. A harmony of destruction. The violence of creation. Part of a bot slides up to my doorway, bits of tuxedo smouldering around a molten cufflink. I consider it a memento, the vision that is. I record such visions and replay them often; I have a collection.

I step into the street where the drizzle sizzles on a scorched helmet, the chin strap is torn but most of the bots blackened head is still recognisable. Its lips have melted into a pout as if it's about to whistle. I kick it towards the remains of its partner squeaking something in bot which annoys me because I don't speak bot, and I would like to have collected its last words.

A gaping, ragged hole is now where The Bakery front used to be, the large window reduced to a powdered chandelier scattered amongst the rubble. It's a dark, wide open mouth and we have just knocked all the teeth out. The gums bleed a dusty white that mixes in rivulets of saliva dripping off tangled pipes and cables. Fragments of the ceiling remain supporting unsteady ovens and sinks in the wrecked kitchen above. A buckled pipe rains down a feint spray on the twisted wreckage that was once a counter. Several large tins are split and their contents, an assortment of flours, trickle down in wafting spirals. Like fine snow, it drifts across the puddles forming meandering paisley patterns of blood, herbs, and cooking oils. The kitchen window on the first floor hangs in pieces, one piece rocks like a crystal pendulum. It turns slowly one way, then back, then crashes to the ground spreading its shards over a fleshy human hand that grips a torn paper bag, but there are no doughnuts.

Above, in the kitchen, a faint orange glow is gathering strength. It begins to flicker yellow, it cracks then pops. Something smashes and a fierce blue green flash is born that bounces against a hard white ceiling. A spinning ball of pale blue smoke escapes followed by a black and grey cloud, billowing and twisting into the night sky. A fire is taking hold.

Ernie's piano has lost its legs and has been blown up against a wall near my doorway. Meka appears out of her shadow and walks across the debris littered space towards me. She stops by my side and we both look at the piano and listen. It rests beneath a fractured rainwater pipe that spits and splutters its contents onto the naked strings so it sounds as if Ernie is still playing, this time a lament.

Meko leans towards me and whispers,
'Water music?'

An intermittent scream, gathering volume, echoes from within the gaping mouth, as if still shouting orders. It becomes a cursing mumble as Ernie's wife picks her way through the remains of her bakery. Ernie has his arm draped around her shoulder and a couple of staff follow behind, looking about, mouths wide open and faces unbelieving. Shreds of indigo pin stripe dripping blood red, decorate the walls, but our targets have definitely left the building. Ernie's piano is playing them into the night.

Above us the whine of four or five SPs builds until their motors begin to herald their erratic descent to the scene. Meka and I amble into the dawn gloom leaving the mayhem and music behind us. There is the sweet smell of baked bread in the damp air, smoke billows in shadows against The City lights and the night is full of ghosts once more.

Turin's dim light will be cutting the gloom for us some miles away and it's the beacon that marks our course. Until we are within a few houses we won't be able to pick it out but its existence is a golden herald in our mind's eye, drawing us safely home. It will only be an hour or so but it will seem an eternity full of railway tracks, culverts, passage ways and dodges, every one of which could hold a dark surprise.

Meka and I walk arm in arm like a couple heading home from a day in The City. We are nonchalant, we give the impression we are only interested in each other, but that is what interests us least. Everything else interests us, but we don't make it look as if we care. Caring is suspicious, someone might notice us caring and wonder why. We avoid any attention, it's a rule.

LEOs can throw a ring around an event just to see what they can catch, but they are the least of our worries. There's plenty of other desperation on the streets at night and the noise and the flames will attract their attention. Now in the small hours of night, the desperate and unpredictable begin to wake up in a mood, and not a good one. In deregulated districts community is strong and nobody has much so street crime is less. Muggers look to more prosperous areas where the risks are increased but the rewards are greater. Muggers can think, not everyone bothers. Some that can't are the alkies, those that don't are the suiciders and the self medicators. Drunks are best avoided, alkies are self-destructive paranoiacs that there's no dealing with, attack for no reason and without warning. They'll use anything they can find, or nothing, drop blocks from bridges or push you off them. Mostly they are unstable and can be deflected into the ground or a convenient wall if you hear them coming. Suiciders don't have the guts to kill themselves so they rush you hoping that you'll do the job for them. They favour armed LEOs but anyone will do, if they're not hurt badly, they'll plead to be finished off. Self medicators sell their drugs as soon as they can, then they can't get more for weeks. After a day or so they revert to the homicidal maniac, sadist, or paedophile that they were before. Any one of these could be waiting around the next corner, timing their attack to the sound of our footsteps.

Meko and I walk down the middle of everywhere, leaving as much space as possible between us and any shadows. This is where shadows, usually a friend, are our enemy. We walk quietly but with confidence, close enough to alert each other by touch. We listen intently and don't talk. If you do that you creep up on things, and things are less likely to creep up on you. We startle a gang of rats exploring a street sleeper. The rats evaporate like smoke and you wonder if they were there at all. We pass on silently not knowing if the sleeper will wake or if he's dead already. There are other peeps about but we travel discretely. Everyone is wary and we take care to see if they turn, stop, or follow. Any unwanted attention is a threat so like them we peep from within our hoods. We do not notice, and are not noticed. Sometimes though it becomes a dance. We pass, then count a second or two, then turn to see if they are watching or have stopped. We see them turn to see if we are watching them and have stopped. There's a way of doing this so you do a complete turnabout without losing pace and is a notice of no threat. Stopping and watching is a threat.

Turin will keep watch like a concerned parent. He'll be alert to any sound that might turn into footsteps on the garden path that approaches the back door. He'll check the dim golden glow upstairs that serves as our beacon letting us know, once we've picked it out, that all is well. Bright enough to be seen if you know where to look, not bright enough to attract attention if you don't.

The cellar is where we meet. It is well hidden and only approached from the back of the house, and only then when we know it is safe and we are not followed. There might be a screen or two turned on but silent. There will be subtitles flashing news in a colour coded everlasting strip that repeats what's happened until something else happens; something that means something. It will have stock market figures, trade accounts, exec quotes on how well their corp is doing, all the news that's fit to print across the background of 24/7 game shows. The news of The

Bakery, a couple of execs and their body guards being blown up, is not fit to print. Suicides are not fit to print because everyone is happy. Happy that there is no crime, happy that everybody is being looked after, happy that the state cares and happy to believe it. Anything that compromises the integrity of the state is not allowed for fear of instilling fear, instilling unrest. If the state says you are safe, then anything which contradicts that is anti-state and is prohibited. It goes without saying. Public displays of anger, which are extremely rare, are dismissed without any need for investigation or enquiry. Riots are always caused by mindless hooligans and protests are always the work of drug crazed anarchists. The people are told this and they know it is in their interests to believe it and to believe nothing else. So they do and they are happy to do so.

  At a junction Meka and I stop before we turn the corner. We pretend we are lovers so she can look over my shoulder and see if we have been noticed, to see if we are being followed. She taps my shoulder, she is not alarmed, it's an all clear.

  At the corner a brothel's neon sizzles as we pass beneath its watery blue haze. Two small boys watch a screen on the wall parading naked figures with their details, what they can do, and for how much. They display their genitalia so you can see how clean they are. If it's a business you can promote it how you like, no matter who you offend or pervert. It's the law and the law is business.

  We turn the corner and pass into the dull red glow that bleeds across the street from the genital pink, arched entrance, that simulates another kind of entrance. It picks out an alkie wriggling in the gutter and clutching at the air as if being helped to his death by some merciful angel.

Alkies are prescribed Alcomed on a compulsory licence. It's a synthetic alcohol combined with a chemical cocktail that is supposed to turn your stomach every time you smell any kind of intoxicating liquor. If you're determined enough, and just don't care, you fight your way through it until your senses become immune. By then your liver has become a mush and your brain is rapidly catching up. Wriggling there in the gutter I wonder why he doesn't just surrender, go quietly, but somewhere in the wreckage there's a spark that won't give up. Some God lit it and it'll be fucked if it will let it go out without a fight. Beneath his slime drenched beard is a face I suddenly recognise. I feel the recognition at first, but it still comes as a surprise when I realise who he is. He was a warden, officious during the day and skulking at night. The job they used to do no longer exists, instead they take other duties. They are the neighbourhood watch, peeking through windows and listening at doors, any way to make themselves useful to the corps. If they can't find enough to report, they'll invent it. If they can't find enough to invent, it's the end of the road, and at the end of the road is a gutter; and that's where he is. But he's unusual, he's still alive. He should have done what most of them do when they get the boot, hang himself somewhere public. They do it partly out of spite and partly so those who have an axe to grind know where to plant it. Once a corp has done with you, you lose all your rights and protection. Ex wardens are too easy a target for those who have a grudge and just want to see them tread that fine line between screaming agony and unconsciousness for as long as possible.

 Lurking in the doorway the whore is dabbing white powder off a naked breast with a damp finger and licking it. She must have spilt some stuff from the small spoon that hangs round her neck. She looks up as she puts her stash away into an iridescent lime green purse hanging on her hip.

'Want some fun, sweetie, it's all legit. State licensed, bug free, guaranteed.'

The bugs she is talking about aren't the charming little creatures that burrow down your piss pipe and eat you from the inside out, or those creepy crawlies that just cling on to your short and curlies for the fun of the ride. She means listening devices, hidden cameras, anything that broadcasts or records. Brothels are required to be swept clean of all such stuff daily so execs, ministers and their like, can party without any consequences. It makes sure that any underage who stars in their own snuff movie, never goes on general release. Going a bit too far may not always be the intention, but there are too many incidents not to know that it's how some get their kicks.

We amble past as some poor bitch lets out a muffled scream in an upstairs room and the window above our heads takes a knock. Right on cue, I think. I look up to see a girl's face thrusting hard against the glass, her nose bleeding, her head then jolts back as she's dragged back in to the room. She'll be lucky to see out the night. If she does she'll be spreading them again in a few days. If she can't, then like the ex-warden, she'll be on that road at the end of which is the same gutter. Goodnight Vienna.

Meko lights up a draw. God knows what she puts in it. It stinks, but it can't be any worse than the air it draws in, at least it's drier, and who knows maybe it's cleaner. We cross over the road and I pin her against the wall. She raises a leg round my waist so it looks as if we're fucking, but we're not.

'Well?' I say, whilst thrusting my hips into hers. She looks back,

'Nothing.'

Beyond the brothel's light we're hidden but she can see down the glistening road and past the dark housing blocks that disappear up into the mist. The same mist that plays a swirling game with the multicoloured light show that seeps across from that perpetual fun park, The City. From this point we can see back to the underpass which is lit and where a solitary light casts an acrid hue across an open space, where anything moving can be seen. We wait a minute or two, then Meko looks at me,

'You can stop now.'

A lengthening shadow draws across the street in the light of the brothel doorway. For a moment we pause and remain close, but it is only the shadow of the door whore. Just her. She flicks a draw at the ex-warden who is now motionless. She stands over him and takes a closer look, then prods him with one of the ludicrously pointed toes of her thigh length plastic boots. She looks up and about, clocks us and decides we don't count. She plays the same game with her chromium heel but presses harder, just to make sure. This time her foot suddenly gives way into the fleshy part of his exposed neck and she hops back to avoid a jet of blood and then swears in case it stains her footwear. The blood stops because nothing is pumping it. She goes through his pockets, there won't be money but there may be other stuff she can sell, maybe a ring. She takes a step back out of the light, stuffs things into the tops of her boots then looks up and clocks us again in the gloom.

'Is that the best you can do, darlin'? Bring him over here I'll show you a fing or two.' It's said like an invitation but it's a threat.

After another glance down the road we decide to move on. Meko slides her leg down and we move apart, then link arms. I look back across the street. The two boys are standing by the motionless body and take turns in kicking him. Deciding he's no threat, they go through his pockets, but the whore has got everything. Angered, they curse him and take his shoes off, decide that they're worthless, then throw them down the street. They loosen clothing, taunting each other till one pulls off his trousers without which he is naked. They find a stick and poke his erect penis, then one of them starts hitting it until covered in blood it eventually subsides and the fun is over. Pulling an arm, they roll him over onto his front. They're trying to get the stick into his arse when the whore comes back out brandishing a long riding crop and tells them all to, 'Fuck off!'

Bodies in the streets are not uncommon, but competition for them is keen and they are picked up quickly. Some free lancers roam the streets on the scavenge and try to intercept requests, so there's often a race to the body. If you're reported as dead, or as near as, they'll wait around like vultures, if nobody's in attendance they'll hasten matters, turn off life support systems just to save time. Well, time is money. If you need care or resuscitation, your health is only worth what the medics can claim off your insurance. I have none, so that's about what I'm worth, until I'm dead, then I'm worth more and then they'll be fighting over my corpse. No one will fight to keep me alive.

At the brothel the whore, or the mother she works for, will have struck some deal with the snatchers and they'll be round for the body, trying to get there before anybody else. Spare parts is a serious business, but then all business is serious. Even the most abused bodies will have useable parts and ones found in the streets are scanned but that's all. No attempt is made to trace relatives or to inform anyone. If there's any ID on the corpse, it might be recorded, more likely it'll be sold on. After a few hours, what's left after they've harvested anything useful, will be as clean as a new born baby. It will have been shaved, flushed out, and perfumed so as to conceal any disturbing odour. Then it will be lying on a steel table like a bleached fish, surrounded by a dozen students from exec homes at some corp training school. They'll all be dead keen to cut up what's left and find out everything they can about this person. Something that didn't interest them at all so long as he was alive.

Meko and I stop again by the end of the street before we turn the corner. Meko leans against a wall as I do and we look back down the street. We check for any movement, listen, engage our senses, gut feelings. It's a rule, listen to your gut feelings. We sense nothing unusual.

CHAPTER 2

Across the urban districts the noise of the sleepless city is a constant background. If you're born to it, it's as natural as your own heart beat and the sound of your own breathing. Only if it stops will you notice it, but then it will be too late. What we do notice is the hum of the filters, clamped to the sides of houses they look like bandaged ears. About the size of a coffin, they suck in the putrid air then push it around the internal air conditioning. They hum with the self-satisfaction that they're helping to save the planet and in the process do more harm than good. Their manufacture produces more harmful gases than they can ever extract. Their grills rattle and their mountings knock. If the building is occupied, by law they have to be operating. The owners breath in the perfumed air (one of a choice of three) and are driven half mad enduring the rattling and the knocking and the escalating costs, in the delusion of better health and a saved planet.

An argument breaks out two or three doors down in a bedroom followed by something smashing, like a window, like someone and a window. Then it's quiet and we can hear the rustling noises in the garbage behind the low wall that Meko and I sit on, rats probably. A feral dog barks and it echoes across the district. A couple of pistol shots crack out and they are then answered by a few more. The dog barks again, and again; then with a single shot it stops abruptly. A siren bounces in and out of the housing, is lost then found again, but each time nearer. Each time closer.

Certain now that we are not followed, we duck into a passageway, past a couple of street sleepers, up and over the service road and down into the darkness of the estate and District 48. There is no street lighting in 48. Except for the hum and rattle of bandaged ears, the houses themselves are in darkness, and you might think they're deserted. Some are, but most have their living room at the rear. It's usually the only room in the house that the occupants can afford to keep warm and lit. It's also more secure, out of sight, and out of hearing; it's the room you live in.

Between two houses, in an upstairs window, there's a faint golden glow in the sliver between curtains. Even in the darkness the glow is barely visible, and not at all if you didn't know where to look. It can't be anything out of the ordinary, but that is our signal, our beacon. If it hadn't been there we would have just walked on like two revellers late home, unusual but not unheard of. We slip unseen into number fourteen that backs onto our goal. It's been boarded up and deemed not fit. We go through the small building at its rear and into the back garden of Ma Brown's. We hear the greased bolts sliding as we walk up the garden path and by the time we are there, Turin has the back door open just enough for us to enter. There's no light, no sound, we don't speak, just touch. Reassuring touches, an okay touch. We pass Turin who waits at the door. Meko heads on through the kitchen into the cupboard under the stairs and down to the cellar. I follow, both of us carrying with us the musty smell of the damp night outside.

In the cellar Chad has draped himself across an old leather arm chair that he has taken to be his. He doesn't respond to our arrival. It seems he is more interested in playing with the pink stuffing, a kind of plastic string, that spews out of one of the arms he sits on. On the table by him is a couple of screens, a mess of cables, a keyboard, and a pad or two. One of the screens is live and pumps out images and titles while a word tape runs across the bottom. It's always on but there's no sound. He's wraps the pink string round his fingers in a weave then watches it unravel of its own accord springing off his fingers and adopting its remembered shape. Chad is in his own world, he has little regard for anyone and less trust, which is okay. Trust no one, that's a rule.

Turin and Chad organise everything but they never talk about events until the time. They get the presents, find the targets, lay the plans; we deliver. We work in couples, The Bakery is my first with Meko. Chad is a home boy, he's never in the field. Turin and Meko go way back, loads of previous. At first I got to go with Turin which was good, learn the rules, how to do things, how not to be seen, not to be followed, the ins and the outs, how to survive. Chad has contacts that only he knows, that's the way it's done. Turin makes sure it's done that way, he says it's safe, we don't want to fall like dominoes he says. Dominoes is a kind of game where one falls down, all fall down. None of us want to fall down.

'Know why this stuffing is better than bot?' Chad says.

'Well, it's not the colour.' I think it's a smart thing to say but already I feel stupid. Looking around there are no takers so I let my smile drain away as if I didn't think it was funny either.

Chad glances at Meko who collapses into the sofa, boots on one end and head lolling over the other.

'Meko? Why better?' Chad wants her attention.

Meko wears a cap, like pilots wear in early films, it has fallen onto the floor and lays there like a buckled bird's egg but with straps. Her hair is dark and short on one side so you can see the burns. She wears them like trophies. They look like a stream running down behind her ear and then disappearing beneath her collar. I don't know how far they go, and whether there's only a stream, or if there are rivers and lakes too, all hidden. I think she's amazing. I want her to notice me, to like me, but she scares me to death. She doesn't move, doesn't open her eyes, just speaks, like she's bored to death,

'Because it remembers what it used to be.'
See? She's amazing.

'Correctacorrecta!' Answers Chad who can't help borrowing from game shows, 'Token galoragalora lady!' He carries on imitating a host's catch phrases while he jots his joke in a little notebook. His mother probably watches game shows day and night. I don't know. We never talk about personal stuff, details, anything that could identify us. Anything that we might have to reveal if we were caught. It's a rule. Turin says game shows are the opium of the people.

We hear Turin's footsteps above, crossing the kitchen and moving along the passageway. There's a muffled conversation, it can only be with Ma Brown who lives upstairs. We hear him return, close the door to the cupboard under the stairs, lift the hatch and then see his Muskrat boots on their way down and his long coat dragging on the steps behind, falling from one to the next like a medieval cloak. Muskrat boots are cool boots but they cost a lot, mine are similar but are cheap copies. My coat is lighter and a bit shorter which I prefer because I can run faster and be more agile if I need to be. Most people have hoods of one sort or another for different reasons. Maybe just to keep the weather out, or so as not to be traced or just recorded. There are cams everywhere and you have to presume that they are backed up with recog and will know who you are by your face, your height, even the way you walk. We often drop hoods if the LEOs are about, as it annoys them. They are always suspicious and don't need an excuse to search you or just beat you up so winding them up is not good. One day I would like to have a leather jacket like the guy in the photo on my bedroom wall. His name was Andreas Baader and he fought the corps too.

Meko swivels round and sits up to make room for Turin to sit on the sofa arm. He reports that everything is clear.

Meko and I were sure but we can't relax until he checked it out. There are approaches that can be seen from the back of Ma Brown's and any tails can be seen too.

'So, how'd it go?' Turin asks.

We nod as if it was routine, which it was, but never is. Events are becoming a format now, but carrying them out is always particular.

Turin needs specifics,

'Targets?'

'Both targets and a brace of BGbots.' Meko was nonchalant, we know we've done well. Delaying the detonation for a while until the body guards had caught up with their clients meant they'd shared the blast. If you believe the promos, bots are infallible, indestructible guardians, but the truth is different and we've just proved it.

Chad and Turin have been a team for a long time, even before Turin met Meko. Turin could handle people and Chad was a data miner. He started out just as a hacker as they all do, but as time went on it became more of a challenge to find out what was really going on. Hackers want it to be known they've got in so they leave some poisonous remnant or obscene graffiti and most importantly a signature. Turin calls them Kilroys. They do this as proof to others that they've been there, it's in their collection. A data miner will dig deeper holes, follow productive seams and hope to come up with something which will rock the world, all without being detected. Chad had got into a chain of supply and had revealed all sorts of underhand practice, kickbacks, under and over pricing, as well as mislabelling, but these were corps so hardly a surprise. Mining some data accounts, he found out something far more dramatic. A leading robotics corp was using the C12 to 14 segments of menial workers that were far more plentiful, and therefore a lot cheaper, rather than the pukka A7 to A9 brain segments that they guaranteed, and which the state authorised for bot enhancement. He thought about telling them, but then he thought why should he make problems for everyone by making the bots on the street smarter. Also there was no proof that some exec didn't already know and was happily making a killing and if so, Chad could be the next. So he kept quiet, jotted it down in his little notebook with his everlasting pencil, and let the world carry on, undisturbed.

'What about collateral?' Turin asks. There's a silence. Turin is always concerned about collateral because killing ordinary people is not what we are about and he tells us that it is just sloppy, and not professional.

'Besides,' he'll tell us, 'it's the worst kind of publicity and he doesn't want his name on it or have to apologise for it when the day comes.'

We know the day he means but we don't know when it will come. So we always make sure that warnings are given and we give people the chance to get away. If collateral is a certainty we should abort the event. However we all know accidents happen.

Meko looks across at me, and I say,

'A piano.' For a millisecond I feel really cool. I look at Meko, and think, 'See Meko, I'm really cool', but there's no expression and there's too much silence then I look at Turin, whose head starts an almost imperceptible nod, then a faint smile.

'Good. Really good.' He's looking at me and he smiles, 'Ash, Meko, good work.'

I look at Meko, her eyes are closed, maybe she didn't even hear. She is so cool. I'll have to mention it later.

The sound of a footstep on the floor above alarms us and we all look up at the ceiling to the source of the noise as if that helps our understanding, or our hearing. Turin rises casually and makes his way to the steps as there's a gentle knock on the cupboard door. We look at each other in silence to see if anyone knows what's going on, then listen until Turin returns. Amazingly, with his hands full of what I think are oranges.

If we don't say, 'Wow!' then we think it. It's not the health giving qualities that fresh fruit is renown for, it's the colour that is a shock. Turin throws each of us one bright orange fruit. Orange juice is available, at least that's what it's called but any real goodness is extracted and sold separately to those who can afford it. The stuff we can get has the goodness replaced with additives and sweeteners. Orange juice is just that, juice that is orange. Now we can see that even the colour is a worthless imitation.

'Argh!' I let out a cry as it is so bitter, and I'm not used to such a powerful taste then, watching the others, I have forgotten that it has to be peeled.

The others slurp and laugh. Meko slurps and laughs. I laugh and slurp now that I have peeled it!

Meko breaks hers into segments which I copy with what is left. Eating the segments is easier and cleaner, as if they have been designed to be eaten that way. Nature is remarkable but we don't get to see too much of it. She looks up and her lips are moist and red as if she's been hard kissing,

'Where did these come from?' She says as some juice runs down her chin. There's nothing but the sound of slurping, and peeling, and you can see a fine spray when the peel is torn off. I bend a piece of peel and it sprays like tiny fountains. Then some gets in my eyes and I wonder if I'm blinded forever, but they all laugh and as my eyes water, so do I. This is family, I think.

Turin tells us between slurps that when the lights fail at the main intersection, until an andy can get there, an ordinary bot, like a surveillance bot, patch programmed, might drop in to direct the traffic.

So before an andy can get to the intersection, an ordinary bots or mechanicals as some call them, do what they can to keep the traffic orderly. Bots though, do not have the agility and their signals are confusing. The locals get to hear, gather about and wait for the inevitable. Sure enough there's either an accident, or some impatient human just drives over the bot. That's the signal they've been waiting for. The locals pour over the barriers run across the autoway while everything is jammed up and make for any cargoes and get what they can before the andys arrive and start laying into them. This time one of the trucks was carrying fruit to an office complex over in 37 and it was a neighbour of Ma Brown's who hauled back a whole crate of oranges.

'Lucky for us the andys didn't catch him,' said Meko examining a piece of peel and wondering whether to eat that as well.

'Lucky for him too.' Turin was mopping up the juice with his scarf, 'they would have beaten him to death for a crate full of fruit.'

'They don't need a crate of fruit as an excuse,' Chad too was finding the sticky juice clinging and was wiping it off on his sleeve, 'they'd do it just for the amusement.'

Turin says that Ma Brown negotiated some veg that was got from another van and she'll make a stew later and we can have some of that too. After raiding the trucks, folk meet up and do a 'divie up', as they call it. Those with children, old folk or anyone ill get priority. The intersection where it happened has a road running to the south-west where the nearest farms are and it's that route that carries a lot of the produce into urbia.

There is a moment when we think of Ma Brown, and others like her with respect and admiration but also some sadness about what they have to endure and for how long. It's confusing because it's difficult to forget that it's they, and those like them, that let this all happen, and did nothing.

'It amazes me,' says Turin, 'that those who have nothing will gladly share the little they have.' And then Meko looks up and carries on,

'While those that have everything will share nothing at all.'

'That's why they've got everything,' I answer. Then Chad has to have his go,

'And how did they get everything? Through theft and extortion, holding people to ransom for the things they can't live without. The state hands the corps the gun and then says they're not to blame when the people get shot. State, corps, finance they're the unholy trinity. At least we're doing something about it.'

Then he picks up a water bottle, holds it up and says, 'Friends against the establishment!'

Meko and I have bottles of water too, and we raise them and shout, 'Yeah!' Turin frowns at us for making too much noise. We smile at each other like brother and sister, and I think we are cool. Then it occurs to me.

'Fate!' I shout this quietly and they look at me and nod, but I know they haven't got it, so I look at them and say it again,

'Fate,' then I have to spell it out to their blank faces, 'F A T E. Friends Against The Establishment.'

There are smiles and nods and Turin holds up his fist with the palm towards us. Meko and I both do the same and then we all look at Chad who seems less keen but does it. Then Turin says it quietly but with such importance that it makes me shiver,

'FATE.'

Then in the same way we all say it.

'FATE. Friends Against The Establishment.'

This is the proudest and most important moment of my life.

When its light we can leave by Ma Brown's front door but we have to be cautious, but not so cautious that we attracted attention. This is a rule. At first, rules are things you must remember, like being followed, trusting no one, always carrying an ED, keeping privacy, and not asking personal questions, or invading privacy. After a while they are just the way you behave. They are mostly just good sense and for your own and your friend's safety, especially when on an event, like at The Bakery, so that we would not be noticed and followed. Walking casually arm in arm when you feel like running like hell is the result of another rule. I asked Turin where they came from and he said they were in an old book about spies, someone called Smiley. Some are the same, others change and some are added.

Ma Brown's house has a small front garden which is unusual as all the other houses in Elm Avenue have just parking places, even though there are no cars.

When Turin and Chad operated on their own they were responsible for the 'Three Car Trick'. The warden's choppers can lift a small car easy, two is pushing it, three is impossible. These are the small cars ordinary people are permitted to have. Turin and Chad parked a car where they knew it would be lifted but bolted it to the road with special anchor bolts through the floor so it just looked like an ordinary single car. The warden sent out a lift request. The chopper arrived, the warden smashed the windows to take the gear, then hooked it up. Staring up at the chopper, the warden sliced the air with his gloved hand which was the appropriate sign that the 'piece-a-junk' was 'good to go'. People gather to watch from a distance. The pilots are always flash and ready to show off when they make a lift and have a crowd watching. The pilot throttled back to max so as to lift the car as if it was made of paper. The cables tightened and the chopper came spinning into the ground, nose first, with all hands. That was a big event and the 'Three Car Trick' became a legend. Ever since that, Turin and Chad had respect everywhere they went, and still do.

CHAPTER 3

The Columbus building stands before me, overwhelming and contradictory.

This is the repository of all personal and public information. It collects, collates, cross checks, and confirms by frequent interviews, inquiries, and surveillance. All state systems are linked and Columbus is at its centre. If Columbus has no record of you, you do not exist. You can only exist if Columbus has a record of you, therefore you are only a record and Columbus has it.

Columbus is the only organisation that uses surface mail. Nobody else sends mail because it gets lost. Columbus denies that mail ever gets lost. Your claim that you did not receive mail is treated as either a lie or a tendency toward delusion, for which medication will be prescribed at a secure unit. Most therefore, admit to lying, or play stupid and say they forgot. As you are already thought to be stupid they believe you. So it is true, mail never gets lost.

Mail is sent so they can tie names to addresses, and everyone must have a registered address. It is a way of controlling and above all Columbus exists to control and to achieve completion. Completion is arriving at a point when all records are correct and up to date in a state of clerical harmony and perfection. This will never be achieved so long as Columbus has to deal with people. This is why people are treated as an irritation and an inconvenience to a point of aggressive indifference.

Steps rise up to the white marble portico that towers over the open space before it. Inside the portico, an enormous glass wall extends in every direction through which many floors can be seen receding on either side of a cavernous void Pillars rise through this vast space and splay out like fans to support a ceiling of crystal tracery. Reputedly the finest ceiling ever constructed. There are few windows visible on the rest of the building due to them being too often the target of protesters.

Set into the thick glass wall before me, hidden from view, is a minuscule entrance door. Like an afterthought, it is concealed in a corner behind a statue. This is so it doesn't interfere with the overall symmetry of the design, which is considered to be perfection. Having to facilitate the access of people is as much an irritation now in operation, as it was during construction. It was then and is still considered, that people, being unpredictable and having an inclination towards individuality, will be nothing but a nuisance and impede the smooth running of the organisation. We do our best.

Below this majestic edifice sprawl a series of paved open terraces scattered with meagre benches on which people wait. There is no waiting inside or near the Columbus building. Nothing should mar the edifice, especially people. Today we are lucky, the drizzle is light and the air is mild. Every inquiry, interview, instruction or request, is referred to as a 'case'. Each 'case' has a number, each number has a person, a couple, or a whole family. They are all desperate enough to wait here hoping that some anonymous clerk can be bothered to process a decision to see, not to see, postpone, or return, a 'case'. It will need to be flagged for instruction. The flagged case has then to be forwarded into a request by the Requestrater who will take a view as to whether any action is justified, and if so, issue an alert. An alert that satisfies the front desk's selection criteria for that period could gain the attention of one of the Alert Reception Clerks on the bottom tier of the front desk. This will make its way slowly upwards until it reaches the desk's pinnacle where it will be stamped by the Supreme Head of Admissions and Reception, if it is one of his rare days in attendance. Once stamped it can then make its way back down again before a Front Desk Interior Liaison Porter can acknowledge its existence. He, because it is always a he, will speedily ensure a reception attendance request is initiated. The meaning of speedily in this context is comparative. When that request is conducted into process, and if the front desk reception team can take time off from polishing, cleaning, and inspecting awards, one of them might transfer the attendance request onto a day sheet, which may become the subject of a Liaison Guard's scrutiny. If he deems it appropriate he will 'vocalise' the case number to the waiting clients outside from his lectern, when he feels so inclined. If that can happen before the allotted appointment 'window' is terminated, then a 'case' may be 'observed'. If not, then it is the client who has missed their allotted appointment 'window' and the 'case' will not be 'observed'. It is the client who is at fault. It is always the client that is at fault. They will then have to re-apply, start again, with the stigma of a demerit having already wasted time, and time as we all know is money. It is worth noting that at every stage, clerks arbitrarily refuse requests or pleas for no other reason than to prove that they can. This is to demonstrate their independence, power, and that they are only human; just like everyone else.

I register with a Liaison Guard on his lectern, and show him my flimsy appointment card which he takes. The material on which the details are printed is such that it barely withstands handling and the weak ink is so diffused as to be hardly legible. The guard reads my details with obvious difficulty for which I am solely to blame, of course. With contempt, he wafts me away so that I retire several paces. With a studied tedium he communicates to the Desk Recording Clerk that case number such and such has arrived for a clerk instigated appointment. This means that the clerk will be told and I will be seen at the clerks discretion which will only be a few hours. This is rather than having to make repeated trips here to wait, which would happen if I instigated an appointment to see a clerk. When a servant of the state wishes to see you, you had better be there, and in good time. If, as a member of the state, I wish to see a servant of it, I might as well wait for hell to freeze over.

The guard looks me up and down and sneers. This is so I should be aware that I am worth little more than something he might scrape off the bottom of his shoe. I smile, which he doesn't like ,and now he would like to punch me. He is waiting for an answer from the desk, but his attention is on me. As I stare back at him his eyes grow larger and his nostrils are beginning to flare. Beneath his taut bloodless lips his teeth are clenching, so that the muscles bulge and throb in his cheeks. I smile again in a 'I would like to be your friend' kind of way. On his lectern where his clip board rests, so do his hands which begin to grip its sides, the knuckles of which are turning white. He gets some kind of communication through his earpiece. He shakily gives me a glossy coloured handout and nods toward the benches. This is an indication that I should wait, but he is unable to speak. The bench at which he nods is already full. The nearest vacant seat is far off so I make it look as if I am thinking about sitting on the steps of the entrance. I can feel his eyes burning into the back of my head. I stop and survey my supposed seat. As I begin to crouch, the guard explodes,

'Don't you fucking dare!' The sound is more like a pipe bursting followed by a splutter, but I am sure that's what he tried to say.

He takes a few hurried paces towards me reaching for his batten, but I skip down the steps out of his range. He stops at the top of the steps, then as I clear them he returns to his lectern and angrily calls out a number. A couple, a few metres away, rise fearfully from a nearby bench and make their way slowly to the steps keeping as far from the guard as it is possible. Way off I notice a figure suddenly rise and start to run, followed by another. I dash the fewer paces needed and take one of the seats vacated by the couple, while the other two race towards me pulling at each other until both fall. One scrambles to his feet but is tripped by the other, still on the ground. He falls, twists, and his head crashes against a marble slab. The other stands up, looks around and makes his way quietly to the seat next to me. The other lays motionless on the ground and no one has seen this but me. At least everyone gives that impression. The bench is in the lee of the portico and is dry compared to other benches, regulars would know this. I don't even know when I am well off. If people have brought nothing to pass the time they sit reading their hands, the backs, the sides, the palms. They check out their nails, their cuticles, the colours and the roughness. There seems no end to the amount of time someone can be absorbed in this way when they are determined to see nothing else.

This is the fourth time I have been to the Columbus building. Amongst everyone else it is where the 'keen to work' go. They are not called unemployed. The PM says, 'Call the unemployed, The Unemployed, and they will be unemployed. Call them 'Keen to Work' and they will be, keen to work.'

The 'Keen to Work' is also a misnomer. The unemployed are never more employed than when they have no work to go to and the 'keen to work' are never less keen than when they have to go to work.

I have read the Columbus glossy handout before, but each time it is glossier and thicker and has the smell of cynical insincerity which is not diminished by the greeting, 'Dear Valued Client'. Of course it isn't meant for our consumption but to give the minister they sponsor something to illustrate his worthiness to the PM. It is the PM who holds the key to his elevated position and which in turn attracts such sponsorship.

If the stepped and porticoed entrance isn't enough to put you in your place, then the front desk will. The front desk sits in the cathedral like foyer, facing the entrance. It is a large, slightly concave pyramid, having several tiers each with less seats until one, by far the most luxurious, rests at its pinnacle. There are about eight tall backed seats at the lowest level, concealed by a long decorated panel. The whole construction is raised so that anyone approaching the desk loses sight of the clerks. Consequently, it is pointless to approach the desk as you will inevitably disappear from sight. The next tier seats about four and is similarly arranged so as you cannot be seen, they too have their curved desk but it is obvious that these are superior to the lower tier if only by the slightly more elaborate carving on the chair backs. So to the next tier, which seats three in more elaborate and luxurious seats until above them all on its own, what can only be described as a throne. The throne is gilded and dripping in red brocade and gold tassels. It is entirely visible to all, having no desk surrounding it, but a low courtesy panel. It is way beyond any reach, being some distance above and back. All this I can remember from my previous visits, but now I read from the glossy handout.

'Entering this remarkable building via the raised portico designed by the legendary Frederico Bestini in the Greco-Roman style, our clients will be impressed by the grandeur of their reception foyer. No expense has been spared in creating for them a foyer of which they can be truly proud. Conceived by the PM's very talented cousin, John of London, the interior design is inspiring, practical, and subtly combines the majesty of commerce with the fortitude of the simple labourer's honest toil, raising their spirits in support of greater endeavour. The central feature of this magnificent reception area is the famous desk itself. To all that approach this work of genius it is a powerful reminder that Columbus spares no effort on behalf of the treasured clients it is pleased to serve. The construction is of immense and elaborate proportions reflecting the very high ideals that Columbus sets itself. Every part of the desk, including the magnificent steps to the rear that were hand carved by DeCerriti, is crafted from the rarest of woods, many now extinct. Remarkable too are the fielded panels on all sides that depict allegorical scenes along the themes of the glory of commerce and the blessing of work.

The extraordinary craftsmanship and imaginative composition is of such excellence that it is a beacon we can all be proud to be a part of.'

I turn another page and it continues,

'The hand-picked maintenance team, who are on hand 24/7, are understandably proud of their award winning desk, and are well aware of their daunting responsibilities. Awards won by the desk are too numerous to mention but familiar to all will be that it has twice won the 'Concours de Elegance' in the Corporate Universe Symposium - Reception Desk Category. All awards are proudly displayed for your pleasure and contemplation in the glass case to the left as you are guided passed to the lift hall. Clients will be reminded that there is no lingering in the foyer so we may be more able to meet your needs as quickly and efficiently as possible. Passing through the entrance foyer, our clients will notice the luxurious feel of the Boccaran wool carpet beneath their feet. An opportunity to experience first-hand, the real luxury that is theirs to share. A visual treat, our clients will find themselves adrift on a sea of carpet in a shade of Gandalfian Grey. This is designed to stimulate the senses on the paraphia level and incorporates the finest materials sourced from across the world, some of which are no longer available. The Columbus insignia, depicted is a double headed eagle encompassing the globe, is picked out in finest blue silk over a rouge panel of textured Quintalay. This visual extravaganza is repeated ad infinitum throughout the reception hall and creates the perfect environment from which the lofty magnitude of the foyer can be fully appreciated. Sculpted pilasters and elaborate friezes carved from rare marbles, many no longer available, adorn every available space. They frame the truly stirring marble panels that have been crafted by experts from across the world. Their work illustrates admirably The Columbus Foundation's unstinting crusade to bring succour and prosperity to the poor and needy in our community family'.

    Now I am back in the real world.
    I am sat on the bench with dozens of other people who are reading their hands. Some put down their hands and pick up a book, or the same glossy PR handout. If so, they soon pick up their hands again and read them, because their hands are real and do not lie, they are the truth and the truth is written on them. I am here because I have been sent for. Others that have been sent for, like me, will be called today, maybe even soon. Others, who have made a request to be seen, are treated as a nuisance and will have to wait. They wait to know when they must return to wait again. They are not given a time, just a day. Their number might be called in the morning or in the afternoon. Who knows? When the number is called at six they could be the last case or one of the several that will have to return and try again. It all depends on the whim of the clerk. There is always an appeal, or a revision, so the process starts over again.
    Now I have finished the hand out, and it is later in the day. The stench of a burger van's rancid oil that has wafted across the terraces all afternoon, begins to sicken. Occasionally one of a couple will saunter off to the public toilets near a disused fountain that fills with refuse and dead rats. You need to have someone save a seat but you

shouldn't trust anyone as they can sell it while you are away. Some arrive early just to get a seat they can sell later when it gets busy. They make a sign by rubbing their thumb and forefinger tips together to indicate they will move if paid.

There is a stream of piss coursing its jagged way across the marble slabs, its source being unable to leave or control themselves any longer. The embarrassment is not as uncomfortable as the need to relieve. For most people, the state has destroyed what little self-respect we started with. Embarrassment no longer means anything. We are all degraded. Even so, no one sees the gently steaming trickle, we all read our hands.

A few days ago one of the guards went to move an old lady who was still there after six; she was as stiff as a board. They reckon she would have been dead most of the day, and people sat next to her. We do not see these things because we do not care, we do not see them because we care too much.

Now I jump. A guard has just called out my number. The guards have changed otherwise the one I annoyed might have said as I got to up to his little desk,

'Ah! I made a mistake. Sorry'

And I would have lost my seat, and he would have said that I was not present.

I am careful not to smile as the guard stamps my paper and issues me with a pass collar which I clip round my neck tight enough for me not to be able to get it over my head should I want to. He points his reader at it and it goes 'peeeep'. It is now me. It has a tracking device so they can tell exactly where I am in the building. I am a dot on their 3D grid and by me, the dot, there is a reference which corresponds to a panel displaying my details. Like The City passes, I imagine that should it receive the appropriate signal my collar might begin to get very hot, tighten and choke me, but I don't know. The guard issues me with slippons which are like little bags which I have to put on my feet before I get inside the door. They say it is to protect us from static and is for our benefit, but really it is just to keep the carpet clean. He leads me to the small glass door in the glass wall behind the statue. The pressure sensor beneath the mat indicates I am waiting and eventually a clerk on the bottom tier of the desk looks up and the door slides open. He is probably in charge of the button which opens the door and has some title which briefly describes his duty in case he forgets. Another clerk on the same level looks up to see I have put on the slippons, his title would reflect that arduous duty too. A third clerk is attending to some paperwork and doesn't look up. I wait just inside the door as it closes behind me, and stand on a translucent plastic square covering the carpet on which is printed, 'Wait Here'. In front of me there is a sign on a moveable barrier on which is printed, 'Wait There'. So I wait here and there. To my left starts the plastic pathway that crosses the carpet and leads to a horizontal steel rail, still some distance from the desk. The rail is about waist high and supported by turned and fluted columns, probably made from rare woods that are no longer available. The plastic pathway then winds round the desk and into the distance. I am devastated that I will not experience the luxury of the Boccaran wool carpet beneath my feet and wonder if what I am feeling are my senses being stimulated by the Gandalfian Grey, on the paraphia level. I decide it is not, but what it might be is the desire to reduce this whole building and everything in it, to a pile of dust on the any level. That will have to wait, but there is one thing I can't resist. I play the scenario through whilst feeling in my pocket. The third clerk moves a piece of paper to a forth one, probably the Paper Receiving Clerk, who turns to one of the two clerks on the next level. Fortunately not all the seats are full. And I wait.

One of the two clerks, looks sneeringly at me, then turns again to his paperwork, mumbles something and without looking at me, beckons with his little finger. This is irritating, he doesn't even consider me worth using a proper finger, and especially not several. I can no longer resist it and I will do it.

I look down pretending I didn't see the demeaning little gesture and remain motionless, staring to one side of the plastic path at the Gandalfian grey carpet and getting my full dose of 'stimulation on the paraphia level'. I appear transfixed, at the same time curling my hand round my little accomplice deep in a pocket, unseen. At last I hear a shout from the desk and I take two steps to the right of the plastic path and onto the hallowed carpet. Instantly a wailing alarm screeches and the clerks as one, are brought to their feet and join in the screeching. A flashing light over a swing door heralds the door bursting open and a team of guards run full pelt, all wearing the bright pink slippons, in my direction. The clerks on the lower tier stand pointing and jabbing the air in my direction with their fingers, while their puce faces look fit to burst. The clerk above them is on his feet too but just glowers, clutching his head in disbelief. The guards, now in a gaggle, make it round the turn of the desk but slide into each other as if on ice. You can't corner wearing plastic bags on your feet. The ones who make it, get to me just as I crouch down. One guard tries to grab my neck but misses as I'm too low and as he can't stop he bounces off the glass wall with a thunderous boom as if a huge gong had just been sounded. From the corner of my eye I can see everyone outside jumping to their feet, but they remain where they are in case they lose their seats. I slowly rise, allowing another guard to grasp the air beneath me and slide head first into the glass wall with similar effect. I hold up aloft what they imagine I have just picked off the carpet. A small bug rolled into a ball, dead. The ring of guards that was about to tear me limb from limb, forms a close circle around me staring in horror at the speck that is between my thumb and forefinger. The crowd parts to let a second tier clerk through, he with the little finger. He mumbles something to the first level clerks who have followed in his wake. They peer round his corpulence to get a look at me, and what I am holding. They pass on instructions to the guards who return to their posts and disappear into the room from where they came. A first tier clerk returns with a small transparent plastic bag and hands it to clerk little-finger who indicates that I should drop the bug into its open top. I am tempted to lose it and create more mayhem, but I have had enough fun and choose not to. It plops into the bag and to my astonishment, uncurls itself. There is a gasp from the clerks, the clutching of heads, if they're not being shaken, and more whispering. I catch the word 'maintenance'. Clerk Little-Finger has a smile on his face, but it only covers his mouth, his cold Gandalfian Grey eyes examine me, then my pass. He is almost tempted to put his hand on my shoulder but it just hovers above it as he invites me to move along the plastic path by pointing with his other hand. Another clerk appears with a piece of paper, hands it to me and takes over from Little-Finger. He leads me to the lift. He presses the floor sixteen, which almost corresponds with what has been written. What I have written is, Rm 1601.

CHAPTER 4

In room 1601 there is a polished faced clerk sitting at a desk who does not look up or give any indication that he is aware of my arrival. We both sit at desks separated by a chest high wall and security glass which fills the rest of the narrow room up to the ceiling; we have no contact. Contact is strictly forbidden. We must not even breathe the same air. His desk has machines and paperwork conveniently placed. His designer seat is luxurious and comfortable. My stool is lower than his seat and bolted to the floor. I look up at him, this ensures I feel inferior. Feeling inferior is the least of my worries. A clunk echoes in the tiny grey room behind me signifying that the door I came through is now secured and there is no way out. I am now already a prisoner, we are all guilty and continually have to prove our innocence; if I answer correctly I might yet regain my freedom. The walls that surround me give the impression of a cell, but there is another door. On that door there is a sign which shouts, 'The Columbus Programme,' It shouts because it's written very large and very close. Then is says the programme will help you, 'Rethink, Retrain, and Relearn Through Active Positivism'. Then it says, 'The Columbus way is your way out'. This is true, it is the only way out of the room I am in.

I sit patiently staring at the clerk's slick backed, black hair. They all have it. Stuck to their heads as if it were thick paint. They wear black suits, and eye glasses. The glasses are tinted grey, you might think because of the bright lights they work under, or the screens they peer into, really it is to make everything and everyone the same no-colour. If there was colour there would be difference, there might be personalities even individuals. A clerk is unable to compute the individual. Over his grey glasses he has tiny beads of perspiration on his brow; he has heating on his side of the glass, I have none. He is tapping away at the screen, he could talk it, but then I might hear what he is writing. What he writes may mean nothing to me and therefore instantly forgettable, but his fear of us learning anything about them or their business fills them with terror. His breathing is shallow and rapid. I hope that he doesn't die, then my interview, like him, would terminate and I would have to do this all over again. To me he is worthless, it's the only thing we have in common, he thinks I'm worthless too.

Columbus makes great claims about their 'human interface' and that you, 'get to speak to a real person, one just like you'. I think not. This clerk has no interest in whether I live or die provided he has filled in all his form boxes and nothing turns red. If he can find a way to sign you off and save Columbus money, he is under instructions to do it, so we play the game.

He starts talking. It's little more than a mumble that the system distorts and delays. The single speaker set high up into the wall out of reach, is only marginally louder than the monotonous drone which I can just hear real time through the glass. It sounds like an echo and does its best to give you the impression you're either losing your hearing, or losing your mind.

He stares fixedly into his pale green screen running at pace through the words and phrases not giving them any emphasis or punctuation. His lips quiver emitting words that he has mumbled countless times before and has ceased to think about. An unthinking human is far more dangerous than a thinking robot.

'You have read the blue notice and have understood it you also willingly accept that all conversations will be recorded and can form the basis of further action if deemed (he takes a breath) appropriate and that such action is intended to assist your betterment as laid down by state legislation the details of which are open for inspection where and when they are accessible a condition of you continuing to receive (another breath) tokens privileges and permissions is that you agree to assist in your 'Columbus Personal Improvement Plan' however constructed and designed for you and agree to perform whatever (a breath) tasks and employments are allocated for your benefit should you fail to satisfy any of the approved criteria under the CPIP you agree to a period of indeterminate duration during which you will take part in the 'The Columbus Betterment Programme' which (breath) will involve relocation to an approved residential centre of your choice from the options provided.'

His monotonous, unpunctuated delivery stops abruptly as he retrieves a cloth with which to wipe his brow. The notice he reads means nothing to him and he cares not whether I understand it, or want to. I play with the idea of asking him to repeat a section so I might appear to be interested. It is foolish to irritate a petty bureaucrat, I have no way of knowing what boxes he might tick and what repercussions might ensue. I sit obediently still and dutifully attentive as he continues.

'You are being advised that abusive language raising of the voice offensive gestures and behaviour deemed to be of a threatening or aggressive nature damage or the attempted damage (breath) of Columbus property however minor by any means including spitting kicking head butting punching or slapping will result (breath) in an immediate termination of the interview and a period of isolation during which you will be assessed and may be detained in a facility for (breath) reports. The wearing of unusual or bizarre clothing including military uniforms period costumes fancy dress masks hats or other paraphernalia is strictly (breath) forbidden and will result in the interview being postponed sarcasm humour blasphemy the use of a different voice other than your own face pulling (breath) including poking tongues or any other in the view of the clerk abnormal disrespectful or inappropriate behaviour will result in a verbal warning in the first instance by written warning in the second and on the third by a termination of the interview followed by an indeterminate detention is this understood say yes or no.'

'Yes,' I say. The first time I heard this garbled notice, which they read out every time, it made me laugh, for which I got a verbal warning. When I told the clerk he must be joking, he punched a key and out popped a slip of paper from a slot in the wall with the time, my number, and in red across the top, Abnormal, Disrespectful or Inappropriate Behaviour - Written Warning!

'Are you fully handed? Say yes or no.'

'Yes,'

'Place your hand on the panel marked 'HAND' and do not move it.' I place my hand on the panel marked 'HAND' and do not move it because there is a notice which tells me I am not to move it.

'Are you visually adequate? Say yes or no.'

'Yes.'

'Look into the optident lens marked, 'Look here'. Are you looking into the lens? Say yes or no.'

I stare fixedly into the lens surrounding which are the words, 'LOOK HERE' and say, 'Yes.'

He taps and machines crackle and whir.

'You are . . . . .'

(And here you must understand I cannot tell you this information)

'. . . . . . Confirm. Say yes or no.'

'Yes.'

He then asks personal questions that are used to cross check. I have told you about names. The names he has are birth names and numbers.

'You have been on the 'Keen to Work' programme for three years and two months? Say yes or no.'

'Yes.'

'The data shows you have had no work during that period. Is that correct? Say yes or no.'

'Yes.'

'Is this because you do not wish to work? Say yes or no.'

'No.'

'Is this because for reasons of health you are unable to work? Say yes or no.'

'No.'

'Is this because you feel that the state owes you a living? Say yes or no.'

'No.'

'Do you believe The Columbus Foundation is committed to help you achieve a useful working life which will be a profit to the community and state? Say yes or no.'

'Yes.'

'Do you agree that The Columbus Foundation works ceaselessly on your behalf for your personal betterment and happiness through being a responsible member of the community? Say yes or no.'

'Yes.'

'Your admiration and trust of The Columbus Foundation is demonstrated by your willingness to co-operate with the foundation in whatever the foundation proposes for your betterment? Say yes or no.'

'Yes.'

This carries on. Later the questions turn into scenarios trying to assess tendencies toward anti-social behaviour, sexual deviation, drug taking, etc., anything which might indicate I am a threat to society. You get a multiple choice answer, you choose the number corresponding to the answer that has the least threat or is the most socially responsible. All questions are in the form that requires yes or no, or a number, one two or three. No explanation is asked for or given, no debate is risked and no opinions sought.

The clerk taps away, the green light glistening on his polished face, unsullied by anything red except the glow of his cheeks. The clerk knows that I am registered in a deregulated district and am unemployable because of it. Nevertheless because it is written, we play the game and he ticks boxes and collects information which is stored and kept just in case it could be used against me, or anyone else, now or in the future, even after I am dead.

The dull green light into which the clerk stares, and he does nothing else, drains the colour from his face and I imagine I can see the circuitry, diodes and mechanicals lying beneath the shiny, lifeless skin. He's a robot in all but flesh and blood. He mumbles on,

'The interview is now complete and we have all the information we require by answering you have taken full responsibility for the accuracy of the answers you have given if you have given inaccurate wrong or misleading answers and now wish to change the answers you may do so now do you wish to change any of your answers? Say yes or no.'

'No.'

More tapping.

'The answers you have given have been accepted and logged by the data system and will remain indefinitely as a record of this interview you are happy for that to happen? Say yes or no.'

'Yes.'

'Further examination of your interview data will take place and cross checked with data already held which may result in you being called back if further clarification is required, this will occur within 28 working days during which you will remain at your current address and be available between the hours of nine till six during weekdays. You agree to this? Say yes or no.'

'Yes.'

'You will inform us immediately of any change which might affect the information which you have given of your own free will in answer to the questions asked during this interview do you agree? Say yes or no.'

'Yes.'

There's a clunk beside me. The door security is released.

'You may now leave.'

The way out of Columbus is not the way in. The way out is not carpeted but it is grey. The walls are grey and the floors are grey but not Gandalfian Grey and not the type that stimulates the senses on any level. The hard walled corridors and staircases have no natural light. The only illumination struggles to light up the way ahead as I walk through. Behind me the lights give up as soon as I have passed. I once turned round and took a few paces back but once lit and passed the only light is the one ahead. There is no turning back, the pool of light encourages you forward at an ever increasing pace. It ensures you do not loiter. The only other things that move are the cams fixed to the ceiling above that check my progress. The domes that house them do not conceal the faint 'wheep' sound that says, 'We are watching you' and it says, 'We want you to know that you are being watched.' Particularly it says, 'We are able to watch you but you can't watch us because we have power and you have none.' When they are obvious, like the ones that watch me now, they seem less of a threat. Elsewhere when they're not obvious, you find yourself looking for them because you can't believe you're not being watched. I follow the light, and turn a corner. The dome above 'wheeps' as I move on to the next light and another cam takes over, 'wheep'.

    I have followed the lights and been watched all the way until ahead is the exit. Before that a security check point houses a single guard who sleeps behind a shuttered screen. If it wasn't for his snoring you wouldn't even know he was there. Woken by my tapping, his bad tempered, bleary eyes direct me to a steel panel instructing me where I should place my head. I place the back of my head against the purple spot, there is a corresponding 'ding' to inform him I have made contact and he thumps a button. There is a sharp click as a frequency pulse releases the collar's connection. I plane it into a tray which has shot out of the wall for that purpose. The tray disappears, but the tingling sensation in my neck does not. It can make you feel sick but my attention is on the exit and I wait for the guard to get permission to release me. Somewhere a clerk might be having a bad day and decides I'm the one that's going to pay for it. Before me is a circular cage with a rotating centre but nothing moves. Any complaint or sign of impatience would be enough to start my downward spiral into rehab. A clunk then a rattling hum and the inner cage rotates noisily until its two slots coincide and I can then walk through. It senses I have left and the carousel continues to a clunking halt, whereupon it locks itself. Columbus has satisfied its requirement and now will have received a large fee from the state for my interview. Once spewed out of the cage I have served my purpose but as long as I am within sight of the building I cannot relax.

    Out on a service road that supplies travel to the Columbus kitchens, their hospitality suites and entertainment lounges, I begin to relax. The stress that clerks are put through demands they have the best relaxation facilities. Working with the public for an hour or so, entitles them to any number of benefits so that they are fit and relaxed enough to cope with another 'client'.

    There are no road signs, or signposts. This is to confuse the enemy within; by that it means me and people like me who want to see change. All change is a threat. An enemy threatens, so by definition we are the enemy. If I hadn't have been here before I would get lost. Being lost is a reason to be arrested. You must always know where you are going and from where you have come and why.

I walk along a blue walkway. There is no loitering on blue, you must keep moving, no stopping. On the other side of the street is an entrance to the underground car park and transit link. Columbus share their facilities with other top execs, ministers and sponsors, so there's a lot of coming and going. As I'm not loitering, a long black executive limo pulls up by the security check point, just before the red and white striped bollards, and I stop to watch; I loiter. A darkened window drops silently down and a slim, gloved hand inside, shows a pass. The guard reaches out and focuses his reader on it. The window raises as the barriers drop effortlessly down into the tarmac. Silently the limo drifts into the subterranean level. The guard settles back in his seat, watches a screen, then another, then looks a little closer. He sees a stationary figure, hooded, standing against a wall and looks up in my direction. He then sees me looking at him. I see his puzzlement turn to a frown and when I don't move it turns to anger. I know he can't leave his station it would be more than his job's worth, but if an exec arrived he might lose it anyway for allowing someone to loiter on a blue area.

Blue areas exist within a specified distance of buildings deemed to be 'at risk' and any building is deemed to be at risk if they say it is. Loitering is generally perceived as a threat whether on a blue area or not, consequently you will never see any stationary persons except in green parks if they are permitted to enter, otherwise you have to keep on the move. I have seen what I needed to see, so before security is called I move on. I see the guard relax and take up his palmer and start keying in for some sex chat. It's what they all do and it's free and reduces stress.

The mist has turned to rain. I draw my hood lower over my face so the rain drips off the edge rather than running down my face. Get enough rain in your eyes, and they begin to irritate. A raindrop catches my mouth and I spit out its bitterness. I draw my necker up over my nose so I see through the slit that's left. LEOs are suspicious of anyone looking like this. It's as good as a mask and if you were a threat, it's how they think you would appear. They imagine you would be concealing a device, something like the size of an orange. They would have their hands on their pistols waiting for you to reach inside your coat. That would be enough for them to open fire even if it does turn out to be just an orange.

Thinking something sometimes makes it so, especially if it's bad. At the end of the street there's an andywagon parked and there is no other way but passed them. They see me all covered up and get suspicious. If I was to suddenly go for my inside coat pocket it would be the last thing I did. The wagons doors slide back and they both get out with their eyes fixed on me. I watch the street ahead and keep well to my side. They have their pistols on kill, the little red light is a tell-tale. They can use stun, but seldom do, it's more convenient not to have another side to the story. One of them takes out a reader, points in my direction, reads the bounce, and is satisfied, and probably disappointed. They'll know I've just exited Columbus, that being so, I'll be clean. Rain will account for my being covered up but there's no guarantee so I walk same pace, same everything, hands in pockets, eyes fixed about two body lengths ahead and no suspicious moves. It would be better if they could see my hands, but it's too late now, if I moved them they'd lose their nerve and shoot. Goodnight

Vienna. Opposite them within a few metres they try to appear relaxed, maintain their cool, their superiority and control, but inside they are like coiled springs. I feel them wishing there was an excuse to blow me away and end their uncertainty. I just walk, I turn the corner and just walk. A short distance and I cross over another deserted street. As I cross I can look back to see if I am being followed and make it appear as if I am just checking the road, not them, anything to avoid raising suspicion. They've both got back into their wagon, out of the rain. Crisis over, for now.

CHAPTER 5

There are still some parts of the District 48 that are pleasant. If it wasn't for the grey skies and drizzle you could imagine how they might have been. Old photos are full of colour but it's not like that now. A few roads still have their trees, but most have found them too expensive and they were removed. There is nothing that a corp can't make a profit out of and the trees were deemed to be a potential risk and therefore needed to be insured. Every year a survey is required to renew the annual Arboreal Licence in case they have become dangerous. They were only dangerous when they came to cut one down and it fell on a house and someone was killed. Each tree has an identity, it's costed and a record is kept. All trees are logged, one way or another.

In a maze of grey streets I turn another grey corner and join the street on which I am registered as living my grey, uneventful, official life. I wonder if these streets were ever anything but grey, and whether the sun ever shone. Ahead of me the road bends to the right, beyond that in a house on the left, is where Carl and Jean live. Carl is my uncle, and his partner Jean live their grey lives there, and where my life is grey and has been since my folks disappeared. It's as if I'm not even alive here. I sleep walk until I get back to the cellar. Of course they don't know about the group and its activities. It makes me angry that they seem to accept everything and do nothing to put anything right. Carl used to lecture in history but since 48 became deregulated Carl, like most people, has become the unemployable. It's a slow death and a pointless life. Give me a meaningful life and a quick death anytime.

As I turn the bend in the street, something is not grey at all. I see a black shiny andywagon parked ahead of me and I instinctively cross the road onto the other side, and drop my hood. We are not policed and the presence of andys in the area is bad news for someone. It's not near where I am registered as living but near enough, and they never park outside the house they are visiting. One of the andys glanced in my direction as I turned the corner, now it would be suspicious to turn back. I carry on casually on my side of the road while the andy on the far side of the wagon watches me. His arms rest folded on the top of the vehicle, his helmet is pushed back and his chin strap loose. The other, on my side, leans back against the door and is talking on his headset and looking up the road in the direction I'm going, in the direction of the house where I live; where my uncle lives. Still talking, his head turns until he can study me closely. Any attention is bad, this amount means they are deciding what to do, what kind of game they are going to play. Andys have the right to stop and search, they also have the right to pursue. In pursuit they can take whatever measures necessary to achieve capture. The PM says, ' The innocent have nothing to fear.'

I am innocent and have nothing to fear.

'The guilty condemn themselves by running.' That's what he says.

Andys will tempt you into running. Besides theft, bribery, extortion, violence, sexual assault and rape, for them the excitement of the chase is one of the few perks they have. If you do not run it just makes them angry having been deprived of their fun. The chase ends when you are dead or as good as and if you don't run, the result is the same, because they'll say you did run.

The andy on the far side drops his helmet down and mouths some words to which the other responds with a slight nod of his head. The intention is to build the fear until I run, even knowing what the consequences are likely to be. As I draw alongside they both clip their chin straps. The one on the far side chews a short thin stick like they do in some early movies moving it from one side of his mouth to the other and making the muscles bulge in his cheeks. He walks round the front of the car and leans back alongside his partner and they both stare at me.

'You!' One of them shouts. He rises up, takes out the baton they all carry and points it at me so there is no confusion,

'Don't I know you?'

I stop and turn, but move slowly backwards watching them and waiting for their move. I shake my head and give a kind of confused expression. It may yet come to running, and maybe if they've other things to do they'll just be happy with the thrill of putting the shits up someone. Otherwise they may just shoot.

'Well, I think I do,' he carries on, 'and my mate agrees.' His mate nods slowly as they both move towards me. They're reluctant to move too far from the car in case I do run for it.

The shake of my head as an answer makes the nearest frown and turn to his mate.

'The little fucker is making out we're liars. That's not very nice is it?' His mate shakes his head and they begin to move apart.

I move slowly backwards trying to watch them both, but they continue to move apart, covering each direction I might go.

'You've upset him now,' he continues, 'and you've upset me. Calling us liars. You gonna have to put it right, isn't he?' His mate nods.

The one to my right draws his baton, slaps it against his open hand and says,

'Your gonna have to be nice to us,' and takes the end of his baton and moves it around his mouth, into his mouth, licking it and making sucking noises. The other undoes his flies, grabs his crutch in one hand, points to it with his baton, then at me.

The farther they are away from their wagon the better chance I have of escape. Neither direction is favourite and they've covered both.

I'm inwardly pleading for something to take their attention and give me a sign. Anything which gets their attention will give me a start.

The one on my left makes a ring with his thumb and second finger, and slides his baton through with a jerk. He does it several times making sure I get the point, and that's what they call it. It's one of the ways they teach someone a lesson, they make sure they 'get the point'. They ram it up so hard it tears you apart and you're lucky if you die quickly. There's just the one lesson. There's no outward sign, other than the haemorrhaging which is put down as drug related. They always carry some bizarre concoction they can plant on you if they feel the need. An overdose of Agridon or Phylamene, can cause you to bleed. Another corpse for the snatchers. Goodnight Vienna! No inquest. No news.

Suddenly they make a lunge on a signal that I missed. One makes a grab for me, he misses as I twist but in so doing I trip. I'm nearly down but I recover and start to run but my coat holds me back. One of them has the bottom of it but before I can get my arms out something smacks the back of my neck and I sink to my knees. Something hitting the middle of my back throws me forward and my face hits the ground and then, as I'm dragged backwards, I can feel blood and grit mixing in my mouth. Then there is a weight on my back, maybe a knee or a boot, and my head is being pressed so hard into the tarmac my ears are beginning to ring. I'm spitting blood and the side of my face stings, my arms are pinned against my back. I rock with a few kicks to the ribs. They're tearing at my jeans but they can't tear a hole big enough for a batten. I loosen an arm and raise myself, then something crashes into the side of my head. I hear it as well as feel it. A second later the stabbing pain sears its jagged way round and round my skull as if it's caught in a cycle bouncing from side to side. I'm being sick but I can't move. Everything drains away, all care, all feeling, every sound. There's darkness, quiet, peace, stillness.

Sensation creeps either inside or outside my head. I don't know. The vision in one eye is stained red, I can't tell if it's in my eye or over my eye, running down my face, or both. I blink and then the lids stick together. I lay motionless with the eye nearest the ground open but stinging with grit. I can see along the road surface, through boulders of grit and blood glistening. My blood. Way off I can make out shapes, bodies, arms waving, voices shouting and swearing and screaming and then things smashing.

I'm in the road and they'll run me over. It's their way to cover their tracks, and it's my body that'll be covered in tracks. I try to roll but nothing works and my ribs scream, so I wait and watch. Two andys are trying to hold someone down in a doorway, two more are joining in. They are fighting over a body which wriggles and kicks. An andy kicks and misses, falls, then is hit by a woman with a bat. She's never played baseball, you can tell, but the second blow is better and just at the base of his skull, he stiffens then drops. Another andy grabs the bat at each end and shakes her like a rag doll because she won't let go. She launches a kick from way back at his balls and scores. She's played that game before. He crumples to his knees, head down. Now I realise the fight is about Carl. He's held on the ground and they are trying to cuff him. He breaks free but falls against the wall by the front window as one of the andys kicks his feet away. This time they've got him. They turn him and push his head through the window but it hits the timber, so they have another go this time the top half of his body is lost into the room before it's dragged out and dumped in a lifeless pile. Now from nowhere, there is a large, long coated figure, maybe from the back of the house, his face is hidden so only his eyes are seen. What he sees is Jean and what he takes is the bat. He strides one pace and draws a long stroke across the heads of two andys. It's slow, deliberate, but his movements are efficient, so he seems to have all the time, and others none. The bat sweeps round and back towards a kneeling officer. Its path is certain, it shatters his helmeted head like a peach, but the bat moves on. He takes one side step and twists. The bat arcs round as the figure turns like a dance, and the radius it describes is exactly that of another helmet which spins away leaving its bloody head in tatters. Half conscious, an andy raises himself to his knees and is allowed to draw his pistol. A long coat swirls, a masked head twists, finds its focus. An arm begins to extend, pistol in hand, another arm raised in defence. But the bat's journey does not falter. It breaks through one arm at the elbow then takes a pistol full of fingers and sends them spiralling across the gardens. The andy's scream is cut short as the bat returns and fills his open mouth with the back of his head. All this I see through blood and grit and as if in slow motion. My head lays bleeding, heavy on the gritted road as truck wheels I cannot avoid swing round and I lay motionless in their path. So I give up and everything fades.

I'm feeling movement. I hear an engine. In my blindness it feels like I'm in a truck, maybe an andywagon. It shifts and I move and I feel the pushing of corners, the going forward and the slowing down. I don't move myself, I can't, other things move me and I can't stop them. Through an eye, a glimmer. There's a woman sat against the side panel. I think it's Jean. If the man that is with her is alive then he is still my uncle. My uncle is called Carl and it is Jean holding his head in her hands and resting it in her lap. There is blood. My blood and his blood, and my uncle's is wet. He is bandaged but still bleeding and I think still alive because Jean smiles to give me comfort. This our journey to Rehab, she thinks I don't know.

Above, the top of the truck is plastic. It's mostly dark in the truck except when we go under street lights or on the autoways which are all lit. The lights pass above us and the shadows move around us. It makes it look as if we are moving but we are not. Outside is moving. We are going somewhere, but we cannot move, we are going to Rehab. I try to speak but my lips are stuck together with blood and I just mumble. Jean puts her finger across her lips so I know I am to keep shtum. Then she makes a look to the side just with her eyes and I follow with the one eye that is open. I see there is an andy further up the truck with his hands tied behind. His head is wrapped in grey tape so there is just a slit for him to breathe. His clothing has been removed and he is in his underwear, which is blood stained, but he is alive. His fat belly moves, and the slit gurgles, and blood and snot runs in spurts over the tape. We are all the same now, just spare parts.

      The street lights above vanish and the roof of the truck is dark and everything is shadow. The truck manoeuvres and the motor echoes as if we are inside a building. The truck stops, then the engine. There are muffled, echoey voices and footsteps, all inside somewhere. They will take us and that will be it. There is a whining, a door or two, closing and then a clunk. Then a sound like locking. The voices echo more now because we are all inside, trapped. The rear door of the truck lowers to make a ramp but it is too dark to see, and I have only one eye and that stings. I feel sick. In pain all over, tired and I am just a piece of meat like a carcass, helpless. Soon it will be all over. They take Carl's body. It is moved by shadows, lifting, placing, a trolley wheels away. I can't see very much, I would rather not see. I think this is enough.

      Maybe because we can't close our ears there is always sound. Before you realise there is light, you hear. The sounds I hear are unclear, distant, perhaps as in a dream and the light is red, all red-orange light. The kind you see when you close your eyes in the light. But this light moves and there are darker patches that move too. Perhaps shadows. Shadows crossing, stopping, and voices. I am covered and warm and not in pain except for my face which is sore. I have secrets. Do they know I have secrets, or is that still secret? I think of how much pain I can bear. Not much. What would Turin do? What will Meko think? I am being touched, my head lifted suddenly there is pain in my chest, burning. There is blinding light and I fear what it is, but then there are words.

'There. Don't open your eyes until you are ready. It might still be uncomfortable. Does your head hurt at all?'

I'm about to say no, but decide just to move my head, which hurts, and I wince. There is a smile, I feel she is smiling, it is a she,

'Okay. Keep still? Would you like some water?'

Suddenly I have never been so thirsty in my life, so I nod which really hurts.

She lifts my head. She cares. The water is cool, but I splutter.

'Sorry,' I try to say but I just splutter. Then I see a little; blurred at first, then I see the glass and a hand, a clean hand, and white clothing like a nurse. The bed is bright and clean like a hospital bed. She moves away and out of sight.

'I'm putting the water on the side here,' she says, 'by the jug. When you are able, have some more.'

I close my eyes, but I am curious, and I mumble,

'Am I in a hospital?' but I splutter again because my mouth is swollen, so I try again, just, 'Hospital?'

'Sort of,' she answers, 'but you are quite safe, you've no need to worry about anything. We've just taken a little blood for analysis.'

I hadn't even thought about that, things being taken. I would have done shortly. Soon I shall check my body for entry wounds.

'How's Carl?' I manage without too much splutter. Clearer, I could understand it.

'Was he the guy that came in at the same time?'

'Yes, he's my uncle.'

'He's not very well but we think he should be okay. Is that your aunt that's with him?'

'No . . .' I suddenly realise I am giving away information. Had I said too much? I'll play for time.

'I'm tired.'

So this is a 'sort of hospital' and she was quick to tell me not to worry. This is a reason to worry. 'Trust no one,' and, 'the enemy has the potential to control everything' these are rules. Another is 'Follow your gut feelings'.

She says that she has not taken anything but a little blood, for analysis. Then they will take, what? My liver, heart, kidneys? What's first, maybe limbs? They might keep me alive during the period of harvest which can be months and it is best to keep donors relaxed, stress free or it can put the organs at risk. That's why she's so nice to me, nice to a total stranger. The function of more and more organs will be substituted by external devices until I have been totally harvested. Nothing will be left except a brain being fooled by pumps and filters while I struggle to comprehend my isolation; then parts of the brain will go. I feel tears welling up in pools that sting.

I have been sleeping. Now I can see a little better, though one eye is still swollen and covered. There is light so I think the eyeball is still in, that at least, has not been harvested. Maybe I'm just not ready yet. I feel as much of my body as I can reach without making it obvious. No pain or wounds, so . .'

'Arghh!' My chest is agony on the left side, perhaps the heart, they have taken it? No, I can hear it pumping, actually drumming, thumping now, or is that a machine. A lung! First they've taken a lung, I can survive with one. Then kidneys, eyes, liver, all to be replaced one by one by mechanical substitutes until eventually, when all the organs have been removed and I am no more than a room full of buzzes, clicks, and hisses, I will just be turned off. The tears roll down my cheeks again. I begin to sob, I try to stop but the more I try the worse it gets. The thought of my body being harvested, slowly, bit by bit, as a living donor waiting for the last organ to be cut out and sold, is too much. The trauma of being beaten up, the loss of friends, family, the helplessness of my situation overwhelms me. I lay with one eye, trying to focus on the ceiling above. Gradually my tears stop flowing, stop stinging and again I sleep. The sleep is full of images. It is all violence and blood, heads being smashed and then bodies being cut up and parts being stolen. They are my parts. They all get stolen by those that live beneath the bed, and in the bed. Then there is nothing left but the depression in the bed where I used to be. That is me. Then a nurse appears and smiles and makes the bed smooth, then her face turns into something horrible, and I wake.

    I wipe the sweat from my forehead and the tears from the one eye that is left. Blinking the eye clears it a little and I can see the room in which I am captive. There is a window opposite, to which is fitted a blind, but it looks as if I am too high up to get out of it, maybe the fifth floor. A door to my left, which would be locked, another bed to my right, unoccupied, several cabinets, a chair on which there is a plastic bag, in which there is clothing, my clothing, jacket, jeans and stuff, looks like washed and neatly folded, which is cunning. I see this now. They have left them for me to see, and my boots beneath in another bag. They want to give the impression I will be able to leave. Everything is painted grey, the walls, the cabinets, the chair, the floor. The ceiling is white squares, a false ceiling with lightweight squares that can be removed, that hang down and twist and spin in smoke. Above them services run, but the ceiling is not strong enough to take my weight even if I could crawl. There are no escape routes. The only way out, is the only way in. I must be calm, think, act when the time is right. If there is any time at all. I will appear helpless, who am I fooling, I am helpless. I wonder what Turin might do. He might say,

'The enemy is weak as it celebrates success.'

I can't remember if that's a rule or not.

The door opens and I noticed there was no unlocking, so they must still think I am too weak to escape. The same nurse, if that's what she is, comes in. She is too considerate to be true,

'If you're feeling up to it here's a little snack, just a couple of biscuits and some juice,'

I nod weakly and look at her through a half closed eye and she smiles but I think that she must think,

'I was born yesterday.'

The juice, obviously drugged, would have to be disposed of to make them think I've drunk it. The biscuits as well, to make it look as if I am the fool she takes me for. I gesticulate feebly that I needed a 'bottle' to piss in. She leaves again without locking the door, but I decided that now isn't the time as she would be returning quickly. Which she does and I pretend to be drowsy, too ill to attempt an escape?

'I'll put it here, okay?'

I make it appear that all the energy I can muster goes into the nod, and that nodding was all that I can do and even that is taking its toll. It does still hurt so it might be convincing. As soon as she leaves this time I see if I can stand up. I do, but any stress to my chest, is agony. It's bandaged where they have taken my lung. Breathing is difficult with just the one and I have no energy. The window has a blind, the sort that prevents any light coming in, and we are on the third or fourth floor of a block. I don't recognise the view so I can't tell which district we are in, but it is part of London Urbia and still south because on the horizon is the old Thames Turbine building. That is to the east and I can see the aircraft over the Estuary Port rising and dropping with their payloads. Nearer are the gas-ship fun rides. I can't have travelled as far as I thought, which is good.

Sitting on the edge of the bed I pick up the bottle and my chest screams pain. If I lift the eye patch, I can see a fraction out of the injured eye now, which helps me focus on the mouth of the urine bottle. In went the biscuits and the juice and some piss, a lot of piss, almost too much. When she comes to take the bottle away I will pretend to be asleep then I will make my escape soon after she has left knowing that she would have things to do.

It works well and as soon as she has closed the door behind her I am up, stifling my groans. I slip my feet into the boots then grabbing hold of my clothing, but with the wrong hand and again my chest is in agony. I change hands and take the clothing with a view to changing when I've put in a bit of distance. The small window in the door doesn't allow me to see whether the coast is clear, so I put down my clothing and will pretend to be sleepwalking or something if I'm noticed. To my relief the corridor is clear but there are voices, and machinery hums and clicks all around. A doorway a few paces away has no window. So I'll try that. I pick up my clothing and move as quickly and as silently as I can. Cautiously I push it. It opens easily and reveals a small room full of empty shelves. Moving toward the room with the voices, the next door is more substantial. I have to push harder and find my chest is hurting. Putting my back to it starts it opening and it continues to do so without a sound. When eventually I can, I turn to see a concrete staircase, bleak and dimly lit. As the door closes I can't stop it creaking. If it's heard, so be it, it's too late to turn back. A dim light struggles through small, soot blackened windows above and below on each landing as the steps turn. There is just enough light to see, so I travel down a couple of flights past one of the small windows, one aching step at a time. Below me the walls are more heavily blackened. A sooty powder clings to them from when there was a fire somewhere below. I take one step at a time and try to avoid contact with everything. Condensation in the moist air forms glistening beads on the walls and handrails. They linger on the handrails but on the walls they break and run down in rivulets, leaving pale streaks that dragging fingers could have made. I can hear voices above, not clear, but they are not raised, and I sense they are not alarmed. I stand by a door on the floor below the voices. I wish it would open but it has no handle nor any means of opening, all round it has been welded. On the next landing by a window, I see the walls are now both grey and black. It is not only soot now but a whitish dust as well that covers everything. It is colder here as the window has some panes missing and I clutch what gown there is around me. The steps have become slippery. It's an oily fat, a grease, that's settled everywhere, on the handrail and every flat surface. The next floor is darker because this sooty grease coats the window. Each step takes me closer to where the fire was. Where the fire is? It's not burning now. It's as if I'm walking down the inside of a chimney, and I'm wondering what it is they burn.

    I feel a momentary breeze from below and it carries with it a putrefying stench. I imagine hollowed out corpses laying on mounds of unusable parts waiting for disposal, waiting to be rendered. Carcasses being fed into furnaces like a Bosch hell; and I am walking down into it. I feel sick and take a few paces back to the open window to breath in less polluted air. Then why there was a breeze at all grabs me as I hear the door above creaking closed. I am breathing hard because of only having one lung, and because of the stench. The cavity on my left side aches where my lung used to be, and I suddenly realise how cold I am. I am still in the hospital gown and haven't got into my own clothes. If I put on my clothing I can think, and not just about being cold, but it's too late. I sense someone is in the same space, though I hear nothing. I don't care to hear anything. I could carry on down and give myself up for disposal or just sit and wait. If I had the energy I would panic. I can't fight any more, and certainly not dressed like this. The pain and tiredness at last drowns me, and I feel myself falling.

CHAPTER 6

'Ash?'

There is light and clean smells, not like the stairwell. I am not in the stairwell, I am in a bed again and ready for harvesting.

'Ash, it's Jean.'

That sounds like Jean. Jean's voice.

' Ash'

Jean I know, but I should trust no-one. I can tell if it is Jean, and even if she is herself or something has changed. I murmur a little as if coming out of a deep sleep.

'Ash. Can you hear me Ash, it's Jean. Carl's Jean.'

I can see Jean's shape. Another shape walks across the light, but not Jean.

'I'll be back in a few minutes'. That was the nurse, she has been listening.

Now she has gone I feel it is safe to open my eyes a little. The light is fierce but slowly the blurs form shapes that I recognise and it is definitely Jean that sits beside me.

'How are you feeling?' She says putting her head on one side so she can see my expression. This is perfectly natural and to be expected. She seems normal, herself, and we are alone.

'Sore.' I say, then a little quieter, 'They've taken a lung.'

'Who has?' She is frowning, I don't think she knows.

'The people here. They took it while I was unconscious.'

'Why do you think that?'

'My chest hurts, I'm bandaged up and having difficulty breathing. What more evidence do you need?'

'Well, a lung would be a start.'

I don't think she believes me, unless she too is ignorant of the real purpose of this place. I ask her,

'Have they taken anything of yours?'

She is shaking her head, but it's the wrong shake.

'No. Listen to me. You were beaten up by two andys opposite the house, do you remember?'

'Yes,' I mumble weakly. She is talking too loudly, and maybe I'm being told off.

'You were unconscious when we picked you up, but you came round briefly in the truck. Remember that?'

'Vaguely.'

'Right. We got you here where you could be looked after. You have two broken ribs on your left side. At first they thought your lung might be punctured but it wasn't. They are likely to be very sore for a while. The only organ that seems to be missing is your brain which you could get very good money for as you use it so little!'

This is Jean. This is how she usually talks to me. She calls it tough love but is just seems like insults. But she is a good sort.

The nurse opens the door and comes in with a tray like before. More juice and biscuits which she hands to Jean. Then she sees my expression,

'It's all right, they're not the same. Though you should be made to eat them, wasting perfectly good biscuits, let alone the juice. You gave the nurse a shock when she emptied your bottle.'

'Something definitely not right with this boy's urine,' says the nurse and they both laugh. I don't because the joke is on me and I think it would be be agony to laugh. I change the subject.

'How is Carl?'

They look at each other. I take this to be a bad sign. Jean looks at her hands, then at me,

'He's still unconscious.' Then the nurse puts a hand on Jean's shoulder,

'But we are hopeful that he will make a full recovery.' The nurse smiles, gives Jean some pills and then goes.

'These are for you.' Jean tells me, then puts the pills in my hand.

'What is this place and is it safe?'

'It's as safe as anywhere can be.'

Now she stands up and goes to the window.

'We are on a hidden floor, and it is better you don't know everything yet, but I will tell you what I can to put your mind at rest.'

'I know what a hidden floor is.'

'You do?'

'If you count the floors on the outside and compare the number of floors that the lift serves there's one or more missing.'

Jean nods,

'And you only look for a missing floor if you suspect there might be one. This has been a medical facility for a while and it's run by a group.'

'A group?'

'A freemeds group, have you heard of them?'

I tell her that I'm not sure.

'People who have professional skills that work in corps but have some sense of humanity and want to help. There are several in London Urbia. It's a semi-mobile unit, each uses a place for a while then they move on. If there's a risk of being found by the state they can move pretty quickly. Usually they're quite safe, there's less risk than you might think.'

'Why?'

'If you or your family need health care which the state says you are not entitled to, what would you do? These people are the same ones that spend their time treating workers, execs, even ministers. They do this for free.'

'So they are always in deregs?'

'It's where the help is needed most and where it's most appreciated.'

'And the nurses and doctors work elsewhere and get paid but they still take the risk to heal people for no reward?'

'Yes.'

'Why do they risk it?'

'You think that only youth has a conscience? And anyone older can't have because of where we are? It's never that simple. When your uncle gets better, and let's hope he does, you should talk to him. Remember he used to teach history when 48 was regulated. Everyone was a youth once, you're not the only one.'

'So it's just guilt?'

'Ash, you are an idiot sometimes.' Jean smiles and shakes her head. Then she sits by my side while I take the pills, drink the juice and start on the biscuits which taste of ginger, Jean tells me.

'That nurse,' she says, 'was telling me that those who have the right to health care do nothing but complain and want more, and want it quicker. There's no gratitude, just expectation and demand. She told me that working the freemeds gives her a real buzz because what she does is really appreciated and she feels needed; and people need to feel needed.'

It's true that since my uncle became my guardian I had resisted his authority. I had never thought of him as anything other than disconnected, occupied with the unimportant and enjoying having someone to tell what to do. His attempts at control were irritating and his warnings irrelevant. I had got into stuff which would be truly horrific on their level if they ever found out about it. It was the kind of stuff he had warned me against, but they did nothing and at least I was doing something. I had little experience of living in a regulated district, being 'responsible' and having the possibility of a job and the drug habit that goes with it. Since deregulation, hope had been taken away, so there was nothing to lose. What if we did blow things up and what if execs did get killed? Life is cheap where we live, and why should their lives be worth any more. Besides it's a win-win situation. If stuff changes, we win, if we die, we're out of here, we win. If you do nothing, you agree, you accept everything like the generations before who did nothing, just let it happen. That's not going to happen again! Direct Action, is Turin's mantra. Route one. That's got to be the way. Bang! Something done, a sign, no argument. KISS. Keep it simple, stupid. You get older and lose the stomach for it, take on responsibilities, children. That's fine, just move over. It's our time now.

Jean leans a little closer and interrupts my thoughts,
'Okay?
'Yeh. Just thinking.'
'I'll leave you with your thoughts then, and the juice and biscuits. Eat them this time. I'll bring in something more

substantial later, in the meantime get some sleep; and no wandering.'

'Okay.' But sleep isn't going to come easy. For a start I'm not used to a comfortable bed. I'm not used to a comfortable anything or safety. If Turin was here he could unpack, dissect, evaluate, conclude. He could tell me what to do, tell me what to think.

After a while I begin to feel really drowsy and relaxed; very relaxed. Also I feel safe and waves of care seem to drift away. I think it must be the pills and I think that was my last thought.

A sound wakes me. A sound that I heard, that woke me, but I can't recall it. It made me jump. Now there are footsteps, some walking, some running. Shadows pass through the dim light of the corridor that I can see through my door's small window. This is the only light. The blind is down and there is no light from outside. There are voices and more footsteps. Footsteps with trolleys that clank. Lights flash in the corridor, doors open and close. I wonder if this is a raid and if there are about to be shots and screams and will it be my turn now, and Jean's and Carl's, and the nice nurse who just wants to help people. Darkness and quiet resumes and so does sleep.

A rolling, scraping sound wakes me and light floods my closed eyes. I keep them shut but it is just the dull light of day as the nurse raises the blind. It is never bright but the blind seals out all light so even this is bright at first. She leaves a drink and a bowl of something I don't recognise. The pain in my chest is better, until I move, and wince.

'Still painful?'

'A bit.' She's caring and has light blue eyes, too old for me really but she has a good figure and I play with imagining her naked and the shape of her breasts without underwear, and then with underwear, and then again without. I imagine a seduction where she is in control and I surrender.

'You're feeling better this morning,' and she smiles. 'There are some pain killers, take them with your juice and cereal, then when I return I'll take you to the bathroom.'

As she goes I begin to realise why she thought I was feeling better, and it is seriously embarrassing. I take the pills and the juice but the cereal is hard work as it tastes like sawdust, or I imagine what sawdust must taste like. I know what grit and tarmac tastes like, and now sawdust.

The morning is spent having dressings changed. My face and ribs have been having ray therapy, which is warming and will speed up the healing. The nurse has changed the bedding and has given me more painkillers for now and when I leave.

'Was there noise last night?' I ask her. 'I thought I heard some, did I? I could have been dreaming.'

'It was my night away, but I think what you must have heard was a problem that Carl had during the night. A monitor set off an alarm and a team was alerted. He's okay now.'

'Is he awake?'

'No but the incident has made his recovery more likely. It was a crisis we were expecting and not unusual. We're sure he'll be fine now.'

As she leaves, the door opens and Jean appears. They have a quiet word, I think about Carl, then the nurse goes.

'Well, you seem to be looking healthier. Enjoy your breakfast?'

'Okay,' I lie, 'how's Carl?'

'Bit of a crisis over night, but he is doing fine. I've plugged in his music and he's on the stimulator. His analyser is pushing normal but he needs rest.'

She pauses for a moment and I know there are things that have to be dealt with.

'Ash, I have to talk to you about stuff.'

I suggest to her that she is going to tell me we can't go back home. She looks a little surprised as if I have no appreciation of what's going on. I don't know the details and why but I'm bound to suspect something. I ask her why.

'After we left the house,' she tells me, 'a friend had it screened and they found a few listening devices.'

'Bugs.' I say nonchalantly and again she seems a bit surprised.

'Yes, bugs. We don't know how long they've been there and how much has been overheard.'

'Don't tell me, you were planning to assassinate the PM?' I joke because I'm not sure how I should react, it's a mask. I suppose I should be shocked, they would expect me to be.

'This is nothing to joke about, Ash. Carl is badly injured.'

'How serious is what they might have overheard?' I ask. It's a fine line asking the right questions and giving the impression you don't know anything about things.

'We haven't been planning anything, we just freethink. Just talking about how corrupt the corps are and how they have control over all the services, how people are held to ransom and have no power. The unfairness of it all.'

'You never talked about that stuff with me.'

'How could we? We didn't want to put you in a position where pressure might be put on you to report us.'

I look surprised but it had never occurred to me that they might think I could be a risk from their activities.

'We couldn't encourage you to freethink because we couldn't allow you to become a risk to yourself as well as others, thinking it was normal. Someone else, even a friend, can have power over you if they hear you say anything anti-state. Then if they have anything on you, even just suspicion, you're marked for life. Then you'll have to give names, and keep giving them, right or wrong, if you want to stay alive. Carl and I decided we had to keep it all to ourselves.'

If only they knew what I'd been up to. Even now my conditioning is telling me to say nothing, play innocent and naive. Same ol', same ol'. I didn't know about them, they don't know about me.

'There's no way we can go back to the house,' Jean says.

'What were you planning then?'

'We know someone who can pull a few strings and even sort us out with new IDs. We'll have to leave urbia and find a place in the rural, then maybe return, or maybe not.'

'How long for?'

'We don't know.'

'You might stay?'

'The trouble is Ash, people like Carl are always under suspicion. He has views and it doesn't take much for him to tell someone. If 48 hadn't been deregulated he would probably have lost his job anyway.'

'Why?'

'Because he's political and there's no room for that anymore.'

'Political?'

'He will explain it to you when he's better.'

'So is that why the andys came round to pick him up?'

'Freethinking isn't illegal, as you know, but it gives the state a reason to detain you while they find other evidence.'

'You mean whilst they find a way of fitting you up.'

'As a . . ,' she pauses, 'an ex People's Rep, Ash, I have to believe there is still some remnants of a legal system; but you are right, once inside there's not much chance of getting anyone out. Unless there's leverage.'

I knew what she meant. If you know an exec or have a good job you can get someone to speak up for you. The spotlight then falls on them, so most are reluctant.

'Why did they came round to the house?'

'They said someone had reported us for keeping a pet.'

'But you don't have a pet.'

'Carl found a stray dog scratching at the back door one night. It was a small terrier type and he brought it in before it could be shot. It took him a couple of days but eventually he found the owner. She was a bed ridden old lady whose son used to take the dog out at night and bring food round. Unknown to her, her son had been mugged and the dog had run off. He'd been taken to a refuge to recover.'

'The dog?'

'No, you idiot. The son! So for a few days the old lady had no idea what had happened. When the son returned he found the dog was missing. He set about trying to find it and eventually met up with Carl. So the dog was returned.'

'Do you know who reported it?' I ask.

'No one, they picked up a dog bark on surveillance.'

'So all this is because Carl's got a soft spot for small dogs.'

She shakes her head the 'there's no hope' way, then explains that having a dog scratching at the back door would have been enough for the andys to claim it was yours. Plus, she adds, it would have been heard and someone would have reported it for a reward or just brownie points. I know that keeping a dog, in fact any unauthorised animal, is a serious breach of the health code and carries the same penalties as if you tried to poison food stuffs, or contaminate the water supply. The dog's bark was evidence of a pet and just the excuse they needed to put away what they see as a potential, if not an actual, agitator. The state thinks there's no one more dangerous than someone committed to an idea, if it's not their idea.

I asked Jean when they plan to go.

'We need an okay that Carl is fit to move. We've talked about it. There's a couple of places west where we have friends, real friends, not just people we can trust, do you know what I mean?'

I nod sagely and it would be nice to exchange secrets. It's harder to remain silent than it is to tell. If either of us landed up in Rehab it wouldn't be long before they had found out everything we know. This has nothing to do with blabbing or how brave you are, no physical pain is involved, the science of getting the truth out of people was always high on the security corps list, and not a penny was spared. You will tell them everything and be glad to.

I ask Jean if they plan to take me with them.

She says it's up to me and tells me,

'You will be able to leave here soon but it might not be a good idea to go back to the house in case they are waiting for Carl and I to return.'

She wonders if I have other places I can stay. I tell her that I do and she pauses hoping that I may be more forthcoming, but it is safer for me not to, so she continues,

'We will travel as soon as possible. We have friends near to the old house and may be able to leave a message for you. It might not be straight forward because we would only want you to understand it, otherwise it could be dangerous. Do you know what I mean?'

You see, she treats me like a child. It's times like this I just wish I could let her know what the group and I do. It might get me some respect.

'Ash,' she continues, 'I don't want you to think we're abandoning you.'

I smile reassuringly and again I'm tempted to give her some idea of what I've been doing and that I can look after myself.

'There's a box buried at the bottom of the garden,' she tells me, 'which you can access through the back fence without opening the gate. It's what my mother and her boyfriend used to leave letters in for each other. We will try to get something left there, and get someone to check it in case you need to get in touch. It can't be something that means anything to anyone else in case it gets found, but a clue. There's an old gate post at the front of the house with a number one left on it. If the number is upside down, it means there's something in the box, Okay?'

I nod.

' You can't tell anyone about it or anything else, Okay?'

I nod again meekly, as if it isn't blindingly obvious.

'And,' she continues, 'it would be wise to keep everything else that's happened secret too, especially this place, okay? It's better that no one knows, no matter how much you want to tell them.'

I know this and it is frustrating to have to keep all I know to myself but these secrets are lives. So I just nod and we continue in ignorance of each other like parallel lines.

I'm in the hospital for another day before they say I can go. Then a nurse tells me everybody has to leave. I walk about this hidden floor and see other patients, but we just nod and do not talk. A special team arrived during the night and they had everything packed and gone in two or three hours. I sat and watched them as I waited for a couple of checks, some painkillers and an escort.

Carl was still drifting in and out of consciousness and we at least made eye contact, which was good. Jean said she had been told Carl was okay to travel and they were leaving for the rural. They would be in a truck so Carl could be laid out in the back. I had some good chats with Jean, more than ever, and we began to understand each other a bit more, for the first time I began to see what Carl saw in her. It sometimes takes a crisis to lower barriers and treat each other just like people.

Out on the street again, I remove my blindfold and hand it back to the driver. He waves and soon disappears between buildings. I stare about me wondering if I can recognise the building I was in, or the view from it but I can't. It's because I have a feeling of loss. You may think you don't need something, then when it's taken away, you realise how much you depended on it. What is it I look back for? Care, kindness, self-sacrifice, and risking so much just to help others? I wonder how it got to be like it is when there are still people like that around.

I turn away, wander towards a cross roads, and take the road which I think will lead me back to 48. Jean could be right about the old house being risky, but I still have some stuff there. I can stay at the cellar tonight if I don't meet up with anyone else I know. I didn't stay at the old house very often but it was good to know that there was a warm bed there if nowhere else.

I feel a cold chill and the mist swirls round the cams which whurr in your direction as they pick up the sound of your approach, or movement. They focus and try to pick up a facial detail so they can cross reference it with their database and see whether you have the nose, the chin, or the walk, they are looking for. For a few nights the hospital gave me some security and warmth, suddenly I feel the paranoia creeping back into my bones like a cold night. When you have to live with something you learn to love it, when it's gone, you realise how much you've been hating it all along. Now I've got to learn to love all over again.

I peep out at others peeping out, we all skulk. We hug the sparkling railings and the glistening walls. We walk bent with the fear of being stopped, tormented, beaten up and left for dead, and half the time we welcome it. The fear of it is so debilitating, sometimes you just wish they'd get it over with.

Nearer home there are dodges we use to avoid the cams but in 48, as it's deregulated, there aren't so many. Most have been blinded and others have just corroded. Anything that's out all the time needs constant maintenance, but when it's in a district like 48 there's no requirement. We're not a priority.

As evening falls, houses are just dark blocks against a darkening grey sky. Soon they'll disappear. There's no colour. In this grey world, colour attracts attention, it's like telling everyone you're different. Being different is not good, you'll soon be made the same. All the houses are now grey but some were once painted bright colours. Long ago they gave up and now hide amongst each other, not wanting to appear different, not wanting to attract attention. Even things that can't think, think that's a good idea.

Reading the shapes I can see between houses, I glimpse the old house. In the garden is the post box where Jean will leave messages. After the last time I was here I have to consider that it is unsafe and probably watched. I scan buildings and roofs for any cams or surveillance. There are several houses that are empty and might have LEOs in, but they are usually careless enough to be heard. If they use an occupied house the owner will make a sign, something propped up in a window or a curtain rolled up, something out of the ordinary but innocent and not obvious. There's a fine drizzle like a mist, not enough to make me invisible in their night sights.

I creep down a narrow alleyway that runs along the back of the gardens that face my house. When you move, you make enough noise so you can't hear others. Then you keep thinking you can hear them, even if you don't. Paranoia doesn't mean it won't happen. I see the houses on the other side through the gaps, each time getting closer until I can look directly at my house. It seems normal, but then it would. I have Turin's words in my ears and his rules. I sit down against a fence and listen. It is quiet, except for the faint patter of drips all around. I feel uneasy though, is there such a thing as too quiet? 'Be guided by your gut feelings' is a rule, but how can I tell if what I feel has anything to do with reality. I'll know afterwards when it's too late. I decide that I am imagining things and reason that LEOs have better things to do.

Rather than walk round, I can get over the fence and go straight across the road. I grab hold of the top of the fence and I am about to jump and haul myself over when I wince with the pain of my ribs and stop. Through tear filled eyes I'm staring at an upstairs window, probably a bedroom. A lightweight flimsy curtain hangs in one pane, the other has the same curtain but it's tied in a knot. I lean against the fence, catch my breath and rummage around for the pain killers that I was given, I take them and think. Even if it is not a sign I will take it to be one. 'Prepare for the worst, hope for the best.' This is not a rule, just common sense.

The alleyway carries on for a few more houses and then opens onto a side road. I scan for cams and the only one I can see has been shot and hangs limply from a ragged cable. They don't usually last long here, but it's new ones I'm looking for. I make my way round to the rear of the line of houses in which mine is about the fourth along. The walls and fences separating the gardens are low enough to step over but I am mindful that the house might be watched from the rear as well. I carefully scale a few walls and crouch down for a last look. I can hear the owners bickering over what they should watch on their screens, and I can smell some sort of vegetable being cooked. Quietly I move through another garden until I can lean against the back of my house. I put my ear to the cold wet downstairs window, but there is no vibration or movement that I can detect. I step back and look carefully at the windows above and to the side. There is no light. I drop silently back up the garden watching all the time. I creep through the garden gate at the rear, into the narrow pathway that runs between all the gardens which are back to back. A few paces and I can feel the loose panel which I lift, beneath it the container is empty. This is no real surprise but now I know what Jean was talking about.

    Some of the fences along this path are still head height so I am well concealed. Should anyone else want to use this path there would be no hiding, or avoiding them. I move along until I can see beyond the house to the houses opposite. Without the night sights they have, it's impossible for me to tell if there is anyone watching. I look and listen, and feel. I see nothing, hear nothing, but still feel uneasy. I move to the gate, open it and walk back to the rear of the house.

    I can see my room on the floor above and the idea of staying the night in my warm bed is tempting even though the house might be watched. I lift the brick and pick up the spare key to unlock the old back door which still uses them. I insert the key and turn it but there is resistance, the door is not locked. Jean would not have left the door unlocked. We know there is a spare key if we need to get in. Someone who doesn't know that, might leave the door unlocked. Someone that we don't know might be keen for us to use the back door. The key is still in the lock and at the slightest sound I could close the door and lock it, which would give me time to get away. I take hold of the door knob and turn it so slowly, silently and hoping that no one is watching it on the other side. I open the door the tiniest amount still hoping it is unseen. I listen, there is silence, and there is no sense of anyone inside, no different odour. Still my gut feeling tells me to close the door and run. I wait a few moments longer. A neighbour's light comes on down the side and on an upper floor, perhaps a bathroom. It sheds its faint light across the gap and in through the kitchen window. Through the narrow slit, no more than the thickness of a little finger, I press first my ear to the gap, then I try to see inside without moving the door. All I can make out are some of the units. What little light there is will be a help inside but then something shiny catches my eye. I crouch down to get a better look. Through the gap I can just make out something running across from the door to the wall at the side, something like a wire or a chord, taught. The neighbour's light goes out and it disappears until my eyes adjust. Now its shininess dimly reflects a red diode indicating that the waiting device is primed. I gently close the door. I guess they wouldn't need to watch the rear of the house. They'd soon know if anyone opened the back door.

Always have at least two ways out, it's a rule. The window to my room has a drain pipe that runs close by. It's a route that I have used many times but it's never been more important. Even with pain killers, my ribs are still agony. As I crawl through the window, the room is cold and damp. I haven't been here for a few weeks and neither has Carl or Jean since I saw them in the hospital. What is rigged up to the kitchen door, I'll soon find out but first I rummage through my stuff which has been rummaged through already. I put some clothes in a sack, some personal photos, some bins and a few other bits. I have an old palmer which might come in useful and a torch that still works. I put my sack over my shoulder and open the bedroom door. There's no light, no noise, no smells, so I move quietly to the front bedroom which overlooks the street. The door is open and I can see the curtains are wide open. This is unusual, even during the day everything at the front is usually closed up. I crawl into the room. I can grab the photos from around the mirror without being seen and stuff from the bedside cabinet which lies on its back. I'm tempted just to see if they're really watching but their scopes would be programmed to pick up the slightest movement; it's probably the same downstairs. I crawl out of the bedroom creep downstairs and make my way to the kitchen, and the back door. Tied to the door handle is the chord I've seen through the gap. Opening the door more than an inch or so and it would have been the last thing I ever did. It's connected to an object about the size of a shoe box taped to the work top. Pull the wire by opening the door and 'Good Night Vienna!' I unclip the wire carefully from the door handle, pull the tape off from the work top and lift the package. As I carry it through to the front, it occurs to me how simple it would be to trip in the dark, or to tread on the wire. To the side of the front door is a table fixed to a wall. I place the package on the table and press down the tape that secures it. I tie the wire round one of the security bolts on the front door. The bolts are already drawn and the door catch is on. Now there is nothing stopping the door opening, even a breeze. I pull a mat up against the inside, enough to make sure all it will take to open is a good push.

    I gather up everything I need and put it outside the back door. I put Jean's photos and stuff in the box at the rear. I put the key in the back door lock from the outside and return to the stairs which I climb in darkness, even though I have my torch. When I reach the front bedroom again, I shine the torch around as if looking for something. I go into another room at the front and do the same, then on the landing and stairs. In all about ten seconds, which should give them time to check why their scopes are flashing, and raise an alarm. I make my way out of the back door and lock it. I pick up my stuff in the garden, get over the walls and fences until I arrive at the end of the street, then I jump into a garden where I can look down toward the front of my house. All is quiet, and nothing moving. I'm beginning to wonder how long I should wait before walking back to a warm bed, when I see a pin prick red light floating about waist level over the road. There are others, brief flashes then concealed; they are the kill lights on pistols. There is a siren some way off and getting nearer. I shrink back into the garden and watch over a wall for what seems an age. Perhaps the device did not detonate, maybe it was a dud to start with, perhaps the wire didn't hold. I am suddenly aware of a dark shape silently moving along the road from my right. An andy combat wagon, in silent mode, has crept up within a short distance of where I hide. The andys empty out, maybe a dozen, I can hear them whispering into their comms, and the soft patter of their boots on the street as they make off in the direction of the house. They'd disappear into the dark if it wasn't for the faint blue glow of their night sights and head up displays. It's quiet and again I wonder if anything will happen.

     A silent crystal white flash blasts all the grey world about. It illuminates the mist and all that stands still is caught in a shimmering brilliance. Then it thumps the air like a huge fist and rocks the solid ground beneath. A millisecond shockwave passes through everything and everyone. Windows splinter and crash, flames punch their way through the billowing smoke and throw up bright shapes that spiral and twist in the scorched mist that swirls around and dances with sparks that fly and fall. The road is laced with glitter and with helmets that have lost their heads and bodies that are pieces and it is death, but it is not mine, and not Jean's and not Carl's and it is none of our friends. This is my doing but it was their event and their reward. This is my success and I did this.

I turn to see a face before it moves away from the window in the house behind me. They're likely to report me in their garden. Not reporting me would be a serious offence and they have no idea who I am, so why not?

If there were any andys in the wagon near me they'd have gone to the scene. There's chaos around the house. Here there are survivors returning, some supporting others. Visors are a mess with messages and information. There are several sirens in the distance and this is their destination. I glimpse a large figure turning into the road, so I draw back, cross some gardens and car spaces, then turn down an alley between houses. The fences at the rear face onto open ground and a car park surrounded by disused industrial units. I feel my way along tall fences topped with razor wire, and maybe electrified. We all live in fear. Across the rubble strewn car park, derelict buildings on a service road reflect a dim light, perhaps a waiting vehicle to the left. A powerful light flashes to my right, from the alley between the houses, hand held, an andy searching, following. The beam picks out a rusting car, bounces off a glass window and everything is visible, especially me. My only route is left. I hug the fence line and work along as the beam narrows to a point. A large human silhouette holds it and its beam scans the open ground in all directions. The beam turns and begins to work its way along the fence line casting shadows against the grey walls of the houses beyond. I back away still in the dark, but the light is slowly searching me out. The fences become a solid wall and then a corner and a trap.

In the wall there is a door, locked and solid. Above it, the wall drops just enough to get over. What is the other side, I don't know; but I have no choice. I scramble over in a panic before the light can find me. I drop down the other side into a small yard and only then realise how painful my chest is. I stifle a groan as I sink to the ground and rest against a small shed. Stark shadows move around chaotically as torch beams search fences and buildings. Soon it will be gardens.

The pattering sound of boots increases in all directions. Extra forces have been brought in. I hear them filtering down the alley, along the fences, across the open ground, checking out anywhere someone might hide, and where I'm hiding seems obvious. Then there is a faint drumming sound which grows louder. I hear rotors cutting the air above. Everywhere becomes a lighter shade. Soon the chopper's lights will bring a brilliance to everything and nothing will remain concealed. In the growing light, I survey the small garden to see if there is anything I can get under, that might conceal my body warmth from their spotters. Doubling back to the street between the houses may be my only escape. Provided the chopper isn't directly above, I might still be hidden in the shadows as it moves slowly over the roofs. Into this small space there is a side entrance by the house but a sturdy metal gate prevents my escape to the front. An impressive array of spikes and razors makes climbing it suicidal, besides it would take too long. If I got to the front countless little red lights would be the last thing I see. Above the gate a cam whirs and seems to have me in its focus, this owner too will be reporting. There are no lights visible in the windows, so I press my ear to the back door and can hear nothing through its solid steel reinforcement.

The chopper has remained stationary over a garden but now it moves towards me. I can hear andys in a garden close by ripping out anything which might conceal someone hiding. The fence next door splinters as they force their way through, nothing stops them if they smell blood.

The light from the chopper intensifies soon I will be able to pick out the choppers rotors. Then the skids on which a powerful array of lights will catch me staring blindly into them, with my arms outspread, welcoming.

Sometimes you just wish it would end; all of it.

CHAPTER 7

'Is it you they're looking for?' I spin round. Then round again, trying to locate the disembodied voice, but I can see no one.

'Up here.'

A balding head with dishevelled wisps of grey hair is poking out of an open window above the back door. Whether through fear, surprise or relief, I can't speak. I stare open mouthed,

'Well, you can stay there or take a chance and come in. I would say you have about ten seconds to decide. It's up to you.'

With that he closes the window at the same time the door in front of me makes a resounding clunk and opens slightly. An intense light suddenly invades the edge of the space I'm in and I have no choice.

I am sat in his front room. There are book shelves all around but only a few books and several ornate little statues. There are two chairs and a sofa facing a boarded up fire place. One of the armchairs is his, into which he nearly disappears. He has a bed against the wall on which are pillows and cushions covered in a similar fabric to the rug that is on the floor. He has the state heater that everyone is allowed that gives out just enough heat for one room, but not if it's cold. Everyone is encouraged to use just one room, Encouraged means you have to have a good reason not to. There are no good reasons.

'What do you think of tea?'
'Bitter,' I reply.

'It used to be drunk with milk in Europe' he continues 'but not in the East. There are still some plantations left but the yield is very poor. Tea was enjoyed everywhere, now governments don't consider it benefits the human spirit. The human spirit is not something they consider worth benefiting. I have an acquaintance who manages a farm and grows a few tea plants. He dries the leaves and from the occasional packet he sends me, I able to prepare the infusion you have tasted. It reminds us that some things were produced for pleasure and not because of the power it gave others over us, or the profit it made out of us. We can have a little soup later.'

A flicker of alarm made me think for a moment. A flicker not lost on this wily old man.

'It's all right, I have no intention of poisoning you. Besides I could have done so already. Perhaps it was the strychnine in your tea that made it so bitter.'

'Maybe, perhaps I'll try it without next time.' I hope I'm being clever and these aren't my famous last words.

He smiles and reveals a truly kind face, but then it closes and I can see his darting eyes are still weighing me up. His old glasses are that dirty, I'm surprised he can even see me.

There's an unnerving calmness about this old man, a confidence. Turin wears his confidence, but this old man just has it in his veins. I would have said that Turin has charisma, now I'm not so sure. I could pass this decrepit old man in the street and not even notice him, but after a few minutes conversation he has woven a spell, well that's what it feels like.

He sips his tea from a delicate cup that has lost its handle, rolls the liquid around his mouth and swallows it with his eyes closed, as if imagining the far off lands he talks about. He holds the cup in both hands, as if to warm them, whilst moving the cup round and round until he sips again from the opposite side. Having done so, and again travelled the world, he returns to see me watching him with a kind of frown. This makes him smile again,

'In a world with so little pleasure,' he says, 'what delight still exists must be taken seriously.'

He looks at me for a moment as if waiting for a response, and when there is none, he leans back again and continues,

'We have made the world, but in doing so, we have destroyed the planet. Discuss . . .'

The word hangs in the air for a while until I realise it is an invitation to answer.

'I can't believe that. There would be nothing to live for if we can't change things. We have to make it better or die trying.'

'And if it doesn't get better?' he replies.

'Seeing everything getting worse, day by day, is not worth living through. I know it may be too late but if we could make a small difference it might be the start. How can we blame those generations before us that did nothing, and then do nothing ourselves? I don't know what we can do, but things can be changed. I have to believe that; it's a belief.'

'And if it is your belief it would be better if it were a faith.'

I asked him what he meant.

'I learned scholar once said that a belief is what you are given, a faith is what you reason for yourself. If the faith you have is something of your own making, conceived and honestly considered, it will be far stronger than anything you might borrow from someone else.'

He sips at his tea and looks over his glasses at me.

'Have you never been tempted to borrow a belief?' He asks me.

'Not really,' I tell him. 'History tells us few religions ever practised what they preached. They were always changing to suite whatever they wanted to do.'

'But that's the beauty of a belief. It requires no proof, no evidence. Evidence just gets in the way and can be contradictory. So it's better for a religion that none exists, then they're free to make up whatever they want. People have been misled and ill-treated for centuries by religions believing the promises they made. Our new religion promises everything in this life if only you believe. If not, like the heretics of old you will be punished. Are you a heretic . . . . . ?

He looks over his glasses and waits for an answer.

'Ash. My name is Ash.'

After what has happened to Carl and Jean, this freethinking is disturbing. I get the feeling I'm being tested, it's a gut feeling and I should listen to it, it's a rule. My instinct is to trust him, but can I trust my instincts? I sip the tea and listen.

'Praying won't mend a dripping tap, a plumber will.' He continues. 'No matter with how much you pray that the dripping will stop, the miracle will only occur after the plumber arrives,' then he adds, 'or if you run out of water.'

'Perhaps the miracle is that a plumber arrives at all.' I say and smile, and he begins to smile as well.

'A good point.'

I decide to take the opportunity while we are in agreement, to ask if it would be safe for me to leave.

'I doubt it,' he replies, 'after such an event I think the officers will be skulking about for the rest of the night. It wouldn't be safe at all.'

'So should I stay here?'

'I was about to suggest it but are you sure you trust me?'

He rises to his feet from the depths of his arm chair and walks towards the door rather stiffly. I had noticed old people often walked like this and wondered why. More I wondered if I would ever get old enough to find out.

'I will show you where you can sleep. I live in the one room so the rest of the house is a little Spartan, which I hope you will excuse, but you will be safe. '

He turns to me and looks over his glasses with a steadfast gaze.

'You are safe, Ash?'

This is unnerving because people don't look at other people with such concentration, we avoid eye contact, it is threatening. I feel as if there is no part of me into which he cannot see and for a brief moment he seems to loom over me, taller and dominating.

'Yes,' is all I can say.

He shows me into a bare room with only a mattress to sleep on and a pile of blankets. A dull light peeps through the slot in some kind of security shutters. It's difficult to tell what time of night it is, but it could be past dawn as at last I lay down to sleep. My ribs are still sore and I have to sleep in a position I'm not used to. Outside is quiet so I presume they have stopped searching and now just watching. When

I sleep fitfully, visions and dreams keep waking me and I'm not sure whether I'm being helped or just a prisoner.

I felt I had been sleeping deeply when at last I woke to find there is a drink in a glass by the bedside. I reach out for it just as there is a gentle knock and the door opens. The old man's wispy hair is what I first see. His glasses are just as dirty and he wears the same clothing as he did the night before.

'I have allowed you to sleep as long as I could. Unfortunately there are some things we have to talk about. Get dressed and join me in my room as soon as you can.'

The failing light of a dull evening filters through the window shutters of his unlit room. They too look like security shutters. I think about the space at the rear, the side gate, the cam over the back door and wonder what this old man treasures so much, or what he has to hide.

Deep in his chair he clutches a mug full of a brown liquid with both hands. He calls it mulligatawny and it smells disgusting. He won't tell me what is in it, just says it is an old recipe and contains spices, whatever they are. I have mug full of the stuff near my chair but there it stays. He looks into his mug for a few moments then eyes me over his glasses,

'I'm afraid you might have a problem.' He tells me then takes a sip which I thought took far more time and noise than it should have done.

'I think I have loads,' I answer.

'You had something to do with breaking one of my porcelain figurines.'

He surprises me with such a trivial matter.

'Would that have been when I jumped into your garden?'

'Hardly,' he says, and he reaches behind his chair and comes up with an ornament similar to the ones on the shelves, but in pieces.

'This fell off the shelf at the same time as an explosion shook the whole street. A few minutes later, you hide in my garden. It could be coincidence but I would hazard a guess that it and you, are in some way connected. Am I right?'

'Go on.' I say, and I think, 'trust no one'.

'Let us presume I am then. You readily accepted my hospitality not knowing who I am. Already one of my neighbours had communicated your whereabouts to the authorities, maybe you didn't know that?'

I recall the face at the window.

'There is a saying,' he continues, 'out of the frying pan into the fire. That could so easily be you, my young friend. You aren't to know what I would do, perhaps already have done, the same as my neighbour.'

'True,' I tell him and decide to flatter him, 'but from what you have told me, you would have as much to lose.'

He pauses for a moment, then puts his mug down on a table.

'You might think so but I could merely be drawing you out. What you don't know is how predictable your presence is here. You know it is not of your choosing, you had no option. I can put your mind at rest, you can trust me, but as a rule, trust no one.'

I'm not sure I understand him, but I can't help reading some significance into what he has just said, does he know about 'rules'. He continues,

'What happened to the building was planned very badly, or it was not planned at all.'

I say nothing.

'Well, if you are solely to blame, I can't imagine that you would make a habit of this, otherwise you would have been through Rehab and back on streets picking up litter or ill-treating innocent passers-by. You have landed in my lap without knowing you were going to, therefore I believe you being here was not planned. Are you safe?'

He stares at me with such an intensity that I am tempted to turn away, but I know that will give the wrong impression. So I stare back confidently and tell him that I am and that I am no threat.

'Good . . .' He is about to say something but pauses. He raises his bushy eye brows as if about to ask a question, which he is.

'What did you say your name was?'

'Ash.'

'Good Ash. I want you to know, I am safe too. . .'

Now I raise my not so bushy eye brows as if about to ask a question, which I am and he answers it.

'I am Goodrich. Some call me The Professor, or just Prof, it's not official and it is done as a sign of respect.'

Trying to decide whether to trust a comparative stranger is totally alien. Even close family cannot be accepted readily. All my instincts tell me this Goodrich is genuine but my conditioning makes it a dilemma.

'Ash, you have a problem which needs solving. I have let you sleep most of the day because what you have to do involves working at night again.'

'Really?' Goodrich nods, then I ask him, 'So what problem do I have that you can help me with?'

I have a respect for this old bloke but he can't possibly know of my problems, let alone solve any of them.

'Where do you live?' He asks me.

'Well, I used to live . . . You mean I haven't got anywhere to live?'

He shakes his head as if I am a hopeless case. I know this gesture as Jean uses it a lot.

'Where are you registered as living?'

'Ah!' Well, it was . . .'

'Indeed, it was, but is it still?'

He has a point, but he hasn't finished.

'I heard about the fight in the street, you were all lucky to get away. When you returned, the house was being watched?'

'Yes, they were waiting for my uncle to return.'

He explains that I am implicated by association. I was now just as likely to be a target as Carl, if only for any information I might have.

'Even so,' he continues, 'let's suppose they are not watching for you specifically. Recog is bound to pick you up, sooner rather than later, and that could be anywhere from a passing vehicle, surveillance cameras, even a local warden. You can't run Ash, and hide at the same time. Without official ID, you are not only putting yourself at risk but everyone you know. It won't take long for them to discover everything you've been up to and with whom. How do you think you are going to live? They'll be no more tokens, even if there were, you couldn't use them. No one will want to associate with you, unless it's to collect the reward for your corpse. Every LEO will be a potential assassin, they won't even need to give you a warning. You wouldn't last a week. As I say Ash, you have a problem.'

Beyond the trauma of last night, my escape and its peculiar circumstances, I hadn't thought beyond just surviving. Goodrich, or Prof, whatever he was called, was right.

'I have a problem.' I admitted.

'Good,' he says, 'this is called the first stage. Before solving a problem it is useful to admit that a problem exists. Progress at last. Stage two . .'

'How do we solve it?' I suggest.

'Not quite. Stage two, is defining the criteria that has to be solved. Do you live anywhere else?'

'No, not really.' I tell him, 'I spend maybe two or three nights a week away.'

'You have a girl friend?'

'Well, no. Sort of. Not that I stay with, yet.'

'So you need a registered address, as well as somewhere to stay a few nights a week. That's the easy part. You are now a persona non grata . .'

He catches my frown.

' . . . A person who is not welcome, and in your case being hunted. You will not be safe anywhere so long as they have your birth name. Do they have your birth name?'

'Yes.'

'Is it associated with that address?'

'Yes,' I say, 'stage three?'

'No. That then is your current identity?'

I nod.

'Is that your only one?'

I nod again.

'You need a new identity. You will also need it to be linked to an address where you are registered and where you can stay when you want to. You need a home, Ash, at least as far as the authorities are concerned. Where's your current identity?'

'It's in my sack.'

'Do you have anything else with your birth name on it?'

'A letter, maybe a form or two I had to take to Columbus. I think that's all with my birth name, and a metal box with my initials.'

'Good that should do. Is Ash your birth name?'

'No.'

'Good, because I've got used to it. Now listen. Go out into the yard and in the far corner there is a metal shed, the key is by the back door. Go into the shed, don't touch anything, just bring back some dry wood pieces you will find in a blue bag. When you come back, bring the things from your sack you've just mentioned. Make sure you lock all doors.'

Without knowing what he is going to do, I do precisely as I am told. I return with everything to find that he has removed the panel which exposes the old fire place.

'Stage three then,' I suggest.

He is shaking his head again like Jean used to.

'Patience!' So, you need somewhere to spend a few nights a week. You need a new identity. You also need an address you can register under your new identity. Okay, stage three.

'At last,' I say.

'It's done.'

What's done?

'Stage three.'

'How come?'

'There is no point in posing questions that cannot be answered. Stage three proposes the solutions to the criteria defined in stage two. I wouldn't have posed a question if I hadn't already thought of an answer. '

'So,' I say, 'stage four?'

'Indeed,' he says, 'stage four is the proposal.'

I raise my eyebrows.

'How we propose to solve the problems that we have identified. First, you must be prepared to go back to what is left of the house. Can you do that?'

'It's probably being watched.'

'Almost certainly and how we get round that is also part of stage four.'

'How many stages are there?'

'Six'

'And what's that?'

'Stage six is what we do when something goes wrong, but don't let us get ahead of ourselves, we are still at four.'

He is making a pile of paper in the fireplace, old pages by the looks of it, and piling on top of them some of the thinner pieces of wood.

'They will have extinguished the fire and dampened down what remains,' he tells me. 'They would have made reports but it is too soon for them to have been acted upon. The site has not been examined yet, but it will be sometime tomorrow, during daylight. If there is the chance that evidence exists that may lead to bonuses and rewards it may be first thing in the morning. You will have to go there tonight, as soon as possible and avoid being seen by anyone. There will be no room for error, can you do this?'

I wonder what happened to the answers that he had before he asked the questions. I suppose he must have not only presumed that I'd do it, but that I would do it well enough not to be traced back to him. This is good but I can feel the trust being a responsibility, and this makes me more determined to succeed. The respect I have for this old man makes me want his praise.

'I'll do it.'

Having said this he lights the small fire and soon adds more of the wood. I joke with him that it's illegal but really I am trying to remind him. He points out that as it is night the little smoke he is making will not be seen. It may be smelt but that will be put down to the building nearby, that has recently gone up in flames. I think in future I will keep my thoughts to myself.

The fire begins a small blaze and he gestures to me to pass him the objects from my sack. I hand them over but I'm not prepared for him throwing them into the fire.

'Whoa! Watch out!' But no sooner has he done it than he retrieves them smouldering and partly melted. The tin remains in the fire until its paintwork peels and flames blue and green and then turns black and parts gleam a dark rich red, like blood.

'Has it rained much?'

'I don't know, I was asleep.' I said this because as far as I can remember, I was.

'Of course. How wet was the garden?'

'Very wet, sort of squelchy.'

'Okay, take the paper and soak it in a puddle or something. It needs to be like its surroundings. The tin and plastic will be fine as they are.'

I do as he says still not understanding what he has in mind. I return with the soggy Columbus letter which is folded as it had been in my pocket but limp and brown with charred edges, and hand it to him.

'Stage Five,' he says as I enter the room. The fire had warmed the room a little and there is a vaguely reminiscent smell which brings The Bakery to mind, and Meko.

'Stage five is the execution. This is the tricky bit. You must place these in the remains of the house where they can be found. They need to imply that you were in the house when it blew up. Do you understand why?'

'Yes, they are to make it appear that I have died in the explosion.' I wonder why older people think all young people are idiots.

'Excuse me for checking, but not all young people have the experience that you do.'

I smile. He smiles.

'Won't they look for my bones or something?'

'If you were important, owned property or had other assets, they may bother. You have nothing, so it's not worth them spending time looking for your remains because time is money and you are worthless. Finding your ID is as good as finding you. Everyone has their ID on them, or very close. They will presume there is nothing left of you. They know, without it, you wouldn't last long anyway. Why waste time looking for your remains, they'll turn up, one way or another. It will be up to you to find an appropriate place to put these.'

He hands the charred remains to me.

'Put them somewhere noticeable but not obvious and if there are other things which might point to your presence and your death, that would be good. Finding some personal effect, particularly an ID, will help them to believe what they want to, that your remains are amongst the rubble and charred to a cinder. One more thing . . '

He reaches down into his chair and pulls out a small scope. A night scope. They are illegal and anyone found in possession of them without a licence, well, it's like having a pistol.

'Do you know what this is?'

'Yes, but I've never used one.'

He shows me how to use it and tells me that on no account should I be caught with it on me. I should dispose of it if there is any chance of it being found and traced to me, or him.

We go upstairs to what was once a bedroom at the front. We part the curtains and peer into the gloom waiting for our eyes to adjust. A helmeted shape passes silently down the street, a yellow light blinking where a pistol might be held in a black gloved hand. The pistol is on stun so they're not expecting to have to kill anyone. He walks nonchalantly past then turns away towards the remains of the house. A similar outline emerges from an adjoining garden and they both disappear back into the darkness of the street opposite. After several minutes a faint light glimmers briefly which I take to be the opening of a front door. This confirms for me that they are not on full alert, their presence is to make sure the site is left undisturbed and to prevent looting, rather than a trap.

We return to the downstairs room and Goodrich asks me what I think.

'They are there to prevent looters. I don't think they're expecting anyone particular and could be presuming that the explosion has already killed their target, or targets. I couldn't see but I think they are in the house opposite, upstairs, front. Which is probably where they were before.'

'Before?'

'Yes. I went to the house to pick up some stuff and found the back door was wired to detonate the explosion if I opened it, so I got in by my window. Before I left I transferred the device from the back door to the front door and flashed a torch about before leaving by the back door. When they pushed open the front door, the bomb went off.'

'Ash, you are a remarkable young man. You must think me a real old fool treating you like an innocent. I apologise, but now we, or rather you, have work to do. Thank you for telling me that, you have put my mind at rest. I think you will do fine.'

I put the evidence of my death into a plastic bag, put on my coat, and let myself out of the back door which he locks behind me. I have the code to the back gate for when I return. It'll be easier than climbing over it and a much less painful. The old units at the rear are quiet, and the open ground is deserted nevertheless the experience I had out here still seems vivid and it's too easy to imagine it happening again. It's experience and I welcome it and I learn. Always have at least two ways out. I know the way I got here the last time, so now I choose another route. I follow the wall round the corner that was a trap, and continue along the backs of the gardens until I reach the road that runs across the top. It's a broad road that used to have trees, some of the stumps are still visible. The first to be removed, are now just depressions in the ground, some about a foot deep. I raise the scope to one eye and do a full circle. There are shards of blue light that creep out from between curtains, windows that have lights in adjoining rooms that fade out when the internal door is closed. All invisible to the naked eye. A torch light in a garden catches my attention but it soon goes out again and I can hear the door shut. It's a revelation to see how much activity is taking place which is normally invisible. The smell of burning is intensified by the dampness hanging in the misty air, a burning house smells like nothing else. I walk to the corner and look down to my left. This would have been from where the LEO we saw, walked past Goodrich's. His house is about six or seven down, where he sits almost lost in his chair maybe sipping mulligatawny. He could also be watching from his upstairs window. I can see the narrow pathway that runs down between the gardens at the backs of the houses. That would make a useful route back out, but maybe a better patrol route for an armed andy, and perhaps the route a LEO might use on the look out for looters. It's too obvious a way to get to the house if you thought the front might be watched. 'Know your enemy', it's a rule. I decide the risk of a LEO strolling down that path at the same time as me was too much. There would be little chance of escape, let alone doing what I had to.

I carry straight on across the top of Goodrich's road. I pass about four houses and between the next two I can glimpse a house with only half a roof left. The next house felt empty and had no side gate. I look at all the windows through the scope and there is nothing, no light or heat, and its bandaged ear is silent. As I lower the scope I can see right to the fence at the rear, several panels are broken or removed for firewood. So I make my way towards it and can see the rear fence of my house. The gate in the middle of it is tempting but I feel it is better avoided. The last time I was here I came over the walls and fences along the backs of the houses but they had the back door wired so weren't too fussed about watching it. I reminded myself how casual they were with the light from the doorway. The right side of the house is gone, except for some of the kitchen. It's blown away at the front and burned at the rear. You can see straight through from the garden to the road and across to the house opposite where I suppose the watchers to be. The left side of the house is still standing, and gives good cover, but to get there I will have to double back. I breathe through my mouth to cut down the noise of air rushing through my head, close my eyes and listen. I raise the scope and do another full circle and see nothing alarming. I step quietly over the remains of the fence. A deafening squeal breaks the silence as a rat the size of a small dog manages to wriggle from under my foot tipping me backwards towards a fence panel, which I grab to save my fall. As I continue to fall so the panel comes with me crunching and splintering, and echoing through the night. I might as well shout, 'Come and get me!' I lie under the panel feeling sure that it will shortly be removed by a ring of officers, their pistols pointed at me with little red lights all aglow.

    After a few moments there seems to be no pounding of feet but in case they eventually decide to investigate, I had better move. Fortunately my grip on the scope had been secure and as soon as I am standing, I use it. I move toward my house's fence and can see down to the house opposite where upstairs an officer paces the room. Another whose head is just visible, is taking their turn with the night site. She stands up and stretches and I take the opportunity. Do not shrink from using the right opportunity; it's a rule. I sprint past my fence to the house next door, over its fence and up to their back door. Even if I trigger an alarm they'll have missed me by the time they get behind their sight again. They may still be curious and here I can abort if I detect the gentle patter of boots. I catch my breath then hop over the fence like I did before and hug the wall beneath my window, then realise I am crunching its glass beneath my feet. Through the window I check out the interior with the scope. There are twisted frames and blackened walls that are still warm. Inside I know everything is charred and black, dull black, shiny black, smooth black, and textured black but through the scope everything is blue as if submerged in a soft blue lake. Through the hole where the kitchen door was, I can see there is nothing left of the front of the house around the front door and above. Blown against the inside of the kitchen wall are some charred remains. An arm with bony black fingers grasps the air and rests against a kitchen storage unit the contents of which have been boiled, fried, and grilled in their containers until they've burst or melted. Water drips from what's left of the ceiling above. Towards the front there is no floor, no ceiling, above or below.

    I drop back to the corner of the house and use the drain pipe again to access my room, this time there's no need to open the window. The floor, walls, and everything in the room is black. The door, still in its door frame, is lying on the floor. Beyond it, most of the landing is gone and so probably are the stairs. The floor closer to the doorway is charred and the timbers beneath are visible, not composite like recent houses but actual wood that burns and so disintegrates. By the door are the melted and scorched remains of a jacket, little more than a sleeve, but I think it's the right one. I can get within about a body's length but the floor creaks. A metal rod from the window solves the problem and I pull it towards me. About to leave, I take out the scope and scan the rear gardens. Nothing more than the usual business I've seen, and that I'm getting used to. I drop the remains of the jacket out of the window, then climb back down the drain pipe.

Back on the ground I move toward the remains of the kitchen trying not to crunch too much glass underfoot. Taking a pace or two into the kitchen I can now see the arm and grasping hand is all there is. Two more paces and I can catch a glimpse of the house opposite and the room in which I've already spotted the surveillance team. By angling the scope round a corner I can observe them without revealing any warmth which their detectors could pick up. The room now appears empty. I check other windows, but there is no warmth or movement. I consider whether they have left or been assigned other duties. I check other parts of the street and risk being seen so I can see more and farther, but there's no sign. I wonder if they are patrolling the area, in another house, just having a break. Are they together or separate? Do they have night scopes?

So far all is silent. Anything close would have to crunch its way about. I take a few steps into the kitchen, then across to the storage unit and crouch down. The finger tips of the grasping hand are red and the bone is visible where the rats have been gnawing. Beside me another unit is charred black beneath a side window, this was where Jean kept her grab bag. She would say if ever the house was on fire grab this bag, it has everything we need in it. Now it was just an empty space and everything we needed had been grabbed. I slip what is left of my jacket's sleeve over the grasping hand and down as far as I can until the melted sleeve is tight. What's left of a pocket, I put the melted ID in, and the paper. I put the tin, face down, under what might be charred bones close by. I take several pieces of charred timber and scorched fabric and lay them

across the jacket so it looks as if it had been there during
the fire. It might not convince someone who was determined
to prove I was still alive but why would they? Pleased with
my handiwork and preparing my story for Goodrich I stand
up. To my horror a torch beam is scanning the garden and it
seems as if it is coming from behind me. Someone is
walking up the side from the road at the front, they might
continue, or they might detour through the building. I try to
see by the torch beam which way they are coming. The
beam bounces all around the back fence and into the
house, its source seems stationary at the front, now it
moves. I could get out of the kitchen door in two paces,
over into the garden next door and across the back of the
houses. Or I could go down to the back fence, over, and off
down the alley way back down between the gardens and
out. If I get caught, there is still the way out sewn into my
coat. I hear the crunch of glass near the front door, it's
clumsy and deliberate. The torch waves about without any
real purpose hopping from one gaping window to another.
There's no attempt at concealment, no creeping, no chance
of surprise, maybe just to scare somebody away, a warning,
to avoid confrontation. All I need is to escape, to get out, to
run. So I turn, lift the scope and check my path so I can run
it in the dark. I see the back fence, sprinting down the
garden would be quick, and concealed from the front. I
prepare to move and take a last look. I don't move. I step
back into the shelter of the kitchen, there is something at
work, it holds me back. I look across a garden or two. Along
the line of the back fences, some rotten, others gone, taken
to burn, seal windows, make chairs, cots, children's toys. I
sense something but can see nothing. I raise the scope
again, nothing. I peer through the gloom. I imagine all sorts,

but then I catch it. It passes between a post and a loose fence panel then disappears. A faint amber glow changes to red, reflected, not direct, shrouded. A pistol changes from stun to kill before its indicator is concealed. An officer creeps silently along the path between fences waiting for a body to appear over one, to land, to be surprised, to be killed. I raise the scope, shading the lens from any reflection. A shape moves to a position just beyond my garden, and to its right. It has a view down to the building next door, my only other route out of here. It is unusual for the LEOs to be so keen, yes they get paid by results, who doesn't, but it's my luck to have found two, or maybe the one, who has a flair for the job.

    To the rear there is no movement, the officer having concealed themselves behind a small shed. To the front there is the sound of approaching feet that are crunching glass. The subtle change in the tone could mean that they are under cover, maybe even in the building. I shrink back towards the charred unit that lies beneath the window. As I do so a strong torch beam sears the darkness and everything is visible. Against a wall there is a section of ceiling which has collapsed making a narrow, triangular void, beside it a partially melted curtain from an upstairs window. The sound of crunching glass footsteps has turned into moving objects, moving them aside, allowing someone to walk through the building. The noise they make covers my wriggling into the void feet first, then I draw the curtain over my head in an untidy bundle. Through the heavy wet curtain I see the torch beam brighten then fade, and footsteps which get closer, seem just a pace away. I hear breathing through a face mask, an andy, far more dangerous than the ordinary LEO.

The light grows bright and is about to fade again when its intensity doubles. It would appear that the curtain is getting its full attention. There's a rustling movement and the breathing gets louder and closer. I feel the curtain begin to move and I grip it tight, but I can't stop it moving.

I feel myself moving with it as the ceiling section moves too. There's a crash and by the sound of it, another section of ceiling has come down sliding alongside the first. A more solid piece hits the floor, a wooden joist perhaps. Now I'm in complete darkness, still covered in the curtain, but beneath more debris. I can still hear but not so well. There is some muffled swearing, then some clearer tones, making a report. I can hear footsteps crunching close by, then they move away until there is silence. They could have gone, or they could be waiting in the next room; or nearer.

I wonder how long I should stay where I am. The wet is gradually creeping through my clothing and I long for the warmth of Goodrich's fire and even some mulligatawny might go down well. I can uncover myself a little and still be hidden by the pieces of ceiling around me. I hear some footsteps, then a woman's voice,

'What the fuck was that?' The voice came from just outside the back door and it was probably the figure I saw between the gardens. She didn't sound like an andy, too confident, she could be a controller.

There was an answer that I couldn't make out. Then she says,

'I said make your presence known, not demolish the fucking building. You checked out all the rooms?'

Another answer I can't hear.

'Get back on station, I'll have a team here tomorrow. Get on the scope and next time I want to know if it's a rat with four legs or two.'

I hear the andy crunch off through the house, then the woman goes down the side, not through the building. I wait. I don't move and hardly breathe. It's a trick I know, you pretend you're leaving, giving up on the search. You say something like, 'we'll come back later,' or 'they must have gone,' then wait close by and see what emerges. I judge enough time has passed, then wait some more. After that I begin to move some of the debris so I can hear better. Then I rid myself of the stinking wet curtain so I can see. Above me there is the coloured reflection from The City. I see it through the few joists that remain of the ceiling. I lie for a while watching the pinks and blues picking out the underside of our dead, grey sky. I listen to neighbours bickering, far off sirens wailing, the sound of a game show's hyped up compere as a window or door is opened. Then it cuts off as the door or window is closed, a brief exposure to someone's tawdry life. A rat scuttles across the floor, I can't see it but I can hear its claws. Then I hear it gnawing close to me and I guess it's having another go at the hand.

As I move, I hear the rat scuttle back across the floor. I pull myself out from under the ceiling panels, then crawl on my belly to the back door. My coat is wet and cold enough not to be picked up by their night sights, but I'm not taking any chances. Outside the back door I lean against the wall and make a precautionary scan of the gardens. Then I hop over the wall and along the backs of the houses. I hear nothing, but even if the andy had spotted something, I was already gone. Andys are dispensable and cheap and are enlisted to carry out anything that is a risk. They're not allowed to use initiative, intelligence or craft. The implants they have control them, they do as they are instructed. She was different, she was a controller. Someone is taking something very seriously.

CHAPTER 8

I feel like it's morning. It's difficult to tell as Goodrich's window faces the City and the light is not much different from the day, so it could still be night. Besides my eyes are still closed.

I have stayed at Goodrich's two nights and both nights have been heavy. He doesn't seem to mind me sleeping in and he's even had all my clothes cleaned overnight. He has told me that he wants me to meet someone, and we need to sort out my new identity. Then I will need to get back to the group.

I get dressed and go into Goodrich's room. He is sat in his chair drinking the tea he makes and with him is a woman who is about Jean's age. Her hair is short and dark, she is slim and looks fit. She has cool boots, and loose fitting jeans tucked into them. She is sitting in the other chair but as I enter the room she gets up and moves onto his bed with a bag that she carries. The room is lighter than I have seen it because one of the blinds is up. She smiles a polite smile at me, but I don't know if I should smile back. She watches me closely, her eyes follow me but not her head which make me feel threatened but I try to look relaxed. I wonder if I have at least two ways out.

'This is Carol. Carol, this is Ash.' Goodrich nods in our directions as he says this as if there is anyone else in the room we could be confused with. We join in the nodding game. I sit in the chair which is warm and I sense that Carol has been here for a while.

Goodrich and Carol share glances which makes me feel alienated and worried that something not good is going on. Goodrich looks over his dirty glasses as if to get a better view,

'You have successfully planted your ID at the site of the explosion to give the impression you were a fatality. We expect that soon the authorities will amend your files accordingly. So, you will have no identity. Without an identity you can't make any claims, you get no privileges, and if discovered you would be killed on sight because there is no record of you and no tedious paperwork to complete. You can be used for target practice, no one will be any the wiser. Without records you do not exist, you are a non-person. You are your records, your records are you. Take one away and the other ceases to be. The old you is dead.'

Goodrich delivers this speech without emotion, and without any affection, like a dispassionate judgement. It makes me feel vulnerable and I realise how much I have trusted him without knowing anything about him. Stupidly I have put myself totally into his hands.

Goodrich turns to Carol, who has been looking at me without saying anything. Then he says to her,

'Well, what do you think?'

'He's certainly burned his boats.' She thinks for a moment, 'Cast him out now with no ID and he'd be lucky to last the day. He has no choice but to trust us, but I'm not sure if we can trust him. If we solve his problems and he's caught, he is bound to give them everything he has and already he has too much. I'm not sure he has the intelligence or the guile to survive and it will be us that have put others in jeopardy with the gamble we have taken; we can't afford that. With what he already knows it's an either, or. '

I'm not liking the way this is going. Don't like the sound of the 'either or' business. Goodrich eyes me cautiously,

'I think he did well yesterday. He managed to outwit the trap they set, and he planted the items in a sufficiently convincing way for the authorities to report his death.'

I'm surprised and wonder how he could know that already.

'Yes, Ash, you are definitely dead,' he says. Then Carol carries on,

'It doesn't take much to outwit two stupid andys. Maybe he had luck on his side, so when it's not, I don't want anyone else to have to pay for it.'

'Actually, there was only one stupid andy,' I tell her, 'and one very professional human. She was a skilled operator, a controller I think. The trap was her idea, and it was part of a whole strategy. And stop talking about me as if I'm not here.'

'Well,' says Goodrich 'in theory you aren't. You died in the explosion you rigged. There is no you.'

Goodrich looks at Carol, a look that requires a response. Carol looks at me. I try to look intelligent and full of guile but she shrugs her shoulders which is not really a vote of confidence.

'As you see Ash, you have not proved yourself totally and we have to decide if we can trust you. I have spent more time with you and believe you should be given a chance. I am prepared to take you into our confidence, a bit. Enough for you to realise you are dealing with something more sophisticated than perhaps you are used to. You need to be able to convince Carol that you can be trusted. We will need to ask you some questions and your future will depend on the answers you give. Okay?'

'Okay, good. I want to prove I can be trusted.'

'Excellent. When you returned from your adventure last night you may remember I insisted that your clothes should be cleaned, particularly your coat with which you have been inseparable since you arrived. I gave them to Carol here, who knows someone who has certain skills? Besides the dirt and filth you seemed to have been lying in, traces of substances were found that are of interest to us, both inside and outside your coat. Do you know what I am talking about?'

Like before, he looks at me in a way that he seems able to penetrate every corner of my mind. He would know a lie, he would even know a lie if it talked like the truth, walked like the truth and even wore the truth's hat and coat. He probably already knows the truth, as she does. She's like that officer, both impressive. I think I might be getting a thing about strong women. I'll tell them as much as I dare.

'You found traces of explosive?'

'Yes.' Carol says, in a way that expects more.

'Surprise, surprise!' I tell her, 'Last night I spent most of it in a building that had just blown up, or have you forgotten.'

'We appreciate that, Ash,' Goodrich tells me, 'but don't make the mistake of underestimating us.' Then he looks at Carol, nods, and she continues,

'There were traces of chemical explosive found both inside and outside your coat. On the outside, amongst the debris you brought back with you, the traces were consistent with what we would expect to find in the circumstances. On the inside, however, there were traces of the kind of explosives that are not used by the authorities, but have been found at various, shall we say, terrorist events?'

'I wouldn't know.' Is the best I can come up with.

'We do,' Carol says, 'and what we know is, you are involved.' She picks up her bag from the bed and moves a bit closer.

'We have to know how deeply involved you are Ash.'

'I don't know what you mean. You need to check out the results. Anyway, you don't have any proof that it was the so called authorities that blew up the place.'

Without taking her eyes off of me her hand reaches into her bag and it reappears holding what looks like a pistol.

'Ash, this is a very special pistol that projects a very special charge. If you make a wrong move, a dash for the door for instance, no matter where the charge hits you, the resulting shock will disable you immediately and you will fall to the ground. You will be conscious but within seconds you will be paralysed from head to toe.'

She reaches back into the bag again without removing her gaze from me, and pulls out an injector.

'I will then inject you with a dose that will give you an overwhelming sense of peace and well-being which will not alter whilst you hear a question being asked. As long as you are able to answer truthfully the euphoria will continue. If you consider replying with what you know to be less than the truth you will begin to experience some discomfort rising to an excruciating agony. It will rack your whole body giving you the sensation of being burnt alive after which it gets a lot more painful. Normally a body is unable to withstand such agony without passing out, but this is all in the mind and the sensation is more intense and indefinite, and will last until you can locate the truthful answer. It contains stimulants which will ensure you experience the very maximum sensation at the highest level. At the same time, we will be spared the embarrassment of your screaming because all you will be able to manage will be a gentle whisper. Now I will ask you questions, to some we already know the answers. Answer incorrectly or prevaricate and I will not hesitate to shoot you and we can continue the way which will guarantee the truth, if only in a whisper. If you are ready we will begin. Okay?'

I have slipped my hand inside my coat to the concealed pocket where my ED is. I am relieved to find that after some time and never needing to check, it is still there. There is a water tight container which pops open if pressure is applied in the right way. Inside there is a quick dissolving capsule containing a fast acting sedative combined with a lethal chemical. It is almost instantaneous and there is no way back. I hold the container gently between my thumb and forefinger feeling for the textured patches that need to be pressed together.

You cannot take chances with groups. Preserving their secrecy is a priority and far more important than the life of an individual. Giving up information could result in the deaths of many. They might think I am a risk to their group but I am a greater risk to mine. A weak link and you could cause the whole chain to fail. I will not be a weak link. I will not be the first domino to fall.

'Okay. What do you want to know?'

Pressure between the two halves of the container releases the dose. I feel the capsule drop and move it towards my fingertips.

'What are the names of the other people in the group and where do you meet?'

'They don't use their real names.' I tell her.

She grasps the pistol, and I get the message

'Where do you meet?'

'It varies. Each time it's different?'

'You're lying Ash. Where do you meet?' She raises the pistol, 'The next time you lie, I will just shoot you.'

'We meet in a cellar,' I am sweating. I know now I have to take my exit, but you keep hoping that something will happen, that you'll wake up, that it won't matter, that the group will be okay, you can tell them, it's okay. My mind is racing and time is running out. The room is swimming, my eyes are filled with stinging moisture and I allow my head to fall forward. I hear Goodrich,

'Ash, you okay? Ash?'

Through my blurred vision I see her stand up, the pistol at her side. I collect enough spit in my mouth, a little pool on my tongue. She leans down. She is loud,

'Where is the cellar, Ash? Ash! Where is it?'

I give the impression I am about to vomit and cover my mouth, when really I am putting something in. With one swift movement my exit dose is in my mouth and swallowed easily as I throw my head back. Nothing can be done. Now it is too late. I feel the warm capsule travel down my throat. Its coating dissolves almost instantaneously and there is numbness creeping through me already. I feel it first in my feet, then my hands. I relax in the chair feeling myself getting heavier and heavier. I can't move. I could have been shot. Figures look into my face, they turn to each other. They talk. I could be smiling. I am smiling. They move away, far away. The tired eyes close and everything is shut out. The dim light fades to red, to blue. Now is the end, but I feel an intensifying peace like water, a tranquillity like waves that wash over me. No pain or regret. My heart begins to thud and echo, I hear a drumming in my ears, it whooshes back and forth like a tide, back and forth, and it too fades. Everything is all right. The red and the orange and the blue of light and sound, all fade, and it's good, and it's silent and it's dark, and it's peace, and the peace is so good, so good, and I know it is the end.

I wake with a shock. I remember the certainty of dying but now there is light again, or the sensation of light, through closed eyes. I wonder if this is the afterlife but I can feel weight, I am covered. It's confusing. I hear breath, my breath. I am breathing. I can't be dead. I am warm. I am in a bed. I have a body, I have thought, I can think and feel. The light grows and a shadow passes. I have some pain, in my head, it aches and my throat is dry. I try to move. My arms cannot move. My wrists are tied that is all. I think these things but I do not know if they are real. I should be dead. I open my eyes a little but it is all brilliance. I blink, and blink again and the brilliance forms a square, forms a window. A wall surrounds the window, and round the wall is a room. An ordinary room with curtains and blinds and homely furniture. I am aware of a figure standing by the bed to my left. I look up at it. Its head is bowed, it looks at me, its concentration is on me and I cannot move. Now I feel my trial has only just begun. Now there is no escape, no ED, I will have the pain.

'At last Ash, we were wondering if you'd ever wake up.' A voice drifts in and out in waves. I try to catch it and play it again until I understand it, but I lose it. My eyes blink and begin to clear, and it is someone I recognise. It looks like Carol. Now I remember Carol and I am afraid. I look again and I know it is Carol. I look around the room there is nothing else, no one else, I am here and I cannot move and Carol will hurt me and it will be painful and I can't understand how I am alive but she will shoot me and this time there is no escape, no exit.

'I expect you are thirsty. Would you like a drink?'

I say nothing, but she sits on the bed side, almost on my hand. She takes a bottle from a small table beside the bed. She removes the cap, and takes a swig.

'There, just to let you know it's safe.'

I lift my head a little and she helps with her hand. I gulp the water and some runs down my cheeks and I don't take my eyes off her. I try to read her but she just looks at the bottle, then wipes my cheeks.

'Up to talking?' She puts the bottle back on the table.

'Surprised to be still here?'

She smiles.

'You probably think you should be dead. That was your intention was it not? Well, it wasn't ours.'

Her manner is different. She is gentle, not harsh like before. I'm having trouble catching up.

'When we examined your coat we found more than a trace of explosive.'

She has my attention.

'Not everyone carries an ED. You must have a lot to hide.'

She sees my reaction.

'Don't worry, we don't need to ask you anything you don't want to tell us.'

I wonder if this is another ploy. Bad Carol, nice Carol.

'Are you feeling okay?'

I try to nod, but my head aches and I frown.

'You are dehydrated which is why you have a head ache.' She offers me more water which I drink then she opens a draw in a cabinet by the bed and takes out a photo frame.

'Now then,' she says, 'I want you to look at this?'

I turn my head, then as my sight clears I see it is me, with her.

'This is you,' she says, 'and this is me.' Well, I'd got that far.

'And this is your room,' she says looking about, 'and you are in your bed.'

I sense my eyes growing larger and a frown. She answers this expression with a smile. She holds my hand which is a shock, but it is not a threat.

'We had no intention of harming you Ash, but we had to be sure how far you would go to protect your group. We do not want to know about your group in detail, they are safe. Do you understand? We switched the ED in your coat for a fast acting sedative, you would have thought you were dying, but you were just going to sleep. There will be no after effects. It's one thing carrying an ED, it's another using it. For us to trust you we wanted to know whether you would take the ED to protect the identity of your group. We felt that if you were prepared to go all the way to protect them, you might do the same for us. Do you understand?'

I look at my wrists and the ties that bind them, then at her.

'We thought you might have tried to harm yourself if you woke up before we were able to talk to you. Ash, I need to know that you are okay with everything, and understand why we had to put you to the test.'

She looks at me and waits for an answer.

I nod and she begins to release the cuffs.

'I suppose it's an interesting experience.' I think she wishes to make conversation and I should help as we are part of the same group, it's what you do.

'Killing yourself and knowing it means death, and not just a cry for help?' I ask.

'I think what you did was very brave. Prof has a lot of faith in you, but I wasn't so sure when he asked me to take you on, but we have no doubts now. You and I are bound up for as long as we have, unless you make a habit of changing birth identity.'

She reaches into a draw and there is something wrapped in paper in her hand when it reappears. She offers it to me, and nods. I unfold the paper and it is an ID. It has my image on it and some basic details and a name. This is how IDs look, but they contain much more information that only readers can access. It is difficult to believe that this can be of any use without risk. So I ask,

'Will this work?'

'Of course.'

'Really?' I turn it over and over, it looks fine but replacement IDs take months and have to match up all existing biodata.

'But how do I know if I can trust this?'

'Ash, do you really think we would issue you with an ID that is not trust worthy?'

'Easy for you to say, I'll be the one that gets zapped. So my new ID is okay, I mean safe?'

'Very.'

'How did you get it so quickly, can you tell me?'

'I'll tell you what I can. We have contacts who can get things done who are a part of our group. You can trust your iD because it is yours, it is new, and yet not new. All I can say is that your records have been adjusted to accommodate your new identity. Everything else is the same, including your biological identification profile. So you, your ID and the records all match, anything else?'

'So this is where I live now?'

'Yes, do you have a problem with that?'

'No, except, where are we?'

'Still in 48, it's a good thing not to change things too much. You know the area, in a different one you may attract suspicion. Prof approached me first to take you on because I'm near, a couple of streets away. If it hasn't occurred to you, Ash, I am now your registered guardian.'

'So, you're my new mum. This must mean that your details have had to be changed too.'

'Yes, but we can talk all this over with Prof when he comes. In the meantime we can have something to eat and I can show you round the house, it is after all where you live. If you are happy with all that, welcome to your new life, ...' She does not call me Ash, but uses my new birth name, just once.

She turns to go but I have a few more questions.

'Why is Goodrich, called Prof?'

'Prof was one of several brilliant students who were thrown out of university for forming a group. They would have all gone on to become very important people in various fields, but they were never allowed to. So as a matter of compensation we call him Prof, short for Professor. It's kind of an honour.'

'What kind of group was it?'

'It was opposed to corporate domination, commercial greed and corruption. It championed free speech, the rights of the individual and free government.'

'Free government?'

'The prohibition of ministerial sponsorship, allowing ministers to decide policies independently, without intimidation, enticement or penalty.'

She sees the look on my face.

'It's true, but it was too late. The group became known as the Apostles, Prof will explain it to you. When the term 'The Apostles' was first used it was with sarcasm and not meant as a compliment, but it was adopted in a gesture of irony. It was after one of the original thirteen students killed themselves, he was a martyr and there were twelve left. However as time went on the irony was lost and some began to believe that the term held some Christian significance. Like lost sheep, they came in hope of finding another shepherd to save them.'

'Save them? What from?'

'From themselves, Ash. Many religions, attract those who cannot help themselves, it does their thinking for them. The state does the same, it demands that you believe, that you do not question, you do not use your reason or your common sense. It demands you suspend your disbelief. You are still free to think Ash, your mind is not in chains. The state will think you very dangerous.'

She smiles and looks at the clock by the bed.

'Prof will be here soon so that will have to be it for now as I have to prepare something for us all. You are easy to talk to Ash, I think we will get on very well. I'm glad we have met you.'

This makes me feel good. I have lost those closest to me, at least for now. I look at Carol and I see her honesty but I am not used to it and it makes me feel uncomfortable. There is contact, and even care, and this is strange. Carol smiles and squeezes my hand as if to complete the moment before she breaks away. She is obviously a strong woman, but now being my mum, even if it is only on paper, is confusing.

'Come down when you are ready. There is clothing in the wardrobe, choose whatever you wish or wear what you are used to, including your beloved coat. One more thing Ash, and this is important, your ED is back in its container inside your coat where it was hidden. It is no longer terminal. We have replaced it with one of ours. It will induce a coma which will give the impression of death to all but the most sophisticated sensors. The coma lasts about twenty-four hours, after which you will gradually regain consciousness. You need to let those close to you into the secret and I will let you have several more. Remember they are not lethal, but use them as if they are'

'Why do I need to let them know?'

'Depending on who presumes you to be dead you may not have much time before your body is disposed of. Your body will need to be retrieved, if it's not, you may never wake up.'

A room at the rear is usually taken as the most secure, where you are less likely to be 'overheard'. Not being in the front of a house means you cannot see people approach. Many have devices that detect the approach or the presence of others, though if discovered the devices themselves may be a cause for investigation because as the PM says,

'The innocent have nothing to hide.'

This means that the innocent can have no privacy. It means that any attempt to have privacy will mean you have something to hide, and the state will presume it's subversive. So privacy is subversion.

Goodrich, Carol and I sit round a table, the sort that families used regularly when they had meals together. We are talking about identity and procedures and what Goodrich calls 'protocols', which is the way to do things. He tells me how I can contact him and Carol, and we discuss how they can contact me, and if we need to make regular times for me to be at Carol's, all that kind of stuff. There is also some details that I need to know about Carol as she is my folk now and I am registered with her. We have to learn the history we share and to carry some images of us together.

I have talked to Carol and Goodrich a lot while I have been here and I think they know more about me than they say. I respect this but when I tell them about Carl and Jean their reactions are not always genuine. This does not worry me, it gives me confidence. Everybody knowing everything would be too risky.

When Carol left for a while in the afternoon I sat with Goodrich the way I imagine someone might sit with a grandfather or an old family friend. I mentioned the Apostles, and he smiled and began to tell me about them and his university. Now all education is tailored towards the demands of the corps, and the universal ambition to become an exec and rise above workers. He told me he went to one of the last independent universities, where subjects were still taught for the sheer joy of learning and the accumulation of knowledge.

'We still thought we could pull the world back from the brink,' he said, 'people were in denial, they didn't want to listen to the doom mongers, they wanted to be aboard the corporate adventure that would sort everything out in the end, and in the process make everybody rich. You can get rich now and still have time to sort out the world before it's too late. That's what people were promised and they were determined to believe it. We knew they were gambling with humanity, do you know what I mean?'

I nod.

'We tried to get people to listen to us, made a nuisance of ourselves. Soon we had other students on other campuses starting groups that were sympathetic. We thought we were winning, thinking that was our big mistake. Our success was our downfall, thinking you are winning can make you vulnerable. Most students even then had corporate sponsors, only those from wealthy families could afford to be independent students, and they were wealthy because of their investments and dealings with corporates too. I was lucky that my father could afford it purely from savings. Corporates threatened the withdrawal of funding from the students, and put pressure on their families in any way they could to stop our protests continuing. Within a few months we lost most of our support, but worse was to come. Before we could sit our finals, the university was told that all dependent students would be relocated to more 'enlightened establishments' if we were allowed to continue to pollute our fellow students. The university couldn't afford that.'

'There were thirteen of us who were demonised as radicals, anarchists and just trouble makers. We were called anti-corporate revolutionaries, many of our former supporters turned against us. There were lies peddled about our private lives, rumours regarding our families, blackmail and intimidation. We knew people, even other students, were paid, offered scholarships, just to accuse us of all sorts of crimes. Eventually we all left but they weren't satisfied and the persecution continued and was relentless. One of our number was accused of rape and other crimes were blamed on his family. He set fire to himself on the college steps leaving the twelve of us behind. This is in the past, but the past, as they say, is always with us.'

Goodrich goes on to explain that the past is still with us because the group continued. The remaining students vowed to keep up the fight in whatever way they could, and that continues to the present day.

When Carol returns I mentioned the conversation I had while she was out and she tells me there is only four left. Four out of the twelve brilliant students who were cheated out of their sparkling careers. Though there might only be four of the originals left, she tells me, over the years some of their sons and daughters vowed to carry on the fight. Many of these have become academics, technicians and highly skilled people working in all sorts of fields within loads of corps. The network is strong and getting stronger, she says that it was through the network that my old identity was altered to my new one. Some are in such responsible positions and are of such use, she says, that they have to be protected at all costs. The work they do is subtle but can influence the systems at the very roots of what maintains the state. Things have been put in place, even so they do not expect to see much change for years. She says that neither Goodrich nor the other three will live to see a climate where birds thrive in The City or roses grow again in our urban gardens, but they are planting the seeds that will bear fruit one day.

Goodrich tells me he fears that if a revolution on the street takes place before they are ready, it will fail. The state and the corps will reap such vengeance that no one will be safe. They would change their systems to such a degree that the work the apostles have been doing will be set back tens of years. This is because, he explains, that it has taken that amount of time to get people into the right places. He's worried that the current complacency, which enables them to operate, will change if any kind of serious threat is felt by the state. He's not even sure how many of them will survive the kind of close scrutiny that might occur in the aftermath. They would all be under threat.

Later I leave Carol's by the front door and head towards the old house. There are a few cams on posts here but they're all awash with paint that has exploded around them. Kids use them for target practice, firing a paint capsule that is small enough to penetrate the protective mesh. You can't be sure they're totally blind so you best not look them full face, just in case. Elsewhere they are power cleaned and buzz and whir as you pass and follow any movement they are programmed to respond to. A more effective method is to fire several petroleum gel capsules and then ignite the mess with a small impact detonator. It makes a splendid display like a beacon and the cams are totally molten and don't get replaced. I make a note of them as I'm not familiar with these few streets and I look for alleys and houses with easy access to the rear. The houses have gardens that back onto little pathways like the one I used to get to my old house. Access to them is by a wider alleyway, every six or eight houses. These houses go way back and they were built the way people liked them to be built. Now you get what you are given and these seem weird. Why do they have gardens back and front? Why all the alleyways? Why the funny pointy roofs? They look cosy and suit old people but you wouldn't want to build one now, even if you could, it would just focus attention on you. People would want to know what makes you so different. In the rural it's not the same, people build anything. Carol's house has an extension to the side so access to the rear is hidden from the front but the rear can be approached from about four different ways. Getting to it is easier than getting out of it.

I turn into Goodrich's road then I turn into the one where the remains of the old house still stand. The left hand corner facing the road where the front door used to be, is gone and the rest though standing, is badly damaged.

There is a couple of old women in bright yellow tunics scavenging with bags, picking up anything they can sell. They rake over the debris. What they rake over are memories. Things that belonged to my mother and father, all that I had. Carl's help over the months after my father disappeared, and his decision to look after me. The goodbyes like distant echoes, the empty promises, the vacuum, the loss and the feeling of betrayal. One parent disappears the other does the same, the fact that the one has gone in search of the other means nothing. They are both gone.

The women's tunics have codes on the back and front which indicates they have a licence and can have whatever they think might be worth salvaging. They drag sacks around into which they put their finds, exchange them for cash, then share the proceeds. There won't be much, Carl and Jean didn't have much. The value to me of worthless things is the memories they provoke. I see what remains of the chair from the kitchen that I used to stand on to reach the cupboards. There's part of a grey coat that my father bought for my mother when he couldn't afford it. The mirror that hangs crookedly by the remains of the stairs is the one my mother looked into just before she left, and the last time I saw her.

One of the women takes out a detector and scans a pile of debris. She then bends down, scrapes away until she picks out something small and bright. She rubs it and slips it into her boot as she crouches down at the same time as giving her fellow scavenger a side long glance to see if the deceit had been noticed. She carries on with a satisfied grin. Any victory, however small, is a thrill. I know that feeling.

At the back of the garden, up against the fence is where the post box is sunk into the ground. The two women are only interested in the house and its contents, or what's left of it, so I pass on by before my lingering is reported. As I leave I take care to notice the old gate post in the front garden by the path. There is the numeral '1' screwed to the post. It is the remains of two numerals, the other, a three, is missing, but an outline of paint remains like its ghost. The numeral is plain except that its base is slightly flared but not enough that the casual observer would notice; I am not a casual observer. The numeral turns around its central fixing and when it is upside down there is a message for me in the box. The numeral is not upside down, so I pass by. I wonder how Carl is and whether he and Jean have journeyed west as they suggested, and how far. Perhaps they weren't able to leave a message because of the house being watched. I reason that they are still free, otherwise why put the house under surveillance and why fix a device to the rear that was sure to kill anyone entering by the back door. I doubted I was the target, besides they would have preferred me alive if they wanted to find Carl. I don't know where they are but the LEOs don't know that.

I take a last lingering look before I turn the corner. It's a strange feeling as if the ground beneath me has been taken away. I have a sense of loss, as if someone close to me has died, maybe it's a part of me. Only a short time ago I walked along the road leading to this one and turned the corner to see the andys. Then stuff happened and another life got tangled up with mine. Somebody took mine, shook it about in a can, poured it all out in a jumble, then tried to stuff it all back. Then when it didn't fit, just threw it away and said just get on with what's left. Maybe stuff has to be thrown away to make room. In a way I really did die at Goodrich's. I have to remember I killed myself, I didn't know I would survive. Officially now the old me is dead. I have a different birth name, a different address, and different guardian. My past is the same, it has to be, but the future is going to be different, if there is one. I quite liked being who I was, it's a pity I didn't realise it at the time. Somewhere my death has been recorded and the recorder feels nothing, doesn't care, just taps the screen, taps 'Deceased'. Then the file which is all that is left of me, the only proof that I ever existed, will become a reference which nobody will ever be interested in. I will have been a waste of time. If it were true it would make me angry, but I smile because the recorder is wrong and their records are wrong. Records are their truth, it is even more than their religion, because they think they have proof. I know it is only a belief, and believing it is truth, doesn't make it so. I know their religion is flawed; this is a very good feeling.

    The route is now familiar to me. From the house I turn towards The City, Ma Brown's, the cellar, Turin, Chad, and the amazing Meko. In another world I would be tempted to tell them about Goodrich, Carol and the things that would gain their respect, show them I'm no kid anymore. That's impossible in this one. I'll have to be happy just knowing it myself. I walk on down the road taking with me what memories I can, ones I can stand on, rather than those that will weigh me down. A new collection.

CHAPTER 9

Ma Brown has two china dogs in her front window. When they face each other it is a sign that all is okay, if they face away, look out, that is how to remember. The dogs face each other, nevertheless I walk past, then round so I can see the back of the house and the route we use at night. Something like the dogs signal is good so long as people have time to use them and only friends know about them, otherwise they are the best trap the enemy can have. Being certain everything is okay is the worst state to be in, so I try to trust my gut feelings. Listening to gut feelings is a rule, whether they are good or bad. I wait for a few minutes before walking up the garden path. I listen at the back door but there is only the faint sound of a quiz show from one of the upper rooms, no voices. I knock the usual signal and stand back just checking everything and eventually footsteps approach. They stop by the door and I let myself be seen, Ma Brown needs to know as well. The door has its bolts slid, the key turns and the door opens,

'Hello dear,' she always calls us dear, if she calls us by anything else that too is a sign something is not right. 'Your friends are out at the moment dear, are you going to wait?'

I tell her that I am and she lets me in. I open the cupboard door, then the trap door, put on the light and step down into the cellar. It's cleaner than I have ever seen it. Usually there are papers, food wrappings, old clothes, and stuff just left about. Chad's gear is nearly always sprawling across the table and at least two of the three small screens are active. Now they are turned off and neatly arranged on a table that is clean and has none of the remains of past meals decorating the surface. The chairs seem cleaner and air itself is fragrant, almost fresh. The stains in the carpet are less obvious. The stuffing that falls out of Chad's arm chair is gone and the gaping tear from which the stuffing spews is covered in tape. Chad's chair is like him, pale leather with too much stuffing that tries to escape wherever it can. He's always losing food in his folds or the chair's, so the two are becoming one. His seat is probably the most comfortable but no one goes near it for fear of what they might catch. That's another thing they have in common. When he's at the screens he sits awkwardly on the arm due to some childhood injury. It's how he always sits, anywhere, he can't sit in any other way. Then when he's finished he just falls back into the chair like a sack being tipped into a skip.

    Ma Brown never comes down here. Turin says it's better for her, and us, that she doesn't know what we do. How Turin and Chad found this place, I do not know, and asking questions, as you know, makes people jumpy. So you don't.

    There are muffled voices followed by footsteps, one or two people. The cupboard door opens upstairs and then the trap door. Immediately I recognise Turin's boots, but the second pair I don't, nor do I recognise this girl's legs. Her boots are a version of Turin's Muskrats, and her legs are more slender than Meko's, she is smaller and I have never seen her before.

    Turin and I greet each other with a hug but the girl is more restrained, which is fine because we don't know each other. Turin introduces her as Sam. Sam has short blonde hair, she has a kind of fairy tale prettiness, her nose is slightly upturned and her eyes are round and blue, very blue. She seems nervous but her smile is genuine and she takes her coat and Turin's and hangs them up on some hooks that I have never noticed before. I get the feeling that the cellar's refurbishment could well be down to her, she seems keen to make herself useful and keeps referring to Turin with looks and they know each other well. She takes a water bottle from her sack and drinks. She notices me watching and offers me a swig which is unusual, even between friends because of what you can catch. I take it as a sign of friendship and I refuse, as a sign of friendship.

'Sam's part of the group now.' Turin says quite abruptly. He has always been against introducing people into the group before we've all had a chance to vet them and done a fair amount of digging. Always something has turned up which gives us doubts, usually Turin, and because one of us is not sure, it's a no for all of us. I was the last in and they said it took them three months surveillance before they were okay about me. Now suddenly she is part of the group, just like that. This is not going to go down well when the others arrive. Turin knows this, which is why he is telling and not discussing.

There's more mumbling upstairs and now I recognise Meko's boots followed by Chad's trainers. If we all wore trainers he would wear boots. He cannot handle being connected. If someone shows consideration he will become awkward until there is a distance again. He is difficult to like. Meko stops at the bottom of the steps as does Chad who has to lean down and forward over Meko's shoulder to see the new arrival. Meko moves in but neither say anything. Chad goes to his table and is fuming that anyone should have touched anything for any reason, he stares at the neatness as if some holy alter has been desecrated. Turin casually takes stuff out from his bag, looking in nobody's direction, as if nothing unusual has occurred,

'This is Sam. She's with the group now.' But before Sam can say anything Chad interrupts,

'Which group?' Chad lays his gear on the table and is busy untidying the neatly placed screens, cables and boards as noisily as he can without damaging anything.

'This group of course.' Turin then looks up prepared for confrontation, 'Anyone have a problem with that?'

Meko and Sam share brief smiles. Meko says nothing, knowing that Chad will do the speaking. Chad has just about finished untidying everything and they are now in the mess they usually are. Out of a pocket he produces something half eaten in loose wrapping that scatters bits of itself as he slaps it on the table. Now he's irritated that one screen has not come up, it's the screen that always comes up late, but this time it's the fault of whoever tidied things up.

'Who is she?' Chad says this without referring to anyone. He looks steadfast into a screen that is busy loading portafiles from the drive he has just slammed in.

Turin looks at us all,

'Before anyone says anything, I can totally guarantee her!'

Chad is typing in entry codes and still does not move his eyes from his screens as they start processing his stored data.

'Oh, well that's okay then. Turin says he can guarantee her, we can all sleep safely in our beds. Who the fuck is she?'

Meko and I look at each other, but there is nowhere to hide. Sam turns to Turin and picks up her bag.

'Maybe this is not such a good idea.'

'Stay where you are Sam.' Turin takes a long hard look at Chad, but Chad doesn't turn round, doesn't respond. Turin then looks at Meko.

'What do you think Meko?'

She is idly rolling a coin backwards and forwards over her knuckles. She watches the coin disappear into her fist like some street magician, the kind you get in The City.

'I don't think it's fair to talk about her as if she's not here and you need to tell us why you can guarantee her. You need to tell us what you should have told us before she came down here, before she met us, before you brought her to the cellar.'

I don't think Turin can argue with that. Now he looks in my direction.

'Well, Ash, what do you think?'

'I agree with Meko, you've always said that before any one joins the group we all have to agree. If only one person says no, then that's it, it's no. If you let us know why you can guarantee her then maybe we can too, but you've brought her to the cellar, you've made it difficult for us to say no. None of us like being put into a corner, that's one of the reasons we do what we do, because nobody ever gives us an option, it's a way of striking back. Your behaving like a corp, you're giving us no option. She might be safe, but that's not the point, we needed you to convince us first. I think it's a bad move Turin, we are all disappointed in you.'

I feel Meko's eyes on me. Chad has stopped and is looking in my direction over his shoulder. Turin is quiet and Sam seems upset. I think I have summed up our feelings and there is nothing more to say.

'Ash is right.' Chad says this and turns round with a respectful nod in my direction and a little surprise. I think Meko is impressed too. I like Sam and want to know her, but that's not the point. We expected better of Turin. You can't make rules and not abide by them yourself, it's one of the things we are fighting against, people who make rules and laws but never abide by them. Its privilege, one rule for them and another for everyone else. 'You do as we say, we do as we like.'

Sam looks at Turin and there seems to be some kind of approval.

'You're right,' says Turin. 'I should have explained this to you and asked you to okay it. The problem is, Sam's not just anyone, she's my sister. '

Chad raises his eyes to the ceiling and Meko just shakes her head. Turin continues,

'We need your help. I know the rules, we don't talk about family, homes, anything personal that might help identify us beyond the group. I'm going to give you the barest details.'

Chad interrupts.

'No! Once you've told us personal stuff there's no going back. If any of us get taken they'll have that information within minutes.'

'I know, but how can I get you to help us without giving you some details. It's a risk Sam and I have to take, and we are aware of the consequences. The briefest details are these.'

Before he can continue, Chad interrupts,

'No! You do what you like, but I won't be held responsible if anything goes wrong. You'll know I knew nothing.'

With that Chad is out of here. He is up the steps and we hear the cupboard door close, and then the back door. I look at Meko and neither of us move. There is a silence and I wonder, as does Meko probably, whether we should follow Chad and leave but we are not the same rank so we go along with Turin and stay to hear what he has to say. Also I want to know more about Sam.

'The thing is,' he says, 'our folks have disappeared and we think they've been taken, but we don't know. Sam lives with them, I have a place somewhere else. Sam returned to find the house empty and in a mess and looking like someone had left in a hurry. Doors left open, food on the table, that kind of stuff. We can't think of any reason why they should leave in such a hurry, and without leaving a message.'

Turin has moved next to Sam who is sitting on the sofa with her head in her hands. He puts his arm around her.

It's strange seeing Turin comforting his sister. The relationship he has with us is unemotional and he keeps a distance. Seeing people in different contexts makes them appear to be different people.

'Did anyone see anything?' I ask.

Turin answers, 'They wouldn't say.'

Sam is upset. It's bad that she is here but I wish that it was my arm around her. She looks straight at me, even though her eyes are wet and I feel I need to help.

'Was there anything missing like coats, or anything they might need if they were staying somewhere, maybe with friends?'

Sam sniffs then looks down and shakes her head.

'I don't know,' she says, 'it looked as if they had left in a hurry, or had been taken. I didn't go in because I was worried someone might be inside.'

'What do you think, Ash?' Says Turin.

'If they were taken, say in a raid, you don't get to take anything and the place is left as a mess. If you leave in a hurry, even in a panic there is stuff that you will always make time to take, and you close the doors after you.'

'Dad would have taken the belt too.' Sam says.

'Belt?' Turin asks.

'Yes,' Sam says, 'dad had a belt made of fabric, woven, patterned. He said if ever there was a fire or anything and I only had time to get one thing, I was to grab the belt. Don't worry about anything else he said, just take the belt and get out.'

I look at Turin but he shrugs his shoulders.

'Where was this belt kept?' I ask.

'At the front of the house there is a small room that dad used as an office. I think the belt used to hang on the back of the door. As you look at the house from the front his office is on the left.'

'Can you remember exactly what the belt looks like?' I ask but before she can answer we hear the cupboard door open upstairs, then the hatch lift and Chad's trainers appear on the steps. We watch him make his way into the room and sit on the arm of his chair.

'Let me make this clear,' he says, 'I don't want to be told any personal information. I don't want anyone to point the finger at me later and say that I knew everything as well, it was me who told them everything.'

Turin stands,

'For fuck's sake Chad if we can't help each other in a crisis . . . Maybe you could try being helpful for once.'

'It's your problem and not the group's. Before you know where we are we become some kind of self-help group and pissing about with family stuff instead of doing the real stuff.'

Chad and Turin stare at each other for a moment until Turin shakes his head and turns to Sam, who has stood up and is raising the strap of her sack over her shoulder; as she does her coat opens and reveals more of her figure. She wears a sweater with some weird design on it, this shows she is edgy. Her breasts distort the design. She catches me looking and maybe thinks I am undressing her but she doesn't give me a 'piss off' look, which would have been harsh. It would have been my next vision if she hadn't turned her back to me. Turin turns to her,

'C'mon Sam we'll sort something out.'

They make to depart but at the bottom of the steps Turin turns.

'Chad, make sure you're here later, we need to talk.'

'I'll be here.' Chad says.

Sam and Turin make their way up the steps and I hear the cupboard door close, then the back door. None of us talk so I start to leave. Meko is no fan of Chad, he's tried it on with her once or twice. Even to try is bad because of the group and not knowing about each other, but it's difficult. I think if Meko gave me the chance, I'd take it, then sort out the problems afterwards. I don't think it will happen.

'Well, I'll see you later then.' I say as I turn up the steps.

Neither acknowledge this and my words hang in the air. The group feels as if it, like everything else, is starting to corrode. We need to plan another event so we have something outside of ourselves to get into. I'm beginning to wonder if what we do is having any effect anyway.

Some time ago, after leaving Ma Brown's one night, I set out towards District 44 where some friends were having a party. Parties are low profile affairs as the LEOs are only too keen to spoil people's fun. On the way there, my path followed Turin's, only for a few streets, but it gave me some idea where he might be headed. At the time I had no intention of using the knowledge but you never know when something might come in useful. We might pretend to have no knowledge of others but you can't help but store what comes your way accidentally.

So even though I'm several minutes behind Turin and Sam, I know their route, I quickly catch up and follow them at a reasonable distance. They are involved in heavy, agitated talk, too involved to notice me or the anybody I could be. I feel I'm doing them a service, watching their back. If nothing happens, no one will know, if it does then I might help. I suppose it's just gut feelings, you have to listen to them, it's a rule. I can see their caution is less, their concentration is on other things. After any unusual event, like folk going missing, you have to be extra cautious, take it as a warning. Carl and Jean, the house being rigged, and now Turin's folk going missing, that's more than enough unusual events. One is an accident, two is a coincidence but three is the enemy. It's a rule.

Turin and Sam disappear into a small tower block which I circle and find a spot where I can cover both exits as well as a walkway across an autoroute into The City. One exit is hidden from view but there is only one route to it, and I can see that. For twenty minutes or so I wait in the shadow of a trash bunker. If a building hasn't got many floors then you use the stairs. If it has enough, like this one, then you take the lift to a floor then walk the rest, up or down. If you're followed it's useful not to tell them which floor you're on. Turning room lights on as soon as you get in is also a giveaway.

I spot Turin alone on the walkway. His clothes have been changed but his walk is unmistakable and he hasn't changed the boots. It's better to learn from other people's mistakes rather than your own. If I had those boots I'd probably want to wear them all the time, but it would be a mistake.

An underpass takes me to the other side of the autoway where the walkway drops down to street level. He gets to the end of the higher level and stops. He conceals himself against a stanchion, presumably waiting to see if anyone has followed him from the building. I can tell him they haven't. He continues walking, less concerned about being followed, convinced of his expertise. He doubles back once or twice and stops occasionally, but the grid system on which these new developments are designed, makes it easy to tail someone and not be seen. Again he doubles back neatly, had I not been prepared we might have come face to face, but it was predictable. He stops on a corner for some time before moving across a road and up a short drive. It's tempting but I wait and sure enough he returns and sets off in another direction entirely, and I follow. Houses here are larger and there are more cars parked off the roads, almost one per household. A street light begins its warning cycle of buzzes and hums before it eventually splutters into life and its cold white light illuminates a few metres around its base and though the sky isn't dark, against the light it's suddenly pitch black. These districts can have street lighting because they are not deregulated, but they still have to pay for them. Year by year, the illumination seems to get less, unlike the cost and the corps' profits. We are not supposed to know this because like all business accounts they are classified. It's their business to light the streets as well as keeping us in the dark.

Dripping cars and wet pavements do their bit to help reflect the antiseptic glare and it bounces around until walking past, it fades to grey, which endures until the next light dimly emerges. The houses, like most houses, sit in solemn dark shrouds with rarely a lighted slither creeping past the tightly fitted curtains and blinds that shield the occupied rooms within. A nearby filter rattles behind me and the one ahead is busy torturing the occupants with its gentle, inconsistent knocking. A gram or two of Pyrapede would soon solve that. I look across to see Turin turn back after several houses, then he enters the gate I can see opposite. He looks round, takes out a key, and tries the front door. Suddenly I have a bad feeling like I've eaten something rotten. He pushes at the front door, then tries the lock again. The door appears to be jammed. He pauses for a moment. Then moves toward the side of the building as if to walk down to the rear. I wonder if his folk have returned and locked up, or if some other, more dangerous game is being played.

I scan the windows around me. There is nothing unusual but my uneasiness increases. Turin returns to the front, looking for signs himself. He takes some steps back and looks at the windows then in at them, then around at other houses and their windows. He too is suspecting something, and I think he's right to.

Turin again tries the front door without success then moves to the side and starts down to the rear.

Like a punch in the stomach I get a feeling so strong that all caution is thrown to the wind by a blind panic. I dash across the road, hurdle the fence and arrive at the back door just in time to leap on Turin and knock him to the ground. The surprise of my attack has winded him and I place my hand over his mouth, until he is aware of who his attacker is.

'What the . . !' is about as much as he can get out before his surprise makes him speechless. I tell him to shut up and listen. All seems quiet and I tell him to stay where he is and not to move. I raise my hand and face its palm towards him to emphasise the point. I then move to the corner of the building and peer round to see if there is any movement from across the road. There is nothing. This time I don't have the luxury of a scope so they might be watching from inside the darkened upstairs room. I ask him if there is another way into the house.

'Only the front door but it must be locked or jammed because it won't open. Ash, what the hell are you doing here?'

'Later, Turin. Did you get to open the back door at all?'

'No, some fucking idiot jumped on me.'

I ask him to tell me about the doors the last time he was here. He tells me that both the front door and the back door were closed but not locked in case Mel and Zac returned.'

'What about the windows?'

'All the windows are closed and locked.'

'Ever had any trouble opening the front door?'

'No, ' he replies, but there is a growing realisation of what might lie behind the back door and my bizarre behaviour.

I take a close look at the back door and then around the garden,

'What's in the shed?'

'Junk'

'Any string, or cord?'

'Definitely.'

I ask him to get me as much as there is, and he returns with a neat ball of the black cord. I pick up a brick from by the path and tell him to get back, just in case. He then moves back and takes cover behind a low wall.

Beside the back door I crouch against the solidity of the adjacent wall which might afford me some protection. I'm fooling myself if I think it will save my life, it might just make less pieces. I reach across and grasp the round door handle which turns easily. It's not locked. The door opens outwards so pulling it from a distance is an option, probably the only one. I apply some pressure and there's a slight groan as the door moves. Over the thumping sound my heart is making I might not even hear the explosion. It'll be impossible to see if there's a wire joining the handle to a device without opening the door a lot more. The spring loaded lock is pressing against the frame. It's stable, but it could slide back into its keep, if it did the door wouldn't open and it'll have to be done again. I nudge the brick up to the door ensuring it won't open any more. I tie the black cord round the handle. I can't see enough to tie any knot so I hope several will do. I then run the cord down and round the brick so it moves too. I drop back to where Turin has been observing all this, paying out the cord so it lies loosely across the ground. I hand him what's left of it.

'I'm going out front,' I whisper. 'After I give you the signal, count to fifty and that will give me time to get across a garden or two and onto the other side of the road. Then pull the door open slowly and be prepared for a bit of a bang. I'll wait to see if we have company. Wait for me to enter by the front, that'll mean we're alone, and we can get what we need before anyone arrives. What's the best route away from here?'

Turin nods toward the front of the house as he starts to unroll more cord and move back down the garden until he is hidden behind his low wall. I check the cord which is practically invisible, and the door. Then I move to the side of the house. I look toward the front which appears all clear, signal to Turin, who signals back. I then creep along the boundary fence, where I'm hidden from the houses opposite, toward the front looking for a way to get into the garden next door. Just as I reach the front of the house a torch beam scans the front wall and the parking area in front of it. I drop back then lie face down and shuffle beneath the horizontal bars of the fence. The torch beam darts all over the place like a berserk fly, flitting from window to door and back to the windows again. The source stands just inside the open gate, then walks up to the front of the house. The figure pauses, listens moving their head from side to side. They move towards me and down the side of the house to the rear. As he passes I see by the outline and some of his kit, it's a warden. In 48 you never see them at night, and rarely during the day. He might just be nosey, he might have heard the occupants are away and has come to see what opportunities there are or he might have specific instructions. One way or another, if he doesn't move soon he might have a surprise; it might be one we share. All I can think of is how close Turin is to fifty. As the warden disappears round the rear, as quietly and as quickly as I can, I shuffle the few feet which takes me through into the property next door. I get to my feet, cross the garden, hop over another fence, cross the road and fall onto the ground by a parked car. I clamp my hands onto my ears and shut my eyes, but there's nothing. I wait a good twenty-seconds. Something has gone wrong. I imagine Turin and the warden fighting in the back garden, the door closing, the cord breaking. Worse though, I imagine the back door opening and there being nothing but the gentle creak of its hinges. I try to think of any good reason why I should be here, why I should have followed Turin and Sam, why they won't think I'm some kind of spy, and why I shouldn't think I'm an idiot. I take a deep breath and I'm about to stand when suddenly the darkness of the night explodes into a brilliant white flash, a deafening crack that expands into a roar and then into a rumble which shakes the ground, and all within a second or two. The windows burst as one and fling their twinkling shards over the road and adjoining gardens. A mushroom of white and yellow curling flame rises into the sky, evaporates and then it is almost dark again. The fire at the rear of the house casts a flickering light across the gardens and pale grey smoke billows into the gloom above. I wait for the commotion from the houses opposite as LEOs pile out to see what their handiwork has caught them, but there is none. After a few seconds I decide there's not going to be any. They'd be quick, hoping to finish anyone off before they can limp away, or be helped. They wouldn't wait. I move swiftly across the road toward the house until I can feel the heat. Flames lick the side walls from a window near the rear, at the front the door is blown out still in its frame. I run up to the side of the house so Turin can see me. Wave an arm then back to the front, over the door, and into a smoke filled hall. Woodwork at the back is smouldering and patches of flooring are alight. The door to what I suppose is the office to my left, is powder black but otherwise intact and opens easily. The room is lined with books and a large old fashioned desk squats solidly in the middle. Behind the door there is a coat hook on which hangs a jacket and a fabric belt, woven, patterned. I grab the belt as a figure appears to my side,

'Got it?' Turin says.

'Yes,' I reply. He bounds past me and grabs a case off the desk and a book from the shelf. We step over the front door and I turn to see Turin taking a last look before we leave. A distant siren announces that something's on its way, so I follow Turin down the alleyways to avoid any cams, then travel back the way we came.

'What took the time?' I ask Turin.

'Didn't you see that Warden?'

'Yeah, I nearly bumped into him. Were you waiting for him to leave?'

'No. The bastard was standing on the cord!'

'But he got off it eventually?' I suggest.

'Only after he pulled the door open!'

CHAPTER 10

In his apartment, Turin's living room has three long sofas and two windows, one that looks toward The City. A view of The City is good and bad. Good if you like to be reminded that some people are having a good time, bad if it is always other people who are having the good time you think that you should be having. It's like not being invited to the party you can hear going on next door that keeps you awake all night. Most people have sofas big enough to sleep on, this is legal unless they can prove you have been using it as a bed. Sofas that can be made into beds are not legal because single people are only allowed one bedroom and any sort of bed in a room deems it to be a bedroom. Blocks that are like Turin's only have one bedroom per apartment but his living space is larger than average. It is a privilege to be allowed a spare room.

Sam sits on a sofa which has her coat and a pile of bedding on it. I imagine that is where she sleeps. By her side is her sack in which is probably everything she now owns. She looks less like someone from a fairy tale and more like a damsel in distress. It makes me feel like I want to protect her, put my arm round her, but you can't do that because she might think I was 'taking a liberty'. I've got into trouble like that before. She is holding the belt as if it is sacred, she smoothes it and lifts it up to her nose. There is a brief moment when a look of alarm comes over her.

'This doesn't smell like my father's office.' She puts it down. 'It smells of smoke; I guess it's smoke.' She thinks for a while and I wonder how honest I should be when she asks the question I know she is going to ask.

'Is there anything left of the house?'

'Oh yeh, there's not much damage.' I lie. She won't be allowed to go there so she won't know and I hope it makes her feel better.

Turin comes in with some toast and other stuff. We drink something which apparently tastes of blackcurrant. I take their word for that having never eaten a blackcurrant. I'm not even sure what a currant is, black or otherwise, but it tastes okay and the warmth is soothing.

Turin tells me that we should not talk about the event because it might put us all at risk. All we need to know is that the belt is found.

I have begun to wonder about all this secrecy. When Turin had a problem it was okay to share details. If it had been my problem, I wonder if I would have been allowed to share it. By sharing I've saved his life, though he doesn't seem to be very grateful. It would be good if Sam knew I'd just saved her brother's life; hat wouldn't do me any harm.

Turin goes into his kitchen. The rooms are separated by a low wall along which there is a bar where you can eat meals. People used to sit round tables, now there is not enough room, so we sit in a line like in a diner. I see him take a packet from a cupboard, remove something from it and replace the packet. The small capsule has a familiar colour. He sits on the sofa next to Sam and looks her straight in the eyes.

'You must always keep this with you, always.' Sam nods her head and Turin continues, 'It is called an ED which stands for Exit Dose. It will send you to sleep for your own safety and everyone that you know.'

'What do you mean sleep?' Turin's expression tells her enough.

'No! I don't want it.' Sam shoves it back into his hand as if it has suddenly got too hot to handle, 'Take it away.'

Turin puts it down between the two of them, and takes Sam firmly by the shoulders,

'Listen!' He tells her, 'If you get caught, they will interrogate you. They interrogate everybody. They will use drugs that mean you will not be able to tell a lie. You will tell them everything about yourself, Mel and Zac, me, Ash, the group, everything. If you get caught and you don't want everyone else to be tortured in the same way, then taken to Rehab and never heard of again, you must take it.'

'I'll tell them I don't know anything, I'm just a girl.'

'It won't make any difference, Sam. Once you are taken they will inject you, its routine. You will experience all sorts of excruciating pain and the only way to make it stop will be to answer questions truthfully. When you are taken with the knowledge you have, you are already dead, and soon they will make you wish you were.'

With this he places the capsule into her hand and closes her fingers round it.

'It's to protect us that you have to take it, and we have to do the same for you.'

Sam looks across at me and I nod. For a moment she opens her hand and stares at the grey plastic capsule in which her ED rests. The word PRESS is moulded on each side.

'You should keep it in a secret place, even make a special place for it in clothing so you can get to it but where it will never be lost. Always remember where it is and to have it on you. You squeeze the sides of the capsule here, and here, then the dose falls out. It will send you to sleep almost immediately and there is no turning back.'

Turin holds her tight as her tears fall down across her cheeks. I'm tempted to tell them about the EDs that Goodrich gave me but I know that would be difficult to explain.

Sam wipes her eyes and she slips the capsule into her jacket pocket, then relaxes back into the sofa and the pile of bedding.

I move to the window and look towards where The City lights glow in the distance. Pods, veiled in mist, suddenly appear out of it with their yellow lamps glowing, while others disappear back in. They buzz around like drunken flies, steering erratically in between tower blocks. They come to rest clinging precariously to a sky line gantry like birds on a wire, but hanging. One arrives, one disconnects, drops, and just before you think it's about to hit a building lower down, it gains height and dissolves itself into The City's iridescent gloom. A thin line of yellow buildings indicates The City limit as if some giant has carelessly painted the buildings, walls and roofs in a rough arc appearing out of the gloom in one direction and disappearing in another. Where the giant's yellow brush has hit the ground walls have sprung up in the same acrid hue, not caring whether they bisect a children's playground, a civic garden, or a market place. Only offices and corps have remained whole. Those with leverage got to be inside the line, and can claim their City address. I follow the line across the roofs and imagine the divided, the mother from child, partner from partner, and lover from lover. Where once they stared into each other's eyes now they're turned to the wall.

Yellow watch towers punctuate The City boundary line and the elevated outlook decks allow the guards to survey comings and goings as if they are on battlements. A brilliant concentration of coloured and animated lights indicate a get through and all the tacky stores, souvenir stalls and tourist traps that line the crowded streets that lead to them. From Turin's other window, I can look across urbia 44 and maybe as far as the unlit 48. The thickening mist conceals anything beyond it making it difficult to believe there is a rural, where there are farms and their controlled environments, and unknown to most of us, a coast line and water as far as one can see. I know nothing about the rural, where I imagine Carl and Jean to be. I didn't give them much time when they were here. Having me thrust upon them didn't help, but they're all I know I have; that's if they are still alive. Sometimes, only when things are taken away do you really appreciate them. You forget they're there, take them for granted. A friend at college whose folks lived near the top of a high rise before security occupied them, claimed that he'd seen the moon and stars. It was for a couple of nights during some strange weather event when the cloud above us dropped to street level. He was prone to exaggerate and would cocktail medicines for effect, so who knows what he really saw. If he thought the weather might be right, he'd chase up any high rise, fighting his way to the roof, hoping to repeat the experience. Seeing it again would mean that he really had seen it, and not imagined it. One night the disappointment was too much. Maybe it was the realisation that he'd never seen it in the first place, or that he would never see it again, either way he jumped. Goodnight Vienna.

    I turn round to be met with a sight that makes my heart drop. In the soft romantic light of the room, Turin is walking towards the sofa with a pile of bedding, which I take to be his. Sam is moving her stuff into the only bedroom. I conceal my disappointment well and ask Turin if we might talk when we are alone. He agrees.

Sam is in bed in Turin's room. I find it hard to resist the image of her lying there. It's important that Turin and I talk and I wait for him to start by thanking me for saving his life. Something he couldn't say while Sam was here. The blinds are still up but the light in the room is low, it could hardly be seen outside, nevertheless it's hard to get rid of the paranoia. Turin sorts his bedding and then goes to a draw. I can't see what he takes out but as he walks back he is holding a pistol. He sits opposite me and places the pistol on the arm of his sofa.

'I'm sure I won't need this, Ash, but if I have to, I will use it.'

I nod but without knowing what or who he's talking about.

'There are a few things I need to know, and I need the truth.'

I find it difficult to take the situation seriously, but he does. There's something I've missed. I maintain a steady, relaxed gaze, carefully avoiding any change in my blinking pattern or looking away while he continues,

'How did you know the back door was rigged?'

I feel remarkably calm in the circumstances. I reason he needs information, reassurance.

'Do you consider me to be a threat?' This confuses him for a moment, I've gone straight to point. My logic is sound, 'If you need that pistol to protect yourself, you must think I want to kill you. If so, all I needed to do was to let you open your back door.'

He can't dispute that, he knows I saved his life.

'How long have you known where Sam and my folks lived?'

'How dy'a think, Turin? I followed you.'

He gives me a surprised stare.

'It was you that taught me how to follow, and how not to be noticed you're following. I could have been dressed like a circus clown riding an elephant and blowing a trumpet, and you wouldn't have noticed me.'

'From the cellar?'

'To here, and then to the house. You should have changed your boots, you're getting sloppy, Turin.' I let my anger show a little, show I'm confident. Having saved his life, I deserve better than this. Maybe he's embarrassed with the pupil saving the master. He knows I'm right about the boots, and it proves I followed him all the way.

'Why were you following us?'

'Gut feeling?' I know this is the weakness in my story. Turin shakes his head.

'You're in no position to play games, Ash. I need to know why?'

'Well, they are your rules, Turin. Trust your gut feeling, good or bad.'

This doesn't satisfy Turin and he's beginning to disengage.

'The whole point about 'gut feelings' is that you can't explain them. You've told us to listen to them and I did.' I'm tempted to say more, but if I tell him about Carl and Jean, I don't know where it will stop. The paranoia that we live under forces us to live like islands and it serves the state. Any shared experience or personal detail can leave you vulnerable. I might have to share something and take the risk, I can separate my actions though,

'You went to the front door which you can usually open, yes?'

'Yes,' he says this like he means, 'So what?'

'So did I.' And to avoid confusion I add, 'At my place, where I am registered as living. It was locked, or jammed.'

'It happens.' He's avoiding the point, because he knows what it is.

'So you go round to the back?'

'Yes, sure.'

'So did I.'

There's no avoiding this time.

'And your back door?' He asks.

'Was rigged, like yours, but before I got to the house, I knew it was being watched.'

'How?'

'A neighbour had posted a signal. You know the type, curtain, something not quite right. Enough to be noticed, deliberate.'

'So what did you do?'

'I checked out the back door and I was lucky. I saw the wire running from the handle before I'd opened the door enough to trigger anything. '

'In the same way as ours?'

'Exactly the same,' I answer him, 'but I had another way in, through my room upstairs. When I was inside I could dismantle the device and move it to the front door, which is the way I reckoned they would come in.'

'Well, they wouldn't come in through the back door. What happened?'

'It was a mess, but that's not the point.'

'No, it isn't,' he says. 'When you set out to follow us, Ash, you couldn't have known what would be found at the house.'

Then I see something occurring to him which doesn't look good for me.

'Or maybe you did? Maybe you knew exactly what had been set up and you had second thoughts. You argue for co-operation, you want us to share information with you. Information which would give you, or somebody else, power over us. As for your place, there is no proof that it happened. If it did, you could already be jeopardising our safety, just by being here.'

He takes the pistol and places it under his bedding.

'I have to get some sleep. I can't deny you saved my life, but that could have been staged to make us feel we owe you, and therefore share everything we know. That won't work, none of us knows it all. You haven't explained why you followed us, I don't buy the 'gut feelings'.'

In silence we both get into our bedding. I go over our conversation and wonder if there was anything else I could have said. How can you explain 'gut feelings'?

Turin's breathing becomes regular and deep. I wait for as long as I have patience then reach under the sofa to where the belt lies, coiled like a snake. I pull it out and it unravels, slowly uncoiling itself as if alive. I wonder why it is so important, it must have something to tell us. I creep into the kitchen area, taking it with me. I turn on a low level spot and lay it out on a work surface which is hidden from view. I filter some water into a glass so that it might appear that I'm just thirsty. Secrecy, deceit, craft, call it what you like, it's becoming a habit. I examine the belt closely. I smooth it out. The weaving is random, a series of multicoloured flecks but

no pattern or design which could be interpreted as code or
language. Exposure to a particular light source or energy
might reveal something, maybe passwords. I turn it over,
the back is plain and padded. The belt is as broad as a
hand but it narrows toward the ends which terminate in thick
metal clasps. The clasps each look like half a disc, one fits
through the other then slides back to make a whole disc,
like a world. The belt is a woman's or a girl's. I can't find
anything unusual about it so I roll it back up, tighter than it
was and as I do, part of it folds into segments like the flats
of a polygon, so I lay it flat again. Along one edge there is a
double seam which is almost invisible. I can feel a
springiness to the top edge, not quite the same as the
bottom which is less flexible. The belt looks folky, hand
crafted and naive. I think that is a masquerade and its
homeliness hides some cute technology. I pass it through
my hands, squeezing, bending, pressing, twisting. Then as I
twist the top edge, a seam opens. It's a finely engineered
seal and inside a thin flat 'holder' made of stiff felt. Working
my way along the edge I try again the twisting grip, but
without success. Then when the twist coincides with a mark
in the apparently random pattern, Hey Presto, another slot
opens to reveal another felt holder. There are six sprung
metal seals, each accessing a pocket. From the first I
remove the square of felt wadding in the centre of which a
hole is cut. In the hole, cut for the purpose, rests a dark grey
disc about the size of the hole made if you pressed your
thumb and index finger tips together. I recognise them
immediately, pill drives. About as thick as a biscuit, these
innocuous looking discs hold phenomenal amounts of data
and possess their own power source. Each has a label
stating capacity, polarity, reference, maker's name and

serial number. Hooked up to the appropriate reader, the world's your lobster. They are mega illegal, and so is any kit that can read them, so they are a rarity. However, I know someone, who knows someone.

CHAPTER 11

A blur walks past that looks like bare legs. My head is on its side, on the sofa, about knee level and it feels as if I've just got to sleep. Sleep? I wish. The thought of bare legs wakes me into imagining other bare parts; my imagination runs the whole picture. I open my eyes enough but not so it looks as if I am awake, that might bring the show to a close. I sacrifice the delicious fantasy for a little taste of the real thing. Sam's bedroom door is open and I can hear the shower running. The legs walk past again and head towards the bedroom door. Something is dropped, not clothing, and the legs stop. The body that is wearing just a long tee shirt bends down to pick something up. The shirt rises slowly, and there is a triangle of pale pink fabric printed with small flowers that defines outlines and shapes but no sooner do I get focused then the body rises, the curtain drops and the sweet gift is gone and the bedroom door closes. My eyes do the same attempting to retain the divine image as long as possible into a deep fantasising sleep.

I awake some time later to the knowledge that there is activity, and it's been going on for a while. You sense it, even in sleep, maybe because you can close your eyes but not your ears. Sam is moving around the kitchen area, but I can't hear Turin. I look towards his sofa, it's a dishevelled mess but there's no body in it. I sit up, change my top and roll up the bedding and consider having a shower myself.

Sitting next to Sam at the kitchen bar we drink coffee, not real coffee of course, and eat toast with some kind of spread. I am not really close but I can smell her freshness. Beneath her jeans are the naked legs that I have seen and that have walked past and that with little effort, I could have reached out and touched. There's more than enough to launch a dream, and I do. I imagine the feel of the pale pink fabric. I imagine my fingers winding in and out of the little flowers until they reach the edge and her warm . . . . '

'What are you thinking?'

'Ergh!' The sharp intake of breathe draws down with it the globule of toast, then the choking that is created projects it, missile like, in her direction before I can turn away. What hair she has is clipped up and just as she lowers her head for another sip of coffee, thankfully it misses her ear but gets caught on the clip. It sticks for a moment then slowly starts a slimy roll down towards her bare neck.

I jump to my feet taking a small plate with me and passing behind her I make a grab for the moist lump and in doing so catch a few strands of her hair which makes her yelp.

'Ouch! What was that?'

'Ant.'

'Ant?'

'Er, fly I mean, it was a fly.' So saying I race round to the sink and make a fuss of flushing it away 'Yeah, they can be really nasty. Er. . . . biting . .'

'Biting?' She looks horrified.

'Stinging, err . . both. They bite and sting. If one end doesn't get you the other end will.' I laugh nonchalantly, okay, nervously.

She stands, picks up her plate, and moves toward the bedroom but diverts to me on the way where I'm standing near the sink. She hands me her plate, plants a kiss on my cheek and whispers,

'My hero.'

And it's me that has been bitten. I feel the delicious warm poison coursing through my body. I take an uncertain step toward her bedroom not really knowing what I'm doing, knowing what I want to do but not knowing if it's right or . . .

My predicament is interrupted by the sound of the button entry's faint peeping and popping, the catch flicking out and the door opening. It must be Turin and I realise I've hardly given him a thought. Now all that stuff starts flooding back and drowns everything else. Turin is not convinced I'm being honest. Maybe he's picking up on my guilt regarding Goodrich. Certainly my impatience with the group and questioning the need for so much secrecy doesn't help. For all the stuff the group has done, nothing has changed. I'm starting to think that the group is ill directed, pointless, random. The paranoia drives me mad, nobody seems to know, or is allowed to care, what anyone else is doing.

Turin moves across to the sofa surrounded by his bedding and sips the hot coffee, or what we call coffee, that Sam has just given him.

There is a silence which doesn't surprise me. The longer it lasts the stronger I find the temptation to revisit last night's conversation, but he must start.

He puts his mug on the floor and leans back against his bedding, folds his arms and starts,

'Forget about the house Ash, for the moment. I've been thinking and I still don't understand why you followed Sam and I? Saying you had a gut feeling isn't enough.'

'It was enough to save your life when you went round to the back door. It's not an exact science, you know that, Turin. All I know is that as soon as you said your folks had disappeared, I saw some similarities and I didn't want the same thing to happen to you and Sam. If your front door had opened, you would never have known I was there.'

'There are rules. No one else would have taken it into their head to follow, on a whim. There had to be a reason why, when we all left the cellar, you decided to follow us.'

'I've told you as much as I can. I could show you the house, or what's left of it, but that would be against the rules, I suppose. There were other things, it's okay I'm not going to tell you what they are. The incident at my house was after those other things happened. After what you said about your folks, it occurred to me there might be a similar pattern. Because of all this secrecy I couldn't warn you, I couldn't tell you to watch out for any sticking front doors, 'just in case'. So it was all I could do.'

While Turin finishes his coffee, I move round to the window. We both relax and perhaps have come to terms. I feel reckless, like walking away from it all. Goodrich and my new family are gaining the respect I once had for Turin and the group. It's essential to have faith in a group and its aims, 'be as one'. This has made a difference but I can't have everything changing in my life. Some things should remain the same otherwise there's nowhere to stand and push from.

'The Bakery job,' I say.

'What about it? It was the one you and Meko did. It was good.'

'You think so?'

Turin nods.

'Did you know what was above The Bakery?'

'Offices, they were empty offices.'

'You counted the floors?'

'Why would I do that?'

'You would have found a hidden floor.'

'You know Ash, this is none of my business or yours. Chad does the planning, that's the way it is, and it's the way it's always been.'

'You have heard of free hospitals, Freemeds?'

'Yes.'

'There was one above The Bakery.'

Turin is disbelieving.

'How do you know?'

'I spent a couple of days there.' Turin is shocked. Some real evidence at last of how we are destroying each other by not co-operating.

'I'll tell you why I was there if you want,' I continue, 'but all you need to know is that I went down some stairs and, had I carried on, I would have arrived at what was left of The Bakery. I got as far as the sooty oils on the walls, the fine white dust that was flour. Even when I arrived there, the doctors and nurses were preparing to move. When I left, so did they, just before it was raided. They'd been operating for weeks without any problems until we came along. Always have at least two ways out and we blew one of them up. Fortunately the andys don't have any initiative, no curiosity, but when a surveyor came to check out the building, well I'll say no more. Can you imagine what would have happened if we'd been the cause of their discovery. How many medical staff, helpers, friends, those being treated, could have been hauled in? Sent to Rehab? Others left with nowhere to go? All that just because there was the opportunity to knock over a couple of corp execs and their tin guards. It will be weeks before the hospital is up and running again somewhere else. In the meantime how much suffering and death will there be to the very people we claim to be helping. I feel appalled at what I could have done. In the end, who wins?'

Turin sits stunned. I hope he is beginning to understand how this secrecy is our greatest enemy.

'What do we really achieve, Turin?' I can't stop now, 'Security corps love us. Some of the very organisations that people are most fearful of, rely upon us to drum up their trade. We put money in their pockets by putting fear on the streets. The more execs we kill, the more others are prepared to pay for protection. The security corps get wealthier, they pay more sponsorship and the ministers turn a blind eye and let them do whatever they want in the name of protection. You really think we will ever bring down this regime? Groups like ours, working alone, independently of each other are no more than a nuisance, an irritation, like a flea bite. If we could work together, co-ordinate, pool our resources, we could be a plague.'

'Groups are autonomous entities,' he tells me, 'they do things their way. Each group has developed its own agenda, initiated by its own individual grievance and customs. It's the way it's always been.'

I know Turin's influence is important and those groups he knows would be guided by it. He is reluctant to force change because the result is unpredictable. If it failed the state and the corps would reap a vengeance on everyone, especially those who are already disadvantaged. He thinks that working separately we have some effect, and those that fail do so without bringing everyone else down with them. They are waiting for Goodrich, and Goodrich is waiting for them.

'Turin,' I ask him, 'how do we measure success? Are we nearer any goal? What goals do we have?'

'Ash, you don't need to know these things,' he says impatiently. 'We move slowly, cautiously. There are others whose identity has to remain secret. They can't know who we are, we can't know who they are. If anyone is picked up everything they know will be found out, you know this.'

We pause for a moment. It's the same old mantra, ask no questions, get no answers, carry on in fear and with a policy of ignorance. Then something occurs to me that he might not be able to refuse.

'Would you like me to find out what's happened to your folks?'

Turin is at first surprised, then confused.

'How could you?'

'That would have to remain a secret.' I tell him.

He thinks about it and he glances in the direction of Sam's room. The implication is clear.

'Okay, but the group cannot be compromised.'

I tell him it won't be and I will not require any more information other than some clarification of what we already know. Regarding anything else, I will give him only bare essentials. He seems to be fine with this.

'The way my place was rigged and yours was identical'

Turin nods. 'Well, so you say.'

'My house was being watched because the couple that they tried to pick up had escaped. They wanted to cover the possibility that those they wanted might return.'

I pause to ensure that Turin is with me.

'If your folks escaped, the device was waiting for their return, like in my situation. If they are being detained, then who was the back door set up for?'

Turin is silent. He stands, walks round to the window and looks toward The City. There's a light mist falling and it's as if we are in a cloud. He looks out into the nothingness that swirls around as if it too is searching for an answer.

'There can only be one other,' he says, 'and it has to be me.'

'Sam is discounted?' I ask this knowing what I know about the belt, and to see if Turin knows too.

'Of course.'

'So there's no way she could be a target?'

'No. No way, she's not implicated in anything we do. That incident is the reason why she is here, not the other way round.'

I ask him if he knew if Chad or Meko had any problems. He shakes his head.

'Would you know?'

Turin knows that if they had been caught and if through the group his folks, him or any of us had become a target, we wouldn't know.

Before he can answer, the bedroom door opens and Sam appears. She looks at us each in turn but her gaze rests with Turin. She walks across the room and the two sit together and he puts his arm round her. He takes her hand in his and looks her full in the face and asks her directly,

'Is there anything that you've noticed, overheard, anything that might help us know what's happened to Mum and Dad?'

She takes back her hands.

'No. No Idea. Really, there can be nothing. I've never seen them do anything anti or even discuss anything.' She pauses, turns and looks about the room,

'Where's the belt?'

I reach beneath the sofa and pull it out of my sack and hand it over. Sam runs it through her fingers then raises it to her nose,

'Do you know why it's so important?' I ask.

'No,' she says, 'dad just said that whatever happens I should try to make sure it's safe.'

There's a pause as Sam goes into the kitchen area.

Pulling her hands away from Turin, moving into the kitchen when asked questions, she is withdrawing. This is a sign she is lying. A big lie or a little one. Trust no one, I tell myself. It's a disappointment.

'Anyone want a drink?' She holds up a bottle that has bands of colour. Turin and I both nod, and then she shakes it until it's a blur. I was thinking that the bands of colour was the labelling, but now I realise, it's the liquid inside.

I go through the list of who else the back door was rigged for besides Turin. I think of Goodrich and having seen him so recently, I know rebellion is not limited to age, sex, class or even position. Amongst the inactive, compliant, silent majority there are some who are just as desperate to see things change. We don't recognise them, they don't wear badges or edgy tee-shirts, but their passion is just as keen. It's not impossible that Zac, or even Mel, were up to something. Sam brings round our drinks gradually separating into pink at the top, fading through green to a red at the bottom, nothing is simple anymore. She stands at the window looking toward The City and leans with her elbows on the cill. The belt lies discarded on the arm of the sofa.

'The belt is really important, right?' I ask.

Sam nods.

'Why?' I ask.

'I don't know,' she replies without turning.

'It would have taken no time to take it and go?'

Sam nods her agreement.

'So,' I ask, 'why did they leave it?'

Sam shakes her head and shrugs her shoulders.

'If you are taken by whatever LEOs are given the job, the first thing they do is a full body search, correct?'

They both agree.

I take a sip of the pink stuff, there's a flavour reminiscent of the oranges, but not oranges. Flavours are invented and 'trend', making new 'friends' until people tire of them and they're shifted, or mixed into another that'll blitz the market. The taste is never as important as the look though, and you choose your drink to suit your eye shade, hair colour or clothing scheme. Mine is grey, but no drinks are grey.

'Then,' I continue, 'if Zac and Mel left of their own accord, say in a panic, Zac would have taken the belt. If they were taken by LEOs, the belt would be left behind.'

'They could have gone out,' Sam suggests, 'thinking everything was okay and then they were picked up or something.'

Nice try, I think.

'If that was the case, why did they leave in such a hurry? Why was the place a mess?'

'Someone knew they were out and broke in.' Not even Sam convinces herself this could be true.

'The doors you said were open, they wouldn't have left them like that, there was a half-eaten meal on the table. There are other things too.' I'm thinking of the set-up, the sticking front door, the device. Someone just happens to vacate a premises so let's set a trap to blow them up when they return? I don't think so.

I watch them both. Turin knows I'm right. What Sam is involved in must be serious, too serious to admit to; so the lie is a big one.

Asking questions and giving personal information is uncomfortable to us all. It creates suspicion, it raises tension. You have to keep asking yourself before you speak a word, if you are signing your own death warrant, even if you are with people you've known all your life. It includes people you love, because that might change, and someone you once loved, and loved you, has you at their mercy. We've grown up with a suspicion of everyone we don't know, as well as everyone we do. There's listening at windows and doors, from another room, even the same room. The obvious, intimidating surveillance, the covert surveillance, the bugs, taps and filters. We fear the consequences of a casual remark, an overheard conversation, a careless reply. The rewards are high for reports that lead to a conviction, it's a growth industry. Neighbours listen at walls, children report their folks, folks their children, children and folks each other; twenty-four-seven paranoia. Now it's like tree rings, it runs through your whole body. Cut yourself and you bleed fear.

In the cold glass before me the green begins to seep into the pink and change the flavour. There are elements of mint and some chemical makes the tongue tingle uncomfortably. The pink tastes like pineapple, and the yellow tastes like the blackcurrant.

Presume nothing, it's a rule.

'Did your folks have many regular visitors?' I ask.

'No,' Sam replies, 'there was never anyone that came from Dad's work place. Occasionally there might be a neighbour, but nobody regular.'

'Nobody that either of your folks knew well enough that they might think of using the back door?' Turin looks at me.

'Mum had a couple of close friends and they sometimes used the back door, but only if the front door was closed and they knew someone was in.'

Turin stands up and starts putting stuff in his bag,

'We better start back to the cellar maybe Chad can make some sense out of the belt.'

I move towards Sam and ask her,

'Do you trust everyone who knows where you live?'

She tells me that she does and that they have nothing to hide anyway.

Turin stops and looks up.

'The group stuff Ash, has no connection with my home life. No one knows what I'm involved with outside of the four of us in the group. Sam too, she didn't know anything before Mel and Zac disappeared.'

'And still practically nothing,' she says.

I leave the rest of my drink. A thin layer is all that is left of the pink which has separated from the green beneath it. At the bottom the deep red which appears to have the consistency of a heavy oil, is busy producing bubbles which slowly rise. When they reach the green they accelerate alarmingly until arriving at what's left of the pink, then they pop and send up a tiny puff of vapour like a smoke ring. Sam tells me that in the right light the little rings are iridescent.

   All I wanted was a drink.

CHAPTER 12

Chad turns on his spotlight and illuminates the ochre brown cellar in silhouettes and the faces that look down onto his table. He lays the belt out, brushing aside various computer ancillaries, cables and discarded food wrappers. With both hands he smooths out the belt, then runs them along its length, turns it over and does the same.

'Where did it come from?' he says putting on a jeweller's eye piece.

'A friend sent it to me,' I tell him before either Turin or Sam can say anything. Trust no one.

'Just need to know what I might be looking for' he says.

'She gave it to me for safe keeping,' I tell him, 'she said I was to look after it for her. She said whatever you do don't lose it, my life could depend upon it. Now she's disappeared and I want to know what's so special about it and if it can tell me where I might find her?'

Sam and Turin seem impressed but Chad holds his hand up to stop any more 'personal' information. He shrouds the belt, does his best to shield it from our view and fusses over it without really doing much.

'I can't find anything, but the kit I've got here isn't the right sort.' He pauses then turns to me,

'Look, why don't you let me keep it overnight and then tomorrow I might have some news for you. I've got some readers, if there's anything, they'll find it.'

'Great,' I tell Chad, 'whatever you can find out would be great, thanks.'

Turin trusts Chad to be able to find whatever secrets the belt has. He seems happy with the arrangement but knowing what I do, I wonder why he hasn't found the discs already. Perhaps he has and isn't going to share his discovery. I feel that knot growing in my gut. Sam seems indifferent, which is strange considering it was she who thought the belt so important. There's stuff going on here and Turin is the odd one out, he seems oblivious to it all.

Chad is still fiddling with a small hand held device taken from his sack. A small screen glows blue, then slowly fades to green,

'Okay guys, at least I can tell you there's no tracker or bug in it.' Turin and I look at each other, in our haste it hadn't even occurred to us to check. Note to self, be more professional!

Chad rolls up the belt and puts it into his sack, spins round awkwardly on the arm of his beloved chair, and gives us a big smile. Chad's attempt to be friendly is nauseating.

'Hey look, you guys,' he takes a pace towards Sam, who looks as if she's preparing to defend herself. She casually moves her feet like pro fighters do so her weight is balanced ready to counter any aggressive move. She does it so naturally it's frightening. For a moment I remember standing in front of her bedroom door this morning. Turin arriving could have been a lucky escape. I do like strong women, and girls, but they are scary. Chad reaches out to Sam and gives her an awkward hug then says,

'Welcome to the group.' He does a kind of fisty thing as if he's about to roll dice. It means nothing to anyone and Sam just applies a smile like it was make up. Then wipes it away.

Just then there's a sound upstairs. Ma Brown's footsteps can be heard going to the back door and we pause and eventually see Meko's boots, then Meko herself coming down the steps. She is often the last to arrive. Chad spends more time than any of us in the cellar, Meko least. There are various posters and cuttings on the damp walls as well as an old planner. There's a small blower that warms the room up but it makes the walls run with sweat, as Meko calls it, so we seldom use it. It never gets really cold and we seldom spend nights here, all together that is. We don't see rats themselves but we reckon young ones get in from time to time.

The old business planner that is by the bottom of the steps leading down into the cellar, indicates the time and date when we should all meet. There are a lot of coloured pins. One colour indicates an hour, another a day and so on. We know which colour represents what and there are about twenty colours, stripes as well, so the code is not easily read, unless you know it.

Sam goes to the corner where there is a kettle to make a warm drink. In our sacks we all have a plastic mug, a plate and other stuff, because you never know where you are going to be from one day to the next. I think we are going to discuss another event. The Bakery was the last one and we need to start planning another, but planning and doing are not the same. My standing with Chad is I'm just a foot soldier, what they used to call 'cannon fodder', he only considers me important as someone carrying out his plans, otherwise I'm dispensable.

I make a suggestion regarding the car park entrance at the rear of the Columbus building, and even accessing the building through its exit nearby. I think it is a great target, attacking the cornerstone of public records and control. It was what I noticed after my interview there. A sloppy guard, the possibility of getting a vehicle close and being able to wait. There would be delivery vehicles, and a van would mask the driver getting away from the scene. The rear of the Columbus building would suffer a fair amount and if it was done at night there would be little collateral. What windows there are on that side would be blown out bringing the work to a stop. There may also be some damage to systems and records which would be a bonus. More to the point, the building is a symbol. Turin and Meko are keen and think it's a good idea and wonder why we haven't thought of it before. Chad says it'll have to wait as there are other events which are planned. He's patronising and I get the idea that he's already dismissed it. It's Chad who decides what we will be doing and what we should be targeting. He has another target which his research has identified as being a possible and checks all his boxes. Some of the criteria will be whether they have a predictable behaviour, patterns which take them into areas which make them vulnerable without too much collateral damage. They include sites where packages can be easily placed without a high chance of discovery, with acceptable impact and detonation characteristics. Lastly, and probably the most important, a good chance that the operatives who set the device, will not be especially noticeable before, during, or afterwards, then not traceable or easily followed by cams, or any other surveillance. There has to be plenty of ways of escape back into the crowd, into the night, into obscurity.

    Without too much ado it is all done and dusted. Chad made all the decisions, no details in case any of us gets caught, so we wait and see. Meko and I look at each other with a resigned expression.

I think we are just smashing windows. When these things get no publicity, what's the point? What we need to do is something that everybody can see, feel and appreciate. Our stuff never makes the news, well it wouldn't, but if it was bigger, word would get about and others would be encouraged.

We all leave quietly in ones and twos after Turin has checked from upstairs. He watches someone go, then signals the next departure. He is always last to leave except for Chad who often stays to organise things after an event is decided.

Above me the mist swirls around a dead street light. It's had its light elements removed. Connected to a power cell, they make a cheap heater if they're put in a tin box with a few holes in the lid. From this road intersection which is on my usual route home across 48, I can still see the back of Ma Brown's a few streets away. We use the front and the back, but it's safer to disperse down the paths and through the empty house at the rear. Chad always uses the back when eventually he does leave, if he leaves at all. Unusually, I catch a glimpse of him hugging a fence line. Out of curiosity I move as if to follow him and to see if it is really him, but I stop and wonder if I should. I will, at least for a few streets then decide. If it was darker he'd be virtually invisible skulking along in the shadows. His brown coat is easy to miss but he insists on wearing pale trainers and they lay a pale dotted line even in the darkest alley. He turns occasionally but he's slow and his bulk telegraphs every move. I have no trainers. I have a grey coat and hood, so with my necker pulled up to my eyes, I just look like a shadow, as long as I'm not caught against a light. There are no lights round here. I follow him to the edge of 48 and decide it's enough and begin to turn. He stops though and rummages through his sack, something falls out and skates across the road. He swears and picks up what looks like a small palmer. It lights up his cheek as it draws close, then darkens as he talks into it. This is startling because none of us dare use anything that can track us. We don't even carry them around, it would be like having an implant. All personal comms are subsidised so they can record everything you say and what anyone else says within range, whether it's turned off or not.

Chad finishes his call and puts the palmer back into his sack with the screen still alight. He waits nervously, checking to see if he has been followed and trying to be as much a part of a shadow that his trainers will allow. By hopping over a few gardens I get closer. We both wait for a few minutes, maybe ten, during which Chad is fiddling with the belt. A car pulls up which is a typical exec car, black, long, expensive. A rear window drops and Chad has a conversation which I can't hear, but I see Chad hand over what I think are the pill drives. He gets something back in exchange and the car drives off. After that he scurries away into the early evening gloom as fast as his pale trainered feet can carry him.

The following morning we assemble at the cellar. Chad has said nothing about the drives but is about to demonstrate. He's a frustrated performer. He could just tell us what he's found, but he needs the attention. We watch as he rigs up a device with contacts, connects wires to several boxes that come to life. Coloured diodes begin to flicker, each with a life of their own. Chad places a tester between two small pads and yet more lights jump about and race round in circles, slowing then speeding up. If nothing else, it's an entertaining light show, but it's just the warm up act for the star attraction, or perhaps I should say attractions.

'Okay Guys and Guyesses, Tops Tokens tokes the tops for tokens for you!' Chad thinks his impersonation of the silver haired quiz show androbotic host is 'fantaba-u-lowsa!' He gesticulates like Lucky Lemonz, but we don't respond with the same screams and calls that his audience does.

'Whata youa gotta here ah, is ah,' and he pauses while he fumbles around in his coat pocket, ' ta-da!' And he reveals the pill drives, six of them, like a game show host. He would have liked to have been more theatrical, juggled with them, or rolled them over a fist. Of the three of us, Turin is most impressed. We take it in turns to inspect them, turn them about, check their weight. Sam takes one and looks very closely at it.

'They're heavy aren't they?' she says.

Chad is keen to impress,

'They hold data, world loads of it. The old quantums have nothing on these. They are totally illegal like. . . ,' and he draws his thumb across his throat in a cutting motion.

'And,' he continues, 'so is any kit that can read them. But,' and off he goes with his impression again, 'just forra ayou, forra one anight only, ta-da!' And he points to the equipment he has been rigging up.

He plugs in his normal screen, which bathes all our faces in its multicoloured desktop. Chad keys in an elaborate code, applies small black and red pads to the pills flats, and keys some more. The word 'Reading' spins out of the screen, jumps, twists, and rolls round like a gymnast on speed until it finishes with its own little ta-da! The screen is full of white space within a directory frame. A series of numbered columns, reference codes and other operating paraphernalia are distributed about the screen, but the columns are empty.

'Don't believe it,' Chad's charade doesn't convince me.

'Ah! Wait a mo' lov-er-ly lady'. And he releases the pill from its contacts, turns it round and tries again, with the same result, blank columns, the upshot is, the pill drive is empty. Eventually he turns to me, shrugs his bulk and with a shake of the head, removes the pill drive from its contacts.

I look around the pale faces searching the screen for meaning. I check out the frowns, who's faking, who's not. Meko breaks the silence.

'Is that right? It's empty?'

Turin gets closer, checks out some of the on screen data, hits a key and the screen reloads, with the same result.

'Nada.' Chad shakes his head and taps a few keys, inserts another pill. The same show starts and then ends abruptly with the same result. He does this four more times until all the pills have moved from one side of the contacts to the other leaving no chance that they were missed.

'Well,' he says, 'there you are, there's nothing on them. Sorry Ash, worth a bit but don't get caught with them.'

With that he closes down, disconnects the boxes, and rolls up the cables and rolls up the belt. With a kind of 'job done' attitude, he hands the belt back to me. Then like a gambler lets the pills drop into my palm like gambling chips.

'No lucky, lucky, mister.' He breathes his game show impression into my face, 'You could barter these they're worth a fair amount but only if you've got the right kit.' Then he adds with a smirk. 'You gonna have to find her some other way?'

Chad irritates me, but I manage to force a smile, to match his. He knew there was nothing on them. In the time he had, and without the originals, what else could his friends have done? What he didn't know was, the ones he exchanged were also blank, but only I knew that. Now I begin to wonder what his friends, whoever they are, will do when they find out. Of all the pale faces bathing in the light of Chad's screen, Sam seems to be the least concerned. With all that her father had said about them, why didn't she appear surprised? Did Chad mean to say, 'Loverly Lady?' Was it just mimicry, or did he know they were Sam's. The questions just pile up.

Back at my new home, Carol is out, but Goodrich and I are sat at the table in her back room. We meet at Carol's, because there's no reason why I shouldn't be here, and Goodrich is unseen by most, just a balmy old man, wandering the streets looking for scraps and a dog he used to own. After we have eaten, he takes out the pill drives that I gave him when I left Turin's in the middle of the night. He lays them out in front of him as if starting some game, and he does,

'You know what these are?'
'Yes.'
'Do you know their capacity?'
'Immense.'
'Wrong. Very immense!'
'Three of these are full, two are half full one only used a little.'

He has my attention,

'Would you like to know what they contain?'

'Would you like to tell me?'

'We haven't had time to go into the files but looking at the directories, file names, signatures and codes, they have been downloaded at irregular intervals over about fourteen months and in differing amounts.'

'Backups?'

'We wondered that but backups have a recognisable file structure, but physical backups are practically unknown these days, who would bother. The structure on these is random, and not even the discs have been used in any order. There are large sections of regular, formal backing up, the type we would expect to find in a corp's security vault. Finding it hanging on the back of a door raises a few eyebrows. Would you like to know to what they relate?'

'Would you like to tell me?'

'They have all been downloaded from the central data vault of CUpal's organotech division. There's a lot of general files but when we did a buzz word search, a fair number of files popped up, some of which were CatSec1. So being as nosey as we are, and those being top security files, we had a look at those first and found a few hundred test run specs. Results, and reports concerning a sub-version AB101with segment spec mods.'

'Meaning what?'

'As you know human brain segments have been used in bots for a while. Technology is limiting the size of the segment that can be used. Only a certain amount of brain tissue can be found work to do, material in excess of function will find something else to do. At best it begins to day dream, at worst, it gets cantankerous.'

'The devil makes work for idle . . . brain tissue?'

'Succinctly put. So find ways of controlling larger segments by giving them more things to do and you get a win-win situation. More control, more functions. AB101is a long running experimental programme apparently, so the press releases would have us believe, achieving astonishingly successful results by trialing an organic interface. It claims to be growing the adaptable organic interface and therefore able to use larger material segments. It also runs a parallel programme, an activity division, called AD, where separate material segments are being given responsibility for different areas of activity. Current interfacing technology has failed so far to handle this amount of material. The organic interface would appear to make this possible. Investment in CUpal has tripled. An organic interface is seen as the way to go, and the pundits agree, where the organic interface controlling a variety of segments goes, the 'total brain' will be the next goal. There are implications.'

Goodrich pauses as he hears the front door open. Carol calls us and we tell her where we are. She asks us if we want coffee and we say we do.

'If the harvesting of brain tissue wasn't bad enough,' Goodrich continues, 'the harvesting of total brains is infinitely worse. Imagine the current crop of bots using a total human brain as their operating system? What residues from a previous life will remain? Can the memory be removed entirely? What evil will still reside in dark corners waiting to be unleashed on us? Then consider the holy grail of robotics, the organic robot. A cloned human grown to a range of specifications, fitting whatever task you can imagine, from sex toys to ruthless assassins, and no one to tell the difference. Fortunately they're likely to take the same time to mature as real humans, but in the future with accelerating growth patterns, it could be less. That's just a lead time though, once the first few are mature enough to be put to work, they'll soon be walking out of the farms in their thousands.'

Carol brings in our drinks then says she has to go out again, saying something about a woman's work is never done. She says this in the same way that Jean would say it, and I think, my mother.

'However,' says Goodrich, 'first they have to grow the interface. As you may know, much of the brain is just storage, it's the operating system, the interface that let's you access the knowledge and use it to good, or bad effect. If they can produce the hardware, a prototype, or just a convincing demo that their organic interface really works, then their corp value will skyrocket. Every other competitor that's not somewhere with organic technology will become practically worthless. Worst case? CUpal, starting with 4U its main rival, could buy up every other security related firm on the planet.'

'World domination.'

'Yes, at least in the security market, but then when you have the keys to all the doors, stationary cupboards and filing cabinets on the planet, it's as good as.'

'Makes you wonder if it's all worth while. Might as well slash my wrists and have done with it.'

'There is something which is puzzling though.'
'Go on.'

'It might take a few days. We are running the drives at the moment and have investigated some recent access dates so we can at least find out what they were last used for. We suspect from what we have been able to access so far that the results have been tampered with. It appears that the experiments are not going as well as their publicity might suggest.'

'So?'

'If they can't come up with the goods in a reasonable time, investors might start to get cold feet. A failure to produce anything meaningful could mean they become the carcass on which other corps prey.'

'Who would most benefit from the content of these pills?' I ask.

'Any competitor of CUpal's. I would add any individual or group who would be against the use of brain tissue, but I think they are all androbots now.'

There was a moment of quiet. I think about the implications and how it might affect what we do next. I'm aware that there is more to come, Goodrich is fidgety like rehearsing a delicate question. I'm beginning to do it too, not fidget I mean, but you imagine what the question might be, and prepare the answer. You even try to prepare for the unexpected so as not to appear thrown and give the impression you're confident and truthful.

'I'm going to ask you something which you may find difficult to answer,' Goodrich says, 'but it is important for me to know the truth.'

'Okay'

'Do the names Zac or Mel mean anything to you?'

I pause before answering. Both the direct nature of the question, and the climate of secrecy that it invades, un-nerves me.

'Yes.'

Goodrich raises his eyebrows, considering their size it's not an easy gesture to miss, and it means, 'Go on?'

'I know someone called Turin and his folks are Zac and Mel.'

'I know you know more Ash, but I understand your reticence, so I'll exchange with you. You may not know what Zac is. He was an androbotic research engineer, one of the very best, working for CUpal. He now works for their organotech division. Now your turn.'

'Turin has been involved in some events.'

'Okay. Mel, Zac's partner, is a friend of ours, and we had reason to keep Zac close because of his expertise and we believe he is also not unsympathetic to our aims. He has access to many areas which might prove extremely useful in the future. We haven't approached him and he doesn't even know we exist. We are on a sort of 'watching brief'. We have no reason to believe that he has been doing anything which might have brought him into conflict with his masters. Definitely your turn.'

'The pill drives were concealed in a belt that was hung on the back of a door in Zac's office.'

'I could be being short changed here,' Goodrich says with a wry smile, 'however, just after we had paid them a routine visit, CUpal's internal security arrived, literally out of the blue, and took Mel and Zac away. Now you.'

'Okay. After Turin had told us that Mel and Zac had been taken, well had disappeared, we went to the house to get the belt.'

'Why?'

'That's not fair. It's your turn to give.'

'Okay. There were no signs, rumours or signals that Zac was anything other than squeaky clean. If that's so then he and Mel, could be released. Unfortunately history demonstrates that once an authority has made a move they don't usually change it. If it turns out to be a mistake, they'd invent a reason rather than admit an error.' Goodrich pauses for a moment.

'The belt?' He asks. 'Who knew about it?'

'I don't know. Turin, of course. We picked it up from the house, from Zac's office.'

'So who knew what the belt contained?'

'No one. Turin knew it was important, that's all. Zac would have known what was in it. He'd be the only one. No one else.'

Goodrich looks over his glasses.

'Perhaps there is someone you haven't mentioned?'

Goodrich can only mean one person and I am reluctant to bring her into this, but I have no choice.

'You mean Sam?'

'I mean Sam.'

'Like Turin, she thought that the belt was important to Zac. Very important. There's no reason why she should know exactly why.'

My mind starts racing. It was she who wanted us to go back to the house to get the belt. Maybe she knew it was dangerous, and why she didn't get it herself. The idea that she sent us back to get the belt possibly knowing that the house might be rigged makes me go cold, I can't believe that. Now I feel she cannot be trusted. Trust no one, always, trust no one.

'She is a talented hacker,' Goodrich continues, and the surprise I show he ignores, 'and we suspect she might have been accessing the CUpal vault from her father's link. Using his private key she would be able to get into the prohibited areas, download files and for the most part leave no trace, which takes a fair bit of skill and daring. She would have used her father's equipment hook up the pills and download what she needed. The belt hanging on the door must have been a convenient hiding place.'

'Why would she hack into her father's corp? Why take the risk, and who would it be for?'

'We don't know. Had we known what she was up to, we certainly would have taken steps to stop her. As it was, she was good enough to evade us, and her father. The trouble is that she must have been careless, and all it needs is a tiny slip up on exiting a vault file and you might as well leave your name, your address and when you'll be in. Her trespassing using Zac's key is the reason he and Mel have their problems. They will presume that Zac is the culprit. If so, not only his freedom and probably his life will be forfeit, but some considerable potential to us is lost.'

'Is there anything I can do?'

'What we need to know is whether Sam is working on her own or for someone else. She might have just been trawling without any specific target, and then hoping to find a buyer. She could have been targeted, and was made to do it under duress. All of this we need to know and fast.'

'Oh, not much then,' I say with as much sarcasm as I can muster, 'I'll get back to you in an hour or so.' Goodrich fails to see the humour so I ask him seriously, 'Can you give me any clues, any help at all?'

'We have made copies of the original pills you brought to me last night.'

He takes out of a draw, what look like the pills I had given him.

'These are copies. We have spiced up the content so that they will appear to operate correctly but then they will begin to degrade, as will any copies made from them. It will appear to be the fault of a bad copy rather than sabotage and shouldn't raise suspicions. We have made them look identical to the originals. They are not, and there is a way of telling them apart. Just beneath the maker's name and reference there is a full stop.'

'No, there isn't,' I say examining one closely.

'That's because they are not the originals.'

'Oh, I see.' I say, feeling like an idiot.

'The clue is,' Goodrich goes on, ' no full stop, incomplete, and therefore not original. Okay?'

I nod and take out of my left inside pocket three pill drives, and the same amount out of the right inside pocket, the ones given back to me by Chad. I place them on the table and slide them forward as I collect his six like a gambler moving chips, then I tell him,

'These are pill drives that I have seen being exchanged. It would be helpful to know where they came from.'

'We'll see what we can do, but it is unlikely that there is any trace of a previous owner. I have to warn you Ash, we seem to have very quickly become involved with matters more serious than we anticipated. The discovery of this belt and the information on the pill drives leads us to the conclusion that we are dealing with something extremely important and therefore dangerous. Corps, as you know, are a law unto themselves and will do anything to eliminate those who get in their way. Even the state is powerless because ministers dare not attempt to kerb their excesses. Whatever practices you have been involved with in the past, remember you are a fumbling amateur in comparison, this as they say, is a different ball game. Know your territory, fight at a time and a place of your choosing, and you stand a chance. Allow them to dictate where, how and when, and you will perish. The consequences will be shared by all of your friends, of which Sam and her folks are now the most in danger. Depending on who it is that she has been working for, will depend on what they do. They will kill her because of what she knows, or because she has embarrassed them, and to show you how easily it can be done. If she did what she did on her own, the same applies. On no account should you get close, or you will be a target too, whether they think you know anything or not. I hope you are not too fond of her?'

Fond? It's way beyond that. I can't believe she would have risked her brother's life or mine, but she's hiding something and can't be trusted. Trust no one. I looked up to see Goodrich eyeing me closely.

'Ah! I see,' he pauses, while he arranges his words.

'Ash, you will have to deal with this and it might be painful but do not let your emotions get the better of you. We are putting our faith in you but we wouldn't let you jeopardise many years of work. No one is indispensable, not even me. I mean it, you will have to grow up quickly, if you are going to survive. I may not see the new dawn but you have a slim chance.'

'I'm just disappointed. I thought she would have been a good friend, maybe more.'

'I suspected it was so,' he tells me. 'Not mentioning her made her all the more obvious. Could it be that you left her out because you already suspected her of something? Don't answer Ash, but you will have to deal with it. I was young once Ash, and I had to grow up very quickly.'

Goodrich and I talk about other stuff for the rest of the afternoon. Carol returns and joins us later. There is a comfortable, homely feel about it. I sit and listen more than I am used to. They enjoy a shared history, like older people do, when they did this, when they did that. Something I will never share because no one has travelled with me. There is only me that remembers when I said this, when I said that, and there's no, when we did that, when we did this. I ask them how things got to be like they are? They both look at each other and their expressions tell me it's a big question. We begin to talk freely which is still strange and I can't get over the feeling that I am being overheard or that all of what I say will be used against me.

CHAPTER 13

Is it possible that Chad's rendezvous with the limo could have an innocent explanation? Are those the contacts that supply him with everything we need to carry out our campaign? I don't want to see Sam as a problem, so my focus is on Chad. As Goodrich warned me, I'm losing my objectivity. I keep telling myself, I must presume nothing, but it's not working. Chad exchanged the pill drives, then pretended surprise when there was nothing on them. Then there's the phone. Just to have a phone contravenes all the rules of secrecy that we all have to obey. Having a phone in the cellar? Someone, or some organisation, knows who we are, knows where we meet and everything we talk about. Using it to make a call? That means that any corp with the appropriate kit can track where the call was made from, and what was said. You'd risk being picked up by any corp, maybe the worst. How can you take the risk unless it was already the worst you were talking to? The thought makes me go cold. How long will it be before they discover the pill drives that Chad has given them are empty? They'll think Chad has double-crossed them. They'll kill him, no Qs. Goodnight Vienna. If they kill him, we'll be next, all of us. Sounds extreme, but that's what they do. They like decisiveness, the big gesture, it looks good in reports, does the share price no harm. A terrorist cell, a bomb factory, the cellar. It will be the cellar.

Passing the old house I check out the gate post. The numeral '1' is still in its normal position and not indicating that anything of interest is waiting in the post box to the rear of the garden. Now, in the evening, there are still two or three scavengers having got under the warning tapes raking over what's been raked over all day. Anything worth anything at all to anybody will have gone. Carl and Jean have gone too, but disappearances are commonplace and no one knows anything. Sometimes they just pop up again, sometimes they don't. It may seem callous but it's what we live with. They are just two more that freespeak, become a target, then disappear. Knowing where they are makes you an accomplice, even trying to find them attracts unwanted interest; so it's better to hope, but do nothing.

Ma Brown's house lies in the distance, across a dip, identical amongst its drab neighbours. In the dull grey checkerboard of streets, any open spaces are like dirty old coats, spread crumpled and threadbare across the ground. Rusting cars stick out like battered brown buttons and one, covered in yellow graffiti, a group logo, jumps out of the gloom like a migraine. Everything is always wet and takes pains to be the same twinkling drabness which is never washed away.

I approach the house from angles that give me sly glimpses so I might just catch something that makes no sense, or sense of something else. I begin to feel an air of expectancy, of anticipation. It could be alarm, or excitement. Feelings don't tell you anything, they just tell you to look harder. 'Are you sure?' they say. I check, double check, wait, listen, feel, all seems okay, but nothing is certain. Presume nothing, it's a rule. I approach the back door through the rear garden, checking the windows for signs, and listening for voices, music, anything. Near to the back door I can hear a screen talking its quiz show jabbajabba. Now the cellar feels like a trap. I think that I'm being watched. Something I do will trigger an explosion, something like knocking on the door. I knock on the door. Eventually Ma Brown answers with the customary,

'Hello Dear . . .' meaning everything is okay.

The cellar is as we left it. The pins tell me that a meeting has been set for later today, who has set it, Chad or Turin? I don't know.

If I wasn't alienated before, I will be soon after I've done what I've come to do. Gut feelings? You either trust them or you don't. I grab an old sack, the sort with lots of pockets, and start packing gear into it. I wrap up the old cables that Chad insists are safer, then the drives and the relays that he so enjoyed being strewn all over his desk. Anything which might have evidence in it I cram into the sack. Another bag I fill with papers, a screen, anything that might be incriminating. I don't do anything without wondering if I should be doing any of it. The more I do, the more I have to do; half a job is no job at all. I work fast and move stuff around and put chairs on tables so it looked less like a place where people get together regularly, less like a terrorist cell where events are planned. Now I've convinced myself the cellar is a risk, I can't rest for fear they're already walking up the garden path. Now every noise is a knock at the door. I pile up stuff as if it's all waiting to be dumped. I sweep up some dust and sprinkled it about so the whole place looks unused.

On my way out I tell Ma Brown that if any strangers want to have a look in the cellar that's okay, it's just where you store old stuff. She nods but doesn't know what I'm talking about and gives a slight smile as I pass by.

On the street with a bag in each hand, if I wasn't paranoid before, I am now. I pause wondering if I've gone completely mad and whether I should put it all back. I feel damned if I do and damned if I don't. I have no proof, everything is deniable, Chad will be believed and the best I can hope for will be a quick death. That's if the LEOs don't pick me up first and give me a lift to Rehab, and a very slow death. Goodnight Vienna. Not much of a choice.

Most people carry a sack, strapped to their backs, or over a shoulder, it holds everything you need. I'm holding another, larger sack, and that makes me different, different enough to give the LEOs a reason to pull you. They'll slow down alongside and say, 'What's in the bag, son?' It's one of their favourite jokes and always makes them laugh putting them in good mood, but not stopping them beating the crap out of you. Twice I see LEOs in the distance, their yellow lights giving them away as they slowly approach a corner up ahead. I stash the larger bag and walk on nonchalantly with the one bag and then doubling back when they've gone. On one occasion, a street sleeper grabbed it and I had to wrestle him for it. My nervousness isn't helped by the presence of six pill drives wrapped around my waist. You're never safe in a deregulated district but being caught with those is just suicide. I'd never even make Rehab.

At the flat, Turin answers the door and Sam is in the kitchen making some kind of stew called a casserole. Turin asks me about the bag, recognises some of its contents. I tell him what I've done. His reaction is what I expected, Sam too thinks I'm mad for sure. They both think I'm definitely paranoid, probably unstable, even dangerous. I explain my fears regarding my place being blown up and the trouble at Zac and Mel's. I tell them if they don't believe in coincidences then it's a precaution worth taking. Neither are convinced. I'm limited in what I can say, so it doesn't ring true. The argument becomes personal, Turin's authority, Chad's integrity, my duplicity. It's a mess.

Again I have no justification for following Chad. If I tell Turin about Chad and the limo, what do I say about the pill drives? Where did I get the duplicates? Turin is bound to go straight to Chad, if only to decide what to do with me. That would warn Chad and any chance of getting to the truth will be gone. I have to accept that Turin, and probably Sam, will think that at best I'm an impulsive idiot, at worst, maybe a traitor sabotaging their efforts.

I sort out what I've brought from the cellar, hoping they'll see I'm organised and thoughtful, rather than paranoid and frantic.

Turin and I sit on different sofas, worlds apart. Then he moves to the window. Sam makes us some coffee, not real coffee, nothing feels real.

Sipping the warm liquid, I begin to list my options, which aren't many. What Sam knows is anyone's guess, but I still want to trust her, which goes against the rules. It's a bad sign.

I begin to wonder how I can find out who Chad's friends are. If I could do that without raising suspicion the facts might speak for themselves.

Turin has picked up my own sack.

'Is there anything from the cellar in your sack?' He asks coldly.

'No,' I reply, 'not now.' He places the sack by my feet then he points to the sack from the cellar.

'Any of your stuff in that?'
'No,' I tell him.
'This is all from the cellar?'
'Yes.'

'I'd like you to take whatever is yours and go.'

Sam looks astonished,

'Turin!'

'Sam! This is nothing to do with you.'

Sam and I look at each other, and I shake my head. She can hardly go against her brother, not in this kind of thing.

I roll up my bedding and fit it into its case as it slowly expels the air. I pile a few other things in as Sam passes with a sorry smile. She goes to Turin's side and I understand the body language.

She mumbles something to Turin, who turns away and looks out of the window, disinterested.

I pick up my sack and walk towards the door hoping for a reprieve.

'Ash, wait! Have some casserole before you go.'

I tell her it's okay and that I'll get something later.

'Well,' she replies, 'take some with you, please.'

I can't refuse her. I leave my stuff by the door and join her in the kitchen.

'Is what you told Turin the truth?' She whispers.

I think for a moment. Then regardless of what I think is best I decide to tell her what I can. It seems more important that she thinks well of me than trying to stay with the group. If I go and say nothing, and Chad's friends reap havoc, I'll always regret it.

I adopt a matter of fact attitude. I talk to her, but I know Turin is listening. I tell her about the black limo and Chad exchanging pill drives, how he must have known they were blank when he examined them the following day, and pretended he didn't. I decide not to mention the palmer, it's too easy to deny. If it were to be found on him then maybe

I'll be believed. Sam takes my word, but Turin is not on my side.

Sam looks at Turin but he doesn't move.

'Well, Turin?' She says.

'You've had your say Ash,' he says without emotion, 'we'll just have to see what Chad has to say.'

Sam doesn't like the idea of Chad being told everything, neither do I, but she can't go against her brother. She moves to the kitchen and stirs her casserole, then without looking up she says,

'This needs to simmer for a while yet, and we need some bread.'

She looks across at Turin who stares out of the window, then at me and nods toward the door as an invitation.

'We'll go to the store, Turin. Do you want anything?'

Without turning he shakes his head.

She moves towards me and the door. I open it, pass through and she follows.

As Sam closes the door behind her she looks at me, 'I'll get him some of that tangy spread in the little brown pots. He has weird taste, it'll cheer him up, always does. You got some tokens?'

'Yes,' I tell her, 'the tangy spread is on me.'

'Mmm,' she says, 'I might get to like it that way.'

Normally that would send me into imagining all sorts of things but I know she just wants to lighten things up. Her strength is underneath, I mean she doesn't wear it like Meko, but it's there all the same and you can trust it.

She's about to get in the lift when I tell her to stop. We walk up a floor and get the lift down to the ground. I pause by the exit before stepping out, trying to sense if there's anything I should know. Sam catches up and I pretend just to be looking about. I don't feel anything bad. My instinct is still to use cover and remain inconspicuous, as a couple it's more difficult. So we are nonchalant but alert, as if we don't have a care in the world, but caring all the time.

There's a faded image of the block on the ground floor of when it was new and opened by some top exec for their workers. Then it was surrounded by green bushes, grass and spaces where children could play. That's all gone now and it's mostly bare except for a low growing thorny scrub that seems to thrive like nothing else. We walk across the open space which surrounds the block, past the rusting shell of a burnt out car that serves as a children's play house and decorated accordingly. There's a public bench commemorating the last real bush. It was about the height of a person, not like the small scrubby ones that are everywhere. It had clung on for years, even flowering once in the middle of a winter, but it was set on fire one cold night by some street sleepers. Since then the site of it is called the Burning Bush and it's where people meet, though nothing remains of the bush. Sam tells me this as we walk past but I want to know something else,

'How long have you been hacking?'

'Me? A hacker? I don't know what you mean.' She says this in a way that admits it. So I move on.

'Tell me more about the belt?'

'It was important to Dad.'

'So you said, but I think you might know why. You realise that Turin and I could have been killed getting it.'

'I know, I'm really sorry, Turin explained. But that was nothing to do with the belt,' she protests.

'And you knew that Chad wouldn't find anything on the pills.'

'Not true,' she replies.

'What do you mean?' I ask.

'When you got the pills there was plenty on them. When you gave them back to me there wasn't.'

This surprises me. Whilst in the kitchen, nobody could have known what I had found in the belt. Now it's my turn to play ignorant,

'I don't know what you mean.'

'You're sneaky Ash, but don't underestimate us girlies.'

We stop and confront each other. She grabs hold of my coat and looks me straight in the eye,

'Ash, you knew pretty soon there was something more to the belt than keeping my skirt up. Sometime after you came back with it, you found out what it was, and what they were. I don't know what you're up to Ash, but when I came to get the belt in the middle of the night, not only was it not there, neither were you.'

Now I understand some of her behaviour. When I had taken the original pill drives to Goodrich in the middle of the night, Sam had come to get them herself, so she had known all along I was up to something but had said nothing.

'Never try to kid a kidder Ash.' She turns away and we continue walking. We carry on in silence then she turns to me and continues,

'You went somewhere with the pills.'

I say nothing, she doesn't need any more help.

'Now let me see.'

She is in analytical mode,

'If you had the skills and the right kit you may have had just enough time to have a look at the directories, maybe check out a few interesting files. There wouldn't have be enough time to read them closely, to see if they were anything more than a collection of all the world's porn or the all the world's literature. Probably room for both. You wouldn't have had time to copy them so you would have needed some blanks to replace them. As they are very expensive . . . . . . '

She pauses for a while, lost in thought, then stops. I turn to see her surprise,

'Oh! My God Ash, you're working for somebody else! Shit! You crafty fucker, Ash! I think I love you!'

I am speechless. I look at her as if the possibility is absurd, it's all I can think of doing. Her outburst is confusing and I'm trying to pick out what is joke and what is a cause for alarm. I replay the bit when she says she loves me, but I know it's just a joke, but I play the sound of it again and again, and can't move on. Then a sense of being caught on open ground when a spotlight picks you out. In reality I'm working for both, but in this climate of mistrust it's betrayal. It's true what Goodrich said, emotions make you vulnerable. I feel a sense of panic but I say nothing. We walk along side by side then she moves ahead and spins round and she looks at me as I look down at the cracks in the road and avoiding her gaze. I tell her not to walk backwards, she'll fall over.

'Seriously Ash, the pills? Do you know what's on them?'

'No, of course not. I thought I might be able to use the kit from the cellar, that's another reason why I went back to get it.'

This doesn't make sense, but she already thinks I'm inept when it comes to computers and stuff. Compared to her I am.

'That won't work with them,' she says, thinking I'm even more stupid.

'What did you mean just now?'

'What about? What's on the pills?'

'No, before that.' She smiles. She knows what I mean.

'I can't remember what I said now.'

She stops, so I do too.

'Ash, be real.'

I think, what a bitch! I'm totally crushed. I hate strong women.

'I hardly know you Ash, give it time.'

I love strong women, 'Give it time.' she says and I try to hide the smile, but it's difficult. All the stuff going on with Turin doesn't seem to affect her. I think she knows far more than she'll admit, but I get the sense it's not bad. At least not as bad as Goodrich thinks.

We get to the store and there's some argument going on over the last small tin of something. A smartly dressed woman apparently wants to pay for an item, though she doesn't have it in her basket. Another woman, who has three children hanging off her trolley, has the item securely stowed in it, but hasn't yet paid for it. Unruly children are usually made to hang on the trolley for fear of losing them. In this case however, it's more likely to prevent them eating the stock of brightly coloured sweet things that are displayed at their precise eye level. By the time we have picked up the things that we want and have got back to the checkout, the argument has escalated to fever pitch. It threatens to turn into a fight involving both women and two of the children, the third child being busy eating the stock of sweets and choking on the wrappers. This would normally be good entertainment, but because I can no longer suffer the piercing screams of the children, I step forward and after getting some quiet, explain that I, being a student of law, which actually I'm not, can make a judgement. They believe me and I begin my summing up. I explain to the small crowd which has now collected that, as the tin is in the basket of the lady with the children, irrespective of the claims of the lady at the checkout, the law recognises that possession of an item is secured, ipso facto, by the action of it being placed, into the basket or trolley or other container supplied by the self-service business for the purpose thereof. With reference to the self-service act, section two, paragraph six, 'Paying for an item does not secure the ownership simple, of an item unless they are also, compus mentus, in possession of it.' I do not know the meaning of the legalese but I use them with such confidence that everyone seems convinced that I know what I am talking about. I then explain to the well-dressed woman that I can get a lawyer friend of mine here in a few minutes to contest the decision but he would be incredibly expensive, and of course the lady with the kids would have the right of appeal. Considering the strength of the mother's case I would be keen to handle her appeal, pro bono, for the considerable costs I could claim from the loser, i. e. her. Unsurprisingly she departs, but not before she has tipped out the rest of her shopping onto the floor.

    Sam is very impressed but she thought, unfairly in my opinion, that in the time it took me to explain the legal situation the two women could have sorted it out for themselves several times over. I agreed, but told her that was the nature of the law.

Walking back to the block we were quiet for a while, but I could tell she was thinking. I was saying nothing.

'Let me get this straight Ash,' I love the way she says my name. 'What you told me at the flat is true?' She turns and looks at me, I return her look,

'Absolutely. Every word.'

We walk a little further before she turns to me again,

'The pills that Chad passed on were empty?'

'That's right.'

'And let's say those were a few that you just happen to have knocking around.'

'Okay.' I am in no mood to disagree, and I still haven't thought of a way of disproving her 'working for somebody else' theory. She continues,

'So the guys in the limo, whoever they were, are given pill drives with nothing on them.'

'Correct.'

'Who were they?'

'Don't know, but I guess they were execs.'

'That doesn't sound good.' Sam says, 'Nobody like that lets people work for them, easy come, easy go. They'll be tracing every move he makes, every minute of the day. They might even know about the cellar.'

'They will. They do.' I tell her.

'How?' She asks and we both stop. Goodrich will probably kill me, but I have to tell her,

'Because he's been carrying a palmer.'

Sam makes a face and takes in a short breath which hisses through her teeth. She knows how dangerous that would be for all of us.

'He's been carrying it around,' I tell her, 'knowing that wherever he goes, he's some one's little spot on a map. They know where he's been and they know where he is now. They may even know everything we say in the cellar.'

'That could be bugged too?'

'Possible' I answer 'finding bugs would be down to him, but his palmer is more likely to do the job anyway.'

We carry on walking in silence, then Sam turns to me, 'Turin's got to know.'

I shake my head then tell her that her brother is in no mood to believe anything I say.

'Unless we can prove something' I tell her 'like catching Chad with his palmer on him, it'll just be a waste of time and warn Chad. As well as anyone who might be listening.'

We reach the Burning Bush and stop. If it was Meko and I we would make a passionate embrace, touching each other up but really checking in every direction to see if anyone is following. Sam and I could and I see it, but it doesn't happen. Suddenly she stops.

'I have a confession.'

From a moment of ecstasy in Sam's imaginary embrace I'm now wondering if Goodrich's warnings will come true.

'Some of this is my fault.'

My worst fears loom and immediately I regret telling her everything I just have. Trust no one, how many times?

There's a pause and Sam looks around as she leads me to the nearby seat. The kind of being led to a seat that means you will need to sit down. So we sit, then she tells me she has been hacking into her father's corp by using his link.

There's an emptiness creeping into what light there had been. The hollowness of being alone again like a shadow grows over me. Even the smallest success is better shared, if there's no one to share stuff with, what's the point?

'You realise what you've done, Mel, Zac?' I ask her how she could have been so stupid?

'It wasn't me!' She says through gritted teeth.

'How can you say it wasn't you?'

'Ash, please.'

I sit knowing now that she must be responsible for whatever has happened to her mother and father. Goodrich was right and I knew it could only be one person, but I had hoped it wasn't.

'At first I was just curious,' she explains, 'it was a challenge. One of the most secure data vaults and it was on my doorstep, well, in my front room. It was a test. Me against the machine, the best machine. One day I would tell, 'Guess what I did? Me! Turin's little sister.' Okay maybe I was a bit obsessed, but by learning and listening, I got deeper and deeper, access all areas, well most areas. I couldn't believe it, so each time I had to see if I could still do it. Prove myself, keep in practise. Then I noticed a trace, like a shadowy footprint, and it wasn't mine. Then footprints, crystal clear, no doubt.

'Sam,' I interrupt her, 'this is pointless, I don't even know what you're talking about.'

'Listen,' She tucks her arm inside mine in case I might leave. 'Someone else was treading the same path, jumping over the same gates, scaling the same fences. They could have been following my footsteps. Maybe I showed them the way. I don't know but if they could follow me, I could follow them. I did and they didn't know it. It was brilliant.'

'I'm not impressed.' I tell her.

'I followed them home. Hacked their system and found what was in their Jamboree bag. It was a kind of, how dare you! Like revenge. There were codes, sequences, formulae, method outlines, but mainly test data. Hundreds of data runs, bracketed runs and variations, a change here and a tweak there, analysis, comparisons. The test results were good, very good and improving. Whatever they were testing was responding and every new programme of testing was showing definable improvements. Not much, but it was proof that they were going in the right direction. Then something went wrong.'

'You screwed up'

'Fuck off! Not me. Them! Whoever was hacking. They screwed up. Data travels both ways remember and when they accessed the vault I could access them. A few days later I decided to play with the results. So I made up a little beastie and set it running, standard stuff that you do, changing codes and formulae to make access easier, so you can always get in when you want to. The test results too we looked at, making them look poor, some even complete failures.'

'We? You said 'we' looked at?'

'Yes, well, whoever it was I was following. We both had seen the results. I made them look as if they were becoming random and would prove nothing. The thing was . . .'

'You screwed up.' She punches me in the ribs, which still hurt.

'No! The programme had to complete, it's the way it has to be. Once it's done its work, you know it's perfect. It has to test itself before opening up what's been altered, otherwise it deletes everything. What I couldn't allow for was the hacker getting access at the same time and then screwing up. It had to be given time, the only risk would be that the hacker gets in during the exchange and screws up. That's what happened, a million to one chance. They fucked up somehow, tried to withdraw but something mega followed them and as it got near their system, its wall closed the part of the exchange that was still live. The programme then withdrew all the data, everything. All the data that they had mined over months was gone, and I thought everything we had. When I checked my directories, there it was, I had it all. Somehow the system had used my link as an emergency backup. Dumped everything in my lap for safe keeping. There was no way they could get back into the vault ever. They must know it was their fault. All it needed was another minute or two and none of this would have happened. Remember I wasn't even in the vault, I was in them. They were in the vault and it was them that fucked up. Okay?'

'Okay.' I repeat. She carries on,

'I tried to get back into the vault myself, but a patch came up every time, 'There is a problem with the system. Engineers are in attendance'. That made me wonder if they were tracing me. I was stuck with all this data needing to be stored. I could have deleted it, but I thought I could exchange it or put it back. It might be important so I put it onto dad's pill drives that he kept in the belt.

'Did you find out who the hacker was?' I ask.

'I thought about trying to contact them, all hackers together sort of thing. I'd know them again though.'

'Who are they then?'

'I mean I would recognise their style, their signature, if I saw it again, probably. I don't know them personally.'

I hit the dull green arrow by the lift doors and they creak slowly open. Sam hits the appropriate floor number and we walk the rest of the way to the flat. Sam buttons the access and the door clonks open and there's that sense that inside is not as you left it. Something has changed. I put my hand gently on Sam's shoulder and she stops to let me walk past and into the flat. It's quiet and there's no sign of Turin. The sacks lie exactly where they were when we left. Turin's bag, that he would take when out, is gone. There's no signs of a struggle. Sam and I look at each other, mouth the word, 'Cellar,' and nod.

Sam goes and checks out the stew she calls a casserole, and fills two bowls. She knows what I am thinking.

'This first, then we go?'

'Yes,' I reply.

Together we look out across the districts toward The City. Always The City. Like old people's chairs that face a screen, we always face The City, its light shows and its tawdry, cheap entertainment, to which workers aspire as a reward for a life well spent. Well, just spent.

'Sam?'

Looking out across the districts seems to be the appropriate place to do this. A place where as much life as there is to call life, lies stretched out before us. She stands by me, close, warm, and every time I look at her I can't help smiling. She smiles back, but because mine has gone, her smile does too. Which makes us smile again, but this is serious.

'This is a replacement for the ED you were given.'

'Oh!' She says,' I'd forgotten all about that. It's here somewhere,' and she eventually finds it at the bottom of an inside pocket. She pops open the container and takes out the cap.

'Don't hold it for too long,' I tell her, 'if the coating dissolves the poison will leach through skin pretty quickly.' She puts it down on the cill and I open a packet with several of mine in.

'Here, take this,' she does. 'These are different.' I tell her.

'Don't tell me,' she says, 'they only kill you a little bit!'

'Almost. They will put your body into suspended animation. Only the most sophisticated sensors will be able to detect any signs of life. It will last for some hours after which you can be woken. Sometime after that you will wake naturally. Try not to be recycled in the meantime.'

'Well, thanks a lot.'

'Yeah, well, then you'll be all over the place!' We laugh, but the laugh is only a mask.

'At least with these there is a chance you'll survive. With the others there's no chance at all.'

'Ash? Don't be kind to me, I won't be able to resist it.' So saying she places the cap into its container and tucks it away. She then leans forward as if to whisper something,

'Ash,' there's a pause which doesn't need filling with words, 'thank you,' she says, 'you may just have saved my life again.'

'I hope it won't be necessary,' I tell her.

We have a bowl each of Sam's casserole. I tell her how good it is. We stand in the unlit room watching the gloom beyond getting darker, and The City lights get brighter, until there are only The City lights, and everything else is gone.

CHAPTER 14

We move silently from shadow to shadow until we see Ma Brown's in the distance. I check and double check for signs, feelings. We stop to hear in the silence any movement, any hushed conversations. Finding nothing is more nerve racking than finding something. I could have missed something and now I have Sam to care for. She wouldn't see it that way but I do, and it makes me nervous. Walking casually past the front of Ma Brown's as if going somewhere else, I clock the china dogs, without a care in the world, sitting in her window facing each other. Either Ma Brown never had the time to change them, or she's forgotten, or everything is okay. Ahead, from beyond the curve, a dull yellow light starts panning across the gardens. Sam pulls me towards her,

'Quick,' she says, 'let's pretend that we're kissing.' The acrid light grows then flashes across us but the andys roll almost silently past.

'Ash, you're not pretending!'

'Sorry.' I wasn't, of course.

If the dogs in the window are right, Chad's friends haven't yet been to the cellar. I rate the chances of them being around as certain. There's logic, but I also have the feeling. I'd prefer Sam wasn't here, I could focus more on my gut instincts. Sam and I walk on until we are at the end of the street.

'It looks as if the cellar is ok.' Is what I say, but what I mean is that that I can't find a good enough reason just to turn back.

'That's good?' She says with a kind of sarcasm.

We spend some time standing close together in the shadows, watching and listening. It's an intimate moment and before I think better of it I say to her,

'I think I know whose footsteps you were following.'

'I think, I thought you did.' She replies.

'What?' I say.

'When you said that I might know them, I thought then, you thought you knew who they were, at least I think I did.'

'What does that mean?'

'I'm agreeing with you. Who do you think it is?'

'I think it might be Chad.' I tell her.

'I thought you thought that, I think I think so too.'

'Just so we understand each other, can we stop thinking for a moment?'

'Okay, why him?' Asks Sam.

'He's the closest to us all, especially Turin. Before the other day I wouldn't have dreamt it could be him. I would have been suspicious of anyone who said it could, I would have thought they'd be lying for some reason.'

'Exactly what Turin thinks,' she says, and I get the point. We are still standing close to each other, but I look out. She looks at me, I feel it.

'Ash, pretend to kiss me again.'

I do. This time there are no yellow lights, not even a glimmer.

Sam relaxes and looks at me,

'You didn't do that last time.'

'What?'

'Pretend! When I want you to pretend, you don't and when I don't, you do. Boys! You just can't take a hint.' She changes the subject,

'So now what's the plan? Aren't we going to the cellar?'

I think for a moment to myself, then aloud,

'If it was Chad's footprints, then maybe he thinks he's got back the data he lost when you were in his drive. He thinks the pill drives contain it, and he would have told his friends. When they find out there's nothing on them, they won't be happy. Worse, they'll think that he's double crossed them.'

'Is that worse?' Sam asks.

'You're right, it won't matter. If Chad has convinced them that he can still get the data they want, they might let him live. I think when they've got what they want, that'll be it for him, and probably us too.'

'It's that serious?'

'It's that serious.'

'Okay,' she says, 'what are we going to do?'

' The first step.' I say.

'The first step?' She repeats like it's a joke, and I wonder if she realises how dangerous this all is,

'You have to give Chad pill drives that he believes to be the originals, so he will pass them on to his friends.'

'You have more?' She says with some surprise.

'Yes,' I take out the duplicate set that Goodrich has given me. This can only confirm at least, that I have contacts, and maybe even that I'm working for others. Before she can say anything, I carry on with explaining the plan,

'Somehow, Chad has to believe that these are the originals from your belt.'

'Okay,' she says, 'but it will make it look like you really are a conspirator.'

'I know, and if I was, this would be the last thing I would be doing. I'm trusting you because I think you trust me.'

'Mmmm,' is all she says, and gives me a hard look.

'I'm no traitor, the opposite. Turin thinks I've been naive and impulsive rather than a traitor. Chad will just be glad to get the originals, and if we are right he will be glad to shift attention onto someone else. Any idea what you'll do?'

'I'll say I thought about what Turin said and decided to go through your pockets, like I do every boyfriend, and found them.'

The suggestion that I might be her boyfriend excites me, but the mention of what seems like so many boyfriends makes me feel ill. Then I tell her that the next problem will be finding out who Chad's friends are.

She asks me if I mean the ones in the limo and I tell her I do.

'I'll just ask him.' She clocks my horror. 'Only joking. Any ideas?'

'Only one but we need his palmer. He might not even have it on him. It'll be his only link, and it's our only proof. If he has it, it'll be in his sack, we just need it for a few seconds.'

Sam is not convinced but I explain,

'Remember he doesn't know we know he's got one.'

'What if he sees me?'

'Don't let him. If you can get into super security vaults a little pick pocketing can't be too difficult.'

Sam gives me another hard look.

'Take your time,' I suggest, 'then seize the opportunity, create a diversion, cover it with a jacket, anything. If there's a chance he'll see you, leave it. Plans are designed to be aborted at any time, it's a rule. If he suspects we're onto him, we'll find out nothing. If he feels cornered, we might all go up in smoke.'

'Goodnight Vienna!' She says.

'Why did you say that?' I ask.

'I don't know,' she says, 'people do.'

'Okay, back to the pill drives. Chad will use them to discredit me. It's typical deflection, he will try to convince Turin I'm a traitor. '

Sam leans forward and I feel her breath on my cheek and her body pressed against mine, I'm sure she is about to kiss me but then she stops and starts speaking again,

'I'll tell him that I couldn't believe the pills were empty, so I thought there must be others and I found them. I searched your coat while you were sleeping.'

'Was, I wearing it?' Suddenly I'm in a fantasy land again.

'Might have been. Maybe it wasn't all I was searching for?'

'Like all your other boyfriends?'

'Don't be silly. I never get what I want when they're asleep.'

I have to tell her to behave. It's no good getting all these emotions. I don't want her to take it the wrong way, but both our lives depend on making the right decisions, and carrying them out. This is no game.

'That's fine,' I tell her, 'say you don't trust me, an instinct, whatever you need to say, whatever makes it real. Flatter him if you need to, Chad's a sucker for that. Make sure he takes the pills away with him, he might make some excuse why he needs them, be reluctant but in the end say it's okay.'

She pretends to look shocked.

'Ash, are you are telling me to say, 'No', when I mean, 'Yes?' I'm not sure I could do such a thing.'

Some way off we both hear a gate hit a fence panel, the one at the bottom of Ma Brown's garden. It's followed by some mumbling.

'That's Chad,' I tell Sam, 'he's probably dropped something getting into the back garden. Your brother will be waiting in the cellar, we should give it a few minutes before you go in.'

She turns and looks at me and I know that we are about to kiss, properly this time. I raise my hand and caress her cheek, then hold her head against me so as to avoid our lips meeting.

'I have to concentrate.' I tell her.

She seems content to rest her head against me while our bodies share each other's warmth. Then as I think we should move, she pulls away and looks at me with a slight frown,

'What do you know about hacking?' She asks me.

'Nothing really, I was a gamer, why?'

'You know that once you've got in, you make sure you can always get in.'

'It makes sense, like having a spare key hidden in the garden.'

'Not really, more like leaving the key in the door, but then hiding the door.'

'How does that work?'

'Because there are lots of doors, and each door has lots of keyholes, each keyhole opens the door, or at least another keyhole, in another door.'

I ask Sam if there is a point to this.

'Let's just say, a door has been left unlocked through which one can see other doors, some of which you've left open before.'

'You've lost me, but look, if those doors have been left open, won't they know? Won't they change the doors, keys, handles, hinges, whatever? Their whole system will have changed.'

'Ash, you don't understand. I'm not talking about that system.'

'Go on.'

'What if they take the door that you have a key to, and use that, say as a new front door?'

'You could use that to get in?'

'Exactly. Any system that downloads the data from those drives makes it easy for me to get into their system. It's like a Trojan horse. The programme I already have goes in, pulls out whatever data I need to access all areas, and I mean all areas, and anything connected, anywhere. If they download the drives I can access everything they have.'

'And it won't have changed?'

'No, because it has been removed from its secure environment. In time they might transfer it into a more secure area, but not until they know what they've got.'

Sam is aware that I'm not as delighted as I should be.

'That's good isn't it?' She asks.

'What about the other data that's on the drives, Zac's stuff?'

'With the right expertise,' she says, and we both know who we mean,

'Chad?' I say and Sam nods.

'He probably could access all the data. It works both ways.'

'How secure is it?'

'Not secure enough to prevent someone who knows what they're doing. It might take some time but they'll get it eventually.'

'What if the data starts to decay?'

'Once they've copied it into their system it will be stable, unless . . . '

There's a moment and all I can hear are the cogs turning. Eventually she raises her head, looks at me and says,

'They aren't the originals are they?'

'No.'

'How . . . ? Fuck it Ash, you really are working for somebody else!' She takes a step away.

'Sam! I've trusted you, now please, you must trust me.' She sits on a wall looking at her boots and not at me.

'I do know some people, they helped me, that's all I can say.' I take her by the shoulders and she shrugs, but not seriously so I try again, until she looks at me with a kind of pout,

'I want us to work together, and I trust you, but I can't tell you everything yet.' She tries to read me, looks from eye to eye, looks for a lie,

'I'm no traitor,' I tell her, 'the others help me, they'll help you, and Turin. It's the start of trying to work together, not separately.'

She thinks for a moment.

'So what are the pills you have?' She asks dispassionately.

I tell her they are identical but the data will self corrupt giving the impression they are a bad copy or one that has been contaminated. It will give us time without giving anything away and may start to corrupt their system too.

'You better be on the level Ash or I'll kill you myself. Or at least call you horrible names which will be so much worse.'

'Trust me?'

'Yeah, all right! Let's just get on with it. And next time when I say pretend I mean pretend, or you'll be going around one lip less!'

'Yes, boss.'

Then I explain that, rather than going down into the cellar with her, I will just go into the cupboard at the top of the steps. When Ma Brown goes back upstairs, I will creep into her unused front room and see if I can hear what's going on. Then when she has Chad's phone, she can bring it to me in the front room, a few seconds, then she can put it back.

We enter with the usual ceremony, then Sam and I go into the understairs cupboard. Sam opens the hatch and disappears below. I wait until Ma Brown goes back upstairs and then quietly make my way into the front room. I sit down for a while then I begin to hear an irregular pattern of muffled voices from the cellar below. Brief sentences being shot across the room in anger, recriminations, blame. I lay down and put my ear to the floor, then the door opens which nearly gives me a heart attack. Sam comes in with Chad's phone.

'Fuckin' hell,' I say still recovering, 'that was quick.'

'Easy,' she whispers, 'he'd hung his sack on the back of the chair and it had fallen on to the floor so all I had to do was sit there with my arm dangling over the side; it was almost on top, the idiot. Then Chad told me to fuck off, and Turin told me I'd better leave for a while. It was a hard choice but in the end I chose to fuck off. They're arguing, yeah?'

'Yeah, pretty heavy,' I put my ear to the floor again and relay the conversation to Sam in whispers.

'Chad's telling Turin he's compromised the security of the group by bringing you into it . . . and that I'm working for somebody else. Turin's saying he agreed to me joining and I've done nothing wrong until now, all the events went okay. Chad's pissed off because no one had any right to move his gear . . . . . . Turin says something about it being the group's gear, Chad says it's his . . . . he is the only one who knows . . . . how to operate it . . . . . something about security and others.'

Sam lays down beside me, ear to the floor and we stare at each other, just as if we are in bed and I smile.

'In your dreams Ash!' This girl reads minds too, but she's right.

I sit up and jot down the number in Chad's phone. There is only one. I close up the palmer and hand it back to her and she gets up to go,

'The three car trick, remind me,' she whispers then goes back downstairs.

Laying down on the floor with my ear to the boards I hear the argument between Turin and Chad. It ranges over all sorts of stuff as arguments do, but Chad has decided that he considers me and Sam to be a risk and that Turin better sort it. Turin says that Chad's trusted him before and there's never been any problems. Chad's tone changes, less angry, and he says that this time it is different and it's not just the two of them, Turin wants to know what he means, just as Sam walks in. It goes quiet, then Chad says,

'What the fuck are those?'

'I found them in Ash's coat,' Sam replies, 'he must have swapped the original pill drives that were in the belt for the ones that Chad examined. That's why there was nothing on them, I couldn't believe it.'

'Nice one Sam,' I whisper to myself.

Chad is silent. He must now be wondering what, if anything, was on the pill drives that he gave his friends in the limo. Chad calls me all sorts, knowing that I was a wrong-un, and that Turin should listen to him in the future.

Then Turin says something to which Sam replies,

'I was sure there was something . . . . pill drives, they couldn't be empty, it was impossible. He's really shifty, those beady little eyes . .'

I notice this is said with enough volume so that I was bound to hear. Cow! I love her.

Chad says something then a pause, then Turin says,

'He's been trying to get us to be . . . . . . to give more personal information so that we . . . . . in isolation . .'

I move my head a little and find a gap in the floor boards where I can hear clearer. Chad then says,

'. . . . obvious, he wants the information to pass on. It must be security he's working for, who else? And where else could he get those pill drives, a barrow market? Do you know how much they're worth? Where is he?'

Suddenly my life is in Sam's hands. I keep saying, 'Trust no one!' yet I keep putting myself in ridiculous situations. All she has to say is, 'Upstairs' and it's Goodnight Vienna. Goodrich's words flood back again about getting involved, then I hear Sam's voice,

'He's back at the flat,' and I kiss a floor board as if it's her.

'Your flat?' Chad says, 'You idiots! He was given the drives by the people he's working for and swapped them, now he's at your flat, how could you be so stupid? How the fuck did that happen!'

Sam explains that I followed them which makes me go cold. Chad must suspect that he was followed too.

'What else did the fucker say, anything about me?'

Chad is fishing.

There's a pause.

I can almost hear Sam thinking, and I'm trying to put my thoughts into her head, 'Don't mention the phone. Please don't mention the phone.'

'Can you tell if they are the originals, from the belt?' Asks Sam, 'They might be blank too.'

I breathe a sigh of relief. I think I know what her game is. She's moved it on to the pills.

'That's right, yeah, your little sister's okay. How do we know? And damn, there's no gear here to find out if these are the right ones. I'm sure they are the right ones. Definitely.'

Now I see what she's up to.

Turin suggests bringing Chad's gear back to the cellar and reading them later.

'No point', Chad says, 'I've got gear at home that'll read these naughty boys. If there's anything on them you need to know then we can use the gear at the cellar when we meet up.'

There's some chatter about when they should meet next. Chad doesn't seem to mind, he's just desperate to leave. His talking in the cellar was odd. Maybe just from where I am listening but his emphasis on the drives being the right ones was said loudly enough for anyone listening to understand. There's a knock at the back door. Our knock, our three then one. The voices stop, there's the knock again. Somewhere upstairs I can hear footsteps and a door opening. Ma Brown comes down the stairs past the front room to the back and opens the door greeting Meko in the usual way. I can hear Chad as he hurriedly climbs the steps up to the cupboard.

I open the door to the front room enough to hear but I can't see. Chad greets Ma Brown, then Meko.

'Meko!' He says nervously. 'All done, we're all leaving, I'll walk you down the garden, eh? Come on, no point going down they'll be up soon.' She tells him she needs to see Turin and thinks that hanging around the back door is not good then comes in.

'Well, Ma B. What can you do, eh?' I hear him say.

'Never mind dear,' she says, 'now you look after yourself.'

'I'm okay, it's them, they can't take a hint. It won't be my fault.'

Chad then says to her, 'Why don't you go out for a little walk. No need to watch the door, just leave for an hour or so. Believe me, it'll do you good.'

'Thank you dear but I'll just watch my programmes.'

'Your choice, remember it was your choice. You're all the same.' His tone is hurried, his voice unsure. He's mumbles to himself as he moves off down the garden path. I close the door.

Ma Brown goes back upstairs. All is quiet save for voices below, and Chads words going round and round my head, wanting people to leave. The tension in his voice and the need to get away. Ma Brown's programmes are louder as she opens the door to her room, then muffled as she closes it. I open the door again and go up to the first floor to where I can see over the back garden. Chad is getting through the back fence and into the shed in the garden of the empty house that backs onto Ma Brown's. In the gloom I will be able to see him walk through its garden, past the side of the house and out onto the road and away. It takes only a few moments but Chad doesn't appear. Alarms start ringing in my head and my guts are churning. I look out each way between the curtains through which our beacon glows at night, everything appears normal. I can see the road that leads away along which Chad will be walking. Chad leaves the shed at last and is walking away up the garden towards number 14. He appears occupied with his sack and I see his glowing palmer slipping back into it. I presume he's just told his friends he now has the original drives, as if they didn't already know. I'm just about to leave to follow him when Chad stops at the side door of the house. He waits but I can't see the doorway. It must have opened because he steps forward and disappears. If they are the same people that were in the limo, they're not letting him out of their sight. Now they have the rest of us in that same sight, all together, in one place. I get that cold feeling creeping over me. At first I dismiss the fears as exaggerated, then I go through the evidence and I'm only left with one conclusion. How long it will take before they know that they have what they want, then what? Think like a corp. Somebody in the cellar knows what's on them. They would have seen us all enter the back door. We are all in the same building, even if we aren't in the cellar, it's too good an opportunity to miss.

I get downstairs not caring about the noise I'm making. On the way I unlock and open the front door. I'm a few steps down into the cellar, when Sam calls my name and Turin makes a lunge at me, it's then I realise what might be the quickest way to get them out of there. I kick his hand away and back slowly up the steps as an invitation. Turin quickly rounds the bottom step. I turn and dash back up shouting,

'Get out. Get out now!'

I'm through the cupboard, shouting still. I feel there's not time to make sure they do with Turin determined to bring me down. I think that Sam is hard on his heels pushing him. I'm through the front door, onto the path at the front. Still Turin is just behind me and a body behind him. I'm just beyond the front gate and turning when a thump shakes the ground and nearly brings me to my knees. I throw myself forward and roll into the street. I'm up again and so are the dark figures behind me. I watch my knees pumping in slow motion, rising and falling like pistons through a blurred vision but there is so much time. I can see my limbs as if they are not mine, in a parody of running. My arms grope forward until I fall into a dark space, a fenceless garden, and come to rest against one of those brown buttons, a rusting vehicle. Another body crash lands beside me. I imagine like me, it is covered with diamond specks of glass and the pepper and salt dust of an expanding blast that sears the skin and leaves it blackened and sore. I expect too if it has ears like me, they will be deaf with ringing. An elderly woman's screams are enough to pierce them though, as she falls through her bedroom floor and into the fiery pit beneath. I see her pink dressing gown, all ablaze, as she drops like a flaming torch into her blazing cellar and her scream is snuffed out. These things I feel rather than see, I don't know if they are real.

Someone grabs hold of me, partially lifts me I see their white teeth clenched in rage, the whites of their eyes, bloodshot, running rivers of pink tears down blackened cheeks and fair hair torn black with smoking embers. An arm slips between Turin and I, and someone whispers the word,

'No.' and pulls him away.

The face moves away and I drop back to the ground. Time passes in waves, a few seconds then minutes. The ringing subsides, the breathing eases, the throat clears. Senses return bringing pain and soreness. Eventually everything stabilises except the ringing.

I sit up still dazed. Sam lays against the car picking bits out of her hair. Turin is motionless curled beside us. I look at Sam and mouth the name,

'Meko?' to which she shrugs her shoulders.

In the distance a siren's wail becomes more disturbing, then another. A few windows showing a dim glow, frame heads and shoulders peering out through parted blinds and curtains. As the sirens that are piercing the night draw closer, the figures draw back and the curtains drop. Move along, move along, nothing to see. They all move along and see nothing. They have never seen anything, they will never see anything. For us there's never enough darkness to be invisible, so we seek it in shadows where we catch our breath and gather our thoughts. First, Sam leaves, then Turin, then I do. We keep an eye out for anything following and don't follow the same path, but like threads we weave our way home.

Dosing in our sofas the following morning, the smell of smoke is still in our nostrils. We had showered and tried to scrub away the trauma on our return. We'd patched up our scratches and bruises, removed molten plastic from our hair and skin, and tried to blow out the soot from our lungs. Eventually without sharing words we slid into our bags, closed our sore eyes and relived every moment on a loop until tiredness took over and we dropped into a fretful sleep. Sam slept in her own bed, in her own room. Turin and I shared the same room but not any conversation or company.

Now in the morning, we drink coffee and we eat toast. We mumble our thanks all the time approaching the moment when somebody has to say something. It's a day to be over before we can say where we are.

To avoid confrontation, we slide round each other and avoid the collision of glances. There's an energy and confusion which swings between anger and despair. The screams of Ma Brown, who did nothing wrong other than ask no questions and tell no lies, and the vision of her plunging to her death haunts me as if it's real, which it might be. And Meko, was she still in the cellar? Did she follow us? You play the pointless game, ask the pointless questions. Was there anything else you could have done? Was there another way? Would you do the same again?

Turin leaves the room and Sam and I are alone for the first time.

After a while I start setting up the kit I brought from the cellar, I have to do something just to avoid doing anything else. Without Chad's drives that he carries on him there's little point. Sam hands me a personal drive, it could be hers or Turin's, there's never any ID on them, just in case. I connect it up as I think it should be, and it bursts into life unexpectedly. The screen desktop goes through its welcome display, then resumes to the vacant directories of the pill drives, the last task it had. I play around with it but an empty contents page is all that I can get and keep getting. Turin comes back into the room and sits some distance away but watches the screen. Every avenue I try eventually brings me back to the same empty page.

'Forget it,' Turin says in a harsh and distant tone, 'there's nothing there. It's wiped, Chad would make sure.'

I back off and look through the window, a few banks of grey, brown, hover over The City but dissolve away to the east and west. The sky is its usual sodden grey blanket, this morning though I seem to be able to see further. In amongst the grey district before me a thin pall of pale blue smoke twists and curls. It's a tormented rise until smoothing itself out, it finds its ease and calmly drifts away and dissolves into a peaceful haze against The City's perpetual light show. Nothing dims The City, everything pales against it, is diminished by it. It is indestructible.

CHAPTER 15

Sam sits at the kitchen bar sorting out her sack into small piles. Each pile sits on the bag in which it is kept, each bag has a different function and that is denoted by its colour. It is usually a matter of secrecy what is in a girl's sack so both Turin and I make sure we look away. Both of us stand looking toward The City, but from different windows and different points of view.

A blank screen waits for instructions. It blinks its offer of help but neither Turin nor I know how to access its secret places. We don't know if it has any secret places, or even secrets.

'You need to look into the shadows,' says Sam.

'What are you talking about?' says Turin.

'Everything has a shadow.' She enjoys being enigmatic and pretends that what she has said has no mystery and requires no explanation. We are not in the mood for games and when we don't play she carries on with much more important things, for instance, on which pile should her sewing kit go. Exasperated, she gives us another hint,

' The shadows are a trace of the what has appeared on the screen stored in a compressed form and helps reloading the screen when you visit those pages again. They're like,' and she makes it obvious she thinks she's talking to idiots,

'When you used to write a message on a pad of paper, you can take the message with you but you'll leave a readable indentation on the page beneath. That's like a shadow.'

'Wouldn't everything have been deleted?' Turin asks. He moves to the kit and starts to tap the screen, slides over the adjacent pad and enters instructions. He reloads the screen several times, tries different directories and different paths as if trying to creep up on whatever is there, unawares. If there is anything, it evades him and like me, he gives up.

'Depending on the capacity of the operating system, the shadows it retains can go back months, and if you know where to look, years. It's surprisingly difficult to really get rid of anything you could call it a conspiracy.'

She has our attention but our expressions tell her we are none the wiser. Knowing that it might be somewhere is not going to help us find it.

Turin tries again. I move closer and the slight adjustment he makes gives me a better view, and some comfort. Sam is repacking her sack and talks to us without seeming to care if we are listening or not, but we do and are.

'Even really skilled nerds don't bother to wipe the operating system, it's like asking them to keep their desk tidy, or wash their hair. They can't imagine anyone else being able to get into the system once they've taken their drive away, mostly they're right.'

She looks over at the tangle of brightly coloured devices and cables wired up so as nothing gets into the air and can be read by any passing LEO.

'That one stores plenty, and it's all there somewhere boys. It's been put together by someone who wanted to know what it was being used for.'

There's a pause while both Turin and I wonder what she means.

'Who built it?' She asks.

'Chad of course.' Turin replies.

'If you can't wipe it clean then there's not as much security as people think there is.' I say.

'It's what I said, a conspiracy.' Sam tells us. 'You think you are trashing all your incriminating evidence and it's still all there and not even bioprint protected. Most affordable units are subsidised, to give you a wireless machine they can read easily. Anyone who wants to can see what you boys are doing, real time. Then as soon as you disconnect, access is opened for a few seconds to a third party. What do you think is happening when they power down? Any logged data changes are copied out to a remote server where it's read and classified. Your screen's blank but the engine's still running. Within seconds some clerk in a security corp is checking everything you've been doing since the last time your machine was turned off. It might look dead, but it's being read. When you could remove your own drive and evidence of what you've been doing, surveillance were desperate to come up with a way to check up on you, and that kit has it. Most people don't care because they don't have anything to hide. If you want to keep secrets then you have to pay for lot better kit that is totally wipeable, and why would you want that? The state reckons it's because you've something to hide. So, secrecy costs.'

'So you can still get security max gear that can totally wipe?' I ask.

'Of course?' she says, 'If you are prepared to pay for a licence. The state thinks that anyone who can afford high end security max gear is rich enough to be trusted. They need all the help they can get to protect themselves, or rather their wealth, from the rest. If you're wealthy you couldn't possibly be up to no good.'

'But that's nonsense, they're the worst.'

Sam shrugs her shoulders.

Turin has at last got a screen full. It comprises columns, lists and codes and a myriad of file descriptions, suffixes and revisions. He umms and errs as he tries different approaches, each new screen loads with another baffling array of symbols, letters and digits.

Sam is trying not to appear interested but can't resist a comment. 'All you have to do is find out where the stuff is hidden.'

I echo her words to myself, 'All you have to do . . . .' She's having a laugh.

Turin relaxes, sits back looking at the screen with his arms in a resigned fold,

'Any idea where we should start looking?'

Sam is doing something with her nails the way bored receptionists do,

'Try . . . '

We both stop and look at her doing her nails and not looking at us. She blows away well, nail dust I suppose, then looks up,

' . . . anything with the suffix, 'Terribly secret files from the last twelve months that I hope nobody ever finds.''

We are just about to search it when we realise she is taking the piss out of us.

'Forget it Turin,' I tell him, 'there's no chance of finding it without somebody who's got the knowledge. We'll have a drink then pack it all away.'

He looks at me and I throw a glance in Sam's direction, he's puzzled but we walk away to gaze through the window for a moment at things in the distance we haven't seen for months. Some old church spires have appeared like ghosts, the ones left for surveillance, and others half demolished, on which pods rest. We can't usually see them but today the blanket has lifted a little. A freak storm or some calamitous event somewhere in the world is affecting it. Observercorp, CUpal, and a few other surveillance corps must be having a ball seeing the ground and all of us walking on it for the first time in ages, without having to swoop down and hover just above our heads. Their shares will be rocketing, then they'll drop as quickly as the mist will. Some will have made billions others lost them but they're just numbers on a screen. You can't help wondering if the rise is down to them.

I'm convinced that Sam is itching to show off, like every hacker or miner I've ever met. They are generally loners but give them a chance to demonstrate their skills and they can't resist it; it's their show, and they are centre stage. Out of the corner of my eye I see her adopt a tiresome expression, like a parent teaching a child who just doesn't get it.

'You could try turning it off, pressing centre screen as it goes through boot phase.'

Turin does as he is told and I go to the kitchen area and try to make a drink for us all. On my return the screen is confronting us with pages full of codes, options, and stuff which neither I nor Turin know anything about.

'Well, great, now what?' Turin says turning round to Sam who can resist it no longer. She packs away the rest of her stuff with studied impatience, says something about boys, the way girls do, and moves toward us.

Turin moves aside and Sam, like the master, takes her seat. Sat in front of a screen she changes into a diva, both devilish and delightful. She slaps a few keys, swipes the pad, taps the screen and no sooner has one screen flashed up that it's gone and another appears. She taps, slides, swipes and slaps so fast that screens are hardly visible before they are replaced by another. She stops, leans back, and watches pages loading themselves up with numbers, words, codes, dates, as if they are all just one infinitely long word without spaces or punctuation.

'This goes back to the middle of last year. Any particular date you're interested in?' She leans back drumming her fingers on the table with a 'Just in a day's work' nonchalance, as reams are being scrolled through.

Turin's face is both pride and unease. He wonders how his little sister can do all this with such practised expertise. I note this lack of awareness with interest. It surprises me that Turin doesn't know about Sam's skill. Maybe there are reasons why Sam might want to keep her skills secret, even from her brother.

Now we all concentrate on a screen full of spaceless digits of every sort. As I become accustom to putting in spaces and skipping characters to try to make words, and doing it over and over, I can identify the word 'cupal' cropping up repeatedly. The rate at which Sam reads this is baffling, it's like being fluent in some ancient language that looks to other people just like a meaningless texture. I might make out a word or two before Sam has worked her way through a page and has brought up another.

'Chad didn't build this?' She says leaning back and putting her arms behind her head. I notice she has small breasts which suit her, they're to the point and not much is wasted. I imagine them to be firm and there I must stop because Turin has just said that he did, definitely, and then he tells her,

'He brought in pieces, boards, drives and assembled it in front of me at the cellar.' He is certain, but even I can see the flaw.

'He did exactly that,' Sam continues, 'he assembled it. There are protocols that I recognise that are like a signature. I can guess who they belong to, and I'm sure it's not Chad.'

Having picked out the name 'cupal' many times, I can't resist trying to impress,

' That wouldn't be an organisation beginning with C U would it?'

Sam looks at me, 'You're right Ash. It wouldn't be.'

She has no idea how much she hurts me. I suppose because I don't allow my feelings to show and carry on without any reaction she thinks it's like water off a duck's back, which is supposed to mean it has no effect. Why ducks? Who knows?

Life at the moment seems to be full of small events which have huge consequences. I wonder if all small events do, or if it's just that I can trace all events of any size back to when they were small. Taking Chad's gear from the cellar had no purpose other than to make the place look less suspicious if it was about to be raided. Now I realise how easily someone with the right skills can access the data, it makes me wonder why we were still alive. Why we weren't prevented from carrying out the events.

As it is we pour over the data, we scribble down on whatever paper we can find, anything that makes sense.

Anything that might explain the events, large and small, of the last few days, maybe of the last few years.

Together the three of us work for hours. Taking it in turns to go half blind picking out a phrase, a date, a place, a reference, anything that could mean anything. Anything repeated, anything that Sam hasn't already picked out as significant, would be pointed out by one of us at the screen, another would write it down. The third would make coffee, not real coffee, and toast, real toast.

After several hours it gets easier, we stop jumping from date to date and begin to identify patterns, apply them, adjust, retry. At first a whole screen full might result in a couple of lines amongst commands and codings that are purely system instructions, but then it starts to break down into messages, replies, a proposed target, time and place; then more specific details. Quantities and which detonator? Steif. Which explosive? Glucosatol, or Pyrapede? Plasticised or liquid? Frequency, audio, or delay triggers? All the event paraphernalia begin to appear as we eliminate unwanted symbols. Abbreviations, codes, initials, all the language Chad used, starts to rise to the surface as if muddy water is slowly draining away. We pick out what we think are Chad's complaints, objections, followed by ultimatums, then warnings and threats. Then an agreement, then a report. Routine events, some I remember with Turin, others mean nothing, then one comes up and I recognised it as The Bakery event. The proposed target co-ordinates, the time, and the method. The objection there might be too much collateral, escape might be difficult. Chad would often be told to comply. All the time there was threatening, nothing definite, no names, but Chad had to be pushed all the way. Sometimes the word 'comply' would be repeated as if to emphasise it. Bots do this sometimes, just repeat a command until it is obeyed. Humans pick up botspeak, at least the LEOs do, repeating the same command until it's obeyed.

Our tiredness is taking a grip just as Turin suddenly sits up, grabs the notes and goes back to the screen. Sam and I just watch as he scrolls through the jumble of words and numbers, stops, then checks something with the notes.

'What is it?' I ask.

'There's a series of letters and numbers with a common prefix. Part of it was familiar, but not in the same sequence. It's not the same prefix that is on the screen, but it's the same prefix that Chad used.'

Sam and I look at each other. Even with tired eyes I swim in hers, but I fear she's not even paddling in mine.

'Explain?' I say, and Turin carries on with enthusiasm.

'Chad's targets always had a particular prefix, a sort of job number. He would refer to the event by the number and when he picked up devices or kit for triggers, etc. He would label them using the number alone, because the prefix was always the same. Looking through these notes nothing stuck out until, two zero two, which rang a bell, but I looked for others and nothing matched except for a seven two seven, they both had the same prefix on the screen. Then I checked out a couple more numbers with the same prefix but the number didn't mean anything until I realised the numbers were reversed. Chad took the target reference as given him, reversed the last three digits and added his own prefix. It was a way to conceal any consecutive numbers, but retain the understanding. 213 and 214 would be consecutive, 312 and 412 wouldn't be.'

'The occasional 313, or 212, would confuse if you didn't know his method.' I add.

'It's not very sophisticated, and when a palindromic number was used, it reads the same backwards as it does forwards,' said Sam purely to illustrate that she knew the meaning of the word palindromic. I reckoned I probably knew the meaning as well.

'Right,' Turin continued, 'what's more, now that the reference can be associated with a particular event, other codes fall into place, some of which I can still remember. An event which Chad raised, AMP 727 was cancelled twice, but in the end went ahead and resulted in the target CE 4978600727 being achieved. That code is a genuine corp exec's personal reference, like their security ID.'

'So the death of that exec was as a result of an event AMP 727, and that the ID pattern is similar each time?' I suggest.

'No,' says Turin.

'They're identical,' adds Sam.

Turin continues,

'CE is one of several CUpal references. Sure the name, CUpal, and their codes crop up repeatedly, and because they are the biggest security corp you would expect it to. Working backwards from some of Chad's references that I can remember, I then looked at the codes, post event. I added back in the corp references you would expect, and found they are not encoded references for places, times, etc.'

'I don't understand.' I tell Turin.

'I took all the codes that Chad used to refer to places, times or personnel,' he replies, 'none of the codes we have so far identified refer to anything other than personnel.

We've only been targeting execs. More, only particular classes of execs. Not only that, we've only been targeting execs that work for CUpal!'

I ask him if he thinks it could be just coincidence.

Sam shakes her head and is just waiting for us to catch up but Turin carries on,

'There's a target back in June that Chad suggests can be achieved simply and he's told to stick to the plan and only achieve targets he's told to.'

Sam is biting her bottom lip. Her eyes are watching some invisible fly make its unpredictable journey around the room. I've noticed she does that when she's about to catch an idea. Then she gets it,

'What if . . ?' Turin and I turn towards her and wait.

'What if we are supposed to find this stuff?' There's a pause as Turin and I try to imagine why that should be, but she continues, 'Chad's no fool and an experienced hacker. If he wanted to totally wipe stuff he could have done it.'

'Maybe he thought he had,' I suggest, 'maybe he didn't look.'

'With something as important as this he would have looked. He would have found it and I know that because I did. This is why I think it's strange he hasn't wiped it. Chad could have set up ways for it to self-wipe.'

'Or,' I point out, 'he may have been instructed otherwise.'

Turin turns to me,

'You're not trying to suggest that Chad is any way responsible for the devices that have nearly killed us?'

'We're not saying that, Turin.' I tell him. 'We just don't know how much Chad might be responsible for.'

'Yes, he was getting the instructions,' Turin replies, 'we worked by the rules, where he got them from wasn't my business. We might have been targeting particular execs but that doesn't mean it's connected to anything else.'

Sam and I remain silent.

'Chad and I go back a long way?' Turin says, 'I know he's not always the easiest of people to get along with, but he would not endanger any of us in the group.'

'What if . . . ?' Sam is lost in thought.

'Go on.' I tell her and she turns toward me. 'What was the last thing Chad said? ' She then turns to her brother, 'Turin? As I came down the steps into the cellar, what was it that Chad was talking about?'

Turin shakes his head.

'He said something about it not being just you two, something like that wasn't it?' She waits for his reply.

'I don't know, something like that, but he meant the group.'

'Then why did he suddenly shut up? I saw the way he looked, Turin, he was talking about somebody or something else. Before that you were arguing, what was Chad saying?'

'We were arguing about you and Ash and how both of you should leave the group. That he didn't trust Ash.'

A light goes on in my head and I see Sam rising from the floor over the cellar and mouthing words.

'Sam, why did you mention 'the three car trick'?'

The light transfers to Sam's face and her eyes suddenly sparkle into life,

'The three car trick! Yes.' Turin is all confusion and looks from me to Sam.

'Turin,' she says. 'What was name of the corp whose chopper went down when it tried to lift the car you had bolted to the ground?'

Turin stares silently at her and gives no answer, so she tells him,

'It was 4U, wasn't it?' There's still no reaction.

'Who did Chad hack into to find out they were using undergrade segments for their bots?'

Turin still gives no answer,

'It was 4U.'

Sam doesn't give up, 'And who do you think traced him, and caught him?'

She has Turin's attention,

'4U! After you had humiliated them, they were never going to rest until they had either you or Chad, preferably both, and one would lead to the other. Somehow they've got him to work for them in exchange for his life . .'

'And maybe yours too, Turin,' I add. 'He may have been doing it to save all our lives.'

Turin turns away from us, but there is no escaping the past and I still have to make it clear,

'4U has been supplying him with targets, CUpal execs every time. No one knew their real identity except Chad, all we did was to carry out the events.'

Sam is searching through some of the notes we have made.

'Turin,' she says and he turns around to face her, but she is searching notes.

'His code name was TINA.'

Standing at the window Turin echoes the name,

'TINA, There Is No Alternative.'

'Chad had no alternative,' Sam says. 'maybe that's why he wanted us out of the group. He knew how it might end.'

'He could have been trying to save us,' I add.

She moves towards her brother and takes his hand. Then explains to him how she accessed their father's link to CUpal and the discovery she made of another data miner who she is now certain was Chad.

He shakes his head in confusion and disbelief.

'Chad has also been carrying a phone,' she tells him.

'I took it out of Chad's sack while you were arguing with him. When I left for a while I went upstairs to where Ash was and he wrote the number on a pad. Then I took it back down and replaced it.'

'You were upstairs?' Turin asks and I nod in return.

'Turin,' I use his name to bridge the gap that has opened between us, 'when he left you and Sam in the cellar, Chad met Meko at the back door and tried to discourage her from joining you. He also suggested to Ma Brown that she go out for a walk, but neither of them took any notice. I think he was trying to warn them. He disappeared into number14 after using his phone. I think he was telling them he had what they wanted.'

'And maybe they didn't need to do anything more,' Sam adds.

'He didn't know what they were going to do Turin, he couldn't have. After the other events I couldn't take any chances, I knew I had to find some way of getting you all out, just in case. I'm sorry about Ma Brown and Meko if she didn't make it. There was no time to explain. If I had been slower, none of us would have made it. I'm sure Chad didn't know what they were going to do.'

Turin is stunned. I look at Sam who mouths the word, 'coffee'. I go into the kitchen. Wash out mugs and go through the mundane business of making a drink.

There is a period of silence during which we drink coffee and wonder what happens now. The group must be over but without the fight we have nothing, we are nothing. The fight defines us, gives us existence, hope. Resistance is living; so the fight must go on.

I look out towards the glimmering City as rain trickles down the window pane and the grey sky-blanket clamps its miserable darkness over everything again. It's easy to be seduced by the bright lights, thrill rides and shows of The City, the rewards for being a responsible member of the state, the privileges and allowances. Did I ever have any choice? Was there ever a moment when I said, 'This is the life I choose and not that one.' At our level, and those like us, the choice is limited. The best we can do is just survive.

Sam comes and stands quietly beside me and fingers the window glass following a droplet on its downward path to assimilation. The path to assimilation is always downward, it is gravity, it pulls. It is the death of the individual.

Sam places her coffee on the window cill next to a dark brown case. For a moment I can't think where I've seen the case before, then I remember. It was in Turin's hand as we left the remains of his folk's home. He dashed across his father's office grabbed a book and the case that now rests upon the cill in front of us. Sam sees me looking and unclips it,

'Photos,' she says, opening it out like a book. On each page are sleeves all attached along their tops like tiles. Photos are usually viewed on the screens or viewers that scroll through all your family photos. Execs are very fond of them, they show off how beautiful they have made their wives and how clever they have made their children. As they scroll you get a general picture, nothing particular, nothing personal. Some, like Mel maybe, do make something of them, put them in a frame and hang them on the wall, just the one and they don't scroll.

Sam is feeling sad for her brother. I would like to do what I can to comfort her but now is too tense. We all know the group is finished. Turin feels it most.

Sam lifts the photos one by one and points out her and Turin as a babies and young people. There are many of Mel and Zac, family occasions and friends. She lingers on some, a screen would scroll on. It would say, 'Get over it, here's the next one,' but some we look at closely. People never look at anything closely, nothing bears scrutiny. I smile when she smiles, and when she goes, 'Ahh', I go 'Ahh' too. Then there is a face I recognise. Someone sat with her mother Mel, in what could be their kitchen. I ask Sam who the woman is whose hand is blurred, perhaps as it moves upwards to her face, maybe to cover it.

'That's a friend of my mother's, Gill. Why?'

'I thought I recognised her,' I say, and I do. I know who it is.

Seeing the person I recognise in the photo confirms the step I have to take. Sometimes it's like there is an invisible guide who nudges you in the right direction. Not like gut feelings that are just a sense, but a physical hint, something actually happens that you should take notice of.

Turin will have to choose his own path now. Goodrich will have mixed feelings about Sam but I trust her and she is too useful to leave behind, well, that's my excuse. We have to work together, forge links, co-operate, it's the only way. Maybe when the dominoes are closer together they will be less likely to fall down.

CHAPTER 16

I lead Sam through the passages and alleyways heading toward Urbia District 23. It borders on 48 but is not deregulated so there are more activities permitted, which makes movement easier and less conspicuous. I show Sam some of the dodges where you can't be seen by any cams and some streets where they are regularly poked out. The grey skies are concealment enough from anything way up but occasionally a mapping drone flies over, they can be used for surveillance, particularly as they can see through to the ground.

'Always work with the terrain,' I tell Sam, in the same way Turin told me. 'It's a rule.'

I check out places to get under cover, alleyways down which we can dash, and listen for the sound of the LEOs in their trucks. I spot a warden sauntering along a line of garages and trying the doors. This might seem like an official doing his duty ensuring all is secure, but really he's hoping to find one that's not. He'll check it out, then later if it promises much, his truck will appear with a few burly associates who will help him recover the contents. Anything unsecured is by law, lost property, and that's what they'll become to the unlucky owner.

'An officer in pursuit of his duty requires access at all times to verify the safety and legality of stored goods'.

This law gives them rights to make access in any way they choose.

'Any goods not found to be in secure storage may be taken as unwanted or lost property.'

This law gives them the right to take whatever they find not locked up. So, unless the owner replaces the lock wrecked by the officer immediately after they've checked the contents, everything of value will have disappeared. Identifying what storage has the best pickings and the time to remove it is the only reason not all storage is broken into. Checking for storage that is already unlocked is in comparison, a generous act. The warden we watch seems like a true humanitarian, but we still give him a wide berth.

Sam and I cross into 23 and the difference is already obvious. There are people on the streets and they do not skulk around like inmates, but walk briskly with a purpose. Their purpose on this, their day off, is to do as much as they can with the little they are paid before returning to their place of work tomorrow morning. Today is a Sunday and it has traditionally been a day of rest, but Sundays are too valuable to use to rest, instead it is the busiest day of the week. Most of the corps are closed otherwise these folk would be working.

We pass a few old cars that have been converted from the fluid energy they used to have. These are rare and very valuable amongst execs. They're only allowed on special permits, so the owners parade them to let people know they have the special permits and that they are thought very highly of in their corp.

Walking around here is not easy because we are used to being watched and about to be abused. Occasionally people smile which takes a while to get used to, but we try to smile back and overdo it which makes us laugh They must think we are mad. It doesn't take long before we get it right, but it's the same every time I leave 48 and encounter lots of people. There are some LEOs here too and they watch us because we are not relaxed like others. Sam links arms and says,

'I didn't mean the bit about the lip.'

I smile at her then she spoils it by telling me that she nearly did at the time, but not anymore. I tell her I'm not going to take any chances and she does a pout like children do when they don't get their own way. I can't help it but I wonder if I will ever have children and if Sam will be their mother. Then I think it's a crime to bring a child into this and that's another reason to change it.

There are some street stalls ahead, they are really brightly coloured like oranges and bananas. There's fruit and vegetables, all sorts of produce from the farms. People sit or stand by barrows full of things they've brought to sell. Some sell children's toys made from wood, somebody else makes jams and pickles. Sam and I only have tokens and these free traders don't have a licence to deal in tokens, so we can look but that's all. We don't even have anything we could barter. Bartering is illegal as it cannot be controlled, or taxed.

In the middle of all these stalls there is chaos. The sellers are on both sides of the street and there is not much room to get past other people so we keep bumping into them which we find really funny. People don't seem to mind and everyone says sorry, so we say sorry too, and to each other. We say sorry to each other and look into each other's eyes and that's when we kiss; then afterwards we both say sorry and laugh.

Honkey Moon is a coffee bar in the middle of all this. We see its brightly coloured sign over the stalls on a building at the side. It looks as if it's been painted by a child who has tried to use as many colours and as many shapes as possible all over the coffee bar frontage. From what we can see through its windows, the inside is the same. We can't easily get between the stalls with people shouting out what they are selling and how much for. There are empty crates and boxes piled high and it's a while before we can find our way to the pavement that runs behind the stalls and sellers all seemingly in the gutter. We get to the coffee bar and stand before its crazy decoration. Outside there are two tables and at one, a couple of heavy looking types sit watching us. As we approach the door a guy opens it from the inside and I'm sure I recognise him but I don't know where from. If he were to stand square in the doorway he would fill it and not even the air could get passed but he steps back to let us in. The two guys outside get up too but sit down again when the big guy opened the door for us as if he knew we were expected. We are, and I wonder who else knows.

      The big guy sits down in the bay window with a small woman who looks like his jockey, in size, not dress. She has a dark skin, tanned and worn, like leather. Her greying hair is drawn back and up into a kind of top knot. She has lots of gold rings and bracelets but I notice her hands are smooth and youthful looking. She has no fat on her, and you might think she is scrawny but it is all faded tattoos, sinew and muscle. The big guy points us to the rear and a bead curtain, then they pay us no more attention. We pass a big chromium coffee machine that leaks steam and hisses like a some primitive engine about to explode. Barely visible behind it, a little old man wearing just a white stained vest over his chef's baggy stripes, gesticulates at us then starts pulling and pushing leavers with gusto. The pipes and cylinders shake and eventually subside as the process concludes and we are offered two coffees, real coffees, that froth and gurgle as if they're not quite dead yet. He waves us toward the curtain as if swatting flies, so we move the heavy beads to one side and pass through with our frothing mugs.

Once beyond we stand in a small hallway with an old staircase, long painted a reddish brown, it now peels to show another shade of reddish brown beneath. It's worn in much used places to reveal other colours, then the bare wood beneath that. A boarded window on a small landing where the stairs turn sheds a little light through its split panels. There is an oriental odour like a mixture of strong spices that have faded through generations. I don't think there are any spices here, it's in the woodwork, the floors and walls. We creep forward, wondering where we should go, but all around us is silence. Then on the floor above we hear a door knob turn and a door opens shedding the borrowed light of day across the reddish brown stairs. Then a female voice I recognise says quietly,

'Come up Ash, and bring your friend with you.'

In the room above, the furnishings remind me of Ma Brown's cellar. Old, well-worn arm chairs and sofas surround a small low level table. It's like a rest room for the coffee bar employees, except there seems only to be one employee and the room could seat eight, or twelve if you include the arms. At the moment there are only four of us.

I embrace Carol. Now that we are on strange territory our relationship has greater significance and our embrace is genuine. I introduce her to Sam, who she recognises, but Sam is all confusion.

'Carol?' Says Sam taking a step back, 'Don't I know you as Gill?'

'Yes, Sam, and so did Mel and Zac. This is one of the things we have to talk about.'

Sam, I can see is trying to catch up,

'The photograph!' Says Sam. ' You knew this Gill was her, I mean Carol?'

'I did, sorry I couldn't say anything. You know how it is.'

Sam is not happy. I'm beginning to understand her and she likes order, at least things making sense. Confusion makes her frustrated, she feels things are out of control and this makes her angry. I take her by the shoulders and look at her,

'Sam, trust me. Give us some time and we will explain.' She sits down calmly, next to Goodrich.

'Sam, this is Professor Goodrich.'

Sam and Goodrich nod and touch hands. I watch Goodrich carefully as his beady eyes dart about watching and interpreting every move Sam makes.

During my meeting with Carol and Goodrich a few nights ago I went over all that had happened since I had seen them. I was able to explain about the belt, about Chad and Turin and of course, Sam. I told them how Sam was using her father's link and how it wasn't her fault it went down. I could tell that Goodrich wasn't convinced that Sam was being entirely honest, though he never said so.

It's important to me that he trusts Sam, trust is as much to do with people as what people do. If someone feels trusted they will not want to disappoint, and if you feel you can trust someone, you probably can. Trust is like an account, you pay in regularly and you get to be trusted. If you make a withdrawal then you have to pay in again, sometimes a lot more. If you take out too much, become overdrawn, your trust account could be closed.

Carol talks while Goodrich observes. He's a wily old bird and doesn't miss a thing. His eyes dart around the room but invariably land upon Sam, he catches her every reaction to Carol's story without Sam being aware she's being read.

Carol befriended Mel because of Zac's position within CUpal, and his knowledge of androbotics, then organobotics, which he was working on when he was taken. They had also become aware of Zac's political irritation, his dissatisfaction with his corp's policy in particular, and state policy in general. Not being obviously enthusiastic and praising the state at every opportunity can be taken as a sign that someone isn't entirely happy with the way things are. You have to advertise your unquestioning support for the corp and the state and everything they do; not doing so will bring attention.

Carol was put in to support Mel and Zac, and to give them safe passage should the faeces hit the fan. It did and they didn't. No one foresaw the sudden arrest because no one knew that Zac's portal was being hacked, why should they. I can tell that Goodrich is still not convinced that Sam is being completely honest.

We talk over everything that has happened and Goodrich makes notes. I know he is concerned about Chad and his whereabouts and whether Meko survived. When I saw him recently he said he would look into it.

'As far as I can see,' Goodrich starts his summing up, 'we have a couple of loose ends, and a thread we must follow.'

He enjoys being enigmatic, but then he is an enigma. He turns to Sam.

'Your brother, if you'll excuse the phrase Sam, is one of the loose ends, your folks are the thread. We must decide what to do about them but I don't have all the information. If I am to take risks I must do my best to minimise them by knowing as much as possible, and nothing should be hidden.'

There is a pause and I can see Sam is uncomfortable.

'Can you do anything about Mel and Zac?' She asks.

'That would depend on the other loose end,' Goodrich replies.

'And what's that?' This is like ping pong, and the rest of us watch, our heads going from one to the other. Now it's Goodrich's go.

'You.'

Sam looks at me and I can see she is feeling cornered but there is no escape, and she wants desperately to help her folks.

'You are a very talented girl,' Goodrich tells her, 'but your folks are beyond your talents. We can help each other. I will be as honest with you as I can be, if you will be honest with me.'

I can feel Sam withdrawing and I wonder what more Goodrich knows, and what I don't. Goodrich relaxes into his chair and sips coffee.

'It's up to you, Sam,' he says, 'I can't help you if you don't help me, we are a community. I'll ask you a question to get the ball rolling.' He pauses for a moment then asks her, 'Why did you alter the results of the CUpal trials?'

Sam looks at me and raises her eyebrows. She sighs, like the games up, and to prepare for some revelation. Now I know that Goodrich has been right all along.

'Zac caught me hacking via his link.'

She leans forward, finishes her coffee and avoids looking in my direction.

'We had an argument,' she continues, 'I left and stayed with some friends for a while but eventually we made it up. I think Mel asked him to. I had to tell him everything, which was difficult, but I told him most. Then a bit later he asked me what I had found out.'

'I told him that CUpal had been a major shareholder in Retrainco, a subsidiary of 4U who hold the licence to operate the Rehabs. He knew that but what he didn't know, because practically nobody did, was that CUpal had bought out Retrainco totally. It was a swap deal with 4U, giving 4U a monopoly in surveillance. No big money changed hands, just names on paper. It had to be secret because at the same time CUpal was buying up Hold Security, the Rehab freeholder. When that was completed, and this is the point, CUpal had total control over all Rehab resources, including all internal policies and actions. Some old Retrainco staff, about eight of them, objected to the new regime and the unwarranted extremes that had come with it. They started to spread dissent and were being difficult. There was an armed break out one weekend by three inmates and eight staff were killed. I don't need to tell you which eight. The three that broke out have never been found. The break out was used as an excuse to lock down all Rehab sites, and restrict all contact with the outside on the basis that it was that contact which allowed the arms to get in; a predictable win-win result. The lock down is still in place. In the meantime the staff have been sifted and any likely dissenters have been removed to lesser duties or retrained, or they've just disappeared.'

'What was Zac's reaction?' Asked Goodrich.

'He wasn't surprised,' she answered, which raised a few eye brows, particularly Goodrich's, but she explained,

'Zac was developing the interface between robotics and brain segments for years, even when he was still officially only working on androbotics. There were always problems with the interface if they wanted to increase segment functionality. What he explained to me was that he had begun to refocus on altering the function of parts of the brain segment to accommodate the interface, rather than trying to develop an interface for an ever changing and volatile segment. His reasoning was that the brain tissue is more versatile and adapts quicker than the interface they were building. In the right circumstances, his theory went, that it was far easier to teach the segment to operate with the interface. When he started to demand more of the brain segment, the results became unpredictable.'

'Some segments didn't learn very quickly,' Goodrich suggested.

'Exactly,' replied Sam, 'as in life I suppose, some didn't learn at all. What puzzled Zac was why the programmes then started to show far better results in all areas. The quality and clarity of response, the stimulation and reaction, the learning speeds and retainment, all began to improve incredibly even though the tests and the procedures were exactly the same. Suddenly the organobot became a reality, larger segments became a possibility as did the ultimate goal of TBOs.'

Goodrich raises an eyebrow, in his case not a small gesture.

'Total Brain Organobots,' she replies.

'So what happened?' Says Goodrich.

'Dad began to suspect that there could only be one answer, brains were being harvested which could meet the appropriate criteria. On the intake registry we found files recording the results of subjects who were being examined on arrival.'

'We?' Asks Goodrich. 'Did you say 'We'?'

'Yes,' Sam answers, 'Zac and I sat at his terminal, and he watched me pulling out the information. What we found was that Rehab intake had initiated a testing regime which would identify the suitability of the subject's mental capacity. We noticed that month on month the number of subjects achieving high scores increased. We then followed up some of the high scorers and we found their stay in Rehab averaged two weeks.'

'And you're not going to tell us they were released?' asks Goodrich.

'I don't know,' Sam replies, 'their records just stopped.'

There is a pause during which Carol stands up and suggests we all have a drink and a bite to eat, we all agree and she leaves. As I hear her footsteps going downstairs I notice Goodrich seems less on edge with Sam who is still avoiding eye contact with me. Goodrich then continues,

'I presume that's when you decided to alter the test results?'

'Yes,' Sam replies. 'Actually it was Zac's idea. He woke me one night, not able to sleep and said we had to do something urgently. It had occurred to him that people of a certain type, with the right kind of brains, might become targets, if they weren't already. Harvesting better brains was a temptation Rehab, run by CUpal, couldn't resist if it meant increasing profits. They would begin to look outside of Rehab for the kind of brains they wanted. Intellectuals, for instance would be sought out for the quality of brain tissue they could provide.'

'This would include people like Zac, and you maybe?' Suggested Goodrich.

'And you,' Sam replied, which made him smile. Then Sam continued,

'Nobody in the chain could see the whole picture. We talked about it all night and that's when we came up with the idea. I got back into the vault and started to change the data as dad told me. We had several sessions but we just had to make the results unpredictable, not change them all. It was during one of the sessions that I discovered someone else had hacked into the vault. We had to make sure they had the altered results rather than the originals so I had to hack into their system as well. I had to make sure their data was the same as the data I had altered in the vault. I didn't know that they were in the vault at the same time. While they were in there, they did something to cause an alarm. The system withdrew all their data and closed so they lost everything. I had a copy of all their data so I could alter the trial results before loading it back into their system as well; but their system never came back.'

'We also decided that if the corp continued to give the impression their research was succeeding, it might encourage others in the same field. So we would have to 'leak' our version to discourage further research from anybody. That's about it really.'

'Well,' Goodrich tells her, 'we suspected that the results had been changed but we didn't know why. I get a scratch . .'

Before he can finish, Carol comes into the room carrying a tray with all sorts of goodies on it. There are slices of pies, and cakes, some fruit as well as the coffee, which is of course, real.

For a while we talk about other stuff, like the coffee bar and how it got its name, the market outside. Because Carol and Sam have met before, they get on well. I hear Sam asking about her folks but Carol avoids giving any answers, so I imagine the news is not good. As Carol goes downstairs to get some more coffee and pressed orange, Sam mentions her brother to Goodrich. He asks Sam what she thinks ought to be done, she says she isn't sure and Goodrich says that it would be good to have a talk with him. Goodrich then leaves the room and it gives me the chance to talk to Sam and I sit next to her on the sofa.

'Are you okay?' I ask her. She doesn't look directly at me but says,

'Still talking to me then.'

'Of course!' I tell her, to which she turns and looks at me.

'I thought that you would be angry with me because I hadn't told you everything.'

I explain to her that I trust her and that when you trust someone, knowing everything is not so important because you know that they must have a good reason for keeping things to themselves. Then she tells me,

'I'm not sure I had a good reason for not telling you. I suppose you can't expect a girl to open up, just like that . .'

I can't help but smile a bit at what she has said, and she starts shaking her head, the same old, 'there's no hope' kind of shake. Then she says,

'You can take the boy out of 48, but you can't take 48 out of the boy!' Now I smile a lot and think she is so cool. She smiles too.

We have all sat down again and I can't remember when I have had such a good meal. The state looks after some districts, or rather the corps do. Without the corps say so, the state wouldn't do a thing, like in District 48. I wonder how much the state knows about Rehab and what they are trying to do? Harvesting the brains of the high scorers would be too good a win-win for any corp to resist. Removing anyone critical, then using their brains to power exactly the kind of machines they were critical of would be the kind of hideous irony a corp could brag about, but they wouldn't stop there. Anyone who puts together a reasoned argument for change, has independent thought, is critical of the state, a freethinker; any intelligent nuisance.

Sam turns to Goodrich who smiles at her,

'You said you had a scratch?'

'Ah, yes . . . '

He is more at ease with her, I can tell.

'. . . I was about to say Sam, that I have a scratch that I can't itch when I feel there is more to a story than I am being told.'

'Don't you mean, an itch that you can't scratch?' I suggest and Prof looks over his dirty glasses and I feel a reprimand coming,

'Like Humpty Dumpty once said,' he tells me, 'when I use a word, it means whatever I choose it to mean.'

I tell him that I think that could be quite confusing and he replies that life is confusing and we had all better get used to it, because it is going to get worse. He has that slight grin which means I shouldn't be offended and he is playing with me, though what a 'Humper Dumty' is I don't know.

Goodrich takes a deep sigh and there is an air of seriousness about things and this affects us all. He has what I think people call charisma. Unless you experience it for yourself it is impossible to explain. It's a power over you that you want them to have and to use.

Nestling in the depths of his chair Goodrich tells us that he thinks we are drawing nearer to the moment he, and his friends, have been waiting for. Then he warns us,

'Nothing is certain. Sailors can become so desperate to sight land that they convince themselves, and others, that they can see it, when actually they can't.'

He stops and takes a sip of tea.

'It is imperative,' he continues, 'that we are more careful, more aware, more sensitive and more intuitive. The closer we get, the more likely we are to be discovered, if only through our increased activity. The corporate fortress has many towers and they all need to be brought down at the same time, as those left standing will prevail and regenerate. We must ensure that when the day comes our energies are directed at every aspect of the system. I include the labs, the offices, all aspects of security, control, surveillance and government. The corps stranglehold has to be severed, quickly and without mercy. The corporate monster will not be slain by just cutting off its tail and hoping it will bleed to death. Co-ordination and timing is essential, we must all play our part, and know what we have to do, and when. Nothing can be overlooked, and paramount will be people on the streets. Boots on the streets draws the eye of the state. They will be a distraction and no less important for that, without them we could not do our work. It is unrest, which they fear above all else. However, on their own they cannot prevail, but it will be their revolution that prompts ours and together we have a chance to overcome. History and experience tells us that in war, nothing is predictable, little can be relied upon and that includes whatever plans and preparations have been made. Be prepared for change, accept it, do not live in the past and seek to retain the comfort of what you thought you knew. Search out new advantages, be alert and adapt. The more we are able to cope with the chaos that will ensue, the more likely we are to succeed.'

Goodrich pauses for a moment, takes a drink, then holds up a hand in case we think he's finished.

'History has taught us that not only do we have to win the war, but also the peace we hope will follow. There will be recriminations, grudges, bitterness, some will desire revenge, even retaliation. There has always to be government, a society needs control for and on behalf of the people, not against it and not by a ruling elite. We govern by consent and we have a duty of care to all, but especially to those less fortunate than ourselves. It is how we treat those, by which we should be judged.'

Goodrich leans back into his chair and closes his eyes. His sentiments depress me. How could we have become the society that we are? There are controllers, and the controlled, and everything is conflict. It isn't a society, maybe there is no such thing, but Goodrich believes one is worth fighting for.

The cellar at Ma Brown's is like another age. Maybe Turin and Chad had a philosophy, but I never saw or heard it, here I feel there is a reason behind what we want to do, and even a pathway to it. As I look around the room I know I am not alone in these thoughts. Goodrich lifts his head and he turns to Sam again,

'You and your brother,' he says, 'must be very concerned about your parents and their whereabouts?'

'Do you know where they are?' Sam gets excited.

Goodrich raises a hand indicating that she should calm herself.

'At the moment we understand they are alive at least.' He pauses for a moment as Sam leans forward encouraging him to say more,

'We think they are being held in a secure facility within a Rehab camp. It's not as bad as it sounds because we think that they want Zac to carry on his work in a controlled environment. Unfortunately, Zac is refusing to collaborate.'

'What about Mel?' Sam asks, and Carol answers her,

'She's fine, but they are using her as leverage. Until Zac co-operates they will be kept apart. Sam, you should know that there is no guarantee that either one will survive unless Rehab gets what they want. The best they can hope for is cohabitation quarters within the unit, but only if Zac does everything they ask. '

'He won't,' says Sam.

'If he doesn't then their stay might be a short one.'

Sam understands.

'If he does comply,' explains Goodrich, 'they will remain in a secure unit and his work can continue, he may even be rewarded by occasional visits from Mel. This is what we would like him to do.'

There is some surprise amongst us at this, to which Goodrich raises a hand.

'We need time. Zac's co-operation can give us some. Even so there are no places more secure than a Rehab camp. With time, we might find a way of getting them out.'

'Is there anything we know for certain,' I ask, 'like where they are, which camp?'

'We are sure the camp is London Southwest. Exactly where Zac is, or for that matter Mel is, on a day to day basis, we don't know. We know that one of the research facilities adjoins some accommodation near the old house, and that would seem an obvious place for him to work and maybe for them to live. It will depend on Zac agreeing to do what they want and them being allowed to be together. No attempt could be made unless they are together, this presumes we can get anywhere near them. The camps are vast and are mainly the old Royal estates, church lands or estates deemed large enough to be appropriate. Their size doesn't mean there is any weakness in security, it's impressive; perhaps I should say impregnable. Internal security has by far the largest budget, not that anyone is allowed to know that.'

Goodrich relaxes into his chair with a kind of resignation which I have not often seen in him. Zac and Mel's situation seems hopeless.

'Sam and I would like to do a reckie.' I announce this as if I've given it some thought. Sam looks at me as if I'm mad.

'A reconnoitre?' I explain. 'We would like to go and see the camp, get a feel for it. Something might occur to us.'

To do something must be better than nothing, besides if I can get to go with Sam on our own for a day, that would be good. Even when things are bad I still find it difficult not to have ulterior motives. Goodrich is not convinced but then I make a movement with my eyes towards Sam and say to him,

'It would be good to do something.'

He smiles and nods his head.

'All right, but you do nothing.' Goodrich says, 'Just observe, make notes. Take a scope and photograph anything of interest. Tell Cassy in the bar to come up and see me when you go, then wait downstairs.'

I ask about sleeping times, if and when they exercise, washing, toilet facilities, Goodrich tells me as much as he can. He tells us about the security, at least what they have discovered, and shows us drawings that they have made. Sam has cheered up a little, doing anything is better than doing nothing.

CHAPTER 17

Cassy drives us to the outskirts of a wood before dawn. On a screen the journey from our drop off point to the concealed area, where we can overlook the section where Zac and Mel are thought to be, looked uncomplicated. I am an urban dweller, tramping through a wood littered with rotting trees is bad enough at any time, but in the dark it is at best difficult, and at worst, embarrassing. Sam keeps shushing me but stuff just seems to jump up at me out of the ground and twice now I've fallen over. Remembering the route that was marked out, there's about two miles of this. Then later when we return, a mile more to where our pick up will be tonight, in the dark again.

Ahead of us there is a reflected luminescence from the camp and behind us the lights of The City can still be seen glowing pink and green.

We will only be able to see one small corner of the camp, this Rehab facility is one of the larger. Carol told us from where we will overlook it, the camp extends south about ten miles and east about eight. Any information in whatever form about Rehabs is illegal, officially no one claims any knowledge of them, or what goes on in them. There is a stock phrase continually repeated about all security measures. They are for the, 'peace and protection of the nation' and must remain 'secret for our own safety'. Then something like, 'the thanks of the people and the government go to the highly skilled and dedicated people who work so hard for our well-being and protection, and to whom we are all deeply grateful'. This is always followed by cheers, the nodding of approving heads and a standing applause. Anyone not cheering, nodding and applauding is treated with suspicion.

There are villages, workshops, farms and everything to make the camp not only self-sufficient but turn a profit. The children that are born in the camp are deemed to be genetically unfit to join society, so they never leave. They make the perfect warders, they have no conscience and obey every command without hesitation, ask no questions and have no guilt. The camp is their mother, father, teacher, carer, their religion and their God. Women who have given birth in the camp have been known to kill their own babies rather than have them taken and reared by the camp.

Sam stops and puts her hand out to stop me too, then places a finger over her lips. We stand behind a tree and listen. All I can hear is the sound of urbia in the background, and the slight crumpling of the soggy vegetation being compressed beneath my feet. Ahead there is the dull, distant drone of machinery, pumps or generators probably in the camp. Every few years there's another camp built, and the existing ones get bigger. Inmates, those that survive, vastly outnumber the warders and together they could take over, if their revolt was co-ordinated. I suppose like the state itself, and the towers that Goodrich talks about, it's impossible unless there is co-operation and all sources of control are hit at once. The inmates are cowed with summary punishments and with intimidating displays of power. The paranoia in the camps is the same as outside, it works. You can never be sure that the person you live, love and suffer with isn't going to inform upon you, and if they are not already doing so.

Above us the greyness is now just visible without The City's reflected light show. The leafless, skeletal trees are stark against it, they are waiting to collapse on us, or at least throw barbed limbs down upon our heads. It's those partly rotten branches, having fallen and missed the opportunity of cracking my skull, that now try their best to trip me up. Ones large enough to be seen and scrambled over are covered in weird bulbous growths that glisten a purple and green iridescence. They have a faint luminescence so you can see the dark shapes that inhabit them slithering and wriggling across their inside surface. There are other growths that are the size of a large plates sunk into the trunks at right angles. It's those that I brush past leaving dusty trails across my shoulders smelling of rotting piss. Teeming down over some roots are what look like hundreds of small white balls, the largest, half the size of a fist. The wood is inconsistent, with frequent open spaces. Some fallen trees have been cut up by those who are prepared to risk being shot just to keep warm.

    I'm about to ask Sam why we stopped when a bushy tailed rat squeals and runs up a tree. Then I hear the faint whirr of an electric motor. About three trees ahead of us there's a cam clamped to a dead tree. There's just enough reflected light to see its outline and get a slight glint from its casing. Another movement on the ground to our left and the cam whirrs round. Then a different pitch of whirr tells me the lens is focusing, then it all goes quiet. It could be motion or sound activated, maybe both. I tap Sam on her shoulder and then try to make a noise like rat and half way through it turns into a choke. We both stifle a giggle which is ridiculous considering our lives are at stake. Sam leans forward to whisper something to me,

    'Fucking amateur!'

'How about a pig?' I reply in a whisper, 'I can do those.'

Sam holds her hand up as the whirr of the cam stops, but there is no secondary whirr as it focuses. I lean forward to whisper, but instead, we kiss, a long meaningful kiss as if it's our last, then I outline a plan. The cam is stimulated by sound, like a human, then turns its lens towards the sound and looks for movement and focuses. It'll be linked to software that will have shape recognition so if it sees us we must try to look as little like humans as possible. Sam says for me that should be easy, I ignore this. I gather some solid pieces of wood and throw one to our left and as the cam tries to find it like some mechanical dog, and we try to creep silently passed it. Twice we had to appear like a tree stump, clutching each other and making arms look like the remains of branches. We wait for some other noise to get its attention. Eventually we get past but there is no way we can be certain we haven't been spotted. After that cam we are both alert to any kind of surveillance, stopping every few minutes and listening. We listen too for anything which might give us warning that we have been discovered. We haven't seen or felt any pressure pads or other cams and we don't even know whether the ground we are covering is mined or trapped. We suspect it is not as we know that the wood is regularly patrolled, what patrols, or how often, we don't know. In these circumstances you have to trust to luck. Trust no one? Luck, you have to trust occasionally.

Sam and I lay flat, concealed by what she calls bracken. We are on the brow of a hill overlooking the London South West Rehab Facility, the sky is a little brighter but not enough for the lights to be turned off. Bracken seems to do very well here so we have to shuffle forward to get a better view. We encourage it to close over us giving us some good concealment, but we are uneasy in case we have already triggered an alarm.

Before us is a valley, about three miles across. Along the valley and disappearing into the distance to our left is the twin perimeter fencing. The fence runs along our side of the valley then to our right where it follows the curve of the valley until it disappears off to the south. Not too far away to our left a road from outside the camp runs up to a fortified gatehouse, it is the only break we can see in the perimeter. A service road follows the inside perimeter fence and the three run together in front of us and as far as we can see in any direction. They turn round the head of the valley to our right and away over the hills. We begin to appreciate the vastness of the camp, or at least the small part we can see. To the right, at the head of the valley, the wood curves round and that too follows the line of the fences. The fences themselves are too far apart to bridge and the killing ground between them is brilliantly illuminated. Through the scope I can identify a variety of armaments installed for both ground and air defence in the towers. They stand like dark sentinels at every vantage point along the inner fence. We presume that both fences are hooked up and all sorts of surprises would be waiting for any unfortunate that got stranded between them. The biggest surprise would be finding they are still alive to hear the shot that kills them.

The fences snake into the distance. They cut swathes over the side of the distant hill and then reappear gouging a trough through forests on hills beyond. Our ridge faces south and we can follow the bare strip and accompanying lights cresting hills and falling into valleys. It crests and falls, crests and falls, until finally melting into the grey of the morning light and disappearing into the mist.

The largest concentration of buildings that we can see, lies before us and to our left. Away in the distance there are other clusters that form captive villages. The buildings nearby are a hotchpotch the largest is an elaborate stone structure with pillars like a Greek temple. It lies like a once proud beast that has been subdued by a host of predators that now feed off its decaying corpse. What look like dormitories have been built on dormitories that have been built on dormitories like an ever spreading cancer, reproducing and reproducing. Dormitories have spawned ancillary buildings that cling like parasites, and they themselves need servicing by yet smaller buildings. Some low level buildings are a collective in their own space, like an old industrial complex with elevated walkways and minor service roads interconnecting. These too seem to have burst their seams and spawn more buildings. There is little sign of humanity in a place that holds, well, thousands, hundreds of thousands. No one knows, no one is allowed to know. What we are watching doesn't officially exist.

Someone in a light purple overall, perhaps denoting the nature of their duties, appears at one door and hurriedly traverses a walkway into the next building. Two more dressed in green with safety helmets appear out of a roof access, walk across the roof and stand for a few moments sharing something which smokes. One of them peers over into a courtyard, the other is disinterested and soon they both return to the access and disappear. Other figures come and go until there seems to be a rising level of activity which is the start of the working day.

As it gets lighter so the pin sharp lamps before us fade and one by one are turned off. Across the hills the lights diminish and their sources disappear into the gloom. The killing ground between the fences remains well lit, while everything else fades. Some way off workers begin attending to some part of the inner fence, and I wonder how much of the fence has to be turned off, and for how long? A device somewhere senses that the available natural light is now sufficient to kill anything that is trapped between the fences. Accordingly it throws a switch and leaves only sufficient light to dazzle anyone trying to take aim at the tower.

In front of us running down to the outer perimeter fence, there is open ground sufficient to give the most inept of guards more than enough time to kill anything before it gets half way across. Within ten degrees, body seeking charges will locate your vital organs, and anyone near you, and blow you apart. For the benefit of anyone attempting this feat the open ground is planted with a herbal ground cover that has tiny white, heart shaped flowers that are quite pretty. The odour that they give off is not bad either, unlike the prodigious amount of thorns like syringe needles they produce. A scratch from just one creates a weeping sore that fills its victim with hallucinatory toxins from which they die. The comfort is they don't know it.

With enough light now, for a few seconds I see a feint ripple in vision above the camp. It's barely perceptible, moves like a wave and shimmers like a thin sheet of flexing glass. This is the aerial grid that Goodrich said we might see. It's just a test, but we can see what he meant when he dismissed our idea of an aerial descent. Any unexpected visitor dropping from the sky would be detected, fried and by the time they had hit the ground, what was left would be little more than toast. That would only be if they weren't expected, it's not cost effective to keep it live. Once down you would have to disable it to rise through it, unless you found another way out. I imagine it works as well keeping people in as it does keeping people out.

On the ground, the only way in and out of the camp that we can see is the gatehouse to our left. We watch closely as, after an hour or so, a van arrives, it stops, the driver gets out and approaches the guards window. Permissions are checked by guards, the driver is scanned then returns to the vehicle. The gate in the outer fence slides open then the van moves into the space between the two fences as the outer gate closes. The van stops on marks on the tarmac, then a self- adjusting sensing device like the structure of a car wash, runs backwards and forwards over the van until it's satisfied. I can see discs in the tarmac that are probably cams and sensors too. Eventually the second gate opens and the van drives towards an inner check point. It hardly stops then makes its way to a covered area for unloading. This is supervised by a couple of guards who appear as the van draws up. Twenty minutes later we watch the process in reverse and as I expect, it's checked again. We presume that the car wash structure uses a variety of methods to detect any prohibited contents, including any life forms. As the morning draws on whatever escape plans we propose, Sam and I recognise they have little chance of overcoming Rehab's security. It would have been tough enough before CUpal took over but now they are in lock down after the protest it's virtually impossible; even so there has to be a way.

About midday a van arrives. This time the driver dressed in white overalls has a conversation at a distance without getting out. A guard waves the van through, the gates open and now the inner gates, strangely without the car wash sensor thing being activated. The inner guards approach the van, then have a brief conversation with the outer guards through the fences, then they wave the van on its way without it stopping. It slowly drives round the inner perimeter road, turns into a short access between buildings opposite us, and stops beneath an extended roof covering a double doored entrance on the right. The driver gets out and walks round to the rear of the van and opens the doors. A device is activated which allows a trolley to be extracted from the van and then lowered onto the ground. The van doors are closed after the device has retracted itself and then the loaded trolley is pushed into the building. Sam and I look at each other with a question mark stamped on our foreheads. Sam lifts the scope up to have a closer look then says,

'Lunch.'

'Great,' I answer, 'I'm starving . .'

'No, idiot,' she replies, 'that's lunch. On the trolley.'

'But don't they have their own farms?'

'Mmmm,' Sam goes and has another look through the scope then hands it to me.

'Check out the van signage,' she tells me.

'There's a picture of food or fruit or something.'

'Caterers,' Sam points out.

'Okay.'

'This is just an idea,' Sam starts, 'firstly it's nearly lunch time. Secondly, Mel has a special dietary need, I think it maybe for her. If we can find out what specialist ingredients are being provided, it might prove they are here, somewhere in those buildings down there. Just an idea.'

It may prove she's here, I think to myself, but not both. So far though it's the best we have and I can see it gives Sam hope.

'I think that's a good idea,' I tell her, 'we might even use the delivery to get a message to them.'

This is going to be the highlight of the day, I can feel it. Sam has the scope again and is trying to make out the supplier's name, the van ID, anything that will help trace it once they are out. If the visits are regular and not as rigorously checked as other visits, maybe it's something we can explore.

Sam seems more focused now than before. I have to remind myself it's her folks in there. It also occurs to me I better shape up, look keen, even if I think we are grasping at straws.

In both directions along the perimeter road we can see pairs of guards patrolling along the road next to the inner fence. Far into the distance pairs of armed figures are doing the same. I presume that each pair are assigned a length of perimeter to patrol, to avoid complacency the assigned length would be changed daily and the pairing would rotate too. Nothing worse for alertness than being on patrol with someone you really get on with, you need silence and a lack of pre-occupying conversation. It also means that nothing is predictable, no pair can be got at, or any one, with any certainty of where they would be patrolling, or who they would be patrolling with.

A small road hugging buggy, with a single guard aboard, stops alongside the pair to our left. The pair salute and after a brief conversation with the buggy's driver, it disappears down an access point into a lower level.

We don't know how many levels there are, all Goodrich's info comes from what people have observed from outside and mostly above ground, rarely a snippet of info gets out. A drunk delivery driver is overheard letting something slip trying to impress a one night stand, or a maintenance engineer brags to a fellow operator, or talks in his sleep. One of Goodrich's team has pieced together what they have gathered over the last few months. That's why we think that Mel and Zac would be in the complex in front of us but it's just a guess. There's no saying that the info is accurate, up to date, or even relevant, nothing is certain. The dietary requirement, for instance, could be for someone else entirely.

The van seems to have been there for ages. I'm about to ask Sam if she has all she needs to trace it when there is an unusual clatter, loud enough for us to hear up here. Something clanging like a saucepan, maybe there's a fight in the kitchen.

Sam picks up the scope and we both watch as the trolley, now perhaps without its lunch, is pushed out towards the van. It actually was a saucepan, well some kind of pan and it rolls across the tarmac. The driver seems in a hurry to get away, can't say I would feel any different, but he keeps looking back. He wheels the trolley round to the rear of the van which we can see, but the device for getting the trolley into the van seems not to be working. The driver has the doors open, but the hook device that lifts it in doesn't come out and grab anything, and the driver can't lift the trolley in without it. I begin to smile as if watching some old comedy but the driver is beginning to panic. There is something not right about it. Then Sam gasps,

'It's Mel!'

I take a good hard look to see that the cover of the trolley has been pulled off and someone, a woman in Rehab clothing, has rolled out onto the ground. They both lift the trolley into the van. Then she gets in with the trolley. The helmeted driver struggles with a number of boxes and equipment then tips them into a convenient dumpster. He then runs back, shuts the rear doors and gets into the driver's seat. The van turns and slowly drives away leaving a bright white cover that had blown under the van, lying stark on the tarmac, it drives slowly towards the gatehouse along the perimeter road to our left. Even from where I am and without a scope, the white cover is obvious, so too the pan that has rolled across the tarmac and lies on the inside edge of the service road.

Sam is scanning along the perimeter road with the scope, then she stops abruptly. I look in the same direction, to our right, and see a pair of guards approaching. The slight turn in the road means they won't see the van crawling slowly away. The trolley cover that is gently flapping in the breeze they won't see for a minute or two, but the pan they'll spot almost immediately. The guard's attention seems mostly in our direction, looking out from the camp. With the intense security surrounding the camp and little chance of any break in, being bored must be a problem. Remarkably one of them picks up the pan and thinking nothing of it, they saunter on. They're almost passed the service road when the other turns to see the flapping cover. He continues his walk, then stops, looks again at the cover and decides it needs his attention. Maybe just to break the monotony.

Just then Sam grips my shoulder, hands me the scope and whispers,

'Doorway.'

I look with alarm. Slumped in the doorway is a figure. Without any uniform I presume he must be the driver of the van, without his white overalls.

'If that's the driver?' I ask Sam. 'Who is driving?'

Sam takes the scope, adjusts the zoom and points it at the van which has stopped at the guardhouse by the inner fence.

'Zac,' Sam whispers, 'it must be him. Oh!'

Sam drops the scope and can't look. It seems hopeless to us both. All she is waiting for are the pistol shots and to have witnessed it all as it happened. There is nothing I can say.

I pick up the scope and see that the van is now stationary between the two fences and waiting for the outer gate to open. They can neither go forward nor back. If it is Zac, and I can't be sure, as he waits for someone to pass him through, the guard has arrived at the loose white cover. He picks it up then turns to the other guard who approaches him still holding the pan. As he does so he sees the figure in the doorway. They both run across and reaching the slumped figure, one of them bends down to talk to him while the other takes out his pistol and scours the vicinity. Something is said and the one standing runs back to the perimeter road and starts walking in the direction of the camp exit. From where he is, he can see a van waiting to exit the camp, but he is too far away. He unclips his comms.

It's not loud, even so Sam jumps and stifles a scream. I notice this but what I watch is the guard falling to the ground, and his comms skating out of reach. The recoil of this pistol is practically nil and it's virtually silent but it's enough to be a surprise, if you're right next to it. She looks at the pistol in my hand then at me, with a kind of relief thinking it was her folks being shot at the exit. She takes the scope and scans, first the prone figure on the tarmac, then at the van that still waits. The guard is moving onto his back, but his comms are some way off. If I knew whether he was in pain, or making a noise, I would finish him off, but he's quiet, so I let him be. He lays out of sight of the other guard, who is still talking to the prostrate driver. I watch to see if he goes for his comms too. Sam nudges me. The outer fence gates are open and the van crawls up to a guard who waves it through as the driver waves his thanks. It slowly picks up speed and heads away, down the approach road, along the valley to our left.

We shrink backwards until, out of any possible sight of the camp, we jump up and start running like hell back through the wood. It's a lot easier with some light and I get to the cam fixed to the tree well before Sam. Two shots into its rear is enough to hear it still whirring madly as we both run past it back to the road. If they think it's a malfunction they'll take their time, if something else, the sky could be full of choppers in a few moments. We daren't pause, even for breath. Eventually, exhausted, our headlong rush through fallen tree branches, bracken and squelching mud, results in us standing by the road side. Not where our pick up point is but we don't need that. The approach road to the gatehouse forks some distance away down the valley. One branch heads towards the rural and miles of open country, and a white van easily spotted, the other doubles back towards urbia, where it's easier to get lost. You don't need a brain to make the choice. No more than a few seconds pass before we see a small white van in the distance. Sam stands nonchalantly by the roadside as I hide behind a tree ready to shoot if anything isn't as we expect. The van drives past then suddenly, it screeches to a halt and reverses.

There's no time for explanations or introductions. Sam and I jump in and I tell Zac to do a 180 and not to ask any questions. A few seconds later I tell him to stop and we all jump out, we get Mel from the rear. Sam plants a hurried kiss on my cheek and I leap into the driver's seat. Now I realise how long it is since I've driven. They disappear into the wood on the far side of the road, as I squeal round in a circle only pausing when I narrowly miss a tree. The van is swerving from one side to the other as I overcompensate and can't seem to co-ordinate forward speed and direction. A bend in the road catches me by surprise and I narrowly miss two trees and disappear into the scrub and bracken between them. Bushes and branches clatter against the windscreen as the van violently tips forward, sliding down through gullies. I glance off several tree stumps and I brace myself for the inevitable full on collision. There's a huge tree stump dead ahead and the van is heading straight for it but just before it hits, the mound and roots around the base twist the van sideways and I burst through onto open ground. My relief is short lived as the smooth wet ground steepens dramatically, making steering and braking useless. The van, with me in it, begins picking up speed. It turns and twists as it gets faster and faster. I'm caught in a helpless gradual spin and then catch a glimpse of what I am heading for. In the distance there is a solid line of sturdy trees, that are getting nearer very quickly. The speed of the van has reached its lethal maximum and is bouncing toward the tree line when it catches something and it twists so the van door is thrown open. At the same time I'm thrown across the seats towards the open door and the ground disappearing fast under the van. I catch hold of a seat to save myself as the van makes another turn this time the open door is on the trailing side and I throw myself out. I roll head over feet a few times and then roll until I stop with every part of me caked in mud.

Laying on my back I begin to wonder just how many bones are broken. It's quiet at least as I wait to find out which part of me hurts the most. I feel as sore as hell but nothing more than anything else. I sit up slowly expecting to see the van, a tangled wreck, having ploughed into the trees but it seems to have disappeared. The line of sturdy trees ahead is intact, no white mangled mess is wrapped smoking around any of them, and no gaping hole between them. I check to make sure I am not overlooking a lost limb or two and crawl to my knees. The greatest pain is where the pistol has dug into my ribs. On my feet I start to take a few steps ensuring blood isn't pumping all over the ground and when I lift a leg, an ankle still comes up with a foot on the end of it.

I start to limp slowly down the hillside following the trail of the disappearing van. Ahead, over the ragged line of solid looking trees, I hear the noise of urbia. The lights always aglow of The City are a good enough bearing and I limp towards them. No more than a few dozen paces my bewilderment is replaced by a cold sweat, way below me I can see what remains of the van, lying near the bottom of an old quarry. It has fallen down about the height of a ten storey building. It clings precariously to a narrow ledge, below which is an expanse of dark water that fills the quarry bottom. Even as I watch, the van twists, rolls onto its remaining wheel and slowly slides backwards. The wheel drops over the ledge, the van rocks, back and forth as if someone inside is laughing uncontrollably, then the front lifts, and the whole thing slides little by little until it drops quietly into the black water beneath. No sooner has it disappeared than the surface is glass again. I have a fear of drowning but I'm comforted by the fact that the fall would have killed me.

After an hour or so I had skirted the quarry and was continuing my journey back towards the lights of The City. I keep seeing Goodrich's face, his dirty glasses like a mask concealing what he's thinking, what he's planning. The word coincidence appears and a huge question mark, but there's worse, I can't separate what Sam and I have just experienced from something planned. Our part in it could not have been predicted, Sam by the road causing the van to stop, me insisting that everyone gets out, and the guard being shot. Now they are all hiding in woods and I'm wandering around with no real direction but The City lights, and no hiding place. 'Do nothing, but observe,' was Goodrich's instruction and he was reluctant that we should be present, maybe because if it didn't go well, Sam and I could've been caught up in the net. I have a dreadful feeling that I have just screwed up everything, they'll be picked up for sure and so will I. Goodnight Vienna.

Though it was only mid-afternoon the grey matter that constantly shrouds us makes it a permanent dusk except for rare occasions when some freak meteorological event makes it lift and brighten. The land here is waste, mainly what they call scrub. Low lying thorny bushes with sparse yellow flowers that are a mockery and the odd tree that hasn't been taken for fuel by an exec with the right paperwork. All trees that are still alive are tagged with the owners reference. The owner waits until their investment is sufficient and then it's felled usually around the Yuletide. Wood fires are the luxury centre piece of a themed room during the winter holiday, so I hear, apparently they add an ambience reminiscent of bygone days and the perfect accompaniment to a romantic evening. They don't need it for warmth, it's just for decoration and status, to others it's life and death. In a cold winter hundreds die of natural causes for want of warmth, more as a result of being damp. It is always damp, that is natural. Therefore it follows that dying of the damp is a natural cause.

I nearly trip over an old metal fence with rings where timber posts used to be. They've long since rotted away and the trail of tangled wire, fittings and rusting barbs, snake across the ground to the corner of an old farm building. Out of curiosity and tiredness, I decide to investigate and lay up for a while. I'm nearly there when a sound makes me hurry the remaining short distance and in through the doorless opening. A half dozen or so pod bikes buzz past about tree top level. They sweep down and do tight circles round anything or anyone if your caught in the open. These are probably Andy riders and are mean and independent. The corp that runs them has little control over them, unlike the ground based variety. What they drive are modified pods, they get them re-engineered, have the covers removed and screens reduced to a token, just enough to afford wind deflection when they crouch behind. They wear special helmets, some polished chrome, they favour being clad in black leather, the real stuff, and imagine themselves to be the reincarnation of bikers from way-back and call themselves 'angels'. Definitely not the type that invest, these types belong to 'Chapters' and specialise in weird initiation ceremonies and are just as likely to kill each other as anyone else, just for the hell of it.

I watch them buzz away into the distance but then to my alarm there's a buzzing close by. The sound of them overhead has masked one of them dropping down to check out the old building in which I hide. I can hear the motor droning down to the muffled click which tells me it's grounded and stable. All is silent. I back into the far corner away from the door. I hear a sound by the doorway, and taking the pistol out, I hold it in both hands, pointing it at the gaping doorway. I wait for a shape to appear and lean against the wall by a windowless opening. It's low enough to get through and see out of, but my attention is on the doorway and sounds that are coming from that direction. Like a cornered rat I brace myself ready for whatever might appear. To my horror I feel something cold slipping round my throat and pulling me back through the open window. A massive arm has slipped round my neck and now it tightens. I can feel my eyes beginning to bulge and my vision is blurring. My brain is being deprived of blood and in seconds I will be unconscious but then I hear somebody speak,

'Ash?'

That's what it sounded like.

I'm unable to speak but I croak and try to nod. The pressure is relaxed a little and I feel the blood surging through my head and reaching my brain again. In a floating kind of dizziness I hear a voice whispering close into my right ear,

    'Goodrich sent us. Wanna lift?'

CHAPTER 18

'How are they?' I ask Sam.

'Good. Well, they're glad to be out of Rehab. Mel's cut is looking better.'

'Cassy had no choice Sam.'

'I know, it just seemed so brutal. Before we could do or say anything she had her knife out and there was mum's blood everywhere.'

'And amongst it an implant that could have killed her and maybe led to us all.'

Cassy had been waiting for the van in which Zac and Mel has made their getaway so as to exchange vehicles and run checks on both Zac and Mel. She had seen the van stop and off load its passengers then drive erratically until it mysteriously took a dive into the trees. She then picked up Sam and her folks but not before some impromptu surgery. She located an implant inside Mel's left upper arm that Mel had no idea was there. Cassy did something to Mel and she dropped to the ground. Before Zac and Sam could find out what had happened, Cassy had cut open Mel's arm removed the implant and was holding her hand over the bleeding wound. A short distance away the implant was fizzing and popping like a fire cracker the way they are designed to do if tampered with. It had looked a lot worse than it was but Sam and Zac didn't know what to think. Sam lost it and had nearly found herself on the end of Cassy's knife as well.

'She could have told us what she was going to do. All Zac and I could see was . . . Anyway mum's okay now. How are you?'

'Carol says I could have another broken rib.'

She actually said it was bruised but the pain is the same and saying it is broken might get me more sympathy.

'We have to leave,' Sam continued without any acknowledgement of my discomfort. 'Carol says we have to lie low for a while, so I thought we should get back to the flat and see if we can sort out the Turin loose end. Goodrich gave me this.'

Sam shows me a pocket sized screen, the sort that kids use to watch vids and play games on. They are also phones which is alarming because any communication can give away the position of the user, and they are easily read and all are monitored for content.

'Goodrich said this is a secure system,' she says, which doesn't convince me.

'How?' I ask.

'Well, he said something about an old coding device called the Enigma.'

This doesn't surprise me as he is one and I tell her so.

'This works in the same way but rather than with codes that change at random so they can't be predicted, or something, this system does the same but with frequencies, I think.'

'You've got a real grip on this technology, haven't you?'

'Well,' she replies, 'I understood it when he told me. It's to do with the rapid and random changes of frequency that you transmit and receive on. Only the devices that are programmed to communicate know the random sequence so, anyway if it's good enough for him.' She shrugs her shoulders with an accepting sort of pout and an inclination of the head.

'Where's mine?'

'Goodrich said you'd want one, but you can't, there's not enough to go round. Besides you've got the pistol.'

'I'll swap you,' I tell her knowing that's a bad idea as I'm probably a better shot. It's just that having a connection is a sign of being further up the chain of command and I begin to wonder if I'm in Goodrich's bad books for not doing exactly as I was told, 'Observe, but do nothing.' Then I wonder what would have happened if I had done nothing.

'Okay,' I carry on, 'that's not a good idea. But it doesn't mean you get to make all the decisions.' She looks at me and I know she's going to take the piss.

'Ah, den. Does Ashie want a little go on Sammy's phonie?' She holds it out temptingly and I make a grab,

'Arrrgh! My rib,' I cry but she just smiles.

'Serves you right,' she says with not a sign of sympathy, 'I got the phone you got the pistol, capeesh?

'Yeh, all right.' I drag myself to my feet and she puts an arm around me, her other is holding the phone behind her back. We kiss. Along warm kiss that is heaven. I taste her breath and it is sweet and has the aroma of coffee, real coffee, and it is fresh and swim in it. Her lips are moist and I hold her tighter and tighter then,

'Arrrgh!' The pain from rib bursts into me and all romance is destroyed utterly. Nothing physical between us is going to happen while I have this agony.

We walk back across District 23 heading for 48 and then turn towards Turin's flat. We could head for Carol's but Sam wants to bring her brother up to date so he isn't alienated.

The streets that were filled with sellers are now deserted and there are several people sorting through the rubbish, the rotting produce and the empty packaging before it's cleared away. Sam picks up an apple but turns it over to see that it's been half eaten by something with two large front teeth.

Nearing the boundary between 23 and 48 both Sam and I begin to feel an air of depression. I ask Sam to tell me about Mel and Zac and she tells me that while I was recovering from my narrow escape, Sam and her folks spent some hours together and the events at Rehab got some explaining.

'At first,' Sam says, 'dad refused to co-operate but they made it clear what would happen first to Mel and then to him. They said his expertise was not so unique that somebody, or a team, couldn't replace him. He admitted that the bottom line was that they would rather be together and face whatever came. Working in the labs alongside each other might also give them opportunities together which they couldn't take advantage of separately.'

'Could he have known others were working on their escape?' I ask.

'No way. They had no idea that Gill, I mean Carol, was anything other than a friend, and they didn't know of any organisation that could help.'

'It keeps coming back to the same problem,' I point out, 'nobody knows that there are other people out there wanting the same thing and are prepared to help.'

'All they wanted to do was to get word out where they were and let Turin and me know that they were still alive.'

'So how did the escape happen?' I ask.

'Mel is allergic to certain foods so one of the things dad said was a condition of him continuing research was that she should have an appropriate diet. They said that they could do that in their kitchens but dad said that wasn't acceptable. They had to be certain of the ingredients otherwise Mel might die and they didn't trust the camp. Eventually they agreed to buy in the food and let Mel prepare it herself, so a delivery was arranged every few days.'

'And that was the van?'

'That was the van,' answered Sam, 'except it was a relief driver who had some device to keep his heart ticking regularly, so the company had warned the camp that they couldn't use the ray detector thing in case it stopped his heart.'

'Was this all a put up job?' I ask.

'I don't know, Goodrich won't say and neither will Zac. All Zac would tell me was that the driver was very co-operative while he was being tied up, but that might be because of his heart condition. He exchanged clothes and documents then made off with mum in the trolley covered with a cloth. The rest we saw.'

'But he didn't know how to operate the trolley lift?'

'Exactly,'

'And the driver?'

'He wriggled free, then collapsed in the doorway, I suppose.'

'He must have been in on it?'

'I doubt it, he was having a heart attack!'

'If Cassy was there that early it wouldn't have been for us,' I suggest.

'There was a tricky moment when they detected some additional weight.'

'Mel, I presume.'

'Yeah. Zac had removed some containers to compensate, but not enough in the time. He had to tell them he was returning some food from a previous delivery which was unacceptable.'

'Lucky they didn't want to look.'

'And lucky you're a good shot Ash.' She stops us, turns to me, clasps my head in her hands and gives me a long warm and blissful kiss. I'm helpless, intoxicated and I think this must be love.

We walk on in silence, arms linked like true lovers, oblivious to the world around, but not for long. The lack of people, colour, light and everything that has made our visit so enjoyable, is about to vanish. Ahead we see the sign that we are about to enter Urbia District 48 (D), beyond which all the streets are deserted, and all the people that live there, irresponsible. A silent gloom descends upon us, and we both give a deep sigh as we pass the sign. Already the air seems damper, the sky darker and the wind sharper. Within minutes we feel a chill as the sound of a siren screams close by as if to say, 'Welcome home', already we feel we are being watched. Our spirits sink as the paranoia returns like a weight and slows our pace to a drudge.

'C'mon,' I say, 'don't let's be down, we've got a job to do, and each other.' I hear it and it sounds a bit soppy but Sam nods and holds on tighter, so that was okay.

We check out the flat from a distance and give it a wide circumference, there are no lights visible but it's not yet dark. There's nothing unusual about the blinds or curtains, no obvious signs, we can't see anyone watching it so we make another circuit closer, and still all seems quiet. We sit down by the path that leads up to the entrance and listen for a few minutes. There are shows we can hear on the screens in every flat, nearly all the same show and suddenly Chad's impersonation of the host comes to mind. How long ago that feels now, I remember him and Meko, really cool Meko and I wonder if she still is.

Sam nudges me as a figure walks across the open space. His head inclines in our direction enough for him to see us watching, but his pace doesn't falter. Sam gives me a squeeze which I take as a signal to move and we do the same routine going up in the lift, and eventually arrive at the door to the flat. There's no sound, I look at Sam and she raises her eyebrows as if to say,

'Why not?'

She pushes the buttons and the door clicks open, we stand in the doorway in the darkness and allow the smells to give us a clue. Sometimes when a stranger is in a room you can smell it, smell the strangerness in the air. But the smell is stale and uninhabited. We enter and Sam goes to turn on the light.

'No!' I tell her. 'Just a moment.'

I go to the windows and look down from the flat at the surrounding buildings, at the shadows, places where I would hide. I feel something's not right. Here I am again, trusting my feelings but seeing nothing that confirms or denies.

'Well?' Sam joins me and we look out across to The City with its eternal light show. Then I see it. Or did I? Just below my vision, a shadow moved.

'Drink?' Sam interrupts my concentration.

'Yeh, got any coffee, real coffee?'

'This isn't the Honkey Moon, unfortunately. We need to go to the store,' she tells me.

'Why?' I ask not really paying attention, still looking, feeling.

'Food, actually. There's nothing here.'

'Good.'

'Really?' Sam replies.

'Yes, it's good we didn't put the light on, and good we are going out. It will put my mind to rest.'

We hadn't even taken off our coats and we were back down on the ground floor.

'Stop,' I said, 'you go ahead, I'll follow. We'll see if there's anyone interested in us.'

Sam walked off in the direction of the store, I waited as long as I could keep her in view then sprinted off on a parallel route. I could see her every now and again but after a while I had to join the same road. There was nothing. She turns into the well-lit forecourt of the store and I wait in the shadows. Two people come out of the store and walk in the opposite direction, soon after Sam comes out, casually heading for home. She walks past my shadow,

'Want a good time, love?' she whispers as she walks past, but my eyes are on the store and someone avoiding the light on the opposite side of the road. I glimpse them, then they're gone. I'm just about to step out to get a better view when I sense someone close and I freeze. Almost silently a figure passes me, walking briskly, hooded, dodging from shadow to shadow in the gloom. It disappears for a few seconds then reappears briefly in enough light to be sure there is someone. Then they disappear again and I wonder if I'm are imagining it. Now I follow, not the same route but close enough to use the same cover. They are gaining on Sam and will get to her before she gets to the flats. I quicken my pace just as they disappear and I stop in case they have stopped. Then there's a scream and I throw all caution away and run towards Sam who is rolling over and over on the ground trying to free herself from an attacker. As I get to her I pull out the pistol and aim waiting for a clean target, Sam frees herself and I squeeze the trigger. The last trigger stage is about to be engaged when a flash of something familiar moves my aim as the pistol fires. The charge hits the ground and the resulting shock is enough to still the hooded figure as Sam is about to launch a kick at his head,

'No!' I scream. She stops, then stands motionless over the figure as shocked and surprised as I am.

Back at the flat, Sam's anger is a revelation,

'You fucking idiot! You fucking, fucking idiot! What the fuck do you think you were doing? Don't you realise Ash nearly killed you?' She paces the floor of the flat with her hands alternately flying about demonstrating her anger then clutching her head thinking of what might have been, what nearly was.

'If it wasn't for those boots . . . ' I say this but let it drift away before I paint the picture, the one we all keep painting for ourselves.

Turin goes into his room to change while Sam and I make some coffee. Then we hear the shower running.

'What do we say?' she asks me.

'Tomorrow,' I suggest, 'if he asks us directly we'll tell him we've had some news and they're safe. That's all. We can't mention Goodrich yet, not until we're sure he's safe.'

'Do you think he might have been followed?'

'I don't know. The more we can find out what he's been doing the better. Let things settle, and we'll tell him tomorrow. If it's all okay, set up a meeting with Goodrich.'

Turin returns after his shower and sits with his head in his hands. I walk round from the kitchen and give him a coffee. The energy of the incident keeps peaking, we try to calm ourselves then reality kicks in and we are back on the street. The vision of a dead Turin bleeding from every orifice is a still frame that keeps popping up as the film rolls on. It's a jolt, breath becomes short and our anger rises again. I look out of the window, trying to convince myself I hadn't nearly killed Turin. His coat is lying by the door in a heap, stained and has the stench about it like street sleepers have. Sam comes to a rest, energy spent, she too sits head in hands. I put her coffee down by her side and return to my window and look elsewhere.

Turin tries to speak but instead just clears his throat. We wait, Sam and I, we are owed an explanation.

He says that he has been sorting things out, things only he could do, it's vague and lacks details. Details maybe he can't tell us, it makes everything sound false; I know the feeling. On his return he needed to make sure that the flat was clean, not being watched, he must have been the figure I sensed was about. He knew that if Sam moved, anyone watching would follow. So he followed Sam to the store and knew someone was following her. His plan was to catch up with her, silently pull her into the shadows, tell her she was being followed and then wait, and the two of them would catch her follower, which was me.

The business with Chad has diminished him, how could I introduce him into Goodrich's network? You can't change people, he'd be too secretive, independent, risk everything, everyone. He'd always be one of Goodrich's loose ends.

We are eating in silence. Sam has heated up the casserole she made and seems better than before. Turin finishes first, leans back and without looking at anyone, tells us he has found out things about Chad.

Both Sam and I look at him, but it's as if he is talking to the air and looking at us is too personal.

'I've been tracing some old contacts, people I haven't seen for years, those that knew us both. Some had stayed in touch with Chad, or at least tried.'

Turin cleared his throat, spoke with more clarity, prepared to share more,

'If what we found out from his gear was true, I needed to understand what had happened to Chad. They said they'd seen less of him and he'd become more difficult to communicate with. When you're with someone, you don't always see the gradual change. No one has seen him since we were last at the cellar.'

Sometime after the 'Three Car Trick', Chad had found ways of getting the materials they wanted to raise them to another level, Chad said. He'd found someone who shared their goals, who could afford to bankroll the group, make a difference. The backer's identity had to remain secret at all costs, not even he, Chad, knew their real identity, the domino theory was quoted constantly.

Turin had found the cellar, formed the group and brought in Meko. Chad would identify the targets, do the planning, obtain what was required. Turin did personnel, logistics and everything else. Turin said he was always curious about Chad's contacts but he understood the need for secrecy. What did it matter so long as their aims were the same and Chad always said they were. There was to be no questions, that was the deal.

The darkening evening prompts Sam to turn on a lamp which doesn't make Turin's drawn appearance any better. He knew about Chad hacking into 4U's vaults, at that time they shared details. Chad used to be funny, loud, always doing impressions, sometimes a pain. It was not long after that Chad quietened down. Turin thought it was because Chad was in a relationship, had responsibilities, getting older. Looking back, it must have been when they had caught up with him. 4U had withdrawn the reward because they said, 'The systems had been upgraded and the perpetrator had gone to ground.' The truth was that they had found him.

Sam and I look at Turin for clarification and he continues,

'Chad had a daughter. Both his daughter and partner moved away about when the group started. It was a plain van that moved them and a neighbour remembers seeing a 4U jacket in the cab. I guess they were making sure Chad did as he was told.'

There's a pause while Sam goes into the kitchen to get us all a drink. When she gets there she takes a long look at her brother,

'Do you think it was them that blew up the cellar?' she asks.

Turin is reluctant to answer but I see dominoes. Through Chad, Turin then Meko, then me and maybe even Carl and Jean. It may not have been the stray dog that caught their attention, but me. It's a thought that makes me go cold.

Turin's head falls against the back of the sofa and Sam suggests he lie down on his bed. She takes him through then returns and sits by my side and we are quite for a while.

'What if Chad had found out what kind of work Zac was doing,' I ask, 'maybe he tried to do a deal. If he was able to get research and test data for 4U from CUpal, that would have been something to bargain with to get his family back.'

Sam is not sure.

'If they approached Chad and asked if he could get that information they might do a deal. If Chad suggested it, they'd just tell him to do it if he wanted his family to stay alive.'

'Good point. But if that did happen, for a few moments he thought he had it, then it was all gone.'

'Then he thinks he gets it all back on the pills.'

'Which I saw him exchange with the guys in the limo.'

Sam drinks her coffee,

'Maybe that's when they decided to blow up the cellar.'

'Why?' I ask.

'They didn't need the group anymore. They'd used the group to blow up CUpal execs, then Chad does a deal to free his family in exchange for giving them Zac's research. If the data was what they thought it was, CUpal wouldn't have an advantage. No need to blow up execs just to see their share price drop each time.'

'When the pills turned out to be blank, they still needed Chad, so they postponed disposing of us all until they were sure they had what they wanted.'

'When that happened, Goodnight Vienna!'

Then there's a moment when I think of Meko and wonder if she made it.

'Meko?' Sam says.

'I wonder.'

'Do you think Chad tried to warn her?'

'Yes, and Ma Brown. The cellar was bugged right? Maybe every word that Chad said, they heard. Maybe a condition was having the palmer with him, hear what he said, know where he was. Maybe if he'd said anything we'd all gone up in smoke. Maybe his family too.'

'That's a lot of maybes,' Sam points out.

'Maybe it is, but they had to make sure the pills were genuine first and had on them what they wanted. There's another thing, when CUpal's vault alarm was triggered, even if they knew Zac had nothing to do with it they could have decided he was too valuable to risk. I think Mel and Zac were taken into, what's it called?'

'Protective custardy.'

'Yes, that's it.'

'In Rehab, I don't think there's much difference.' Sam says, 'besides they probably knew he wasn't totally 'on side' and couldn't be trusted in the long term. Perhaps they wanted to make sure he didn't take his knowledge to someone else.'

Later that night we have something to eat. Turin is looking more like himself, but he is quiet, preoccupied.

We watch the small screen in Turin's flat. It's reporting a minor disturbance in North London following the shooting of a man by the LEOs, nothing unusual. In the background the flash of a banner proclaiming the dead man was unarmed, it's soon torn off the holder who is bundled into an andywagon. The commentary goes on about proving that enemies of the state are hidden in the most innocent of urban districts and no effort will be spared in rooting them out. Every disturbance will give them more reasons to brutalise anyone they don't like the look, or sound of. It's the usual consequence, any event that can be used as an excuse to abuse, intimidate, or instil fear into people, irrespective of their guilt or innocence. The innocent are only that because their guilt has not yet been discovered.

Sam walks over and sits by Turin.

'And all this started with the chopper incident?' she asks.

'We did something that was so good, so smart it became folklore, a legend. We made 4U look stupid and that hit their value and that, no corp will ever forget, or forgive. A chopper can easily be replaced, a few human lives, even easier. Reputation is something all together different. Chad and I made them look like fools, they were never going to rest until they had killed us, or as good as, and made sure everyone knew.'

'What now?' Sam asks.

'I don't know,' Turin replies, 'those lists we saw, detonators, explosives, 4U were supplying everything. All the time I thought we were fighting for a new order, we were just unpaid assassins.'

I ask him if there is any way we can find out about Meko but he shrugs his shoulders. He pauses for a moment, looks at us both, then a sadness overcomes him which only he can disturb,

'Meko and I go back a long way. What you don't know is how much I felt for her, and I think, her for me. We couldn't take it further, it would compromise the kind of security we insisted, Chad insisted. If anyone needs to know what's happened to Meko, it's me.'

Sam asks him if we are really safe in the flat.

Turin replies with a less than comforting shrug, but then continues,

'I don't think any of us knew about Cilla, Chad's partner, and Mia their child. Some people there knew them and remembered me and the 'Three Car Trick'. They knew that Chad had moved away and wanted to help, they liked him, liked his silly impressions, 'Correctacorrecta' they would say. They found out for me where they had moved to, that's where I found this.'

Turin dug into an inside pocket and drew out the small black notebook.

'Remember how he wrote stuff down with that weird pencil? This is his book, it's all in here. When I got to their place the door was open and everything inside had been trashed. Someone had been through the whole place and nothing had been left intact. All the tech stuff, drives and storage had all gone, anything on the walls had been torn off, anything on the floor had been ripped up. Anything standing had been reduced to a pile of splinters in the middle of each room. In the bedroom, the mattress had been torn apart and bits of the bed were thrown in a corner by a pile of woman's underwear that some weirdo had shat on. Behind the door was an upturned pot and peeping out of the dust was a corner of this notebook. Whether he meant to leave it behind or not, I don't know, but these notes help make sense of what we've heard and what we already know.'

'I would like to think Turin,' I say to him, 'that Chad wants us to know what has been going on. Remember 'TINA'? There is no alternative,'

Turin relaxes against the sofa and closes his eyes. Sam gets up and takes his bedding into his room and returns with her stuff and places it next to Turin who opens his eyes. He then gets up and goes into his bedroom.

Sam puts his clothes in to wash then she joins me on my sofa. She opens up the player, takes out the cell, turns it round and it activates Enigma. She reports that Turin is alive and with us at the flat and we have good information about Chad. She asks if there are any instructions. The reply says that we are all to rest and contact will be made in the morning.

'That suits us fine,' she says and we make up our separate beds and fall into them as if they are real beds and the most comfortable ones we can imagine. Sam is the first to fall asleep and for a while I listen to her breathing, until I too am gone.

The dull morning light it still enough to shun and I turn over on my sofa and pull my bedding up. My ribs still hurt and strange dreams fade as soon as I try to remember them. Morning, as it usually does, has come too soon. I sense movement in the room but I keep my eyes closed in case it's Sam wandering about with hardly anything on. I'm desperate to open them, but I still have Goodrich's warning about involvement and how it can cloud judgement. It's too late for that.

Only having oneself to worry about is enough, sometimes more than. I know that Sam is more than capable of looking after herself, but if you care you can't help but want to protect, I'm engineered that way, I can't help it; I'm genetically programmed.

I hear Sam pouring coffee. Three mugs, one for each of us, and I am reminded that we have to decide what to do about Turin, it's difficult to know if he could fit in. I will get Sam to talk to Goodrich on Enigma, see what he thinks.

Sam puts a warm drink on the floor next to me and then one by her sofa, then she takes the third into Turin's room. As I stretch and open my eyes as much as they want to, I hear her knock on his bedroom door. She knocks again and calls his name telling him she has a coffee, but there is still no answer. Suspecting something is not right I sit up draped in my bedding and see Sam return with the coffee, she looks concerned,

'Turin's gone.'

She has a piece of paper torn from Chad's notebook which she hands to me. On it is written,

'Had to leave. I know now what I have to do. Look after each other. Turin.'

'What do you think it means?' I ask Sam. She thinks for a minute, re-reading the message.

'Chad?' Is her suggestion. 'What do you think? You know how he works, I just know him as a brother.'

I tell her I don't know but I try to put myself into his shoes, into his Muskrat boots. I don't come up anything that might put her mind at rest, so I agree,

'Yes,' I say, ' he'd be looking for Chad.'

'What do you think he'll do when he finds him?'

I'm just about to answer when her screen player starts streaming a movie, the sign that someone was trying to reach us. She stops the movie, removes the back, turns the cell around and the screen starts scrolling.

'It's Carol,' Sam relates, 'we are to meet at hers.'

Then she says, 'Ah!' which I take to mean there's a problem so I ask her,

'What?'

Sam reads for a bit, replies and shuts down. So I ask her,

'Well?'

'They suggested bringing Turin.'

'Ah!' I say. 'We'll go anyway. We can tell them everything about Chad.'

Sam looks at me,

'Goodrich won't like Turin going off on his own will he?'

'Probably not.' I tell her. ' I also think that the sooner we leave here the better. They may be following Turin, so they may soon want to have a look here.'

'Like they did at Chad's?'

'It's possible.'

I think it's more than possible and suddenly the realisation that they may be even now be coming up the stairs and the lifts, checking rooms and breaking down doors makes me want to run, and take Sam with me.

We look around the flat and realise we have some work to do before we can leave.

'We had better take all the tech stuff, or at least destroy it if we can't carry it.'

We start in Turin's bedroom and Sam begins to find a reason she can't possibly leave anything. By the time we have made a pile of the personal stuff that Sam wants to take, and all the tech stuff which is essential, we will be walking through the streets looking like we are moving house.

Loaded down with stuff in this district will be a temptation no officer could resist. Then as a bonus there's the full body search which is an ever present threat to both sexes. They are permitted to use whatever method they choose to ensure orifices are not being used to conceal or traffic substances. The fear of what might happen to Sam in such circumstances makes me glad I am carrying a pistol, although that in itself is a liability.

I realise that after having lost most of her stuff in the explosion and the fire that resulted, we now might have to leave the rest of her stuff behind. Not everything precious is stored in the clouds.

'We have to get rid of stuff that is incriminating,' I tell her, 'Stuff that might be of use we have to take with us, and then if there is any room left, personal stuff.' I say this in hope rather than expectation, trying to separate a girl from her stuff is impossible, so I give up.

Besides the bag which is always with me, there is little at the flat I need to take. I examine the kitchen area and cupboards for food stuffs it would be a shame to leave, but find little that Carol won't already have. As I am doing this I hear a splintering sound followed by several cracks, I look towards the source of the noise to see Sam is breaking into the processor,

'Whoa!' I shout, 'We need that!'

'I know,' she replies, but carries on regardless.

'Then why are you breaking it?' I approach her to stop any further destruction, but too late, the system suddenly disintegrates into a pile of circuitry, fine wires and other bits of electrickery.

'Sam! I needed that to give to Goodrich!'

Sam holds up some shiny black capsule that looks like a many legged insect.

'That's all we need.'

'What about the rest?'

'We can burn it, then it'll look like we've destroyed it and they won't need to look any further.'

'All right, smart arse, but tell me next time.'

With that she picks up the photo album and waves it at me.

'Yes, all right.'

We are about done. I gesture to Sam and she turns off lamps so my silhouette can't be seen. Thinking that we are making our way out, I look about to see if anyone breaks cover. It's the usual procedure like taking the stairs to a different floor, before taking the lift. There's no feeling of anything other than an eerie tranquility as if everyone is waiting, but not watching.

Opening the door to the corridor is the same as entering the flat. There's a musty smell of condensation, rat piss, and food from somewhere above, nothing clean or military.

To the rear of the block is an area where trash, too rigid to pipe away, gets dumped. There is a bizarre collection of furniture, set out like some one's living room. It's arranged in the same way that it might have been when it was surrounded with walls, a floor and a ceiling. The rusting remains of an old steel drum, not worth recycling, serves as a fire place where anything that will burn gathers the street sleepers around it for warmth, the evidence of last night's revelry still smoulders. We remove several rat kebabs that are left overs, and lay on some paper documents which begin to smoulder then flare and engulf the techie stuff as we put it into the flames. It spits and crackles, small blue and green flames burst, then something pops, fizzes and whee's, like a miniature display. Four or five rats suddenly jump out from somewhere getting hot, and dive into a hole in a sofa, it's not good for them either to be caught out in the open. I peep out from my hood at Sam who peeps out from her hood at me, we stand dressed in the dull, lifeless tones we choose so as not to stand out. We too move like grey shadows from cover to cover, little more than rats seeking shelter that doesn't get too hot.

We load our sacks onto our shoulders, walk away across the open space, then by the Burning Bush we stop and look around. There is a pale blue thread of smoke rising up to the right of the block. The two elements, water and fire, seem to punctuate life's chapters. Whether it's the destructive power of one or the cleansing nature of the other. Looking back they seem to link one stage to another, and always herald change.

CHAPTER 19

There's a nervous energy about Carol as she points us through to the back room. She runs up the stairs saying she needs to get some things before we all leave. Sam and I say nothing but have a silent conversation with questioning looks and shrugging shoulders while we wait for Carol to join us. When she does, she looks at us, from one to the other, as if we are party to some secret.

'You've not heard?'

We both shake our heads but with expressions that ask for more.

'Something has happened,' she says.

On the basis that things often do, I ask her to be more explicit.

'There's movement in North London.'

'Much?' I ask.

'We know a few hundred but it could be a few thousand, but it could be more, lots more.'

'I'm guessing that because you use the word 'movement' that this is a bit different from the usual half-hearted demo?'

'Yes, it looks more organised. Prof thinks we need to be there.'

She turns and puts things into a sack.

'Hang on!' I say, 'I thought we were into careful planning and networking, making contacts over years, building relationships, low profile stuff. Suddenly we are off on a demo.'

'And if it turns out to be more?'

Sam gives me a look and I can see I'm outnumbered,

'Good point. Let's go!'

We follow Carol into her front room. She parts the heavy curtains so she can see the road.

'Cassy is picking us up in her van,' she says looking out as far as she can in the direction she expects Cassy to appear. 'We have to work with the people, neither of us can do this on our own.'

I agree with her, and it was what Goodrich was saying, a few people shouting is just a protest, but a few thousand doing the same is a political movement. It's the hope of it being the latter which has alerted Prof. If it doesn't grow it will be just another riot by mindless hooligans and no one need worry. If it does, then we could be on the brink of something incredible. I seem to remember something about there being a tide in affairs and if taken at the right time, leads on to greater things; I hope that this is the tide.

I take the pistol out of my sack.

'Should I take this?'

Carol turns, looks at it then turns back to the window.

'Better not. Prof will have everything we need and on the way there they'll be check points.'

Sam looks alarmed.

'That's a good sign,' Carol tells her, 'check points means they're taking it seriously, no check points, no serious threat. Here she is.'

Outside is what looks like a laundry van, the writing on the side makes me smile and I point it out to Sam. It should read, 'Stay Bright', but the 'y' has been worn out and now reads 'Stab right' and reminds me of Cassy's fondness for knives.

Sam and I lay down in the back of the van and prepare to cover ourselves in stuffed laundry bags if there's an emergency. A laundry van is excellent cover and we can get within a mile or so without suspicion, especially as both Carol and Cassy now have laundry uniforms on.

While Cassy drives, Carol tells us that a few days ago a man was shot by the LEOs, both Sam and I wonder what is so unusual about that? Then Carol tells us that this has happened in a prosperous district where everyone toes the line, does what they are told to do without question. In all respects, Urbia District 4 in North London, is the perfect example of a law abiding community. So I ask Carol what went wrong, and she replies the LEOs didn't bother to inform the family that a member of theirs had just been shot. When they complained, they were told no senior officer was available to talk to them. The disrespect and pain that the family suffered, stirred friends and supporters into action, and a few gathered to protest. The LEOs responded with their usual heavy handiness and a young girl was struck and injured. Eventually after a lot of running battles between the police and locals, andys were drafted in. The LEOs claim he was armed, as they always do, but there were enough witnesses to prove he wasn't.

Carol complains that even when the people do as they are told, no Qs, they are still abused; it adds injury to insult. She tells us that builds anger and resentment until they have nothing to lose, even their own lives are worthless.

I feel this is normal.

While we are travelling, Carol tells us that it's quiet at the moment but they know that there are people coming into the area from other districts. There is definitely something building, LEOs are taking up positions all over the area so they've received intelligence too. There are a number of signs, not just one incident, but others too and preparation, this is what has made it different, and why Prof has called it.

Sam is aware that LEOs shooting to kill unarmed citizens is hardly news, even cowed people can become desperate enough to think the risk is worth taking. From under the laundry she makes a gap so she can be heard and says she can't remember this happening in a regulated district before, so it must be different,

Carol agrees, then says it's why we need to judge the commitment of people and the nature of the protest.

'We need to see if behind the frustration and anger there is any structure, a line of command, tactics, anything which can be organised into a real threat. It's no good if people are going to be on the streets just to break a few windows then go home.

'So this could be it, really?' Sam asks.

'Really?' Carol replies. 'Last night there were about three or four thousand people of all ages on the streets. There were a few skirmishes and some looting but most were prepared for a serious engagement. We've heard that some groups from 9 have been drifting across the boundary in small parties. We think that other groups will have reps here from other cities, even abroad.'

Sam points out that it sounds more like a rally, then Carol says,

'Our info is from official sources that we've intercepted, so we know what the LEOs know. Andys are being deployed at strategic positions so that proves they are taking it seriously, which is why we should. LEOs might handle minor disturbances, but the seriousness of a situation can be judged by the amount of andy involvement.'

I wonder about Turin and wish he could be a part of this, seeing how people working together can do anything.

I can see Sam is not comfortable.

'We don't need to get too involved,' I tell her, 'we just need to observe, maybe make contact with anyone who looks as if they have responsibility.' She is not convinced.

'What about the wardens?' I ask Carol.

'That's who we've got to watch out for. They'll have a better idea of the terrain, they'll know the streets, and they'll be running the check points. It's too soon to search every vehicle, there is still too much traffic. That's why we need to be there before it gets shut down.'

Sam asks her if she thinks there may be a curfew.

'Not yet,' Carol replies, 'too much impact on business to do it on the threat of unrest, they need it to start affecting business before they'll think of safeguarding lives. They'll want to bring all the troublemakers, as they see them, out into the open where they can have go at them. A curfew affects business, takes a lot of enforcing and the people you really want are getting a well-earned rest in store for the next day.'

'Check it,' says Cassy as she nods in the direction of a cross roads ahead, beyond which there are several warden's patrol vehicles parked.

Carol stabs a finger toward a parking bay.

'Hand me one of those blue bags.' Carol says nodding in the direction of some of the laundry, I hand it to her as Cassy pulls the van in. Carol gets out and takes the blue Stay Bright bag stuffed with clean laundry with her. She walks over the cross roads, nonchalantly past the warden's parked vehicles, then disappears into a doorway. She's a few moments and then appears with a different bag, a yellow one, just as stuffed, and I wonder how this could have been arranged? Carol walks back round the other side of the wardens and back to the van. She gets in and throws the yellow bag on top of the blue ones we are under.

'Take a right,' she tells Cassy, then turns to us, 'We'll find another route to get closer. They're monitoring cars with some device, I don't know how sensitive it is, you might be safe but it's not worth the risk.'

'Where did the yellow bag come from?' I ask Carol.

'It's in the blue bag, just change them round.' She says with a smile.

'Durr!' Goes Sam, whose support in these things can always be relied upon.

Three attempts and each time we spot wardens on the main routes. Presuming they are using similar gear, we take a maze of side streets. Eventually we arrive at a car park surrounded by several housing blocks from where we can walk. We park where we've spotted other working vehicles so ours won't be out of place, it'll look like someone on a shift or a part timer. We all get out and Cassy and Carol exchange their uniforms for day clothes. If this was in 48 the wardens would clock the van within a few hours and then soon after it would be gone. I can't help but think it's risky, it's in the blood, I won't believe it's still here until we return; if we return.

Cassy leads the way and we walk towards the commercial centre. We walk past a themed mall that houses all the Touchyfeelies under one roof.

Cassy stops on a corner. We stop too and look into a shop window full of sex aids and several screens demonstrating their use. Across the street is a small Statebank outlet next to which are two money shops. The rest of the street is full of similar outlets, investor agents, power and supply brokers, finance advisors and share exchanges. The local Exec Club sits proudly on a corner and then there are corps rep shops scattered around. On our side, the pillared entrance to an Interbank Mall takes up most of it. This will be a target area as it most accurately reflects the aspect of the establishment that people hate. We move on nonchalantly like bemused visitors from the rural, Cassy with Carol, and Sam and I. Sam stops to look in a jewellers, through the bars we can see down an alley way reflected in a mirrored display. There are several andys sat on the ground leaning their backs against a shop wall, parked up the service entrance is their vehicle. They have a variety of vehicles to choose from depending on the damage they wish to inflict, this one has a mounted turret fitted with an assortment of crowd pleasers. The most obvious is the water cannon, but there are gas launchers, two baton guns and a device that fires capsules. The capsules can contain anything from a harmless dye, so you can be traced later, to a substance that causes paralysis should it come into contact with skin. Interestingly, it is a synthetic version of a spider venom, if any of it gets into the mouth it has a habit of paralysing the throat and lungs, suffocating the victim. This is not something I share with Sam. She and I move on not wanting to attract any attention. Several jewellery outlets, symbolic of conspicuous wealth are here, and by the mustering of other andys nearby, they think this area will be a target too. On a corner Sam and I catch up with Carol and Cassy, we haven't seen any evidence of last night's disturbance. We all walk on and turn several corners where most outlets seem to be open and operating normally. Then we pass a fancy frontage advertising high end style footwear that is boarded up, the windows having been smashed and we presume missing some, if not all, of its prestigious stock. It's not high on the list of political targets so we reckon it was just opportunism. A few doors away there's a shop displaying cheap footwear and corp workwear, it's open for business, so much for mindless hooliganism. Another shop close by is a burnt out shell being cleaned up. We turn a corner and nearly walk into the rear of an andywagon, these are the armoured vehicles that the andys travel in, about twenty of them at a time. The rear lays down and forms a ramp so they can all rush out. There are no windows and the inside of the wagon is pretty bare and uncomfortable so when they are released from their incarceration they are already pissed off. After that we see more of them with their commanders standing around chatting casually with other LEOs, arms folded as if they are just waiting for a game to start; it's a game to them. In one wagon there are a few andys cleaning weapons, charging up stun rods and battens. They have their head sets off and look the mean fuckers they are. You can imagine each of them has a fondness for a particular kind of sadism, without their implants not even their controllers would be safe. When they are directed they are in harness and their state licensed brutality is more focussed, more efficient. You don't often see an androbot without the helmet and visor, it's a human face but one that seems born to violence and sadism, and the corps have found a use for it.

    Suddenly overhead a whining hum reaches a scraping crescendo. We dive into a doorway as the sound of smashing glass above us is followed by a brief waterfall of glistening shards crashing onto the street between us and the andys. They leap about cursing a pod that we see drifting unsteadily away over the buildings on the other side of the street. One andy grabs a pistol, fits a long sight to it and takes aim but he's too late and the pod is lost amid roofs, filtration boxes and disused chimneys. Another pod is above us now, but some distance higher, making for the same direction. They are surveillance bots spying out the area and seeing where there are people and seeing how easy a target they make.

We return to our task and decide to split up taking different sides of the street in case, thinking we are a foursome, the andys call us in for a closer look. If they did we'd probably make a run for it and start the riot we are here to observe. I make this observation to Sam and all she says is,

'Bring it on.'

I'm not sure I find that encouraging or a cause for concern. We get a glance from Carol and a nod in our direction and we look down a side street. There's a doorway just closing that conceals a small crowd of what looks like ordinary peeps, in hoods mainly. Someone has just gone inside and the door shuts quickly. It seems to confirm the suspicions that troops are building up on both sides.

For the next hour or so we criss-cross the area, then meet up in a coffee bar serving real coffee from one of those elaborate machines. We don't sit too near the window so our curiosity isn't obvious and we can talk as a foursome, we watch everything while sharing our thoughts and observations. Carol is the first to point out something that has occurred to us all.

'We're not the only visitors from out of town,' she says, 'and it looks like there are groups here in support.'

If that is true, it's extraordinary and another reason why this event might be different from those in the past. I keep thinking that Turin should be here to see it.

We are just about to order some drinks when there is a solid ground shuddering thump. I know what it is and grab Sam by her shoulders, wrap myself round her and fall to the floor. Cassy pulls at a startled Carol just in time as the window glass splits, opens up and allows a deafening blast of heat to push us, and the furniture, across the floor towards the back of the bar. Then it sucks. We are drawn towards the window as the glass which appears suspended in mid-air is sucked out, rising into the street taking with it napkins and table cloths as if in some kind of bizarre tornado. Then as if in slow motion, everything drops to the ground silently, because I cannot hear, and what is not broken in the air is then dashed to a thousand pieces when it lands, if it can be. These are glimpses that I piece together to explain the events of a few seconds. Each glimpse and feeling is expanded into time so as to explain and understand it but, like a dream, it's doubtful that it takes any time at all.

I feel someone fighting me and realise I am still clinging on to Sam and my protection has become her suffocation. I locate her beneath my coat and the table cloth that was caught up in our dive for cover, she comes up gasping for air and clings on to me as I remove a spoon from her hair. She wipes away the dust from her mouth with a dustier sleeve, then spits away the rest. She says something which sounds like a neighbour's drum solo through a brick wall, and I point to my ear and shake my head. We are sitting on the floor against the front of the bar as the owner unsteadily picks her way past us. Above, the ceiling looks intact, the light fitting hangs crookedly but maybe it's been like that forever, now it has a good reason. The upturned table in front of us moves as Carol emerges, blinking away some grit, Cassy pops up too surveying her arm which is bleeding. She picks out a small splinter of glass, sucks a good mouthful of blood from the wound and pinches its sides together trying to stop any further leakage. As she spits out another mouthful, Carol tears a strip from a table cloth and binds Cassy's wound as it dribbles red again. Other than the window, any furniture that wasn't bolted down and an assortment of table linen, the bar is mainly intact. Even the chairs when we've put them back on their legs have only suffered a few scratches.

Outside the owner stands looking across the street to where the andys were stationed. We join her rescuing her tablecloths, napkins and menus and discretely watch the andys that have just arrived, picking over the debris with their batons. Near me an andy headset lies in the gutter revealing its inner workings, the head up display is scrolling out of control and the word 'Alert' flashes intermittently. There's a strange lining inside the helmet, a light brown, woven, ragged fabric, out of place and different in character to a black helmet. Then I realise what it is. I wonder that there was at least one andy with enough self-awareness to want to hide his baldness.

There are smouldering bits of tunic everywhere. The nearer one draws to the source of the event the more they are filled with unrecognisable bits of flesh, until I see a gauntlet with an intact arm. Now there is a line of andys with their rods held horizontally, making a moving barrier that approaches, while others behind them pick up pieces and place them into carts borrowed from a nearby store. There's a resigned, matter of fact attitude to the task, indicating minds that have been turned off to the suffering of humans, however grotesque; even those like themselves. I look at the carts dripping with blood. I look at the andys mindlessly carrying out someone else's commands, and I see the wig. I wonder how deep one has to dig to retrieve what's left of the father, the brother, the son, the boyfriend or the lover.

Sam tugs at my arm,

'Do you think we should stay around here for when things get busy later?'

Her words sound as if she's speaking underwater and her expression tells me she'd rather not be where it gets busy. I visit again that dilemma of Sam's safety and what needs to be done that may harm her. Goodrich, as ever, is right, there is no room for emotions but the corporate world that we live in has no emotions, is amotional, and we have had enough of that world.

'We need to split up.' I tell them, 'It's not good the four of us to be seen together and we need to be aware of any build up.' I say this but I'm also thinking that we might all have been killed, and splitting up might be safer.

'Okay,' says Carol. She turns to Sam, 'you've got your player?'

'Yes,' Sam replies.

Then Carol tells her she'll send her a signal which will be a game show prize money update. That will be the signal to communicate through Enigma. On the player their position will be 'Mr. Fu's Sushi' if we need to find them. Ours will be 'Sublimetime'. It's a sex shop she tells us.

'Nice,' Sam replies.

We split up giving the impression we are acquaintances thrown together by circumstances, that are now going our separate ways. The street behind us is crawling with andys. A violent breeze suddenly picks up, I look at Sam who is clutching her head and gazing skywards. A huge four rotor chopper is darkening the sky and straps are descending on cables ready to haul up and away one of the andy's mangled wagons. The andys fix on the strops, the winches take up the slack and as the chopper rises and turns, its payload does too. The rear of the wagon, torn and twisted, swings into view as it rises. Bodies lie piled up inside, maybe eight or ten that I can see, with four or five carts strapped in with their gruesome contents. I watch it float away, wondering if they'll bother to put the pieces back together before disposal. Then I see it, an andy's head lolls from side to side, pale, helmet-less, and bald.

Sam and I move away. Having cleared most of the debris, the andy cordon has retreated and as expected, reinforcements are arriving. There's a team with red flashes on their bulky tunics that are waving detectors, they walk like cheap robots made from a kiddies kit. Their bulk is to protect them from explosions in case their detectors detonate a device. The detector squad check out an area then signal to a commander who then gesticulates and a half dozen or so andys file along the pavement and take up a position. There's something familiar about the commander, the way he moves, moves his arms. Moves her arms. She was at the house. Suddenly a wave of stuff piles in and I clutch onto Sam who takes me into a shop doorway, I sit on the ground as the sickness overwhelms me. Sam lifts my head and looks into my face and mouths some words.

'Speak up, I can't hear!' I mumble.

'I thought you were deaf!' She says.

'What?'

'I thought . .' She is stopped by my smile and retaliates by digging me in my ribs which doesn't help.

'I feel sick.' I tell her.

'Probably from the explosion,' she says but I shake my head.

'I've just seen someone I recognise, from the house.'

'Which house?'

I tell her that the commander out there in the street, is the controller who blew up the house where I lived, trying to kill Carl, or Jean, or me, who knows, all three. Sam has never heard any of this so I have to explain briefly that is what led me to Goodrich's back garden, and the man himself. She asks me what happened to them and for the first time I find the tears welling up and all I can say is that I don't know. Sam takes a bottle out of her bag and I take a drink, we are both dusty and must look like street sleepers, so sitting on the ground in a doorway is nothing unusual.

We relax for a while before moving on carrying out our reckie. We walk away from the doorway and take the first left, opposite to where we saw Carol and Cassy and different to the way we arrived at the andy lines. We ignore a turning or two then take another left and start a circle with the financial district as its centre. Each time we cross a road that leads in that direction we see in the distance a collection of andywagons and other crowd control machinery. We walk until no andys can be seen and turn left again. Some way off there is a familiar thump followed by the momentary silence which follows it, when everything prepares for the pain to kick in. It's soon followed by sirens which I didn't hear before. Sam gets a vibrate from the screen and takes it out, opens the back, turns over the battery and up pops the message.

'Did you hear that?' She reads out. She types in 'Ys. Wr u nr?'

She gets the reply to say that they weren't near and they are reporting this back to HQ.

'What's HQ?' Sam asks.

'Headquarters.' I tell her.

'So what's Quarters then?'

'When there were troops, that's when there were armies, on the battleground they were positioned in quarters and where the commander happened to be was the headquarters.'

'How do you know that?' Sam asks.

'Because I was a gamer for a year or two.'

Another thump, this time nearer and from a different direction.

'Sam?' She turns and looks at me, 'Write to Carol and copy in HQ. Ash thinks . .'

'Yeh!'

'. . . That the balloon is going up.'

'What?'

'Just write it. Then add, require instructions immediately.'

Sam writes this and sends it.

'What's all this about balloons?'

Before I can explain another thump, this time ground shaking, nearer followed by alarms, then sirens. People begin to meet on the street talking to neighbours. Neighbours they've had for years but never talked to. They look up into the sky looking for palls of smoke as three or four pods fly shakily past. Then someone from an upstairs window points a finger, and we look to see a rolling cloud of smoke rising over some offices.

Sam looks at me, enquiring,

'The first thing you do before you send in the troops is you soften up the enemy.'

Sam frowns.

'Artillery? Bombs?' I explain, with a gesture that points to the smoke drifting over our heads.

She shrugs, so I begin to explain further.

'The idea is to sow confusion, fear, give a prepared enemy something else to deal with, something unexpected, so they have to rethink their strategy. Dealing with casualties is time consuming, it also makes people lose confidence or get emotional and careless.'

Sam looks down at the screen and reads a message out as it comes through,

'Now is the time for all good men to come to the aid of the party. Does that mean what I think it means?'

'What do you think it means?'

'I could mean the balloon's up and gone!' She says.

'You are such a fast learner!' Sam looks back to the screen,

'See you at Mister Fu's. I thought that was wherever they were.'

'It is,' I reply, 'Carol and Cassy will be heading for a safe place. Bring up the map,'

She taps and slides and a map appears, not the sort I've seen before, it's simpler and the colours are different. I smile to myself at the depth of Goodrich's preparation, one of the first things the state would turn off would be data and comms.

'Are they moving?' I ask.

'Yes.'

'Okay, pick a point ahead of them and we'll make for that. Have you got us?'

'Yes.'

'Which . . . . ?'

Another crunching thump, the closest so far, then pistol firing. More pistol firing with a different acoustic, from a difference place, and someone else. Then a small explosion.

'. . .which direction do we need to go?'

Sam indicates, slicing the air like a commando, I smile and follow as we move briskly, keeping close to a long wall, and stopping at junctions to check all directions before crossing. There's no traffic, there's an ominous silence without it. Down one junction we see flames leaping from a building and several andywagons turned over by a large hole in the road. Windows down the street are broken and some confused people are venturing out into the street.

'That was a biggy.' Sam points out.

'And I tell you what.' I point out, 'That device wasn't left in a shopping bag by a passer-by. Someone knew exactly where the andys would be stationed.'

'What do you mean?' She says.

'That device was right under them, as it was with the others, someone knew where the andys would be. Devices have been planted beforehand, and to do that with any accuracy, someone must have known where they were going to be.'

'They've stopped.' Sam shows me the screen.

The symbol indicating 'Mister Fu's Sushi' hovers over a building near a junction. We make a mental note of where it is and where the screen indicates that we are. We proceed hugging walls where we can and cross another junction just as there is another explosion, this time a good distance away. The air seems full of sirens and little else other than a pungent smell like burning plastic. The darkening sky above us has mixed with it traces of smoke that light up with the flashes of subsidiary explosions. A flash, like lightning, is silent but you feel it in the ground, then you hear it. In the distance a store is burning, pressurised chemical and gas containers burst like incendiaries and their metal containers are jettisoned high, spinning into the sky. They trail a stream of ragged flame like a malfunctioning fire work, fizzle out, then return to earth through a neighbouring roof, still hot enough to do what an incendiary does best.

I hear the sounds and record the images. There's enough of it to be a start and I'm here in it; right in the middle. I feel a rising thrill, come what may, survive or not, I am witness. Before, there were just small skirmishes, disorderly protests, The Bakery. These were just shouting, a nuisance, an irritation, now stuff is happening that nobody can deny, ignore, or dismiss; it is also make or break. The state and the corps will use this as an excuse to crack down on everything and everyone, it'll be death or glory. They'll not allow any middle ground, there won't be any safe haven, no neutral. If you're not corporate, you're anti, and you're dead. Like Goodrich was saying, it has to be all or nothing. Now the choice has been made.

I look at Sam who is turning the screen round to point it in the direction we are heading. All girls do that. We will either celebrate a victory or we will die quickly during, or painfully afterwards. I lean over and touch an icon that automatically orientates the screen to the geography. Sam touches the icon again,

'I was happy the way it was,' she says.

Girls eh? What can you do?

Above us a pod flies faster and straighter than usual and makes us both look up and follow it as it darts ahead. It banks sharply to the left, then accelerates until its motor is screaming. We watch it until it crashes into the middle of an office block, about the eighth floor. The windows are filled with one billowing yellow and crimson cloud that gilds its way across the building. For a moment the whole floor is a golden glow. Then the glass walls burst into a shower of glistening shards that rain down and crash onto the walkways. From where we are, we can already see a glow in the floor above. Sam and I just look at each other with raised eyebrows and a look of only mild surprise. I begin to suspect such things are not accidents.

CHAPTER 20

On the player, our icon hovers over Carol and Cassy's, and we wait. A solitary hooded figure drifts past but pays us no attention, no peep or ceremony. All around us is an air of expectancy, down the usually bustling streets as far as I can see there is no light but the cold white street lighting. All the shops and offices are closed. Those that have them, have drawn their shutters and either wait deep inside or have left for their comfortable regulated homes. Other than an occasional shadow passing across an upstairs window, there's a stillness, it's like everything is waiting. High up in the exec suites of some office blocks there are still lights, they think they're too high to be affected by what happens on the ground; down here is somewhere else. Below them an odd floor or two is well lit for the poorly paid cleaners who can't afford a revolution to interrupt their work. Even freedom fighting has to conform to their shift work.

Sam and I look about us, waiting for a door to open, but there is nothing; then the peep returns. From beneath his hood he catches our attention, then with a subtle inclination of his head, suggests we follow him. He does this with a practised art without really pausing. We follow discreetly and travel a circuit down alleyways and back onto the street. I imagine our little procession is observed, just to see if we are being followed. Almost back to the spot where we were picked up, we duck into a dark, narrow entry. A steel panel slides to one side, one of many that we just passed, all identical. Beyond it a dull light makes the passage we are in seem a lot brighter, but it's a matter of degrees. Once through, the panel slides back easily and locks itself.

Derelict rooms and passages strewn with rubbish and the remnants of office life come and go, the way is never obvious. Sam and I are caught out presuming the path lies one way when it's the other. We descend into a subterranean catacomb then rise into an airy disused office with views over the streets before descending again. Sam and I share glances, hoping that they are who we think they are, and we are who they think we are. We seem to descend for ever until we sense activity ahead and soon pass a room that hums with machinery. After that people begin appearing, then blank screens burst into life, loading figures and images. A large wall screen with a still image begins to pan alarmingly across deserted streets, focuses down, then pans out again. We step through a small door in a steel wall, ahead of us there is a long tunnel shaped room that disappears into the dark beyond. Beneath its arched roof, work tops are arranged on either side, and on them ranks of screens are being attended to by a dozen or more operators. They sit with faces coloured in the changing patterns of the screens they monitor. Sam and I still follow our guide and now, ahead, there are clusters of people, standing, pointing at things on screens, doing calculations, giving opinions, making decisions. We have to squeeze our way through but no one pays us any attention, they are all focussed, intelligent, dedicated, busy.

Ahead of us a large segmented screen is edged with scrolling updates. Each segment is at first a different cam view, then as we approach one cam view is enlarged to fill the whole, this spins away to reveal an aerial map of London. Beneath this I see a familiar outline, a thin cloud of wispy grey hair surmounts a round head on a slightly stooping figure. Even with his back to us there's no mistaking Goodrich, he is talking to Carol. It occurs to me the months that they must have spent organising this place, and in total secrecy. Then Sam sees someone in the distance and moves on, she throws her arms round a figure, then there are three in a hug, cuddling like a family.

'Ash!' Sam turns to me. 'This is my dad, I mean Zac, and this is my mum, Mel.'

'I think we've met,' I say.

'Yes,' says Mel, 'but we didn't have time to meet properly.'

'Well, we get to be introduced at last.' I reply and we formally shake hands and introduce ourselves. I use the name 'Ash' to avoid confusion, I will tell them my birth name when the time is right. It seems a very ordinary thing to be doing when the world might be on the brink of destruction, meeting your girlfriend's parents. Things don't change though and I'm nervous and not wanting to appear a complete idiot even though I look like a street sleeper.

Zac sits down and is busy with a screen full of digits, tapping instructions then waiting for the screen to load, then scroll. While he waits for another screen full he turns and looks at Mel beside me. She takes my hand,

'We have to thank you Ash,' she says. Mel's hair is longer than Sam's but her eyes have the same sparkle, and, like Sam's, her smile is full and genuine.

'Do you have to?' I reply.

'Okay,' and Mel smiles again, 'we would like to. Sam has told us how narrowly we escaped rehab and had you not been such a good shot we might . .' She's tempted to think of what might have happened but it's best not to. '. . well, we owe you a lot.'

'That's okay, I'll just settle for your daughter.' And I look at Sam, who digs me in the ribs. Then she does the 'no hope' shake of the head.

'Well,' says Mel, who at least smiled, 'it's something that we can talk about later.' I know what she means, and what she means when this is all over, and if we are still alive. She glances at Zac then turns back to me,

'We've got something to do here, Zac and I. Well, you tell him Zac.'

Zac taps and slides one of two screens he has, then starts to explain,

'During our stay in Rehab,' he begins, 'various groups contacted us. There's quite a few, which is not surprising judging just from the size and population. There are escape committees, sabotage groups, all sorts and all committed to bringing down the Rehab system, no matter what it takes. It's what keeps them sane, if not actually alive. Some do escape, they are usually rounded up pretty quickly. The handful that have ever escaped have never found the support outside and exist in a kind of limbo. Those inside still exist in hope that somehow a way can be found to help them that deserve it.'

'And we have the keys' Sam interjects.

'We think we do but that doesn't mean we are just going to open all the gates. There's a lot in Rehab that need to be there, psychopaths, sadists, serial killers, every weird and demented criminal type you can imagine. Rehab thrives on the conflict, there are public floggings, hangings, decapitations, not all run by the institution but with their consent. That's why there are groups, you can't survive on your own.'

'And dad thinks we can get into both CUpal and 4U.' Sam tells me. 'CUpal is straightforward, but without the Trojan Horse those pills gave us, 4U could have been very tricky. There's a few minor security issues, and we're working on them now.'

Sat with her family, I can see Sam is in her element, working with her dad on something that makes her expertise invaluable. They sit with their backs to me looking into screens whose content has no meaning to me.

To my side a pair of eyebrows appear,

'Well Ash, what do you think of our 'war room'?'

'Very impressive, Prof How long have you been here?'

'Coming up to three hours.' He sees my surprise.

'It's been one of our sites for more than a year, this is the first use we've made of it, we try to keep our options open. Not being able to co-ordinate action, or predict what happens on the streets, has kept us on our toes. This is our third code red, on the first two occasions we never got to go live, this time I think it's different.'

As we walk back to where I saw him first, he puts his arm on my shoulder the way I have seen fathers do with their sons.

'We have been planning for an event for years Ash. Even now, I don't know if this is really it. Our technology and expertise has never been greater and more able to the bring the system to its knees and help the people.'

I look at him with some surprise as we stop by the large screen.

'Do you know what a metamagnetic pulse is?'

I shake my head.

'You know how data can be corrupted by coming into contact with a magnetic field?'

I nod.

'A metamagnetic pulse is a brief magnetic field which creates the same effect but on an infinitely larger scale. A simultaneous triggering of devices that have been in place for years will delete all the data within range. Rapidly installing some appropriate systems can reintroduce a basic level of control and protection. Sam and Zac are able to work with that and the access they have already gained to the various security systems. Once they are in, they will pass that on to others. Zac has mentioned Rehab, and he is keen to help some of those he met. But that is not all that he, Sam, and others are working on, before we start removing data, we need to break the fiscal system so that money has no power.'

'Isn't that impossible?'

'Removing money is very difficult, yes, but not paying it in.'

I tell him I don't understand.

'We access security systems and enable the creditisation of accounts so that all accounts have an infinite balance. The result is the same, equality, money becomes worthless. No one has more leverage than another, it's the unequal distribution of money that gives some power and others none.'

'But some will have gold and other valuables.' I point out.

'And because everyone has an infinite amount of money to spend, anyone can buy it. There's no point in selling it when you already have more money than you will ever need, like everyone else?'

'And they have an infinite amount . .'

'Exactly. Removing data from certain institutions is also essential. Like money, information is another form of control.'

We arrive beneath Goodrich's large wall screen and join Carol. He spends a moment examining the information, the images and the icons that flash and don't.

'You are still uncertain?' I ask.

He gives a thoughtful smile, but one that's seems more positive.

Carol hears my enquiry and turns toward me,

'We started intercepting information a few days ago. Only yesterday did it begin to look like the state was taking it seriously enough to get involved.'

'In a big way,' adds Goodrich without removing his attention from the screen. 'They routinely wipe out minor incidents, a few dozen people here and there is not a problem. A group finally decides it wants to make a statement and because it acts independently the state has no problem in neutralising it. In fact it's encouraged so that the security corps have an excuse to root out collaborators.'

'We think this time is different though,' says Carol

I look at both enquiringly.

'There's been a lot more abnormal activity on the streets than usual,' says Goodrich.

He picks up a small palmer and taps it. The screen above him changes to an aerial view of London, then he traces an oval on the screen.

'This is roughly the financial district since The City was enclosed. Activity over the last twenty-four hours has intensified.'

A few more taps and slides and the screen plays a series of event icons indicating time related activity.

'What are the green squares?' I ask.

'People,' Carol answers, 'areas where footfall has intensified indicating activity way beyond normal. We think that this indicates people are gathering.'

'I know,' I tell them, much to their astonishment, 'we had a brief glimpse of a sort of collection point as a door was closing. As we passed the end of an alley way, a door opened to let someone in and inside was a crowd of people.'

'What you have just told us Ash, is the only confirmation of what we suspect. With all this technology, I feel distanced from reality, maybe I'm just old fashioned, but there's no substitute for seeing it with one's own eyes, or in this case yours.'

Goodrich looks at the screen, then looks at me, then at Carol. I'm sure he has something for me to do and it doesn't involve me sitting at a screen, number crunching. As much as I would like to join the ranks of illuminated faces around me and be close to the ones I care for and care for me, I guess my work is going to be outside.

'You have something for me to do?' I ask.

'I do,' Goodrich replies as a note is passed to him. He looks at it then at the red haired girl who had handed it him. He ushers her toward Carol, then takes me to one side where we can sit down and speak privately. We both relax for a moment and I look around in amazement at the efficiency and dedication that surrounds us.

'We have had places like this for years, set up ready to be occupied in case they are needed,' Goodrich tells me. 'With so many vacant buildings we are spoilt for choice, but they need to have certain qualities so when they have been identified they are prepared, so all we need to do is select the appropriate one, and move in. Well, it's a little more complicated than that but you get the gist.'

I nod, still impressed by what I can see.

'What do you know of this bombing?' Goodrich asks me.

'I told Sam I thought it was the precursor. Like a softening up.'

'Why do you say that?'

'Because it has a precedent in history. When I was a gamer, it was how you started an assault. I don't think there would be any point unless it was followed by something else, something big.'

Goodrich thinks about this.

'And, I think it was planned with some expertise,' I add.

'Why?' He says.

'Because they knew where the andys would set up their road blocks, and where their alternative positions would be. And what's more,' I tell him, 'the devices were planted well before the andys took up their positions.'

'How do you know that?'

'By the nature of the result. The devices were hidden, beneath or near to, the andy positions, not thrown or dropped or left by a passer-by. The andys deployed in confidence and the devices were detonated at the right time, in the right place, for greatest effect.'

'Well,' he thinks aloud, 'they would have had plans in place to protect various commercial interests, and they have carried out exercises which we have observed, but never thought of making use of. Not in this way.'

Prof scribbles a few lines on a note pad with a pencil that he keeps in an old, handleless mug with other pens and pencils, the way artist do.

A low growling thump shakes the ground. Over Goodrich's shoulder the screen displays a new bright red flashing icon on a map displaying a ring of dull red icons that are not flashing. Goodrich turns round to look at the screen as a woman joins us and reads from a slip of paper,

'Another detonation at 20/34. Junction adjacent Columbus Square. Flashing now.'

Goodrich turns to the woman,

'Thank you Terri,' he says with a smile and turns back to the screen. She continues with some hesitancy,

'It's the second on deployed unit 13, even though it's moved.'

Goodrich asks her to explain.

'Unit 13 was one of the first to be targeted. They pulled back to a secondary position about an hour ago, and they've just been hit again.'

'Unit 13,' Goodrich observes, 'unlucky for some. They must be a little confused. '

Then he looks at me,

'I mean their controllers Ash, the androbots are not allowed confusion, life is about dealing with the unexpected, we can all cope with the expected. It's how we cope with the unexpected that tests our metal.' He rubs his chin in thought for a moment.

'It is interesting that there are some other initiators out there. That's excellent news, more than we could have hoped for, it will encourage people to join the protest. We need boots on the streets, Ash, without that our chances are slim. What do you think?'

'I think there will be a tipping point,' I tell him more in hope than expectation, 'when people think there is a real chance of change, they will join in. I don't think we are there yet but there is too much going on for it to be ignored. Sam and I saw a pod crashing into an office block, that's not easy to conceal.'

'Excellent!' Goodrich's eyes lit up as his eyebrows moved alarmingly, 'That would have been north east of here? About twenty minutes before you arrived, yes?'

'Yes,' I reply but Goodrich is already walking away and slapping some operator on the back. There's a fevered conversation and I can see both parties and several others celebrating the news. As they move around I see part of a sign and I realise where we are. How apt I think that we should be in The London Underground.

Goodrich grabs me by the shoulders.

'Excellent news, Ash, you have confirmed what we hoped. We had taken control but before impact we lost visual due to a power supply interruption at security. We halted further attempts, but now we can resume.'

'Resume what?' I ask as we both sit again.

'We've had access into 4U signals, not their vaults unfortunately, but we could pick up and monitor what their surveillance bots were up to in their pods. We've been able to see what has attracted their attention. Zac is getting us deeper into their operations and we've carried out some simple manoeuvring hick ups just to see what control we have. Your observation has confirmed that there is nothing stopping us interfering with the pod's giros and creating havoc.'

'They'll soon catch on won't they?'

'If we use it sparingly we can allow them to think it's incompetence, but eventually, your right, they'll stop using them, but that's fine. Before they do we'll have to pick our targets sparingly, let some irrelevance get through, and when others operate normally maybe they'll think it's ground attacks.'

Another resounding thump from above, followed by another further away, then another.

The screen behind Goodrich has six or more red lights flashing, more than I could account for in thumps. The area, like a rough circle is filling in and dull red spots are overlapping.

There's a commotion further down the tunnel and a distinguished looking man walks forward and shakes hands with Goodrich. They talk quietly and agree something, the man then walks away and leaves Goodrich with his thoughts until he sees me,

'A bomb has exploded injuring some people and they need some help setting up a hospital in that sector, or moving the casualties.'

'Can I help?'

'No thank you Ash, I have something else in mind for you. We expected casualties and there are facilities nearby, they just need some personnel. Hutch will sort it out.'

'Hutch?'

'Yes, your biker friend, who picked you up, remember?'

'How could I forget? I had the feeling I'd seen him before.'

'You have,' Goodrich is being enigmatic. 'He was a friend of Carl, your uncle and his partner Jean. I think it was his team that took you to the hospital with them.'

'So he was the guy who fought off the andys when they came for them.'

'That does seem to be his mission in life, each to their own but he was also instrumental in us meeting.'

'How?'

The question hangs in the air as a neatly groomed kid, who seems too young to be involved in all this, approaches and Goodrich looks in his direction.

'We've spotted movement, sir.'

'Ash, this is Claude.'

We introduce ourselves but I can't think of him in any other way than as someone's little brother who just gets in the way.

'Claude keeps an eye on things,' Goodrich tells me, which sounds as if he's been given something to do to keep him out of mischief.

'He gathers their visual,' Goodrich explains.

'Oh! I see, excellent.' Claude ignores my surprise with adult disdain and continues,

'There's several groups of people emerging from side streets, alleyways, old buildings and even from drainage systems. We've blocked signals so they can't be seen but the numbers are increasing and soon it may become obvious, and . .'

'. . and they'll smell a rat,' Goodrich finishes his sentence. 'Okay, re-run forty minutes of recordings from before there was anything too memorable and merge another sequence at varying intervals then if they do react the groups will have moved on.'

'Yes, sir,' Claude says dutifully and returns to his post where he seems to be appraising a small group, most of whom tower above him.

'I always think he's about to salute,' says Goodrich smiling. 'This is phase two I think and where I will need you, Ash.'

'I imagine it will be out there and not in here?'

'Does that worry you?'

'No, I'm more use out there. Just tell me what you need me to do.'

Goodrich emphasises timing saying he can see much with the surveillance they have, but actions need to be co-ordinated. The groups appear to be working together which has never happened before but he cannot tell who, if anyone, is in control.

'They too need to know they are not alone,' he tells me. 'We need to let them know what we can do.'

'I'm to be a kind of envoy, offering assistance?'

'Yes, more important Ash,' Goodrich tells me, 'is finding their command structure on the ground. We can handle the technology from here, all intelligence and communications. Another concern is paramount, if it becomes a fight from street to street, house to house, the people will be massacred if the andys continue under control. There is no army to turn and support us against them Ash, I need to know if they will still be taking commands. With the firepower they have at their disposal, all this might count for nothing if someone rallies them and they respond.'

'You don't know what they will do when they are no longer being controlled.'

'It is an unknown, and a risk, but we may have to take it.'

I pass down the increasingly busy tunnel to where I can see Sam sitting next to her folks. In the dim light the screens brilliant colourful displays, scrolling and loading, constantly moving, it reminds me of an old gamers arcade. In reality it is not that different except the consequences are real lives, and whatever lies ahead. Perhaps it takes meeting someone you really care for to make you take the future seriously. As I reach them, Sam stands and puts her arm around me. This is very good as it indicates there is no conflict with her folks.

I draw Sam to the side so I can look at her directly,

'I have a mission.' Sam looks down to see where her coat is and the implication is clear.

'Just me.'

'I'm coming too!'

'No! You have things to do here.'

'So what's the mission?' She asks.

'Oh, just observing, just reporting back to Goodrich what I can see, feel. Nothing tricky.' I can see Sam is not convinced, but understands.

'I'll need your player, I have to key in my thumb print,'

'Better wash your hands then,' she tells me.

Sam hands me the screen and we kiss politely - well, parents watching. Our lingering look into each other's eyes though, says all we need to say.

I pass back through the tunnel and look back to see Sam blowing a kiss, I snatch it from the air and plant it on my lips, then return the favour. I have a brief chat with Goodrich who has been joined by two other people of a similar age to him and who I enjoy thinking are other apostles. He hands me a package which I can feel includes a pistol. Our conversation is constantly interrupted with reports and the screen behind him is a confusing litter of symbols, references and other indications of activity. An operator pans back on the map of London, and the extent of activity is a shock. Everywhere it seems there is some disturbance. I overhear another report saying that looting has broken out along the South Bank, another that crowds of people have broken through barriers on two bridges, one has been repelled with heavy casualties but the other has made it into The City. Tower bridge is up and another has been blown to prevent a massive crowd crossing it. Development is slower further south because all forms of communication have been jammed. Hutch and his fellow bikers are acting as dispatch riders taking reports and dropping leaflets at the same time as dodging fire from the andys on the ground. There are some flashing red lights in 23, and several in adjoining southern districts; there is a single dull red light in 48.

    We are in the centre of a revolution ignited by a malicious act, the sort we have had to suffer every day. On its own, nothing extraordinary, but every load has its last straw.

CHAPTER 21

I follow one of Goodrich's 'runners' through the catacombs which are filling up with personnel. His 'runners' carry messages from one area to another and guide anyone who needs it through the maze of rabbit warrens to and from his HQ. There are now dozens of people down here. My path is different from the way I came in but still underground. We pass a large store room being turned into an improvised news centre with a desk being assembled. A geeky looking youth is helping some engineers rig the broadcast equipment while several presenters rehearse their lines. I stop momentarily but I'm soon hurried along by my guide who tells me she has other work to do. A few corridors later reality kicks in as a large show room on an upper floor is now full of mattresses awaiting the injured. An adjoining room serves as an operating theatre where that same distinguished gent is talking to a group of attentive assistants. As I pass, a door opens and I glimpse the armoury and I instinctively feel for my pistol, then the lump in my coat where my ED is concealed; just checking.

My escort holds up an old hand-held and checks with an observer as we approach the exit. Apparently this is 'D' exit, how many others there are I don't know, there may be no others, other than the one we came in by. We wait several minutes until his hand held gets a buzz and I am thrust out into the street like a para out of a plane in an old movie. The feeling is similar, I too am hoping I land on my feet.

My nostrils are the first to notice there's something in the air. Grid lighting is out and I remain in a nearby doorway and acclimatise. There is sporadic pistol firing, no more than a few seconds pass of quiet before another exchange of firing. There's a harsh repetitive crack some way off which must be an old type pistol, maybe a gun or even an old rifle, an untidy but effective weapon albeit inaccurate and cumbersome. An andywagon trundles past and an andy riding on top fires indiscriminately a what appears to be a shadow as it goes past. I thank them for the warning.

    I make my way from shadow to shadow, doorway to doorway, as I seem to have all my life. I worry that I am so used to it that I no longer think about it and it will be then that I miss something. Before me to my left the glow of The City is still relentless and I fear it always will be, it's my bearing and I head across streets and imagine my path on Goodrich's screen. My palmer will give me all the information I need, where I need to go and what I need to know. I can visualise Goodrich's screen and my avatar, a pale blue star, being watched over, as if by guardian angels. It comforts me.

    The sounds and smells around me are a constant reminder, if I needed it, that I am in a war zone and that very little is predictable. When a gamer, I often wondered how close it was to the real thing, now I am in the centre of a war I realise there is nothing to compare. Everything is extreme, fear, exhilaration, weariness, life and death. There are no lives other than the single one I have, and being shot hurts like hell. This is all too real.

    I run on and on, from shadow to shadow. Every few streets I turn down an alley and conceal myself just to see if anyone follows. More concerned about being followed or observed, I turn a corner and stupidly I nearly run straight into the rear of an andy barricade. I freeze against the wall with one hand on my pistol, for a few seconds I remain motionless, waiting to see if any of them have noticed my blunder. Their attention is in the opposite direction, down a broad high street, with four and five story buildings on either side. A dull light illuminates the street from several large stores whose emergency lighting has been activated by the power cut. Behind the andy's positions there is a gantry above with an array of unlit floodlights. They point down the street into what I now perceive to be a killing field. The andys are banked on both sides of the street like the sides of a narrowing funnel. They won't be seen until the crowd is almost upon them, the sides will draw in, better able to direct their fire down the street and into the crowd. The floodlights will blind the crowd and give the andys a well-lit view of the unfolding massacre; the bodies will just pile up.

Once views of this horror hit the screens what will people do? Cower in the safety of their homes and suffer the perpetual torment with the dignified quietude of the silent majority? Or with anger, rise up and overthrow the oppressor no matter what the cost? What have they done so far?

I move as if to find another route, but then stop. The certainty of what's about to happen can't be ignored and what's a life worth, knowing I could have prevented it? To do nothing because I think my mission is more important, is the kind of philosophy we are fighting against. Every life is sacred.

I shrink back from the andy ambush and move down a service road that turns and runs parallel to the high street, along the back of a line of touchyfeelies that front onto the killing field. A gap between them appears and is a convenient access back to the high street. Approaching with caution I can see a team of andys have taken up a position blocking off the escape by wedging two andywagons alongside each other. A dozen or more andys sit on top joking and discussing the best way of killing the most in the shortest time. They fantasise over what valuables they might like to find on the bodies and argue over how severe wounds would have to be before making it undesirable to rape an injured girl or boy. I wonder how many andys I could kill before they got me. The odds are not in my favour.

I move silently across the access and continue down the service road unnoticed until it bends, following the course of the high street. I stop at a road that runs across me and joins the high street to my left, to the right it disappears into the dark. Looking left, I can see the end of the killing field clearly and there are no andys blocking my view, or anything blocking this escape route. Diverting the crowd this way seems a way to avoid their massacre. Odd, I think, that this route should be left open. The muffled click of a truck door closing some way off to my right stops me just before I step out into the road. I can see nothing, but I feel there's got to be some horror waiting for whoever escapes the killing field.

It seems darker here. At first I presume it is the buildings that prevent the perpetual glow of The City reaching the streets below. Looking up it's dark and lacks the iridescence that is usual. I lean against a wall and smile, and can't see anything for tears. The dream is real, for a moment. For a moment the sky was dark, The City was dead. Then as the smoke drifts away, so the lights resumed their indestructible display.

Caught on the same breeze, a wave of chanting, far off, wakes me from the dream. The sound fluctuates due to its course between buildings. Its harshness changes to a roll like thunder, then rises to a shrill again with beating drums and whistles. In and out the sound is twisted but each trumpet call and answering chant grows that little bit nearer. The andys must hear it, they will be checking their weapons, turning them on to kill, taking up their positions.

The road from the high street on my left drops away to my right. The reflected light from The City having resumed, I catch a reflection in a visor, so brief and faint you could have imagined it, but I know better. The andys down there are looking uphill and will be invisible to the crowd and once the lights are turned on and the pistols start firing, the only escape will be down this road. Another glint, another clue, another rack of lights ready to be turned on. A ground shaking thump some way off and a ball of flame is enough to glimpse what waits. Perhaps twenty, maybe twice that number, four or five trucks, at least two with mounted machine pistols. I drop to the ground thinking there must be a few night sights. Now the rise in the road conceals me. Use the terrain, it's a rule. I roll over the road until I rest against the gutter on the other side. Then I roll over the pavement and into an alley way, out of sight. I stand, then listen to see if anything is occurring as a result.

I take a breath before moving on. I can feel where the pistol has dug into my side, the player too was uncomfortable at first and I was worried I might damage it. I feel the weight of the pistol at my side and check the screen. I check another pocket, then all the other pockets. The screen is missing. I haven't used it since I left HQ, it could have dropped out anywhere and the realisation I might have to retrace my path torments me, until I look across the road and see it black and dull, screen down, in the middle. I creep to the edge of the alleyway with my back against a wall and to the andys, and I prepare to roll out and get it. Suddenly yellow lights bounce off a sidewall leading to the high street, the light moves down as the sound of tracks and a throbbing exhaust thrusts the vehicle into view. I can see the player as it disappears between the tracks. Then as the armoured wagon passes it reappears behind it intact, lit by the vehicles rear lights. I fix its position waiting for the lights to fade and the wagon to drop down the road. I dart across to the other side of the alleyway so as not to be seen. It's a tracked command vehicle, a kind of mobile compact HQ. The engine note drops to tick over and I hear voices, checking signals, positions. On the road the player is near the middle of the street undamaged, still picked out by the wagon's rear lights. The wagon has halted within a short distance of the waiting ambush, and not enough yet to conceal me rolling out into the road. With a burst the engine note picks up, the exhausts pulse, and the tracks begin to move in opposite directions turning the wagon around on the spot like some bizarre carousel. The tracks skid and grind as the wagon's dazzling lights turn back towards the high street and pick out the small, flat object lying in the road. My only chance now will be after it passes. There are more voices then the engine note picks up, tracks skew and slip as it pulls itself forward. The wagon levels out on the far side of the road and crawls slowly toward the high street. It's light on my side picks out the player lying in the road. Then it disappears beneath the vehicle's protective forward apron, but not in the middle like before. Briefly it sparkles a million shorts, bursts, pops, and is then dark. Crushed beneath the track and the road, from the glow of rear lights, all I can see is an iridescent trail of fragmented crystals.

A blast of drums is a jolt. Whistles and answering chants have turned a corner somewhere. Echoing between the office blocks and other prestigious monoliths, they sound as if they could be in the next street. I can feel the weight of the crowd, the chants, the chatter, the feet on the ground. Without the player my choices are limited. Heading for the street where the andys are in force would be suicide, then the noise and energy of the crowd has its own momentum and my voice would just be lost and I would perish in the massacre along with everyone else. I look along the backs of the shops and stores, then up to where the buildings merge with a sky still patched with drifting clouds of smoke. Close by a large steel shutter, a fire escape leans weakly against the rear of a store, making its uncertain way up four storeys to the roof.

Its rusting frames creak as I go up past doors that have long been bricked up. No need to risk security and the loss of merchandise just for the safety of the workers, all that protection was repealed decades ago. On the roof the sound of the crowd approaching is thrilling, it rises up in waves like marching battalions. A trumpet strikes up with cheers following, then chanting. I feel the history of a thousand revolutions, people on the streets. The oppressed unleashed.

On the roof I make my way in between ducts and round a large skylight still with a dim glow beneath from an old emergency lighting system which has been triggered by the power out. A vast carbon filtration system, serving just as much use as it ever did, squats uselessly on an adjoining building, It's stark against the lights from a district where power still lights the streets and drives the filters. How much brighter shines a light where everywhere is dark. I move in the shadows and stop by the parapet toward the end of the high street as it curves round. I can hear the occasional smashing of a glass window in the wake of the crowd, then the drums start again, followed by whistles. The banners and torches appear like some host that has arisen up from the ground and awakes before me. There will be a few minutes before they turn into the high street, then a few more before the lights come on and the andys open up. Another trumpet call is answered with cheers and the drums again start up, and now some pipes. I blink tears from my eyes and wipe my face across my sleeve and as I turn my head I see a crouching figure to my right. It is behind the parapet but on a lower roof. I blink several times to make sure but when he lifts a launcher to a shoulder there's no more any doubt. Launchers deliver a variety of surprises. There is the canister that explodes above you and stains you and everyone else with a radio sensitive marker dye that makes you instantly traceable for later arrest and processing. Other canisters incapacitate in various ways, and yet more that maim, burn, or gas you, and anyone in the vicinity. The fun is, you never know which it's going to be until it's too late.

    I look in other directions, on other roofs, this side of the street and the other. I count seven others that I can see. To my left there is a higher roof over which I can't see and there may be one or two there as that is the highest point with the best vantage. I check to see if my pistol is secure then scramble up a sloping roof. The noise of the crowd, the chanting and drumming is enough to hide any noise I make. Sure enough as I reach the top, along the higher level there is another crouching figure. By his side I can see a neatly placed battery of grenades as well as his launcher and a pistol with the long site already fitted. His job will be to drop the grenades into the crowd as it turns, as it will when the andys at the other end of the street open fire. That will get them panicking, they'll realise that they and those about them are all trapped and are being summarily executed. If that carnage wasn't enough then those on the roofs would tidy it up. They would shoot everything that's still moving, and after that everything, moving or not. Playing dead doesn't work.

    I fold out the site on my pistol and as it clicks quietly into place, it activates. Through its optic I can see what nobody else can. The fine green beam along which the charge will travel. Just as the andy sneaks a look down at the pavement below, the nape of his neck becomes visible, and that's all I need. At this distance there is no need to wonder. I don't bother to look up and check the result, just make my way across the roof to where he lies.

    The dead andy is void of torment. He lies warm and at peace with that hum, a faint vibration, that is the remnant of the charge ebbing away. As soon as he is still, I shift his body so that I can get to the parapet and survey the killing ground beneath me. The crowd and their banners are just turning into the high street. I put the andy's pistol to one side in case I need it, but mine is smaller and quicker. I crouch beneath the parapet, take one of the grenades, activate it, then hurl it towards the andy barricade. A few seconds and there's a flash of brilliant white light and that expectant silence that is a millisecond before a shuddering crack and the sound of windows being sucked out. The crowd is silenced, and their progress slows, but doesn't stop, it has its own inertia. I've already hurled another down the street, before it can do its worst and in case I've been seen, I've let another grenade hop, skip and jump across to the roof below. Before I take cover, there's enough time to see the andy with his launcher stand up to see what's clattering in his direction. That was the last thing he did see. The grenade takes out part of the roof, he and the parapet are blown clear across the street, at least they will be by the time they've landed. But I don't watch that. Two more grenades I throw across the street onto the roofs, but only one makes it. The last two, with some carelessness for my safety, I stand up and hurl up the street to catch the andys as they move forward from their defences. I drop down, then peer over the parapet to watch one explode just short of the andy lines taking out half a dozen. The other rolls into the rest before it detonates and covers them all in a harmless blue dye.

The crowd has got the message and is retreating back the way it came, runners down the flanks are telling them to turn. Sporadic firing breaks out down the side street and some andys are still waiting to pick off any that make it into street, which is now brilliantly lit, but thankfully, deserted. Those in the vanguard of the crowd are retreating over those behind them who have not had themselves time to turn. Several pistol shots echo above the screams and shouts. I look through the andy's long sight and see on a roof across the street, an andy's pistol and its site scanning in my direction, seeking me out. Before it can stop, I let off two shots, then another, but I needn't have. In my sight I can see the first charge cut through the flesh beneath his helmet strap, then, as his head is thrown back, the second charge hits the underside of his chin. The charge will go through his head with the inside of his helmet taking the full force. This is why his helmet disappears behind him taking the rest if his head with it and tearing away what was left of his neck. From where I am, I can't see the blood, but it must be a mess. Being a college gamer has some uses after all, at a distance the games the same. Unless interrupted the third shot will travel on slowly disintegrating until it becomes no more than a gentle breeze, about ten miles away.

    I can hear a high pitched angry voice behind me, it's the andy's head comms, I listen in. The firing has stopped on the roofs and the crowd has all but gone save a few limping stragglers. Some seriously injured are being hurriedly scavenged to their safety by fellow protesters. Two or three bodies remain. Fires have broken out in the buildings opposite. On my side in the top floor next to me, the fire is beginning to get interesting, the filtration unit is looking precarious with flames leaping up one side. An andy runs across the street below and into the alleyway beneath me. I decide I'd better move, so I make my way down and back across the roof to the old fire escape. I grip hold of the top rail and wonder why it's shaking, I look down and to my horror see about twenty andys piling into it, coming up to meet me. A couple at the front had got over half way up and then halted when the weight of the others had started it shaking. Unsure of the structure they had stopped but those behind had just kept coming until now it is jam packed full of andys, some still wanting to get onto the bottom steps. Two pistol shots is all that's needed to loosen the top fastenings and the whole staircase suddenly drops to about half its height trapping the andys in a kind of collapsing concertina. Sinking like a guillotine it severs any limbs and body parts it catches as it teeters away from the building. The improvised cage leans motionless for a few seconds packed with blood soaked tunics and any body parts that remain. Slowly it topples over and crashes onto the ground crushing any life that was left. In amongst the chaotic tangle of metal and limbs, helmet displays flicker and fade, garbled commands become mute until there is nothing. What's left of each andy is given its last rite, they stiffen and shake with the terminal pulse that puts them out of their pain and misery, then at last they relax.

I turn towards the building on my right when a canister of some sort whistles past me and disappears over the side. At first I think I am under fire and drop to the ground as another spins into the air then falls into the street. The fire on the adjoining building has got to the andy and his small armoury. The heat is detonating the small charge that projects the canisters. Before a nasty one goes off I had better find a way down. Even a dye grenade would not be helpful; blue is not my colour.

The glass of the skylight is tough but eventually a whole pane gives way and I can look down into the top floor of a touchyfeelie. The drop is further than I would like but the bed beneath is solidly sprung, so much so that my rebound brings me neatly onto my feet by the bedside in a position of attention. All this and no audience, no one will believe me. So cool!

I make my way down through the store using the immobile autostairs that transport customers between floors. There are large windows to the front on each floor and no exits to the rear. At the bottom of an autostair I freeze. For a moment there is nothing else but me, and what I stand in front of. The whole corner of a floor is dedicated to the one and only, 'Muskrat Boot Company'. Its logo runs like a triumphal arch a few steps ahead of me, like the entrance to a temple. Before me are displayed all of Muskrat's superb products, but centre, on a raised plinth, tilting seductively towards me, a pair of Muskrat 'Supreme Flight', the best boots in the universe, and by the looks of them, my size. But I can't move, it's as if before me are all my material wants, no, needs. With these boots I will have made it, they will make me the person I want to be. My life would not have been in vain. I will have been a success. At the very moment I am about to take them from their display and try them on, something stops me, I take a step back and smile. Now that they are for the taking, their appeal diminishes, besides I am worth more than just a pair of boots. There is nothing that I can have that makes me greater than the person I am.

Below, somewhere in the building I can hear an impact; a vehicle crashing into and pushing metal. The loading bay shutter, I can hear it groaning and giving way. There are shouts echoing and beams of light reflected through the store all bouncing off walls and crowding in. I scamper up several autostairs till I'm back in the beds on the top floor, there are about twenty laid out like a dormitory. Above me is the skylight through which I dropped, too high to reach but it's the only way out. Ridiculously I think of hiding under the bed, it worked before, when her parents returned unexpectedly. But they didn't know I was there, and they weren't armed. I grab the bed I landed on, then heave it onto its elaborate headboard. I lean another bed against it, to give it support and to make it easier to climb. Balancing on the bed's foot board I can reach a louvered vent and the glass strips are easily broken. Having climbed through, I fire three shots into the mattress below but its fire resistance only makes it smoulder. A couple more and it bursts into flames.

I feel safe until I look around me and see how many doors there are, locked to me, but not them. They'll soon find them, gain access to the roof, and me. The roof on the adjoining building is alight. Where flames are not actually leaping through, the surface is already smouldering, soon it will all burst into one inferno. The higher roof on the other side is intact but it has no features other than a dead andy, but from there I can make a last stand firing down. I'm trapped, with not even one way out, if the andys I can hear below don't finish it, the chopper they'll call in will do it for them. I'll take as many with me as I can, it's not a rule, but it is now. I scramble up to the higher roof where I can hear chanting has resumed, the pipes too and the drums. That's good and as a final gesture I raise a fist.

The dead andy will afford me some cover, I won't be seen immediately. The headgear is still barking orders and the display scrolls pink and blue, I hear the word 'roof'. I pick it up to hear better how they are going to finish me off. Then I put it on.

'So this is what it's like to be an andy.' I look down at the dead figure and particularly what he's wearing. Blood saturates his tunic, but that's not going to be unusual.

I stand uncomfortably between two access points onto the roof. One is a hatch that I presume lifts, the other a door set into a raised roof section, perhaps at the head of stairs. Above my eye line the display scrolls across and down. The night sight frame in the centre is not operating due to the camera being smashed, a precaution I took in case they felt like giving me instructions. A voice does keep requesting a response from several andys, and any one of them could be me, or at least the one I'm dressed as. It's ill-fitting but in the dark and the mayhem I should pass as one. The sound of andy boots on the stairs gets louder as each section is cleared. Voices become clearer from the bed department immediately below. Then I sense a real closeness. Rather than listen at the door, I make my way round until I lie on the raised roof section over it. There is a heavy thud and the steel door beneath me flies open. Through my visor I can pick up their beams, scanning what area they can see. Then a sudden rush of four or five andys, followed by a stream of them. Making it look as if I have been covering the rear, I back round to the doorway adopting their crouch and join the fan shape as it spreads across the roof. The idiots are about to give up so I have to point out the hooded body lying on the pavement beneath, wearing my boots. The andy with bands on his helmet pushes us aside, decides that his mission is accomplished and cuts the air with his gauntlet in the direction of the steps down. I fall into the rear of the procession as we trundle down the stairs. Reaching the first floor again, the andys ill-fitting boots are working like a vice on my toes. I let the rest of the andys get ahead, then I stop and turn towards the front of the store, to where the Muskrat boots are,

'Bollocks,' I mutter, 'I'm 'aving 'em.'

CHAPTER 22

From the top of the autostairs I could hear the commotion surrounding the collapsed fire escape. Andys are expendable human units recruited for service from Rehab, there are plenty more so it's always a toss-up whether they are worth mending, or recycling. If they were bots there would be a dozen hygiene clad engineers out there picking up every neurone driven diode, tracing which bot it came from and making sure they picked up all the pieces. I can hear cutting devices and the sound of pistols on kill finishing off any that managed to survive their terminal pulse. Not worth mending then.

I move back into the Muskrat display nursing my new boots, waiting for the andys to go or to start up the autostair to this floor. I crawl into the display and listen in on the headset. In between periods of dozing, I try to make sense of the codes and jargon that they use. There's a lot of other crap being transmitted too which just sounds like interference and random signals. I take them to be communicating with my implant, if I was an andy and had one.

I wake with a jump, hearing the coarse scream of an andywagon heating its intakes. By my side the helmet is still garbling messages. An andy reports in and asks for clearance to proceed somewhere, leaving the area. The reply is affirmative and advises him that the store's own security personnel will be arriving shortly to secure the building. Then I hear the andywagon pull away and I decide it's time for me to move too.

I'm about to step out of my hole then wonder if looking like an andy on the streets is a good idea. Across the floor from the Muskrat corner there are racks of coats. A hooded one in a display looks good, the right size, and grabbing that one is quicker than searching through racks in an unlit store. I take it then stuff it, and a few other things that I collect on the way, into the andy's backpack.

At the rear of the store the buckled loading door has been pushed to the back of the bay. I walk past it and peer outside. It's clear of andys as far as I can see in between the drifting banks suffocating, caustic smoke billowing out of the adjoining store. The ground is spattered with blood, dark red streaks carve shapes and flashes like a twentieth century modernist masterpiece. There are pools, still bright red at their centre, that darken towards the edges. The collapsed fire escape rests like a twisted trellis and is decorated with pieces of blooded skin and tunic like an exec gift tree on Corporate Day. I no longer take pictures, mental ones, my album is full.

I turn left down the service road but I don't get far before I've had it with the andy boots. I duck into the darkness of a service entrance and rest on some steps. I get rid of the andy's boots and put on my own genuine Muskrats. Black or grey are the only colours to have, these are black and because the Muskrat insignia is black, they are more subtle, less showy, and I think that is cool. Andy boots are black so mine don't look obvious, but they feel like heaven. In the darkness of the doorway I can rest for a while wrapped up in my new coat, and guess what, it's grey, my favourite colour. I see what I can find in the andy's backpack pockets. I take out a ration pack, tear it open and eat a bar of some sweet stuff. There's loads of chatter on the headset, teams of andys are heading for zone 72, which doesn't mean much but apparently that's where the protests are converging. I imagine ranks of andys waiting to mow down the protesters and no one there to warn them.

I drift into a dozing rest. I feel partly guilty that I am not active and doing something, and partly knowing that I must rest if I'm going to think straight when I need to. Distant sounds herald slaughter and the sky above depresses me further with its usual City light show, as perpetual as ever, though the colour has changed and the rhythmic patterns are less defined. None of this is enough to stop me falling into sleep.

The thump of a device wakes me. Two pods fly like arrows overhead and seconds later, two explosions. I wonder if I'm dreaming. I see The City sky light flickering a dull orange-red, but it undulates chaotically. It brings me to my feet if only to prove I'm awake. I stand on some steps near-by and what I see is the reflection of fire raging a few streets away, either it masks The City lights, or it's The City itself, but I daren't believe it. The ancient ritual of rebirth is bound to be accompanied by fire. How can a phoenix rise without ashes?

Moving away from my service entrance I can now see there are other areas of the night sky that are aglow. I can see the top of an office block engulfed in flames escaping from the windows below. It resembles a beacon but it's no good to me, what I thought was The City light is just another glow in the sky, as one fades so another starts up. I'm lost, the glow of the City has always been the beacon by which we have navigated our lives. It has been our lodestar. Now from east to west the dark grey sky has beacons everywhere.

I try to remember the landmarks on Goodrich's screen, the high street with a turn travels north and south, and it turns to the East, the financial area lies to the South East of it. I walk back the way I came. In front of me now is the road which the andys blocked and in the middle of the road lies the shattered player, I kick over the fragments for nostalgia's sake.

I turn left and head away from the high street and continue in the direction of where I might find the main body of the protest. There I could make myself useful, make contact with some groups, let them know that they are not alone; tell them about Goodrich. There too I might get some idea of the andy's structure and what might happen if they lose their comms with their central control. There may even be some of Goodrich's folk there.

I dodge along checking front and rear, things have moved on from here. I wear the helmet loosely and sometimes just to my ear. The constant prattle dulls my senses and I start listening to that rather than just listening. The power grid is still down so all office blocks are dark monoliths against the dull grey sky. The emergency lighting has faded to insignificant, so if there is anybody up there, watching, reporting, I wouldn't know. Ahead of me, a group of people are gathered around the entrance to a food store. The store is dimly lit with candles but the till, which has its own power pack, is tinkling away. Nothing, not even a revolution, should interrupt the taking of money. Turning a corner there's commotion by a token machine, more than a dozen, some of them street sleepers, are jostling each other in a queue. The machine seems to be shelling out as many tokens as they can carry. One passes me with his loot wrapped in a table cloth, partly ecstatic that he is now rich, but predominantly fearful of those who were his friends and the envy they have for his fortune. He skulks away looking behind him, swearing and threatening everyone whilst clutching his hoard. I scare him and he runs off and I realise that part of the andy's tunic is showing and I'm carrying a helmet. I do up my coat and approach the queue. A big guy looks at me, then the helmet.

'A souvenir,' I tell him. He smiles then shuffles forward. By the way the machine is paying out there won't be any tokens left by his turn, or mine. There seems to be no limit on what anyone can have but people are impatient and after a few goes they get pushed out of the way. The big guy gets to the machine, puts his thumb on the plate then presses the fifty key. The machine hums into action and spews out tokens like it's a jackpot, he does this three times but half way through the fourth it stops. The guy grunts, then starts kicking the wall beneath the machine. He's about to launch into the machine itself when someone from behind wearing a cap walks forward,

'Whoa! Hang on, it's okay.'

The big guy is not in a mood to be stopped and lifts him off his feet, but not before he's plucked a slip of paper from the cash tray.

'Look big fella,' he says fighting for air, 'this money too.'

The big guy lowers him to the ground and loosens his grip.

'See. It says on it,' he points to the fancy calligraphy printed in a dozen shades with coloured borders and little pictures.

'All you have to do is take it to the store, and they'll give you tokens or goods,' he says, 'it's the same as money. Believe me.'

The big guy is appeased but doesn't loosen his grip, presses keys and another few slips of brightly coloured paper spew out on a roll. He lets the little guy fall to his knees as he snatches the slips then walks away. He looks back at the little guy then at his notes, still not quite believing his flimsy pieces of paper have the same buying power as tokens.

I take my turn and I'm issued with several slips of paper every time I press the button. The paper curls as it spews out as if its stored on a roll. The background of each slip is the same, only the amount changes, printed in a different colour and embossed. Indentations on one edge differ too so you can tell what they are in the dark, or if you are blind. Nothing must stop you spending.

As I walk away the little guy winks at me from near the front of a queue that now disappears round the corner.

'Our grandchildren,' he says, 'will never believe we are printing our own money!'

I smile and head back to the store.

I sit on a small wall with a few things that the store had left in stock, I take a good long drink from a bottle. There are noises far off that I take to be protesters. Sporadic gun fire and when the breeze is right, what I think is cheering, but I can't be sure, it may just be some live game show still recording. Who knows if this isn't all a game show.

The street map I've bought is wrapped up tightly and the hardest part is getting the protective film off it. I activate it and it rolls out flat then a cartoon ad show presents itself that I have to endure before it asks me what I want. I've bought and paid for it but what I've got seems a low priority compared to the chance to sell me something else. Doubtless that something else would be less important than the chance it gives for them to sell me something better and improved. And so it goes, there's nothing that can be bought that there isn't something better and more expensive that we should have bought instead.

    I touch the button, 'Where am I?' It lights up, goes through some performance telling how much quicker, more accurate and better defined the upgrade is. In the time it has taken me to buy this product it is already out of date. Overcome with consumer depression, I watch limply as characters morph into cross hairs to give me my position. I expand it to see a larger area, then close in on some roads I recognise. I tap a street in the financial area, then 'Route', and streets throb yellow, from there to me. I memorise some landmarks, street names, then I tap 'Close'. It tells me it is closing and while it is, I have to endure more ads. Then no lesser person than the chief exec thanks me personally, telling me how important my business is to him and his family of workers. It then asks me if I would like to file a review? I decline and then have to explain my reticence. I change my mind and give a five out of five, answer yes to a few questions, and the map closes. Anything less than a max and the interrogation would have been endless. If you want to get on with your life you just say the product is the best, give it a five out of five, and a 'Yes I would certainly recommend it to a friend'. Only then does the thing shut down, roll itself up, and let you go.

    As I walk, I pick up more of the jargon from the headset. The andy's repeatedly fail to understand instructions, have to have long explanations given to them and then take everything literally or misinterpret them. There's no initiative shown, no common sense applied, but since I saw the andy's wig I wonder if they're all as stupid as they make out. There are operators who give the orders, they interface between those andys on the street and the commanders. Occasionally an angry voice in fever pitch interrupts the conversation and balls some instruction that the operator has been trying to initiate for some time. Bots might be far more expensive but at least they are biddable, but then you pays your money and you takes your choice. I wonder if it isn't pure human stubbornness that makes the andys take things so literally. Once an awkward bastard, always an awkward bastard, there may be hope yet.

One of the commanders in the field reports that they have located an enemy control centre and have it under surveillance. A reference is given, he says they have taken up a position in office block R223, overlooking R772, a disused station. He wants four more units to take up a position on a flyover R91, and a further six units along the main street RA213 as backup. The operator replies that the number of units he wants is unnecessary and he can have three more units only. There's no answer.

It occurs to me that the 'enemy control centre' to which they refer, must have people Goodrich wants me to contact. If I can get there before the andys, I will also be able to warn them.

A disused station is easy to find. If I had spent more on the map I could have got it 3D and would have found the office block and the flyover instantly. There is only one area that I think fits the criteria, but it's a guess. I activate the map as I travel in the direction I think I need. I don't have time to suffer its ads, when it eventually shows my position, I stop and confirm my guesswork and plan my route.

After a street or two I can see another token machine, there's a blue currency logo on the pole above it otherwise I wouldn't know it was there for the dozens of people round it. People are running away with wads of paper notes, dropping some and not even bothering to pick them up. Out of curiosity I pick one up and give it a close look, it seems fine; fine enough for my pocket anyway.

A local homewares store is besieged with people of all sorts who are coming out laden down with goods in trolleys and carts. A young girl and guy bump into each other and the guy's new screen perched on the top of a pile crashes to the ground. He swears at the girl but then they laugh and she gives him a bundle of notes then they pat each other and shrug. I begin to think I'm having some kind of drug induced hyper reality trip, but this is all real which makes it so much more bizarre, and unbelievable.

Between buildings I can see there is smoke rising and occasionally through it flames leap upwards. Another explosion rips through a building in the distance; it's seen but not felt until a second or two later. Then one closer and that's immediate, like lightening overhead. Everyone I can see ducks, as if that would help. I pass a store that is closed but it has had its doors smashed and stuff has been taken. Someone has left money, old habits I suppose. There are sellers on streets taking advantage of the money that everyone has, despite the risks. Another token machine is on the rise ahead of me, there is a lot of fighting and injured people are all over the place. There are mothers with children pleading, but no one's queuing, they must know the machine could run out any time. As I get closer, some people have formed a collective and attack the group that is round the machine, emptying it for themselves. Just as they get to the machine, a small crowd appears from a nearby junction. They see the machine is still paying out, and run headlong into everyone, wealding sticks and anything else that will carve their way to the machine before it's printed its last note.

I leave the screaming and shouting behind me, following the route I can remember from the map, a few blocks, then a left and a second right. On the breeze I can hear chanting, drifting in and out and only a few streets away. I turn down the next street that travels in its direction. The drum beats grow louder and then there are pipes; the thrill is inexplicable. When marching to war what more stirring sound is there but pipes and drums? You would lay down your life just for the music of it and only later would you ask what you were fighting for.

When I think it can't get any louder I turn a corner and it nearly blasts me off my feet. I've come out at a junction some way ahead of the vanguard but the buildings retain the sound and it bounces back and forth until you're deaf with the passion of it.

Proudly held aloft is a small bird painted onto a cotton sheet, and raised on two poles. A small bird has brought these thousands together.

As they march past, images of the 'Sparrow' are everywhere, and though I am not a member, I join in to show my solidarity. We travel several streets, zig zagging toward the commercial centre.

I leave them and move down a side street so I can check my route in a secluded doorway, then I carry on toward the disused station. There are signs of damage on most streets wherever the crowds or a splinter group has passed. Windows are buckled and pushed in, goods thrown into the streets, a few premises still burn. Some vehicles are burning too, where they were parked, or where they have been rolled into the street. The nature of vandalism varies. Much of what the capitalist state produces is symbolic, so the vandalism is symbolic too. Some premises are just vandalised because the protesters feel the owners have ignored them, patronised them or treated them with contempt. If the state doesn't care about you, why should you care about it? It's a deal, and it's the state that breaks it. Stores that have anything of use have been looted so that what some see as their rightful share can be taken. The token machines now are mostly deserted having run out of anything to give. A drunk clings on to one, persistently pressing his thumb against the panel and requesting what the exhausted machine cannot give.

Turning a corner ahead of me I can see the station. I hop into a doorway and orientate the map to get an accurate position for the office block and the flyover that were mentioned on the headset. The street to my right runs up to the offices, from here the flyover is not visible, but lies on the opposite side of the station. I wait for a few moments, listen and see if my gut feelings tell me anything. Demonstrations are everywhere. Occasionally there is a burst of firing, the sound of people screaming and shouting either as they are being massacred, or as they are charging, or both. The silence, or the cheers that follow, tell you which.

There's nobody on the streets; here there is only desolation. I catch a glimpse of what I think is a lone figure, I shrink back into my shadow by a pillar and watch as the figure moves on the street opposite. It slides from one doorway to another, then disappears into an alleyway at the far end, just as my vision is obscured by an overturned van. The figure was not an andy, and dangerously I presume the opposite. Where the figure came from or where it went to puzzles me. Its body language is one I understand, an ease of moving smoothly through shadows with a natural air of awareness and caution. I feel an immediate affiliation too strong to ignore. Having so observed, the coin then flips and I wonder if I too am being observed.

    The van in the road can give me cover halfway across. I could stay there for several minutes so that if someone had only thought they'd seen me, their attention might be diverted. How good is their peripheral vision? If they are looking down a sight, they won't have any. How long will they wait for my next move? The long run should always be made first, it'll be a surprise. They will expect the next run and be ready. Given time, their concentration might lapse, but the second run is more likely to be your last. Too much thinking is not always good. I sprint across the road and pause only briefly at the van then sprint to the opposite corner and into cover. I don't know if anyone saw me, even if anyone was looking. Paranoia? Perhaps, but it doesn't mean they're not there.

    I move along to where I first saw the sliding figure. I check every door, every access, anything that might conceal an entrance, there's nothing. I'm well into where I saw the figure so I turn and take it slower, using my senses, everything. I'm almost back to the corner when I smell coffee, not real coffee, but coffee all the same. I creep along the line of windows, sniffing the air, until by an inactive advertising screen, set back a little from the line of stores, the smell seems strongest. I stand breathing in the faint aroma and then look down. On the floor is a footprint, barely visible and even as I watch, its sharp patterned sole relaxes into a mess of blurred edges then disappears into the surrounding dampness. I wonder if that's what I really saw but the smell of coffee is real enough. I move to the right of the screen, where it's tightly bolted onto the wall and sniff along the seal. I imagine I can smell coffee. I move over to the left of it, to where it isn't so hard up against the wall. The smell of coffee is unmistakable. Near the top and bottom, I can see through the slight gap to where catches are waiting to be engaged, the pressure of the closing mechanism has weakened slightly. On the ground by a trashed window next to the screen are several metal strips. Inserting one of these lifts the internal bolt near the top, and with it, the bottom one too. The seal opens and I can pull the panel away like a door and I can slip inside. I gently allow the door to relax back onto the catches as it was; I just feel it is best to leave things as I found them. In the darkness beyond, a dull light is reflected into a narrow passageway that is easily defended. The creamy coloured walls are cold and moist and the wet footprints travelling each way could have been here for hours, or just a few minutes. I move cautiously along the passage way with my own small pistol at the ready. The andy's pistol with its long site is too cumbersome in a confined area and protrudes ominously from the sack. Every moment spent in this passageway there is the risk of someone using it and running straight into me from either direction. Ahead are some concrete steps going up, but the passage diverts to the side and continues straight on. I stop at the bottom, here at least there is a space beneath the steps that afford some seclusion in which I can hide if need be. I take the opportunity of listening. There is no sound from any direction other than the sound of regular dripping, and its rich, clear echoes. The stairs are not so wet, more traffic carries on the level past the steps, and that's the route I choose. Beyond the steps the light is less and the cream painted walls turn a drab grey that are foreboding and promise some horror beyond. I carry on and soon reach the source of the dripping. No sooner am I being dripped upon then for a second a reflected light dances along the walls. A door closing sends an echo as the light diminishes, followed by footsteps coming in my direction. It's impossible to judge how far or near they are, or how soon the owner will be upon me. I back track and throw myself against the wall under the stairs and collapse into the corner covering myself, hoping to look like a shadow, or a bundle of rags. Somebody strides past, I hear the double click of the advertising panel echo as the two catches fall into place, then steps as they return and go up the stairs over me. Before I can decide if I should make a run for it, the footsteps return. I hear them on the steps, but they stop abruptly, they take a single step, then another. Then I hear sniffing, someone sniffing the air. They suspect something, and someone. Down on the level I can hear them taking steps slowly, then not at all. My face is in the corner and I can't see if they are looking away into the depths of the corridor, or are about to plunge something into my back, or shoot. For all I know they could be squeezing the trigger right now. My senses are at their most acute, waiting for the faint mechanical sound just before something hits me. A pico second of well-being before transportation to the next realm. Goodnight Vienna. But all I hear is a rumble, like thunder. Like boots, like andy boots, and lots of them, then silence. Whoever it is standing near me hears the same, they perhaps heard it before me, they then run off in which direction I can't tell. I raise myself from my cramped position just in time to feel a deadening thump somewhere in the building, then I'm knocked backwards by the blast of hot air and a very familiar smell. That in turn, after the usual pause, is followed by glass smashing and heavy objects falling back down. A thin pink and blue cloud billows down the steps as if it's falling, and then drifts in every direction. It's nothing to fear, however the appearance of pin thin pistol beams cutting through the smoke, may be. Timed to perfection the door I came through has also been blown and andys must be making their way along the corridor as well as down from above. I crouch by the bottom of the stairs and wonder for a moment, whether to use the andy's headgear and see if the clearsight works, but with such a narrow passageway, I don't need to see them to guess where they are. I move back to the cover of the concrete steps. The beams move around too shakily for anything other than pistols. I fire a couple of charges blindly down the passage bouncing them off walls. They will lose some power by the time they hit anything full on but they will still break bones. Only one light on the steps and the beam is at a slight angle, so I send another couple skimming off the floor to where I guess he's lying. I send along a few more just in case they think I'm fooled by them not firing. Then above me I hear a doorway being rammed. As I move to get a clear shot up the steps, a charge whistles past me and cracks into the floor behind. I throw myself back to avoid any more, then as the sound of boots above gets louder I decide to see what's at the end of the passageway. It is, after all, my only way out.

I run blind down the corridor, concrete walls on both sides, hoping not to run into anything, or anyone. Eventually a dull light appears much like the one near the entrance, beneath it a steel doorway and a large handle. I throw myself against the doorway and push the handle down at the same time, nothing. So I pull the handle up and it moves a little, but the door doesn't. I hear a pistol shot and drop onto the floor as a charge hits the steel framework. I fire four shots down the passage, two bouncing off the walls, turn while still on the ground and fire three more into the seal by the door handle. I spin round while still on the floor and thump the door with my boots, it's solid. I fire repeatedly until the pistol's indicator oscillates. I sit up and take out the andy's weapon and fire another three charges, then try the handle, it moves down but not enough. There are pin beams above me, and for all I know, in the middle of my back. I drop and roll to one side because two heavy charges, the ones you can hear coming, are bouncing off walls and whining towards me. I cover my face with my arms as I hear them slam into the door, buckling it and shaking the metal frameworks and the ground around me. There's a strange rolling sound like a ball, clanking its way through the thinning smoke. A large grenade wobbles into view, I have no choice and waste no time but scoop it up and bowl it back down the corridor into the smoke. I turn, pick up my bag and with both feet drop kick the buckled door which gives enough for me squeeze through. I don't know what's on the other side, I don't care. In one movement I'm through and rolling to one side covering my head with as much of my coat and back pack as I can. Somewhere along that corridor there is a blinding light and a deadening thump which sends a shock wave like a piston in every direction. I feel it coming down the corridor, then I feel it burst into the space where I am.

A second or two is long enough and I'm making my way down some steps through dust and smoke in a chamber the size of a small chapel. A blackened skylight way up sheds a dull light through several missing panels. I cling to the wall on my left and avoid a corroded hand rail on my right. At the bottom I look back up to see that the door and its frame have been blown clear across the chamber and lie by the stream that runs in a channel beneath me. I cross a narrow steel bridge which takes me onto more steps down onto a path at the side of the stream. It reminds me of an old canal, but underground and smaller. As the smell of the explosion gives way to a familiar pungent odour, I realise I am in the sewers.

The path is well used and must have been one of the routes used by protesters seen coming out of the ground. Now they are all above and I am all alone, below, but not for long. There are voices, but it's impossible to say from where as the sound reverberates and circulates. What light there is comes from above, down drains and culverts, then reflected off dripping walls that are ancient and crumbling. There are passageways running in all directions, most with sewers, but it seems, all with voices. I feel I'm in one of Escher's works of art. I must move on but no one way is better than any other. I pass several entrances that have no light at all, then one that has a glimmer of light in some distant part. I cut the corner and trip, falling into the darkness and I sit exhausted listening to the voices, commands, a female voice, headset talk, reports of nothing found, no one here. The ancient brickwork surrounds me, arches and vaults, like catacombs. At the corner where I fell a stone is prominent, not enough to notice but enough for me to fall over. On it there is a rough chiselled mark, the same on the two faces that show. Resting next to it I am at the junction of the vile stream that trickles past and just another branch tunnel. The splash of a rat jumping in after some tasty morsel echoes in the silence. Now I notice them, they're everywhere, biding their time, in spouts and outlets, peeking out of cracks or just sat at the water's edge.

In the silence that has crept up on me, there's a faint crunch. Too heavy for any rat, it was a boot compressing the grit beneath it as it takes the weight of its creeping owner. A whisper, so faint it might have been a breeze. I push myself up the slimy wall and delve into my sack and remove the andy's helmet, pistol and long site. The helmet is still active and now it's in the open the squawking commands are obvious. I place it carefully upside down onto the edge of the stream and give it a little shove and off it floats. It squawks into the darkness until all I can see is its head up display, like a light show on a City fun boat, drifting downstream.

I rest the andy's pistol against the tunnel wall as I put the back-pack over my head and onto my shoulder. Another faint sound is felt rather than heard. I creep slowly into what I hope is total darkness. Eventually I turn and study every small part of the archway I'm backing away from, waiting for a shape, a gloved hand, a toe at the base, anything which will give me that millisecond advantage. I raise my pistol, fully charged again and curse silently, the andy's pistol with its long site lays by the archway where I've left it, not against my back where it should be. Such things may turn a battle, and if I needed to leave an indication of which way I'd gone, I couldn't do better. A dead end will be just that.

Something moved, about halfway up the wall on the left hand side. There it is again, briefly, something, something like the end of a pistol. I shrink closer to the wall in case there's a rush. A figure dashes from one side of the archway to the other, loud and careless, then seconds later another, and then another. Coming from both sides at once will make it more difficult for me to aim. Another two dash across, so there will be at least four a side when they charge. Behind me too now, there are noises. As I edge backwards, keeping to the left and waiting for the charge, my left hand finds a void. I turn with surprise but it's just another passageway and I'm suddenly in a pool of dim light that's being reflected from a short distance away. I turn into the passageway, but the hushed voices that way are louder, I have no choice but to go back. I take a step out and hear the pistol shot. I pull back instantly but too late, my left hand is thrust to one side but there's no pain, it must have been close, a lucky escape. Then I feel the stickiness of warm blood running through my fingers. I shake off the blood and hold my hand up but the warm stickiness is uncomfortable as it runs down my arm. Then what starts as stinging soon becomes a racking pain. I feel trapped, but above all, angry. I stand back from the light as best I can and fire shots down to the archway, count to three, fire two more, three shots are returned, I still count to three, get them into thinking there's a rhythm to this, fire two shots. The voices behind me are louder, they've heard the shooting. Another count then fire two shots, two return, now run like the wind! It's a dry bed I'm running up, a storm drain down to the main sewer, with my Muskrats I'm almost silent.

All hell lets loose behind me and above me charges ricochet and thump into buttresses and other supports. The andys are storming my position filling the air with charges and hopefully meeting up with another load of andys doing the same. My tunnel climbs a little steeper making it hard going, eventually I come to another steel door. Behind me the clammer of boots and shouts is growing nearer, unfortunately, they didn't manage to kill each other. I push on the handle, and to my relief this time it moves. I put my shoulder against the door and it creaks open. The space inside is intolerably light, there are spotlights, a blinding light. I try to move but something on the floor stops me. I look down, a body. I try to shade my eyes to see, but my arms are grabbed, pulled to the side, then twisted so all I can do is bend head down and stare at the floor. Someone speaks and there's a sharp pain in my neck, a sting, an injector. A numbness creeps round my face, my mouth is dry and I can't support the weight of my head. It hangs down and all I see is the floor and shadows moving round and round. I am moving and trying to stand but my feet drag. The light fades and there is darkness and just weariness, such weariness and sleep, and I welcome it.

CHAPTER 23

I hear a woman's voice.

I am sitting with my arms secured behind me. Ties are cutting into my wrists. My eyes are bound shut and my head is pulled tight back.

She comes closer,

'So, his name is Goodrich?'

The realisation that I must have already given that information makes me fearful of what else I must have given away. This is why we carry our EDs, but I can't get to mine.

I am about to say, 'Yes', and I have this ethereal feeling which is warm and comfortable and it is where I would like to be. Then, 'No,' appears as an option and with it a burning sensation at every nerve ending. The more I want to say, 'No', the more the pain builds. If I could convince myself it is the truth then the pain would subside, but I can't.

'Yes.' I gasp, and the pain subsides. My blindfold is wet with my perspiration. There is no hope of passing out, you would go mad first. Stimulants ensure you remain awake and sensitive.

'Tell me about Goodrich?'

I'm tempted to say, 'Who?' As the thought occurs to me, so does the pain. This time it starts from where it left off. I hear a scream, and wonder if it's me. My mind and my body seem to be drifting apart, losing control.

I ask her what she wants to know. The choice is to eventually tell the truth without knowing you are doing so, the pain being so intense that you never recover your sanity. Or tell the truth, and remain capable of taking advantage of any opportunities that might occur later. There is no hiding the truth, this is reality.

'Describe Goodrich.'

'He is about seventy maybe older,' I dutifully say and any temptation to depart from what I know to be the truth is accompanied by the familiar stab of burning pain that my silence increases.

'He's untidy with silver hair but the top of his head is bald. He's quite short. He has bushy eye brows and dirty glasses.'

There is something familiar about her voice. There is a pause and she is telling someone else to make a note. I can hear gentle tapping, someone entering details.

'Where is he Ash?' she comes closer, 'You know that every wrong answer will be increasingly painful. That is without the pain that I can inflict.'

'I like strong women.' I tell her without any pain because it is true. Then something smashes into the left side of my face. I feel that brief numbness you get after a blow, before the pain kicks in, as it does this time, and I feel blood filling my mouth.

'Was Sam a strong woman? What about Carol, Ash? Is she strong too?'

I'm shocked at how much in my unconscious state I must have told her.

'You've been telling me about these people Ash, but what I really want to know is where they are, Ash?'

'At the HQ.'

'With the man, Goodrich?'

'Yes.'

'That's better, you see how pain free the right answer can be?' She says something to the other person in the room, I think there are only two. Then there is a knock on a door,

She makes a noise indicating her impatience and opens a heavy door, maybe steel. There is some mumbling. I hear the name 'Goodrich', then a man's voice, obedient, 'He knows noth . . .' More mumbling, There are others being interrogated. Everything will be revealed, it is impossible not to.

Something is said, not by her, but then she shouts, 'Then find somebody!'

The door closes. I hear another door nearby open and close. While it is open there is a brief cry, someone being hit.

She comes nearer, I can smell her breath, it is sweet and she is perfumed. Her hand is on my crotch, gentle, caressing, I expect pain but the temptation to enjoy it is too great. The physical tightening of her grasp and the massaging begins to block out any sense of danger. I find myself enjoying it, I can't help it.

'There,' she says, her voice is soft, friendly, seductive.

'This is a lot better way to gather information. I can do all sorts of exciting things for you. All you need to do is tell me the truth and we can enjoy each other. Pain is so uncivilised, each correct answer will get you more enjoyment, but you must control yourself, we don't want it to be over too soon, do we?'

She is close. She presses her softness against me, I hear her heartbeat and her warmth, my face is between her breasts. She pulls my head into her cleavage, then her hands run down and sink inside my clothing, searching.

'Now tell me, why are you wearing this uniform under your coat?'

'I used it as a disguise to escape from the roof of the store.'

'So it was you, was it?'

There is another crashing blow into by face from the other side. This time I feel my teeth biting into my cheek.

'You only delayed the inevitable, the streets are now piled high with those you were trying to protect. You are responsible, you have their blood on your hands. We would have let them go home quietly but you changed our minds and they are all dead. The only inconvenience you caused us was having to recycle so many bodies all at once. We didn't have time to tell whether they were still alive. Some said they were but you can never believe the lying scum. This Goodrich, where is his headquarters?'

'It's at a cross roads and the entrance is . .' I feel the pain starting as I look for an answer, but the intensity is not as great, I wonder if the drug is wearing off. Now, as long as I think the answer is right, the pain fades away, if I think the right answer is wrong the pain increases. It's only to do with my perception of the answer, if I can believe my answer is right I will not have any pain.

' . . at Mr. Foo's sushi bar.'

She moves away from me,

'Mr. Foo's, find it!'

There is frantic tapping, a pause then a mumble. She comes back to me. Her face is close to mine, again I smell her sweet breath and it mingles with the taste of blood in my mouth.

'Tell me again, my darling, where is Goodrich's HQ?' She sits astride me pushing her breasts into me again, and rubbing her crotch against mine.

'Now look what's happened, you've made a mess. Your blood is on my tunic, some of your bodily fluid is over me, I may have to take it off, get undressed. Would you like that? Then we can have some more fun. But first just tell me where the HQ is.'

'The entrance is at Mr. Foo's Sushi Bar.'

She is still close, watching my reaction, seeing if there is any pain. Then she turns away.

'Try again. This time find it, try Sushi Bars. Bring up the map, see if there is any near a cross roads.' She paces the room. There is a knock at the door.

Impatiently she opens the door and a man's voice whispers,

'We've got as much as we need, sir. This is their only command centre we've been able to find. There are about sixteen groups and each has sub groups. Names, places, details are on this sir.'

'Excellent. Good work,' she tells him, 'this can be loaded into the system here and later into our network for execution.'

'Sir, there is a problem above with comms, and we can't get a signal. Units are having difficulty communicating with each other.'

'Okay I'm nearly finished here. Clear everyone out and I will see you on top. You've primed the gas?'

'Yes, sir. What do you want doing with mine, sir?'

'Nothing. Neither of them are of any more use. Go up and start planning the search for the other leaders, I want them identified and killed. If you cannot identify them, kill them anyway, and any close to them. We'll have them running about like headless chickens. I will see you when we have finished here. I will sort out the comms then I will need to talk to all deputy controllers. Now leave.'

The door closes at the same time as I can hear the momentary whirr of a printer. Suddenly light bursts upon my eyes as my blindfold is removed and painfully I can raise my head. I blink repeatedly, try to focus and gain some idea of the room. It's that same cream, and a low ceiling, with a steel door set in the same kind of frame, no windows. I guess we are still in the sewer complex.

Without making it obvious I try to get an idea of my bindings by resting my head forward onto my chest as if in pain or recovery. I'm sat on a wooden chair, like those in cheap restaurants, each ankle is flexitied to the front legs, and my arms to its rear uprights. My wrists too are tied to the chair back but not to each other.

I don't look in her direction but I can see her andy boots. I look up as she turns, and I can see the rest of the room, a rubbish collection of random furniture. Across the room, beyond her, there is an andy at a screen sitting awkwardly on an arm chair in front of a small desk. She collects something from the desk, images, and brings them over to me. She stands behind me then grabs me by the hair and jerks my head back.

'Now take a look at these and tell me which one is Goodrich.'

She presents me with one at a time and asks me the same question,

'Is this a photograph of the man known to you as Goodrich?' It's the right way. Any question that can be correctly answered will be pain free. If she had asked me. 'Is this Goodrich?' I could have said, 'No.' Because it would only have been an image and I would have been correct and pain free.

She shows me about six and each time I answer 'No.' Because it isn't.

Then his face appears before me. Even as she is asking the question the drug induced pain starts collecting itself and making for my nerve endings as I think about lying. She finishes her question and every answer that tries to avoid a 'yes' builds the pain, not as immediate as it was, and not as intense but still enough for me to say,

'Yes.'

'There, that's all we need. Now you can relax.'

She knows that the drug is beginning to fade, and a second dose will be less effective until I recover. She walks round me, back to the andy.

'That one,' she says pointing at the screen, 'I want his details on every screen, he must be found, killed, and everyone with him. Top priority. Stop at nothing. Clear them out like rats.' There is some frantic mumbling from the andy.

'Okay, pack up your gear, shoot him then shoot the one next door and then report to me above.'

She turns to go, but hesitates. She walks slowly towards me, lifts my head with one gloved hand and brushes my hair back with the other.

'How mean of me to think of leaving without saying goodbye Ash.'

She has long eye lashes surrounding her light hazel eyes, but they are cold. Her sweet breath is on my cheek then on my lips, then so are hers. A gentle, almost loving kiss. I'm tempted to bite, but she might yet have some feeling, I'm nothing if not an optimist. I try to look lovingly into her eyes to make contact. She draws her face away and focusses for a moment,

'You'd like to fuck me wouldn't you?'

I nod, then she whispers so close,

'Well, my pretty boy, you're the one that's fucked.' Then she moves away and stands looking at me, 'If I had the time I would get you stripped naked, hung from the ceiling and then I would shoot you myself. Watching you piss and shit yourself would be a treat.'

She moves back to the andy who is now standing with his case under his arm. His visor is down now and his right hand rests upon his pistol. She stops by him, turns towards me and folds her arms. She is taking a last look.

'Kill him. Shoot him there first.' She points at my crotch. Insanely I wonder how she got to hate men so much.

The andy looks at her for conformation. She stands there motionless, watching me. She glances at him briefly.

'Shoot him I said! There!' And she points again.

I can't help but start to wriggle in the chair stupidly thinking that I might yet avoid death. The chair moves at least making the crotch shot more difficult and a quick death more likely.

'You bitch, you fucking frustrated bitch, you can't even do your own fucking killing.' In the treacle slow, adrenalin filled moments, my mind is racing. Thoughts, images flash past, then one slower, the cellar. A vision germinates, a tumbler falls into place and there's the solid clunk of a realisation. The andy turns his visored head toward me and raises his pistol through the swimming air to fire. When the two focus on me that will be it. Goodnight Vienna.

'Correctacorrecta!' I shout as loud as I can to reach a distant memory. If andys need to wear wigs and can still sit awkwardly on the arms of sofas they just might be still in the building,

'Correctacorrecta!' I shout again.

The andy's head twitches to one side as if bitten.

'Correctacorrecta!' I shout again, then. 'Token galoragalora lady!'

He clutches his helmet with both hands, then the fists clench and the pistol fires into the roof bringing down a shower of concrete.

'You fool! Kill him. Now!' she screams but his head is racked, the implant that they all have hooked into the nervous system is going berserk. She tries to wrestle the pistol off him but it fires again into the ceiling.

I use what strength I have to raise the chair then drop with all my weight onto one leg which splinters, releasing my right leg I do the same with what's left of the chair and it disintegrates leaving me with flexitie bracelets on all my limbs. The bitch is screaming commands at the same time as trying to unclip her pistol. She stops as I pick up the andy's case and smash it into her face. I can hear the bones crunch and she drops to her knees facing the two of us. Her body falls slowly backwards from her knees as the andy too collapses against the door. As he slumps heavily to the ground he puts his right hand down to cushion his fall, the pistol that's still in it fires along the ground. Then all is motionless.

I raise his visor, and then remove his helmet. There before me is Chad, patches of red where the sensors make contact. His mouth is moving, but there is no sound. I imagine they could be words but I don't know and I can make no sense of them. His face is dripping with perspiration and one side is deep red. Dark blue patches blossom in the pale skin, veins still pulse in his neck, and a trickle of blood falls from his ear. His eyes roll around, once or twice. I think they focus on me, but then they roll away and one gradually fills with blood. I take his hand and look into his eyes,

'Well done Chad, you are tonight's big winner.'

I speak loudly as if calling him back. A flicker of recognition maybe, and his mouth opens as if to speak, but it says nothing. His blank staring eyes move less, his mouth ceases its silent chatter, and his hand falls limp. I see his chest sink, and then the pain drain from his face, as all care is being lifted. Whatever he tried to say, I understood. I wished him peace, and not only that we shall forgive him, but he should forgive himself.

Blood saturates my knee. I can feel its sticky warmth all the way down my leg. Standing up I realise a piece of chair leg is sticking out of my arse. I pluck out the painful wooden splinter about half the thickness of a finger but about the same length. It's not all my blood, behind me lies the bitch, and it's in her blood that I'm kneeling. She had sunk to her knees when I hit her with the case. Then she had fallen slowly backwards, onto her heels with her knees apart. As Chad collapsed to the ground he had put out his right hand, still holding his pistol, to save himself. With his finger still on the trigger, it had fired straight up her main avenue and entered her where there was least resistance. I'm consoled by the fact it's the way she would like to have gone.

I pick up both pistols, open the door and check the passageways, all is quiet and appears deserted. From the open door I turn and fire back into the room at the case. The lid springs up as it spins round and I send another into the contents. The case somersaults backwards with the data sets popping and whizzing like indoor fireworks. Another charge and it skates across the floor into the far corner leaving a trail of purple and grey smoke.

I stand in the doorway, not sure which way to go. The large area before me has rooms and disused offices leading off it. Seats like the one I was tied to are piled in a corner, some stacked, others broken. There are fragments of maps dotting the walls, a large table in the middle covered in pieces of cloth and paint, different colours. There are data leads and cables connected to sockets but no machinery, no screens.

To my right an echo reaches me, a sound reverberates up from the sewers. Then above a ringing sound like a steel door hitting something as it opens, not the sound of it closing. I hear it echo below and that confuses me, I'm suffering the drug after effects and the order in which things happen is not clear. I'm confusing echoes with the sounds that make them. There is activity above me, low pitch rumblings, like heavy vehicles. A doorway above, somewhere to my left, is open through which I can hear an andywagon. Suddenly there are footsteps. I can't make out whether they are coming up, or down. Up is where the andys are, I think. Down is to the sewers and the gas they were talking about, now perhaps active, filling the subterranean levels with a poisonous fog.

Another metallic sound from above, maybe below. I reason that soon some andy is going to be sent down to see what's happened to their commander. I gamble that there is more than one way up and turn in the direction of the distant stairs. I run to the bottom of the steps prepared to chance it and go up, when a door above slams open. It echoes below and again I'm confused, I stop. Now I can hear booted footsteps hurrying towards me. There may only be two sets but the echoing makes them seem more and closer, but I can't tell from which direction. Taking them by surprise I might have an advantage, but more would come. I dash back into the room where the commander is still pissing blood onto the concrete floor, and everywhere are my bloody footprints, literally. I hear an andy calling out for the commander. I quietly close the steel door, then hold the handle up hoping he will think it's locked. If it opens they'll only be one option.

I lean against the door pulling up hard on the handle. I can hear very little and put my ear to the cold steel. There's a knock which nearly deafens me and my head jolts back. I have the vision of the two of us either side of this door, ear to ear.

'Commander! Captain 772 reporting for orders, Commander.'

There's a pause, I keep the pressure up on the handle to make sure there's no give. I feel a slight pressure on the handle, then it relaxes.

'Commander! Are you here Commander?' Another pause, I can't hear whether he is standing by the door or has gone. I hear a muffled voice calling down to the sewers. There are two deafening thumps on the door, then some pressure on the handle and I nearly give in preparing to shoot, but the pressure relaxes again. Then as I put my ear to the steel I can hear them,

'No, the commander's not here. She's locked this door.' A dull voice I can't make out. There are at least two.

'No, she said just leave them. Check that one, knock first to see if she's in there, you know she doesn't like to be disturbed.'

I hear knocking on another door, then a different voice. I press my ear to the door to catch as much as I can.

' . . . lively one. . . . to be taught some . . . .'

'Serves you right if you don't catch something one day.'

'No . . . can't give me . . . . . already got. . . tied up?'

'On a chair.'

'Fuck, we'll have to get him off that. Is there a . . .?'

'Yeh, a table.'

'Good. We'll . . . over that. You . . . ties?'

'Yeh, loads'.

'Good.'

There's some noises I can't make out, then a pause, dull, muffled voices, then all hell breaks out. I hear an andy cursing, and the sound of splintering. A door bangs closed but I can hear the mayhem continuing. I open my door again, pistol in hand and peer out. Two doors along is the source of the noise and on a table nearby, the andy's jackets, head gear and stuff. I move silently along to the door which is slightly ajar. I push it open until I can see the back of an andy boot is about to stop it. I put my shoulder to it with all I've got and it thumps into the back of the andy just as a pistol fires. I stand in the open doorway as the andy that I've just hit, turns, and starts to swing his pistol round towards me. The result was never in doubt. The blast hits him under his arm where there is least protection, ripping the shirt and tearing into the flesh. He drops to the floor and into the middle of an expanding pool of blood. I step over his body into the room. In the middle of it stands an andy with his back to me. On the floor, in the far corner, lies a figure still alive, resting on its elbows, and breathing deeply. I watch the andy as he slowly sinks to his knees, his uncoordinated hands trying to reach his neck. I walk towards him, looking at nothing else, with my pistol held out in front of me. He falls to the floor as I move round him. He has come to rest on his side and has a broken chair leg thrust into his neck, just under his chin. His eyes are moving, they catch me with a pleading stare, blinking away sweat and filled with confusion. His blood drenched mouth gapes rhythmically as each pulse pushes more blood onto the floor beneath him. This slows to a trickle as his pupils slowly lift upward and become fixed. Life ebbs away like a receding tide until all is still.

'That was fucking close!'

The figure on the floor behind me has rolled over onto his back, and stares up at the ceiling, exhausted.

'I thought I was a gonna. If you hadn't pushed the door open when you did, he would have killed me for sure.'

I turn slowly with more hope than expectation. The hair is matted with dirt and blood and sweat, but there are wisps which could be described as fair. The boots are the same. I daren't believe it but as he looks over there's no denying it,

'Well fuck my boots it's Ash!'

'Turin? Turin! Is it really you?'

'Is it really you?'

'Yeh! It's really me. Is it really us?'

We laugh and as I pull him wearily to his feet we hug like long lost friends, which is reasonable.

'We should make a move.' I tell him, 'These two came down to see what's happened to their commander, they'll be more coming down soon.'

'Commander?'

'Long story.'

Turin looks around the bodies then picks up a pistol from the floor.

At the doorway we stop, then check out the corridors for any noises.

Turin stops and I look at him.

'Just in case anything happens,' he says, 'thanks Ash, you saved my life.' This embarrasses me, so I make light of it.

'That's okay Turin, I knew it was you in there.'

Turin looks at me with surprise,

'How?'

'Oh, gut feeling.' I lie.

'Don't fucking start that again!' He says and we both laugh.

'How's Sam?'

'Fine.' I answer, 'And the other good news is so are your folks, they're all back at HQ'

'HQ?' He asks.

'Long story,' I reply. 'Do you know how to get out of this place?'

'I should do, it was our HQ.'

'HQ?' I ask.

'Long story. Right, this way.'

We head towards the open door and the steps which take us down.

'The andys have put some 'heavy gas' down the sewers.'

'Okay, right, then we'll go . .'

We turn and head in the other direction.

'And above is filthy with andys that are going to come down here any minute.'

'Ah!' Turin pauses for long enough to give me concern.

'No problem,' he continues, 'always have at least two ways out, it's . .'

'. . a rule,' I interrupt, 'yes, I know. Wait!' We both stop. 'If this is really going to be the way out then we should take our boots off, unless we want to leave them a trail of bloody footprints.'

'Good point,' he replies as we remove our boots, and he looks at mine, 'Nice boots, They look new.'

'They are.'

I follow Turin to some double doors set into a box about the height of a person. He opens both doors,

'A cupboard?' I observe, 'this is the master plan for escape, we hide in a cupboard?'

'More like a wardrobe,' Turin replies, then he points at an innocent looking fitting in the roof,

'Pull that catch out,' which I do.

'Then,' says Turin stepping into the cupboard beside me, 'Just slide along the back,' which he does, 'to reveal a passageway. Ta dah!'

He then turns and tells me to wait for a moment while he goes to the door leading up and jams it open.

As he returns an acrid odour begins to fill the air.

'Quick,' he says, getting back into the cupboard and closing the outer doors behind him. We both step into the passageway beyond then slide the cupboard's back panel into place.

'Whenever those two doors were open at the same time,' he tells me, ' it created an updraft from the sewers. There would be such a stink we had to close one or both of them. It will be enough to pull the gas up and fumigate the whole area.'

Having got our boots on and checked our pistols we start along the dimly lit passageway. The cream painted walls still run with moisture and at intersections or junctions we turn at signs known only to Turin and the groups.

'Whose idea was it to have an escape route in a cupboard?'

'It was just another passageway but it was the gamers that made it look like a cupboard. Apparently there's an established history of secret passages through wardrobes, behind bookcases that spin round, trapdoors, and walls that move. We thought a wardrobe would be out of place, and a book case, well we didn't have any books. The model makers and the kite flyers built it.'

I ask him what happened after he had left the flat. He explains that on his search for Chad, he had changed his mind. Meeting old friends, some of whom were leading their own groups, was a revelation. Many had initially been frustrated by the same lack of co-operation and stifling secrecy. They had started to form links, just passing on information about corps activity, road blocks, raids, detentions. No operational stuff, but alliances began to build. He reminds me, not that I needed it, that it was Chad who was keen that nobody should know anything about anyone else, and that now we both know why. I point out that it was for our protection as well; what Chad didn't know, he couldn't tell. I avoided mentioning I'd seen him and that he was dead, there was time for that later.

Some of the leaders that Turin knew wanted the groups to co-operate more with each other, but there was mistrust amongst them. There were security issues, and some of their aims were different. Some groups had splintered and the various factions wouldn't talk to each other. Then an incident sparked unrest, the one we first saw on the screen at Turin's flat. It became a tipping point, there comes a moment when people's frustration and anger over-rides their self-preservation. They are prepared to put their lives at risk, even sacrifice them if they believe there is a better future for the ones they love. The groups knew that if they couldn't form a united front, they would be destroyed. Turin and Chad's names had been mentioned and Turin particularly was someone they could rally round, but no-one was in contact. It was hardly a surprise that Turin was asked to lead them, they were groups without a leader, and he was a leader without a group. Turin explains what a revelation it was when they first met, so much was already in place set to go. Information regarding LEO defence and attack strategies had been known for years, there were even androbot informers which seems difficult to believe.

'There was a problem though,' Turin says, 'now that the groups were working together, the threat of infiltration, a careless word, or an arrest of someone for an unrelated incident who was then interrogated, could result in everyone finding themselves in Rehab.'

'Goodnight Vienna!' I point out.

'Quite,' Turin replies, 'so we had to act immediately before anything like that could happen. It was a risk because we didn't even know if we had informers in our own ranks. If we moved fast it might not give the LEOs enough time to react. It was a gamble, I know, but it was also an opportunity, and if an opportunity occurs you should make the best use of it.'

'It's a rule,' I add.

'It is, but it shouldn't stop you preparing for failure.'

I pointed out that we didn't have any idea what was happening on the ground above us. Then I asked him if he'd ever heard of Lawrence of Arabia. He said he hadn't, so I explained on our way how a foreigner had managed to organise quarrelsome tribes into a successful army. He asked me where Arabia was, but I didn't know.

It grows lighter as we walk up sloping passageways, climb flights of steps and eventually pass through some disused offices that have windows in their ceilings. Another flight of steps and Turin opens a door onto a secluded section of roof, the sky gives me no clue as to the time of day. There is no City light reflecting off the perpetual grey blanket above us that tells us where it is, and therefore where we are. It is confusing. It's dimming has been an ambition, now the lack of it is alarming and heralds uncertainty and maybe chaos. For all it signified, it was our beacon, our Mecca, now we must find our own direction.

Neither of us know how long we were unconscious for, before being interrogated. Beyond our roof, below and around us, all seems quiet. Sporadic interruptions lift our gaze, but there is nothing major, nothing shakes the ground. If the battle is lost, there will just be pockets of resistance being mopped up. A skirmish, a last defiant act of rebellion, before an eternity of retribution.

Smoke still fills the air and from this roof we can see fires burning both near and far. Some are still fierce, others almost out, many more that smoulder. We look down upon an aftermath, like warriors at first light, after some medieval battle. Except we do not know if we are the victors or the vanquished. Below us the bodies have been plundered away, but the field still wears the scars of war.

'What's happening?' I ask Turin.

'I don't know,' he replies.

We walk towards the edge of the roof and look down upon upturned vehicles, torn banners, and burnt out stores. Everywhere there is broken glass that frosts the road and spews across pavements like crushed ice. What sounds like distant skirmishes still puncture the strange silence. Somewhere, something gets too hot and a ball of smoke is vomited into the air. Is it success or failure, or just a pause between battles?

'Do you think we have lost?' Turin asks.

'Is it that simple?' I answer. 'Win or lose? We're alive aren't we? As long we are alive we are not defeated.' I pause to consider the consequences of failure, and they are too great.

'Blowing things up is good therapy but you need an idea to make changes.'

Turin turns and looks at me.

'Don't you have to destroy something before you can rebuild it?'

'Maybe,' I reply, 'but it's good to have some idea of what you're going to put in its place. Some kind of vision.'

We turn away from the small parapet and walk across the roof, down and across another into a raised doorway and down a concrete stairway. Each floor is labelled until we arrive at a pair of steel doors, labelled 'GROUND FLOOR'. They look like old fire doors for an escape and there's a bar arrangement which locks the two doors together. Turin releases the bar and tries to push the doors open, but they appears to be jammed.

'We had trouble with this before,' Turin says.

'Great,' I reply and together we both put our shoulders to them and on the second attempt the doors burst open and we are projected out onto a service road, and into the middle of a group of about thirty andys.

'Shit!' If we don't say this we think it.

We stand motionless side by side and slowly raise our arms and wait for the beatings to start if they have the time, otherwise they'll just shoot us. Goodnight Vienna. But they don't.

As we look around nearly all of them are eating. None are wearing their headsets, helmets, jackets, even their pistols and harnesses are strewn carelessly around, several by our feet. If it wasn't for our bewilderment we would pick them up and take as many andys with us as we can, it's a rule, I think. Someone eating is hardly a threat, even an andy, so long as they continue eating. One of them stands up, a particularly nasty looking one, the size of a barn door, as they say. He walks slowly towards us and looms bigger with every step. We edge backward, not daring to look behind us in case that would be his cue to grab us both by the neck and suspend us until we are dead, or at least stop wriggling. As our backs come into contact with the fire doors behind us, this Goliath holds up a flask and offers me a drink. I'm not accustom to accepting drinks from strange people, and this andy is one of the strangest. I look at Turin and suggest, by way of a gesture that he should drink first. After a momentary glare he smiles at the andy whose broad smile is almost beguiling, in a friendly monster sort of way. Turin takes a sip and begins to hand it back when he changes his mind and takes a decent gulp, before handing it back again.

'Actually it's not bad, it's quite nice,' says Turin nodding his head slightly in approval and in thanks to the andy, who now turns back to me.

'Thank you very much,' I say, treating him as you would any monster who could swallow you with one gulp if you gave him the slightest offence. I hesitate at the 'Mmmm's' and 'Delicious' in case I overstep the fine line into patrimony. I take a sip, then as Turin did, surprised by its pleasantness, take another. I hand the flask back with much nodding and smiles. Another andy noticing this, picks up his flask and offers it to us. We both decline like fat ladies pretending to be on a diet, saying things like, 'Couldn't possibly,' and, 'No thank you, really, I'm full up.'

Having been through this ceremony, we wait for some effect to take place which would result in us being carted off to Rehab for recycling. We stand aimlessly and watch the andys tucking into their food wondering what is in store. Judging by the packaging that lies strewn about, I now realise that they are not eating regular andy rations but what they have just looted from the adjacent store. One of whose doors is hanging twisted in the doorframe it once filled.

Turin and I are still rooted to the spot for fear any movement will be interpreted as an attempt to escape and some painful retribution will be our reward. I catch Turin's glance and with a sideways movement of my eyes, indicate we should make a move. He frowns severely, indicating that I, 'Must be fucking joking!'

I repeat the gesture with my eyes at the same time turning to look aimlessly at the building behind me. I examine the structure of the doors and how well the hinges are set into the brickwork.

Turin looks at me as if I am completely mad and indeed now suffering from whatever intoxicants, drugs, or poison, we have just consumed. Cautiously, I move a pace or two away to examine a sign saying, 'DELIVERIES'. I call Turin over to take a closer look at the excellence of the sign writing. I draw imaginary lines over the lettering at the same time as watching every movement the andys make. Which is none, except for the routine eating of their booty. More false interest in brickwork, then the fascinating details surrounding some shutters, and a large loading bay, all serves to take us a small distance away. Enough to make a run for it, but we slowly turn our backs and start to walk, when what we both fear, happens. There is a shout of alarm and the sound of boots. Surprised to be still alive, we turn to be confronted by an andy offering us two plastic wrapped, sausage rolls. We take these and thank him, he smiles and walks back to his comrades, two of which now stand and wave. We wave back, give broad smiles and turn, still not certain that the sound of two pistol shots will bring down the black curtains on this bizarre event.

'What the fuck was that all about?'

'I haven't a clue,' I tell Turin, 'maybe they've lost their comms, certainly their control. Could be temporary. Don't know.'

The implication is clear. Any minute they might return their former sadistic selves.

We turn left into a passageway then pause. Peering back round the corner, I check on the andys. They're still chillin' and seem to have forgotten all about us.

CHAPTER 24

Turin and I are confused, our brush with the andys only made it worse in the face of no other information. Afraid of any presumption we must be alert to any threat in whatever shape it make appear. We presume nothing, it's a rule. Dodging anything we feel is risky, eventually we arrive at a deserted precinct, at a corner we rest in the dark beneath a solid ramp.

'We should get back to HQ,' I tell him, 'then we might have an idea of what's going on.'

I tell him that Sam is there and his folks are too. He wants to know more but I tell him there is no time to go into details and he will have to be satisfied with knowing they are all safe and well.

'What about yours?' Turin asks and sees my reaction, 'I've never asked.'

'Don't know,' I tell him, 'they had to leave for the rural before this started. Maybe when we know more, we might all have to leave urbia, then I'll look for them.'

'And continue the revolution eh?'

'If it's necessary,' I answer.

'It's never over 'til it's over.'

'Could be a rule?' I suggest.

'Might have to be.'

I try to sense the direction we should be heading and I lead the way. After a few minutes I don't recognise anything and start to worry I might be taking us in the wrong direction.

The street ahead of us is strewn with debris, several burnt out vehicles and a couple of abandoned andywagons.

Toward the end of it there's a few people hanging about near a small store.

'We need a map,' I tell Turin and I head for the store with him following.

Around the entrance there are exhausted people sat leaning against the store front, others lying flat out on the pavement, even on the road. Some are nursing injuries and have others helping them. There are people standing in the doorway and inside is packed with more standing, sitting perched on empty shelves, all watching a screen over the counter, just inside the door. The remains of the till lies behind the counter and wires lead from its powerpack to the screen. It seems the need to make money has been replaced by the desire for knowledge.

A dishevelled presenter is trying to link reports and unsteady images, reading from papers being handed to her. There's a fascination in this amateurishness which charms everyone watching. Each time a hand appears in shot a shout goes up but is silenced by others so the news can he heard. This abrupt change in presentation is confusing but we dare not presume it is any indication of success. A live report is the caption and all we see is tall stone buildings and glass offices. The camera drops down so we can now see many thousands of people in a square before the camera and filling the streets beyond, chanting and waving banners. As the camera pans round the scene, people have taken every vantage point, and a large fountain is hidden by people trying to get a view. It seems that every building is occupied and proving it by draping banners and flags from everywhere they can reach, then picture clunks back to the studio to find the presenter unready, much to the delight of everyone. The scene switches back and now we have a different view of Buckingham House, the London home of the PM. A shaky handheld views the ranks of the PM's personal guard and above it the famous balcony from where he gives his speeches. From the currently deserted balcony the camera pans round and we see thousands of people, as far as the camera can see. Several leave the shop saying they just have to be there on this day.

Still we presume nothing, perhaps this is the time we shall look back upon in some miserable future and remember thinking we were winning. The disappointment would be too much to bear, so we presume nothing. It's hard to believe anything has changed. It's like not knowing if it's a dream, and fearing you'll soon wake up, back in the real world that is the continuing nightmare.

'Do you have any maps?' asks Turin. He asks a little chap who has the only seat, and sits behind the counter beneath the screen. The little chap raises his eyes to the ceiling and shakes his head,

'Another map!' he shouts across the store.

There is some movement and the word 'map' is passed around until something flies through the air from the far corner.

Eventually it arrives with the seated man who then says,

'One Map' and throws it in our direction at the same time as a chorus of,

'No charge!' echoes through the store with much laughter and nudging, except from the little chap who now we take to be the owner, still shaking his head.

We leave the store and stand outside eating our andy sausage rolls.

'Well,' says Turin, 'do you think those pictures were real?'

'I don't know,' I reply, buttoning the map. It springs to life like the previous one did and eventually I get a view of somewhere with a coast line.

'Bollocks! This is no good, it doesn't tell you where you are!'

Turin takes it, and turns it round,

'It's broken, look it can't even tell which way round it should be, I'll take it back.'

Turin returns with the same map and tells me that all the maps are like it because there's no signal. We'll have to find where we are by just recognising streets and buildings.

'It's been like that since the morning,' he tells me. 'They say there's no signals, no comms, nothing.'

We sit down and move the map around until we find London. Then by identifying roads, landmarks and using the view selector, places of interest and other controls we find what we think is where we are. Without the cross hairs we are used to, it's just guesswork. We mark it and where I think is the place we want to get to, Mr. Foo's Sushi Bar. I have to explain that it doesn't really exist but we head for it anyway.

The path that the crowds took is obvious by the devastation, it's travelled like a storm that burns and smashes much in its path. Side streets are almost untouched, but where there has been conflict, the walls are scorched, there are blood stains, and occasionally areas stained blue or red. As we draw nearer to Goodrich's HQ, there are more andywagons and other armoured vehicles burnt out, or just turned over and occasionally one covered with graffiti, as if it had changed sides or had been commandeered. Crowd control vehicles and machinery lie dormant, some are burnt out shells, some still smoulder, others are illuminated from within as their corpses burn like candles.

Andys, when we spot them, congregate in small groups. They have removed their tunics, or at least wear other things over them. In a small square several chairs have been set up and two or three women in blood spattered coats are carrying out impromptu surgery. A queue of thirty or so andys are waiting to have their implants removed. A spray anaesthetises the area then quick work extracts the interface. The body of the implant remains but it's dead. Each Andy walks away holding some torn bedding to the wound on their neck or a shaved patch on their head and wearing a big smile. They wave and smile at everyone, even as the anaesthetic wears off. Some of them break down and weep, but not because of the pain.

Without too much trouble we get to the high street that I looked down upon and where the andy ambush was set up. We even pass the street off it where I can still see the glistening fragments of plastic and screen, all that remains of the player that was supposed to be my lifeline.

I try to retrace my steps exactly to find the way into the HQ but it is some time before I find it. I stand before it but without any visible means of opening it. All I can do is knock, then I remember. I turn round and look up at the windows across the road, I raise my hood and a figure appears to stare for a moment before excitedly speaking on his comms.

'I think I'm a bit of a surprise,' I tell Turin.
'Why?'

'Because within a few minutes my comms got accidentally trashed. So this is the first they've seen or heard of me for a while.'

Some sounds behind the door result in it opening and another surprised face which is just about able to say,

'Hi.'

'Not much of a welcome,' Turin observes, 'are you sure this is the right group?'

I hesitate at a junction, not remembering which one to take and the girl who has let us in goes forward, leading the way. Eventually we arrive at the main room which is all but deserted, six or seven people are gathered in a group at the far end. As we approach there is a worrying silence and I begin to wonder if it's because of something I've done, or something I've forgotten to do. At last, a face I recognise,

'Carol,' I say as we hug.

'Ash. Oh Ash!' she says almost in a whisper. It's a subdued welcome, and I was expecting more. Her embrace is full of sympathy and I can feel she is searching for the right words, which begins to alarm me.

'This is Turin, Sam's brother,' I say to her, and watch her carefully. Carol embraces him with the same reserve. I move through the doorway to where I last saw Sam, the girl I want to spend the rest of my life with.

The rooms are empty. Some screens are blank, others linked into more professional news stations that have got themselves back up and running,

'Turin! Look here, this is Goodrich.'

On the screen Goodrich is talking to some interviewer.

'Can't be him!' I call out, 'his glasses are almost clean, must be an impostor.'

I turn to see Turin at the doorway with Carol's arm around him.

Something hits me like a truck. I'm totally winded and sink onto the seat, Sam's seat. I can hardly breathe but already I cannot accept what I fear I'm going to be told. It won't be true.

'She went to look for you.'

'No.' I say. 'No, they wouldn't have let her. She's lost, she'll find her way back. I'll find her. . .'

'They found her.'

'It's not her. Can't be her. Why would she . .'

Your signal immobilised, they tried to make contact, all they got was. 'Signal not receivable,' they didn't know . . . .'

'It fell out of my pocket, it got trashed, that was all.'

'When she found out, we told her it was too dangerous, and she was needed here. We sent someone else and when they couldn't find you we couldn't stop her. Goodrich, Mel, Zac they all tried. Two others went with her. '

'Where are they? Where is she?'

Carol looks down, then at Turin.

'Where the fuck is she!' I scream, as if it helps, but it doesn't.

'They're all at the funeral. Zac, Mel, everybody who could go . . . '

My head rests in my hands. I feel the tears trickle through my fingers. I try to see her face, to kiss her lips, to hold her, but it all keeps fading away.

I pretend it doesn't matter, I pretend it isn't true. How else do you cope with something so painful and so real. I tell myself I would have known, somehow she would have told me she was leaving. A reasonable voice tells me it's not true and I shall look up and she will be there, or I shall wake up. The world however changed, cannot change so much, that she is not in it.

'Ash?' Turin crouches beside me, 'I am going to the funeral. I have to be there for Mel and Zac and Sam. I'm needed, will you come with me?'

'No, I can't. I'm no good at funerals. I'm a mess now, hell knows what I'd be like . .'

'Ash?'

Turin moves away as Carol sits by me. She rests her arm on me, I feel the soft warmth of a woman and it feels like Sam. It will always feel like her. Every woman.

'We thought we had lost both of you.'

'Who found her? Where?'

'I think it was Cassy. When they knew they couldn't stop her they issued her with a player, so she could keep in touch. One of the guys came back badly wounded and said they'd run straight into an andy blockade. Her signal was stationary. It was on the high street for an hour or so. They kept on trying to contact her but she didn't, or couldn't respond. We were just about to send someone out to check and she moved, so we thought everything was okay, but still no contact. We thought that there may be a comms problem, but by the time we had found out it was fine, it had stopped moving again. That's when we sent Cassy out to check and she found her in a side street. Zac and couple of others went to help recover the body when it was safe.'

I look at Carol with a look that she will understand.

'No. There was nothing. There were no marks. They examined her but she had been dead for a while. She must have died before Cassy found her.'

'What of?'

'I don't know Ash. The doctor's at the funeral, if you want I'll ask him when he gets back. Can I get you a drink?'

'Yeh, I'd like a coffee.'

'Real coffee?'

'No, just coffee.'

I sit still numb. I try not to think about anything, but I sit where I last saw her, last saw her with her folks as I left. I can remember the look we had and all it had said. We knew the risks and it might be the last time, but 'might be' is not 'will be' until 'it is'; I can't believe it is. It doesn't make it easier sharing a last moment. Last is so like the word lost, tears fill my eyes again, I drop my head into my hands and can't stop the sobs.

When I look up, and after I wipe my eyes, there to my left is a coffee. In front of me, is what she would see, I look around as if her point of view is her, and she is still here. I run my fingers over the screen she used, I imagine it still warm as if she has just left and will soon return. There beside me are two seats, and the two that sat there, are now watching her take her last journey. On one seat some clothes, some in a bag. I hear Carol tapping away close by.

'What are these?' I ask.

'Oh! Sorry, those . . . well her folks wanted something a bit more . . . for the . . . not what she was wearing . . You know what folks are. I'll take them.'

'No!' I say too sharply. 'No it's fine, really.'

She carries on her tapping and I dream I could turn round and it would be Sam. I don't because I know it's Carol, and that would spoil the dream.

I reach out and take the small pile of clothing as if she is somehow there or at least somehow to let her know I am here. It hurts not saying goodbye, not telling her how much I loved her, that she must have known is not enough, nowhere near. I feel the coarseness of her jacket, and hold it to my face and I relive the way we used to pretend to kiss, then she wanted me to, then she said she'd never let me again. I smile though I can't stop the tears flowing. The tighter I hold her empty jacket the more the tears just flow, but . .

'Carol?'

'Yes Ash.'

'Where's the funeral?'

'It's somewhere near where they live . . .'

'Exactly?'

She brings something up onto the screen as I stand behind her, then she writes it down.

'It will have started, you'll never get there in time!'

'Where's Hutch? Get Hutch to pick me up and take me there.'

'It'll nearly be over . .'

'Just do it!'

'Okay.'

I imagine the old churches are not as easy to find as they used to be. Since the state sold off all their church properties, they've had all their spires removed because pods kept hitting them. Now they're just another idiosyncratic building from the past looking for a use.

Hutch drops me off in the road by the church. Having just delivered Turin, he knows the route and where the entrance is.

As I walk briskly towards its doors beneath an arched stone entrance, I hear the solemn music that accompanies most of these events. I pass a couple of attendants by the door that appear as solemn and bordering on tears, as they are instructed to be. Inside there are about thirty people arranged round the casket resting in their centre. I can see Zac and Mel in arms together consoling each other. A figure looking like the grim reaper clad in gold, conducts the ceremony standing at the far side by the door through which Sam will soon be sent to eternity, if anyone stops me. The figure raises his arms aloft in some glorious salutation which heralds the journey to begin. A few tearful well-wishers pace forward and kiss the casket, others lay objects on it as it begins to move towards its destiny. Head bowed, I make my way round the outside of the congregation to the right while everyone with respect is silent with eyes downcast. I pause by a large candle stick, a religious relic that has some significance even today, and who knows, maybe even some use. Nobody notices me remove the monstrous candle to reveal a spike about the length of a finger. I round the far end at about the same as the casket has travelled beyond the outer circle of people. Now there is nothing between me and it and I rush silently forward and plunge the spike into one of the fittings. The first to try to stop me is the grim reaper. He leaps back as I take a swipe with the candle stick. It's heavy enough to have to make another circuit before I can slow the thing down. This second pass is enough to make the grim reaper fall backwards over his robes into the path of the attendants who, I must say, were very quick off the mark; perhaps this is a common occurrence. I shout as loudly and as profanely as I can through gritted teeth trying to give the impression that I am at least possessed, undoubtedly merciless, and bent on murder and,

'I will fucking kill any one that gets in my way,'

Turin moves forward and I thrust the spike at him and tell him.

'That includes you Turin!'

As he backs off I wink at him which I can see fills him with confusion, but he stops and holds his arms out, thinking that there must be some method in my madness.

'Ash! What's going on?'

'You'll see, Turin or at least I hope you will.'

So saying I remove another fitting with the candlesticks spike, then another. I plunge the spike into the conveyor belt and jam it just as the doors are about to open. With three of the four fixings gone I can open the casket and as I let it go the last fixing snaps and the lid clatters to the ground.

Turin has turned around and is quietly pleading with everyone to stay where they are for their own safety. His mother, Mel is in tears and I know, given the chance, Zac would like to kill me.

As I lift Sam by the shoulder and support her head I know there is life. I hold her close and plead with whatever deity cares to listen to bring her out of her sleep. I nurse her, speak to her, call to her to come back, hoping she hasn't left at all. Then my heart leaps as I'm sure I felt her move her head, and a slight pressure on my arm is a prayer answered. Then suddenly a gasp and she throws her head back and gasps again. I feel her lungs fill and her breath on my face. Another gasp as if coming up for air. Then her eyes, blinking, stare, blink again and focus on my face, on my eyes. Then I look up and smile, need I say more, and what face isn't streaming with tears of joy, is still in shock.

'Ash?'

'Yes, Sam.'

'Are we pretending to kiss again?'
'No, it's the real thing.'
'Where am I?'
'Don't worry about that now.'
She looks around, and then down,
'And what the fuck am I wearing?'

CHAPTER 25

'You know, as much as this park is very nice,' I say to the others, 'it looked so much nicer when we weren't allowed in.'

'Human nature,' replies Turin, 'the grass on the other side of the railings always looks greener.'

'That's because it's plastic,' says Sam digging her heel into the synthetic covering.

'I particularly like the water feature,' she adds.

An army of attendants used to keep the park in good order, they would polish the fittings, paint the railings and re-lay the plastic grass if it showed any signs of wear. They would ensure the seats were safe, clean and the name of the seat's sponsor, emblazoned for eternity, remained unblemished; something seldom achieved during their lifetime. The brightly coloured floral displays would be renewed each week with replacements from the farms, but the trees excessive greenery was never convincing. Sponsored by the corps, their execs were the only ones allowed to use any park. Like all recreational facilities, admissions was restricted to those with the appropriate permissions and allowances. An allowance gave you the right to enter, but you needed a permission to stay. Shows would be put on for specially invited execs, and games played for their entertainment. It was not unusual for a park to have a ring, which was actually square but still called a ring, where two fighters were pitched against each other until one was beaten to the floor, unconscious. Occasionally, execs who had some kind of dispute, would enter the ring and batter each other for the amusement of their colleagues. There was never any guarantee that the stronger case would prevail. Victory usually favoured the stronger fist and seldom the more logical argument; might was always right.

The park was spotless, and its orderly sameness was ruthlessly enforced by the attendants popularly known as, 'Parkies'. They would appear from within the darkness of their huts to retrieve anything dropped or discarded. Several would be waiting to zone in after an exec picnic to scavenge what remained. They'd leave other things too, sometimes hidden in the food, but that's execs for you, or was. Now people come and go as they please, there's no security, no 'Parkies'. Now the place is a mess.

Turin, Sam and I sit on one of the park seats, the type that has horizontal slats and elaborate curly cast ends. The name plate bolted to it is large enough to make the seat uncomfortable, so we cover it with our coats; a small victory but one that makes us smile. There are seats like these throughout the park, now people can come and go as they choose, some choose to stay. Some seats support a solitary figure swathed in bedding, others have become the centre of a small community. The plush plastigrass carpet undulates gently off into the distance but locally it bears the swirls and rucks of a large vehicle turning, probably the one that has become the nearby water feature that Sam observed. It's a half-submerged andywagon on the edge of the lake to our right, on which two small boys are sitting.

Still here are the open fronted huts in which the 'Parkies' would shelter. Some of the more secluded ones have been converted into homes, have names, emblems and fly flags bearing witness to the occupants individuality. Some have been painted and several express their individuality perhaps too forcefully but who would begrudge them their freedom of expression after generations of it being repressed. Unfortunately you can never legislate for taste, or if you do, where do you stop? And whose taste?

The park is dwarfed on all sides by tall office buildings. Some have physical security just to preserve the buildings and prevent looters. When the metamagnetic pulses were activated nearly all data was erased but Sam and Zac, with the help of about thirty others, had backed up enough to be able to reintroduce some security aspects. Some buildings, most museums and galleries, remained secure. Those caught inside, mainly staff couldn't get out, such was the lock down. Teams went out to release them but the heritage volunteers, comprising mainly historical groups, searched them as they came out. They put back all the stuff they were trying to leave with. Parks and open space restrictions, as well as a host of other regulations were instantly removed. Anyone likely to enforce them was not going to show their faces. Groups of people gathered on blue areas everywhere and ritually danced round and round as a symbol of their new freedoms. The Columbus building was an obvious target, a section of the carpet had been torn up by people wanting a souvenir but the desk remained intact. Some said it was such a powerful image of control and repression that it was still unapproachable.

Turin rests with his legs straight out in front of him, hands stuffed into in his pockets and his head lolling over the back of the seat as he contemplates the grey sky. I tell him he'll still have a long wait before it turns blue, if ever it does. Sam sits between us, upright and neat, both hands holding a coffee, not a real coffee, in her lap. I sit bent over my palmer, my cleaned Muskrats tucked back under the seat.

I scroll down and read the news out loud as I have been doing on and off for nearly an hour. I continue,

'I couldn't, with an easy conscience, be a candidate in an election that I have helped establish and from which I might benefit.' Professor Goodrich, who chairs the transitional committee, stated this morning, 'In the event of any success, there would inevitably be accusations that I had engineered a system from which I was bound to be a beneficiary.'

There's a picture of Goodrich and several other elderlies.

'Look,' I say to the others, and point the screen in their direction. Turin is motionless but Sam turns, raises her eyebrows and nods approvingly. Then I continue,

'Professor Goodrich has stated that it could be six months before elections can take place.' I rest the palmer on my lap and relax against the seat.

Already prominent figures from the regime are queueing up to return. Some were claiming they had always championed the masses in the face of corporate extremism. Ministers who had been exposed as corrupt had retreated to their country estates to prepare their defence for the forthcoming trials. Typically their defence was that they were operating within agreed guidelines, it was an accepted practice with which they did not agree, but were powerless to change. Others only defence was that they could have behaved far worse and the fact that they didn't is surely a reason for praise not condemnation. Many just plead ignorance and claimed that they had no idea of what was happening, one even put forth her poor attendance record as evidence. Several employed teams of specialists to prove that they were either mentally or physically too unwell to attend court proceedings. To avoid prosecution, one tried to convince a committee that he was insane but they threw out his case saying he must be mad to think he would be believed. His defence team tried to use that as evidence proving their client's case.

The most ardent supporters of corporate excess and the least likely to find any sympathy, came out fighting. They said that the claims were wildly exaggerated, and anyway you can't make omelettes without breaking eggs. The PM and his inner cabinet all denied that they'd had any personal involvement whatsoever in any atrocities, however minor, and that anyone who had evidence to the contrary should come forward.

I lean forward again and pick up the pad. I scroll it down to where I can read what the PM actually said.

'Enough!' says Sam, 'drink your coffee.'

'I took Chad's ashes down to his partner and daughter last week,' says Turin.

'How are they?' Sam asks.

'Glad that they are no longer in Rehab but sorry he's no longer around. They said to thank you for what you had written about him saving your life, Ash.'

There is a pause during which we all think about Chad and try to order our confusing thoughts. Then Sam turns to me and says,

'Zac told me that it was reported that most of the andys just sat down in Rehab wherever they were when their implants were deactivated. It took others an hour or so before they got the hint. No one knew what was going on.'

'I can understand that,' I add, 'we felt the same way when we suddenly found ourselves in the middle of a couple of dozen or so.'

'The ones that offered you a drink?' says Sam recalling our story.

'And a couple of sausage rolls,' adds Turin.

'Real sausage rolls?' Sam asks.

'Of course not,' I tell her.

Behind us, we hear a vehicle drive along a road just outside the park. We all turn round to look at the spectacle weave in and out of the debris. The body of the truck is decorated with birds, more are painted on banners flying from the windows.

Turning back and settling down again, Turin asks how long it is before our lift arrives.

'At least another hour,' I tell him, 'Carol's running Goodrich all over the place.'

'It was lucky you jumped into his garden, otherwise none of this might have happened.'

'Not as lucky as you think.'

'Explain?' he asks.

'I never knew Goodrich and Carl knew each other. They'd met through a history group before 48 was deregulated. Goodrich was watching over Carl and when the LEOs got heavy, it was Hutch that stepped in and took us off to hospital. They had to leave, Goodrich suspected I wouldn't because I was involved with other things. He had spies everywhere and when things got hot Hutch shepherded me into Goodrich's back garden. I never saw him, just the light of his torch waving about.'

'Do you know where Carl and Jean are now?'

'They managed to get a message to Goodrich so I'm going to find them. They say there's some weird stuff happening in the rural. Estates are building up their private armies, carving up the countryside and claiming rights of heritage. Some say one day they'll march on urbia and take it back.'

'Like a civil war?'

'Part two,' I reply.

There is a noise and running feet behind us and Turin turns round,

' Talking of which . . .'

Suddenly a few dozen people appear to our left, running across the park toward the lake.

'It's the birders! They're rioting again!' says Sam.

'No they're not.' I say, smiling, 'Look, by the lakeside, some one's spotted a bird. I wonder if it's a sparrow?'

'Of all the things we've had to endure,' Turin says, 'and what we've had to overcome and the dozens that have died, their joy is seeing a little bird.'

'Maybe it's those little things that really count,' Sam replies,' It's those little things that make it all worthwhile. I wonder why?'

'That's just the way it is,' I reply, 'and the way it should be.'

YOU SHOULD KNOW THIS
Footnotes to the text.

Chapter 1

1.SENTRY BOTS AND PODS - Observation gantries are sited around the twelfth floor so that sentry bots can monitor below them. Sentry bots are low grade and used for observation and control. They buddy up in pairs and argue a lot. The pods they operate are cheap end and malfunction frequently. The pods dock on the gantries to recharge while the bots themselves, power down and wait to be alerted by a signal that detects a problem on the streets below. You used to be able to see them undock and drop down to check out some misdemeanour, now in the perpetual gloom they still skulk around but are mostly invisible. They say they watch us to make sure we come to no harm, but they harm us all the time. They're not cut out to resist the acidic moisture so they corrode, de-laminate and warp. This primarily affects their navigation and proximity devices, so they kill a few hundred people each year by landing on them or just falling off the gantries. The corps who operate them always claim it's sabotage and it demonstrates the need for more units and more vigilance, and a greater freedom for them to operate. This is just corp speak because their angels refuse to finance upgrades and instead demand increased dividends. It doesn't mean to say there isn't sabotage. The mild acid drizzle that falls plays havoc with all machinery. The bots joints are particularly susceptible, excess humidity can cause a few diodes to go on the blink. For a few months they programmed them to avoid getting wet at all costs. That resulted in kids using water pistols on them or just dousing them with a cup full which sent the bots into a blind panic. A bot in a panic is hilarious and great entertainment, until their pistols start firing. In this atmosphere everything corrodes, and everyone, inside and out. Each new mayor promises to legislate a standard upgrade for all bots. They suffix the model number, add another PR slogan, and reprogram the interface. They herald it as new with a no expense spared ceremony to which all the sponsored ministers and their friends are invited. Nothing changes except now the bots can speak at you whilst wearing a hideous grin fixed from audio receptor to audio receptor. What you have to wonder is whether the malfunctioning, unpredictable, often lethal behaviour of a bot, is worse than the predictable corrupt sadism that is the hallmark of the average Law Enforcement Officer working in a deregulated district where they get rewarded by results, have the worst job, and no supervision. It's a close call and the lower you are in the system, the closer it gets. That's just the way it is.

2. THIS IS ABOUT DRUGS - If you want, you can get a licence to purchase the drug you like or need. To get a licence you have to show you are a responsible citizen, and apply for a Rem Licence. Rem means a responsible member of society. To be a Rem you need to prove you are in an approved occupation. That is an approved position within an approved organisation or company, fulfilling an approved role, and most recently, in an approved district. Each approval procedure can take at least six months. The PM said he would, '. . . help the poor unfortunates that through no fault of their own have become dependent on the evil we call drugs. This demonstrates we care. This demonstrates we have understanding. This demonstrates we love.' That is what he said.

Genuine addicts cannot wait that long and get it illegally. Most of the stuff on the streets is made and circulated by the state. If they intercept consignments, it's the same, they process it and put it back out on the street, but it's not what you think, it's what we call 'haunted', there's a ghost in it. Take more than a gram, and who doesn't, six days down the line and you wonder why you can't focus, another couple of days and your skin begins to itch, by that time you need glasses. A week later you lose your taste, bowel and bladder control which is very embarrassing, but you don't have to put up with it for long because within a few days you're snatcher meat. Moral? Don't touch anything unless you've seen it made! Better still don't touch anything.

Most real dependants die waiting for their licence. Those that eventually get their free monthly ration don't need it anyway, it's recreational. So the state rewards its Rems with a monthly score. They in turn often become dependent and are the perfect worker, never do anything or say anything against the corp, who is also their supplier. They'll fulfil their quota, live the quiet life, take a pay cut, do anything they are told to for fear of losing their monthly dose. About twenty percent eventually cease to function, lose their Rem status and join the dregs, if they can still crawl to where the dregs are. They take 'ghost' and die, or land up in Rehab from where nobody returns. Goodnight Vienna. That's just the way it is.

Chapter 2

3. MENIAL WORKERS - C12 to C14 cover those doing menial work and it is the lowest grade and has no rights or protection. This is so the labour force can be mobile and not constrained and go where the work is. Workers usually queue for the work knowing that it will be low paid and often dangerous. Compensation for injury is at the corps discretion and investigation is self-regulated which means that injuries and fatalities are the always the fault of the worker. C12 to C14s are the most common source of parts due to environmental factors, illness, drug and alcohol dependency, suicide, etc. The wasteful destruction of corpses has long been illegal due to the demand for organs. Everybody is recycled. That's just the way it is.

4. LEOS AND ANDROBOTS - The default LEO is an androbot, or andy, abbreviated android/robot from

commercial development. LEOs are Law Enforcement Officers and include all sorts, andys, bots, wardens and any others with power to arrest, detain and pursue. Andys are humans, predominantly male, under control, acting and programmed to do whatever is commanded of them by a controller, male or female who may be near or distant. They are predominantly male because the males used are more aggressive, are already less inclined to have any emotional issues and are expendable. Andys are recruited from extreme categories within Rehab, where there's no shortage. Female equivalents, if suitable, are re-trained for a variety functions in the service and entertainment industries, often within Rehab.

Andys are under control and have a variety of implants which are used to modulate temperament and incentive. They are fully suited and have comms sets and head up displays via which they receive instructions. They have helmet pin lights that illuminate their range of vision, night sights, cams, and other visual and audio receptors. All this information is transmitted real time to their controllers. Further implants affect both nervous and muscular systems so that the andy can be paralysed partially or completely, or subjected to a range of sensations from a feeling of nausea to that of being burnt alive. Controllers do not issue requests, they issue commands which must be obeyed without hesitation or question. Any variance can be met with a lethal pulse which terminates. Goodnight Vienna! That's just the way it is.

5. CARS AND WARDENS - Hardly anyone has any form of transport 48 so most of the car parking places are empty. Some vehicles might be owned by people that club together but you daren't leave it on the road because of the wardens. Only if you are a state official, an exec or manager, would you be allowed to park in the street, none of those live round here. Wardens can get credits for traffic misdemeanours if there's any traffic. In theory you can park a car in the road for up to twenty minutes. Unless you can

prove it's been there for less than twenty minutes, and nobody can't even with a room full of witnesses, a warden will report it and it will be lifted. A chopper drops down, they smash opposite windows and run a chain through, or just clamp a magnet on the roof and up it goes. Up, up and away, with or without you and the family. Kids sometimes push a car out into the street and wait inside hoping to get an aerial trip of the district when the magnet takes them away. When it's gone, it's gone, no fines, just gone. It's unlikely in 48 but if it's a collector's model, it will belong to an exec within hours, otherwise it'll be recycled that night.

The wardens won't be seen here at night but they do skulk around in disguise trying to pick up information which they can use during the day. They might listen at windows, follow you, make notes, that kind of stuff. It's what they do now because there's no traffic. They get paid for information so they patrol during the day, spy during the night. If they get something on you, like you are keeping an animal, they check to see if you have the right permissions. If they catch you out, you can pay them to keep quiet, but they will be back for more until you can't pay, then they'll make something up and report you. Like everyone, they've become desperate, but there's no sympathy and it doesn't stop them disappearing besides they sometimes carry a valuable surveillance kit which is easily reprogrammed. Goodnight Vienna. They were replaced with bots in one district to save money but the bots were expensive. It was far cheaper to replace a dead warden with a live one instead of buying another bot. So they sold the bots, it made financial sense, and everything's got to make financial sense. That's just the way it is.

Chapter 3

6. WORK AND ALLOWANCES -There is an average of forty percent unemployment. The State secretly encourages this to enable a mobile and enthusiastic work

force but really it is to ensure people are desperate and will do what they are told to do, no Qs. In deregulated districts unemployment is much higher, at least double, but the state does not issue any figures. There are no statistics gathered or recorded in deregulated districts. The PM says,' Though we love them and they are part of our family until they see the error of their ways they are beyond the pale', he says this because he knows what it means.

Some years ago the New Employment Strategy was brought in to 'enable the unemployed to join the wonderful world of work', but it was really brought in to save money and to reduce the risk of violence by the unemployed and to make it easier to penalise wrongdoers. It works like this, you are not credited with any privileges unless you register for work. Privileges include everything you can get from the state and permissions and allowances, but not entitlements as they come with a job. Privileges for the 'Keen to Work' are level 'low' which allows them to reduce it to a level 'minimum', and then to a level 'zero' if you are a problem. The level is designed to supply the nutritional requirements of the average person. It makes no allowances for those who are overweight or on special diets or who have any food issues. You are allocated a certain number of tokens per week which you exchange for food, clothing, etc. no luxury goods. Only certain places are licenced to accept tokens, so you have little choice. Also the tokens are registered to you and are readable so the state can record what you have used them for, how many you have left and therefore they cannot be used as barter or saved. There are token dispensers which also dispense paper money but not to the 'Keen to Work'. The dispensers are common but only a few ever have enough tokens and there is no point in complaining because if you are 'Keen to Work' you have no say because you do not make a contribution, because you do not work. By not having a say, you cannot register any complaints, you are not covered by any insurances, and you cannot vote. You cannot vote because you have nothing to lose and will only want to make things worse for everyone else. The PM says, 'How can you have the same rights as those who are a credit to society?' He is always right and that's just the way it is.

    7. GOVERNMENT 'SPONSORS' - Columbus, is what they call a 'Preferred Prime Provider', and it is so because it is one of the home secretary's sponsors. Sponsoring is normal and has been so for many years. All party members are sponsored by corporates so they can afford to do the state business. A company like Columbus, actually there are no other companies like Columbus, that sponsor a minister or secretary, is in a powerful position and does what it wants. What it wants is to hang on to as much as it can from the state in levies and taxes and pay out as little as possible. All PPPs are self-accrediting and are always successful, which is no surprise. They do not need to show figures as these are confidential and could be used by competitors. In Columbus case, there are no competitors. Columbus claims improved success year on year in all areas, and a drop in the 'Keen to Work'. They do not need to show if the drop is due to anyone finding work, they only need to show there are less people on the books. Verification of this success is provided by a subsidiary, whose findings are also confidential, for the same reason. It is unlikely that the success they claim is due to clients finding work. It is mostly due to irritated clerks asking questions to which there are no correct answers, or answer that they can, and will, interpret as wrong. You score less than the minimum required and are 'signed off'. If you are 'signed off', Columbus gets a bonus. If that is too much work to a clerk, they can lose records, or send a 'Request to Attend' to an old or wrong address, so you miss the interview. Anyone missing an interview for any reason, is reported dead, or has been removed to Rehab, is recorded as having found work, for which Columbus gets a bonus. That's just the way it is.

8. GENETIC ANCESTRY PROFILING - All corporates including prime providers have data bases which are linked. All information is stored indefinitely, even if you are dead, in case it is relevant to those living afterwards. Scrutiny levels take into account Genetic Ancestry Profiling (GAP), so you might die, but how you lived your life will affect your descendants, as your predecessors will affect yours. This is why you may not be allowed to procreate even if you can afford the licence. Information is made accessible to all corporates that purchase a Central Data Licence. The licences are not intended as a safeguard because the information can be used in any way that is seen fit. Licences are just a way to gain leverage and revenue. If you or your predecessors are considered irresponsible by one corporate, past or present, you are classed as irresponsible by them all, now and into the future. That's just the way it is.

Chapter 4

9. SURVEILLANCE - Presume you are being watched. Presume that your image is being sought and will be identified, collated, and your actions monitored. 'The enemy's weakness is thinking they are strong.' It's a rule but not one of Turin's. They trust what they see and think they have control, no Qs. Like names, we can change appearance and because there is mist and drizzle, the visibility on the street is poor, which is a help. High surveillance cams can read through mist and rain but buildings get in the way if you know how to use them. We use and remember 'dodges', where we can travel without our movement being recorded. Images are processed by data handling machinery that can recognise characteristics. We can swap or change appearances to imitate someone else. Walk differently and it fools the data handlers. Surveillance is not for our protection but for our control. It is

a reminder that someone else has the power to watch us and we better watch out. That's just the way it is.

10. POLICING - In a policing rationalisation plan it was decided only designated areas could be policed. Policing used to be the responsibility of several corps when it was first sold off by the state. As one corp became more successful, usually through bribery and intimidation, it bought out the others. So eventually there was only one corp doing the job on behalf of the state which paid for it. Because they could, that corp demanded a premium to police troublesome districts, where it was more costly and it was difficult to get a good return for their shareholders. Shareholders had their own policing and security arrangements protecting their gated communities and estates, so weren't affected. A district could pay for policing, of course, you could always pay, or you could apply for a private policing licence and organise your own, or contract in one. The corp's preference was to police affluent districts where crime was very low, so poorer districts got policed less and less until they had to find, and fund, policing for themselves. Between the various policing organisations, conflict began to grow, along with a lack of co-operation. Some began to behave like private militias and during the 'Bloody Spring', battles were taking place every few days.

The PM was recalled because the situation threatened the 'peace of the state'. The 'peace of the state' is very important if you have it, it is used as a reason to do anything and to do nothing. It's not a reason we can use, it is only used against us, the people that is.

The PM decided that all groups should be abolished, and only policing approved by him would be allowed. So as to simplify things and to reduce 'red tape' policing became the sole responsibility of the state's major supplier, which happened to be '4U', which was also the PM's principal sponsor. That's what you pay for.

Districts make arrangements with '4U' as to how much policing they can afford. It is illegal for a district not to be policed but in 48 (and several others) we cannot afford even the basic package and are still in negotiations. Legislation states we cannot be penalised as long as negotiations are 'on-going', so District 48 is exempt from penalty. District 48 is also exempt from any policing. That's just the way it is.

Chapter 5

11. DEREGULATED ZONES - Because we are registered as living in a deregulated district the chance of being employed is almost zero. Even if you wish to travel outside into districts that are not deregulated where the employment is higher, you won't be employed because of the district you are registered in. The corps call this the 'The Bad Apple' principle. Employing a 'Bad Apple' will contaminate all the good apples who work without complaint or protest. Those who have work, live in fear of losing it, and all the other benefits, drugs, etc.

There are agencies that specialise in finding people work, even in a deregulated district. They are 'Proud to Help', is what they say. They are mostly crooks and can only get you a job by supplying you with a false identity which is not traceable to them, but it is to you, and they deduct extra for the privilege. You have to take whatever work the agency gives you and jobs vary from unblocking public sewers, cleaning out chemical tanks, disposing of hazardous substances, etc., all the jobs nobody else wants to do because it's either dirty or dangerous. Probably both. The state pays agencies and rewards them for every worker that gets a job and a lot more if they have to retrain you. Most workers are registered as having been retrained, but no-one ever is. You are encouraged to 'kick back' some of what you earn to get a better class of job. Women, young girls, and some boys pay in kind, others deal or steal, to afford the bribes. If you try to leave, or make a fuss, they report you for having suspicious documentation, which they have supplied but can always prove they didn't. Possession of a false ID means Rehab. That's just the way it is.

12. URBIA DISTRICT 48 D - I live in Urbia District 48 which was deregulated some time ago. An Urbia District which meets targets and satisfies criteria is a district that behaves and is deemed 'responsible' and is regulated. This encourages investment and corporates, and over half of the

people who live in those districts have jobs. Failing to meet the targets and criteria for three years in succession means that the district will be deregulated. All investment is withdrawn and the corporates move out. There are practically no jobs, and responsible districts will not risk employing you. It is not possible to forget that we live in a deregulated district. All signs, street names, warnings and instructions in all districts are suffixed UD then whichever number Urban or Rural district it is. Our suffix, UD48 is followed by a large red D so we not only know where we are, we are reminded that we are deregulated, and we are all irresponsible. The PM says, 'This is a comfort because knowing what you are, will help you come to terms with your problems.' That is what he says.

We know what our problems are, and we have come to terms with them, and the fact that they won't change. Without investment and corps, people cannot get jobs, without jobs they do not have hope. Without hope, the people do not care what happens to them, or others. Why should they care about the state when it has turned its back on them? Corporates control everything, ministers, the state, everything. All corporates left UD48 (D) when we were deregulated. We even had to compensate them for having to leave through a poll tax.

A deregulated district is at the bottom of the pile. The people that cannot leave are made desperate and have to rely on each other which can draw them together more than in regulated districts. For the LEOs, a posting to a deregulated district is usually a punishment. They are at the bottom of their pile. The best jobs, perks and pay are in The City, followed by highest regulated districts. Those here have mostly been demoted because of insubordination, bribery, extreme violence, (violence itself by any licenced authority is not a crime) or they are just crap at their job. There are some that prefer deregulated areas because they enjoy the freedom they have to do anything. They regularly rape both sexes, carry out acts of violence, burn, loot, take bribes, run prostitutes, and carry out 'disposal' for both the living and the recently dead. All this for agreed sum about which, later, you will be blackmailed. The LEOs and the snatchers have corporate links and you are worth much more dead than alive.

The PM says, 'Districts get the policing they deserve,' and he says, 'We will help these districts to make the tough decisions needed to become useful members of our valued society and gain the respect and the co-operation of other districts, because we love them and they are part of our family.' That is what the PM says.

There were 67 districts in the London Urbia, but there are now only 52. Fifteen districts that had been deregulated, were colonised by a responsible neighbour. This was the 'Adoption Strategy' for returning failing districts to prosperity and happiness. They were called 'Prodigal Sons' by the PM who knew what that meant, and it was hailed as a 'great success'. The responsible district, with state help, plundered the failing district of all worth. The property and infrastructure were taken over, and the people forced into virtual slavery. They worked for a minimum alongside others whose reward was quadruple and had privileges but they were no longer irresponsible and could vote,

'Voting is the right of all free people', says the PM when he welcomes them, 'back to the fold.' Because he knows what that means.

Voting in our one party state means nothing but it is seen as legitimising the administration to do to us what they want. That's just the way it is.

Chapter 8

13. THE GREY AND THE MIST - At night in District 48 there is very little light. There are some licenced premises that can have a limited amount, a screen, some advertising, but these are few. There's no street lighting but the lighting from neighbouring districts that are not deregulated and are responsible, brightens the sky in places. That's reminds us

that we are deregulated and are all irresponsible. Then, of course, there is The City. The City is ablaze and lights up all the urbia districts around as its sparkling iridescence is reflected down from the grey blanket above. In deregulated districts people are in the shadow and lurk about in dark places. This is because of the people we are, or because of the people we have become. We live in a world that is grey and misty. Sometimes there is a breeze which lightens the sky but it is always grey and when it is not misty, it drizzles or rains. Occasionally the mist is laden with a black dust which leaves a dirty film on everything. You stay in, or wear a mask which collects the dust and makes black patches where you breathe. The PM says it is harmless and due to freak atmospheric conditions, so it must be. Sometimes there is an electrical storm which breaks the monotony but can be dangerous. We don't mind this as it plays havoc with the bots. They start jabbering, hold their heads as if in pain, and have involuntary spasms which makes them incapable of driving the pods. So when a storm is expected there are no pods about, unless they are caught out, in which case watch out for falling pods. In a deregulated district like 48 the light is unpredictable. Day can be darker than the night, and night, lighter than day, which makes it difficult to tell whether it's time to get up or time to carry on sleeping. That's just the way it is.

14. ABOUT GROUPS - It is difficult for ordinary people who do not work for a corp to survive without the help of groups. In a deregulated district, or dereg, it is impossible. All groups have to be registered with the Department of Social Activities, otherwise they are illegal. To register you have to buy an annual licence and agree to regular inspections, both of which are expensive. In a regulated district where there are people in work, groups can be afforded but they are not needed. In a dereg where there are only a few people in work, groups are needed but cannot be afforded. Only groups that are considered a

benefit to the state are permitted. Anything which attempts to replace services which a corp can supply, whether it does or not, is forbidden. In a dereg all groups are considered actually a threat, or a cover. The most severe penalties are reserved for anti-social, anti-state, and anti-corp groups, which include all forms of protest and dissent.

Groups are not allowed to deal with finance, rewards, exchange of goods or profit. In theory they do not exist in District 48, but it is where people get their support, safety and their protection against the state. If you don't have a family, and many don't, it's a surrogate. A group's security is essential if it and the people are to survive. So there are ways to find out if you can be trusted and this is called 'being put to the test.' Being put to the test is a good thing because it means that there is nothing else preventing you from joining the group other than demonstrating that you are trustworthy. If you are not put to the test, the group and those in it, cannot be trusted. That's just the way it is.

Chapter 10

15. ENTRANCE TO THE CITY - To go into The City you have to arrange for an advance pass. All sorts of checks are made on you, so there's no point in applying if there are any risks. By this I mean you will get permission and think everything is okay, then when you are at the get through, you will be detained, etcetera, and the etcetera means Rehab. If you are responsible and get permission, you are given a day for your visit. On the day you go to one of the many get throughs where you are fitted with a wrist cuff which glows green as you enter. A cuff is green for the first 22 hours then it changes to yellow, then red. At 24 hours exactly it flashes red and begins to heat up until it burns through your wrist. Only the get throughs have the equipment to remove cuffs, so nobody is late unless they want to lose a hand. Chemicals released in the cuff generate enough heat to melt the cuff as well, so the cuff is

ruined as well as burning through your wrist. The pain must be unbearable but it doesn't stop them billing you for the melted cuff. That's just the way it is.

Chapter 12

16. ABOUT RATS - Adult rats are about the size of small dogs so they leave traces. The ingenuity of people is amazing, so much creativity and original thought. You can see it in the variety of traps that people make, decorate and even exhibit. The State encourages it only because it is a nuisance to the corps. There's no money to be made out of offering people pest control. Only specifically targeted traps are permitted. The state doesn't allow anything which could be used for other purposes like guns, bows, catapults, etc. Rats generally avoid us. You may glimpse a monster at night but rarely during the day. Signs of their burrows are common and people have good sport catching them with nets, caging them and feeding them until they have enough flesh on them to slaughter. The meat is like chicken but tougher unless it's fed with a special diet whilst in captivity. Some monsters have gone on to become unofficial pets after being kept for some time. Sometimes they're used to guard the house and squeal frantically if any one approaches. They can be trained to attack, and there's some who breed them for fighting, though I've never seen a rat fight. They can make fearsome guards if allowed to roam, deterring even andys until they're shot. Goodnight, Vienna! That's just the way it is.

17. MEDIA DEVICES - We don't use phones, or palmers, and only screens that are safe. This is why. When all media competed with each other for viewers they were funded by corps and agencies who had agendas and

needed to know how many viewers were watching, listening, using. Viewstat was a benign corp that gathered statistics by tracking viewer's usage across all platforms. Every technology had ways to record and send usage information to Viewstat who also carried out customer surveys and opinion polls. This was okay until Viewstat was taken over by a surveillance conglomerate called CUpal because they realised the surveillance potential and could extend monitoring to everything that was watched, loaded, and communicated by any device, anywhere, in real time. CUpal convinced the state that there was a considerable risk to security and consequently the 'Peace of the State', and that a number of terrorist attacks were imminent. The state issued permissions for them to monitor all wave comms for sensitive words and phrases, and investigate users. The attacks never happened, they never were going to happen. CUpal claimed it was their surveillance which prevented 'carnage on the streets', and preserved the 'Peace of the State'. CUpal's shares doubled. The permissions remain in force.

 CUpal were the first to develop 'clever' technology, which not only monitors all wave comms in real time, but also incorporates deceit detection, emotional profiling, risk potential, and motivation. CUpal continually raises levels of alarm and demands further state investment and permissions to combat the threats that only they are able to perceive. Now anyone deemed by CUpal to be putting the 'Peace of the State' at risk, is routinely detained and interrogated. This includes anyone critical of CUpal.

 The popularity of non-wave comms, like old phones increased because the technology to tap them no longer existed. Soon though, the old network apparently failed and it was said by the Department of Communications (now part of Internal Security, wholly run by CUpal), not to be financially viable to repair and was scrapped. We knew it was dismantled to prevent its use.

 Clever technology or CT, reads between the lines so that it can detect a lie, emotional instability, and subversion, anything which can be interpreted as a threat. A threat is anything which CUpal says it is. They state, 'The words you use is what you say, the way you use them is what you mean.' CUpal sponsors several ministers in the Department of Internal Security and therefore has preferred status. Their PR department invited them and the media to the release of WIT, when they had achieved liberty to do anything to anybody, where anybody means those who cannot defend themselves. WIT comprises 'Total Surveillance', 'Interpretation' and 'Administration', and was greeted with much appreciation from the government and the fiscal corps. Some corps were uneasy, they thought is was too much power for one organisation, but only because they felt threatened. WIT stands for, 'Whatever It Takes'. You have to be very uninteresting or very stupid to use a device that can be monitored by an organisation that is bent on your control and harm, and it prepared to do, 'whatever it takes'. Freethinking on comms is a one way ticket to Rehab. That's just the way it is.

18. SOME HISTORY - This is what we talked about and what was said when I asked them how it all happened, because I have read stories and seen videos about when it was different. Some time ago, there was a financial collapse around the world. The governments blamed the people for taking too much, and the people blamed the governments for giving too much, and not controlling things. The corps blamed nobody and just made money. The people in desperation got the government they deserved who claimed to have a solution. The solution was that the people should pay for the mistakes that the corps had made whether the people could afford to or not. The less power you had, the more you had to pay. The government gave everything they could to the corps, so they could make money and prosper and in return they changed things so they could stay in power and finish the job. They needed the corps and they thought the corps needed them. Together they limited those who could vote, to those who were responsible. Criminals

were not allowed to vote, then immigrants, then the unemployed, then any others that they suspected as irresponsible and not their friends. It became the one party state which the government said was better for the people because of continuity and it was cost effective. The links between the state and the corps were strengthened so that ministers could be sponsored by corps and represent them because the people were already represented by the corps that they worked for. The corps then had bought the government and the state, the ministers, the workers, and the power of life and death. Anyone not bought just had to be controlled and the corps could do that too. That's just the way it was. That's just the way it is.

Chapter 14

19. ABOUT THE CORPS - The relationship between the corps and the people was always subject to the strain that the angels put on the execs. Carl, my uncle and I had little in common but he said to me once, 'No man can serve two masters'. I now know what he meant. The angels demand high rewards for their investment into a corp. The source of the reward is ultimately the people. The reward has to be maximised to ensure adequate profits. Profits have to improve year on year so that there is growth. The percentage profit has to increase too, so that the business is seen to be improving and becoming more efficient. If the percentage profit remains the same the corp is seen to be stagnating. Competition was seen as good and that the people would benefit from what was called, 'Margaret Forces', which are supposed to force prices down. In reality, corps in the same market are able to see what prices the market, which means the people, can bear. So prices are driven up and up as one corp sees what another can charge. If the product is not popular, demand falls and competition is consolidated into a niche monopoly. The product becomes very expensive for the small amount of

people who wish to buy it. If the product is essential, demand is high and corps fight over the guaranteed rewards. Ministers will be 'bought' with offers of executive positions, entertainment, and 'perks', in exchange for state preference and influence. Some corps will be hindered through legislation then absorbed by others, competitors will be sabotaged, until one corp becomes the preferred supplier and has a monopoly. The state says this is efficient and cost effective. Efficient means that the corp has no competitors to worry about. This reduces advertising and marketing costs and minimises the need for research, improvement and innovation, unless it is to make further savings or promote expansion. The corp can charge the maximum the 'market' will bear, reduce PR, customer services and complaint procedures. The only thing that threatens a corp is another one. Challenging a preferred supplier, which has a monopoly is impossible without an advantage. An advantage can be achieved by A, Better in-house research, innovation, or development, or B, Stealing it from the corp, or C. Sabotage. The second is the preferred option, along with the third. To steal or sabotage another corps data, a corp will do whatever it has to do. No Q's. That's just the way it is.

Chapter 15

20. PRIVILEGES, ALLOWANCES AND PERMISSIONS - Corps look after their own and dispense privileges, allowances and permissions. These benefits are awarded to good workers who are toeing the line. Merits also accrue with service. Service can mean just attendance and punctuality and efficiency, but also pointing out wrong doers and reporting anticorp as well as antistate attitude. Merits can bring rewards and promotion for the individual and relatives and known associates. Being reported for anticorp or antistate attitude will mean at least demotion and some loss of benefits for the individual but also for relatives

and known associates. Corps are self-regulating so they decide the rules, managers are the jury, and execs issue sentence. A minor punishment may be the removal of merits, privileges, allowances or permissions for a period of time, a severe one would result in the state turning its back on the offender. This will mean the individual has to move to a deregulated district because they are irresponsible. Relatives and known associates can avoid severe punishment as long as they have helped the prosecution and they too turn their backs on the offender. Those who are suspected of bad behaviour can also be punished. These are known as pre-bad apples, not yet bad apples, but the effect is the same. The corp's decision is final and there is no appeal. Some choose to leave Urbia and live in the Rural where they will never be heard of again. That's just the way it is.

Chapter 18

21. PEST CONTROL AND MUTANTS - All vermin, particularly rats, carry any number of diseases lethal to humans. Over time and as a result of dozens of extermination programmes, they have become immune to all but the most advanced and most expensive poisons. Consequently these poisons are not available to the general public. Genetic exterminants created some bizarre forms, always after being hailed as the solution. The subsequent generations of rodents that survived, mutated and developed coping mechanisms that resulted in them changing shape, colour and behaviour. One of the most successful was a rat that took to nesting in trees and changed its colour to a rusty red. The animal was able to hide its normally aggressive behaviour behind a chirpy, cute exterior that had the addition of a bushy tail and 'cheeky' wisps of hair extending from its ears. So successful was its disguise that people began feeding them in parks and gardens. Another mutation resulted in a sub species

glowing in the dark as a result of an experiment to make them easier for the wardens to shoot at night. This habit was picked up by anyone who could throw a spear, fire an arrow, or use a catapult. Shooting 'Glowers' eventually accounted for nearly twenty percent of all domestic accidents. Rising insurance claims eventually meant that legislation was passed making it illegal to shoot them. There's now a reward for them. They are farmed for their luminous coats, which like their ex-owners, glow in the dark. As an experiment, genetic attempts to control rodents, proved invaluable to anthropologists. Scientists recorded the various forms and sub-forms that the rodents took. Then with careful studies, followed their development as some died out, others did well, and some better, as they adapted to take advantage of their environment, like the rust coloured park rat, or simply overcame their problems. On some ministerial estates where pets are permitted, the rats grew to such a size that they began to chase the dogs and develop a taste for cat meat. In the towns they often shrunk in size allowing them the kind of access that only mice had enjoyed. Some, where there was a plentiful supply of fish that had themselves mutated to overcome the local chemical pollution, grew webbed feet. Not to be confused with the sort found recently in urbia. They could swim fast enough to catch fish, and were able to stay submerged for prolonged periods. New varieties of rodent are being discovered all the time but their major threat still lies in the diseases which they carry. That's just the way it is.

22. PERSONAL POSSESSIONS - Possessions have to carry with them proof of ownership. If you cannot prove you own something with the appropriate paperwork, backed up with recorded purchase information, purchaser identity confirmation, times, dates etc, then you have no proof of ownership. If you have no proof of ownership, it is not yours. If you are caught in possession of goods of any description or value that are not yours, they are deemed to have be stolen. Being in possession of stolen goods is a serious

crime which can (and therefore will) result in a custodial sentence (optional), and the confiscation (certain), of all other possessions whether or not proof of ownership can be supplied. This is to compensate the state for the expense that the criminal has incurred. Possessions so obtained by officers of the state may be disposed of as they see fit for whatever remuneration may be forthcoming. Information concerning the disposal and remuneration resulting from such activities, requires security clearance which is unlikely to be granted (which means it won't be). You do not have a right to anything without proof, and often not even then. That's just the way it is.

23. TELEPATHY - I have told you about rats. What I didn't tell you was about some experiments they were used for. New born baby rats were dropped into boiling water at recorded intervals. The mother rat, some distance away in a sealed container, was plugged in and her brain patterns monitored. Her reactions corresponded directly with the precise moment her offspring hit the bubbling water. It was the first laboratory indication of the existence of 'Telepathy'. If rats can do it, we can, and do it all the time, but we just don't know we do, and we have no control over it. There's something now, like anticipation. It's people sensing there's something brewing. Somewhere, something's happening and a part of you is tuning in to find out if it's going to include you, whether it's good or bad and whether you should stay, or run like hell. What the corps have been up to, they only know, but it would be something that was in their interests and not ours. That's just the way it is.

Chapter 19

24. DISTRICT POLICING - The policing of a district that is Regulated and is deemed to be responsible, is very different to 48 for instance. Where I am registered you are guilty until proven innocent, which never happens, your guilt

is a given. Harsh regimes, including curfews and other inconveniences, are encouraged by the state and by the corps that supply security and policing. It is in the interests of the state to hold up deregulated districts as an example of what happens if you do not behave responsibly, as the state sees it. It is in the interests of the corps, like 4U, and CUpal, to make out deregulated districts to be as big a threat to the 'peace of the state' as possible so that more money is poured into keeping the peace everywhere. No policing corp wants to see their efforts succeed in case the threat is perceived to be less and funding is withdrawn. An example of a self-fulfilling philosophy in a deregulated district is regarding the carrying of weapons, especially pistols. It is LEO policy that pursuing an arrest is a life risk because of the possibility that the target might be carrying a weapon. It is generally accepted that if a person is wanted by the police then that person is guilty and is prepared to do anything to resist arrest. The excuse for shooting the target, in effect a summary execution, is to ask them for their identity, in case they have the wrong person. As the person goes to get their ID, they are shot. All that the officer has to prove is that they thought that the target demonstrated a malicious intention. The request for ID has only ever been heard by other LEOs. The target's behaviour is seen as justifying the action and confirming their guilt, so no further investigation is deemed necessary. The judges, who are employed by the same security corps, say that actions speak louder than words, so who said what and when is irrelevant, and, the action of the suspect is paramount, and it is their action that warrants the consequences. There are a few investigations that have taken place into such an events, on every occasion it was because the victim's close relative was a high ranking exec. The large compensation paid also included an apology for mistaking the identity of the victim.

In such circumstances even totally innocent people, knowing what is likely to happen, will defend themselves with whatever and however they can. When they do, it adds to the demand for more extreme policing methods which will result in more extreme forms of resistance. More innocent people are presumed guilty and get killed. Goodnight Vienna. That's just the way it is.

25. TOUCHYFEELIES AND SHOPPING - In prosperous districts people like to 'go into town' to do their shopping. It may not be a town and they may not have to go into it. They will go from outlet to outlet and be sold things by assistants, mostly things that they don't need, called impulse buys. It's a social event rather than a necessity as everything can be bought from home and delivered there without stepping out. It is also a way to impress the people they are with. It is a good thing to say, 'I'll have both', or 'I'll have one of each.' It demonstrates you can afford not to have to choose if you are undecided. It demonstrates you have more money than sense. When people 'go into town' they also visit the Touchyfeelies where they try things on, smell fragrances, all the things you can't yet do in the comfort of your own home, unless you can afford a rep. Then they can order them immediately to be delivered later or go home and think about it. They will then 'eat out' and 'do the rounds' which means going from bar to bar trying foods and drinks. The centres are most busy at night, but business builds up from midday and peaks about midnight. The bars are then centres for entertainment which cover every sort from music to theatre, film, sex, and anything that makes money. There are streets, even areas, that are dedicated to certain types of activity and will attract a particular type of business. There are always streets and areas dedicated to casinos, sex, and sport, where the gamers go. There are also genres, cults, and cultures. Whatever interest you have, however weird or unusual, provided you are prepared to pay, there will be a street or area dedicated to it somewhere. One minute you can be in a foodie street, the next you are in Mardi Gras, or on a pacific island. It's disorientating, even if you are not taking anything. All town centres are the same because they have

little to sell but entertainment. The bigger the town, the bigger the rides. That's just the way it is.

Chapter 22

26. BIRDERS AND OTHER ASSOCIATIONS -There is an association which goes way back whose members are called Birders and their interest is birds. They have a proud history having tried to preserve birds for centuries and to encourage interest in them, all sorts of birds, large and small, some you can eat and some you can't. The corps discourage all forms of infestation. rats, cats, dogs, and birds have been prohibited for some time. The keeping of any pet is prohibited unless you have the appropriate paperwork, and for most common people it is not appropriate for them to have it. It is appropriate for execs, however. It is to protect us, the people, that these measures are taken. Exterminating all forms of life able to carry infestation, contagion or infection, is carried out for us by the state to keep us healthy because the state loves us. This is what the PM says and is therefore true. Unless you have a large estate with staff and adequate boundaries, the keeping of pets is an activity which endangers life.

Birders secretly organise trips to see them, at the sea coast for instance or areas where birds can live and breed safely without contaminating people who have not the equipment or personnel to protect themselves. Some execs have vast caged areas where thousands of birds, and other animals, are kept for their own amusement. The amusement of the execs that is, not the birds or the animals. The caged areas are under tight security because it is suspected that the Birders have a militant wing that might try to break in and release the birds. There is at least a consistency in the execs attitude to birds and their fellow humans. However no one is likely to break in and let us go free.

Some time ago a bird was sited in Urbia District 42 and word got out and dozens of birders flocked to see it.

The LEOs took exception because more than the regulation amount of people were congregating in less than the regulation amount of space. At first they tried to catch the bird, which was called a 'Sparrow', so it could be given to an exec, but all the execs said they had similar ones, so the LEOs killed the bird. This angered the birders, it started a riot and seven birders were killed and four LEOs. Several more birders were imprisoned and were known as the 'Caged Birders'.

Minority interests do not conform because they are not enjoyed by the majority. The PM say that, 'it stands to reason that minority interests have no place in a democracy, where the majority hold sway.' And so it does.

The birder's association, along with many other associations, have all been declared illegal and have ceased to exist, at least in public, but evidence of their existence is common if you know where to look. In the case of the Birders, a motif or a logo with a stylised bird or wings, a name, certain colours, even a sound, can all signify the owner's affiliation. A strange or unusual emblem, of which there are hundreds, can indicate an association of one kind or another. It has become a pastime in itself, guessing which prohibited group is represented. Collectors exchange photographs and maintain albums of secret associations. They too may soon be banned but so far they have not chosen their emblem. All of these illegal activities can result in detention, and examination. The examination will find that you are not normal, if only by the mere fact you are having to undergo examination. Not being normal is more than the first step on the way to Rehab. That's just the way it is.

TURIN'S RULES

Trust no one.
Do not share personal details.
Listen to your gut feelings.
Make no assumptions.

Don't attract attention, especially by avoiding it.
Blend in with your environment.
Work with the terrain.
Vary your behaviour within your cover.

Prepared for things to fail when you least want them to.
Plans are designed to be aborted at any time.
Prepare opportunities but use them sparingly.
Make full use of the right opportunity.
Keep your options open.
Have at least two ways out.

Once is an accident, twice is coincidence,
   three is the enemy.
Allow the enemy to underestimate you.
The enemy has the potential to control everything.
Make your actions your choosing, not your enemy's.
Fight one battle at a time.

(The Moscow rules were referred to in the spy novels
   concerning the character, George Smiley of MI5,

written by John le Carre. These are a version.)

GLOSSARY

ALLOWANCES
Permissions, credits and favours automatically bestowed in conjunction with position or work benefits.

ANDROBOT
Abbreviated android/robot. A commercially developed desensitised Human Law Enforcement Officer subject to exterior control. The description references humans sourced out of REHAB, subjected to robotic control. Controllers maintain command by an array of implants that control nerve and muscle response as well as overriding human instincts, decisions and emotions. Implants also simulate physical pain as well as psychological patterns and can be used to terminate the officer if necessary. Androbots are usually selected from extreme criminal categories within REHAB for their psychotic tendencies usually having a history of crimes involving extreme harm, premeditated and serial killing. These types have been proven to be the most biddable, most enthusiastic, and ideally suited for adaptation. They are also the cheapest to recruit. Due to their expendable nature, they are used in situations where violence is likely thus avoiding any expensive damage, in the case of BOTS or in the case of humans, injury or death. The androbot programme attracts a state subsidy. An Androbot is often referred to as an 'Andy'.

AUTOWAY
High speed route for permitted grounded vehicles only. Used by the executive class and permitted corporates.

BEGEBOTS

[Bee Gee Bots] Body guard robots - corporate. [BG Bots] Promoted as having high defence and protection skills. In reality are ineffectual and considered just as a status symbol and perk by execs.

BIODENT

Biological identity profile [BIP] contained in ID cards and other aids to confirm the carrier's identity. Is cross referenced with instant DNA, cornea recognition, finger printing, etc. All records are owned by Columbus. If you do not have a record you do not exist. You are your record.

BOT

General term applied to non-human devices, particularly those that appear in humanoid form. Mechanically robust but control mechanisms unpredictable. Synthetic bots require extensive programming and continual updating, they are subject to viruses and other interference. Bots using human brain segments are becoming more common though the interface is still not without problems. Human brain segments attract state subsidy. The ultimate goal is a total organic robot, the organobot. Several corps are carrying out trials in this area.

BOTSPEAK

A high pitched, simulated voice process used by most bot manufacturers. It is not easily understood and is irritating to the human ear. Bots do not need it to inter-communicate. Its purpose is to provide a physical back-up to other waveform methods of communication, and to carry out conversations in front of humans as a form of intimidation, manipulation or torment.

BOUNCE

Receive info after pointing a reader or other device at a person or object which stimulates a response from implants, ID cards, etc.

CARTRIDGE

Removable ancillary computer drive containing portafiles. Computers do not carry any data, only the operating systems and drives for ancillary equipment. Data cartridges are user secure and possess user input, physical and biological identification interfaces.

CORP/CORPS

Abbreviation for Corporate/Corporates. Most 'corps' are large autonomous commercial businesses, who sponsor one or more ministers. Corps are invested in by 'Angels' who demand higher profits and returns, year on year. Without their continued support, share price falls and makes the corp subject to absorption and take over.

DATA MINER

Term used to describe 'hackers' who seek only information by accessing secure data storage facilities. Their intention is to leave no trace and their 'trespass' [q.v.] to remain undetected.

DODGES

A dodge [dodges pl.] is a route which can be taken without being under surveillance.

DRAW

Cigarette probably herbal and often containing drugs in a mild form if used regularly. They can be scented, spiced or contain ingredients considered beneficial to physical or mental health.

ENTITLEMENTS

Associated with work and position

FATE

Friends Against The Establishment. An acronym coined by Ash and adopted by the group.

EXECS

Abbreviation of 'Executive'. A broad class of corporate employee above worker including managers and directors. Responsibilities include decision making, control, and corporate policy. Execs attract large remuneration packages, entitlements and privileges.

FREETHINK

To express thoughts and views without fear of consequence. Whereas freethinking itself is not actually illegal, it can be used as a reason to investigate further, and to detain until evidence of more serious crimes is found, which always is.

FREEMEDS

Semi mobile volunteer medical teams that occupy vacant facilities for the care of people mainly in deregulated districts. Considered anti-state and therefore able to move rapidly to avoid discovery.

FREQUENCY FILTER

Protective shield which allows the operator to select which frequencies are permitted to enter. Can be personal, vehicle or local and assists in detection. Used to protect official comms from overspeak or third party interhearance.

HACKER

Computer expert/enthusiast who is able to bypass security measures enabling them to carry out a variety of activities within a system. A hacker will often leave evidence as proof of trespass. Subdivision - Hackanista - Anarchist motivated hacker - sole intention to create mayhem within a system[See also DATA MINER]

ID
Identity, usually in the form of a plasticised card which the owner must have on their person at all times. Failure to do this can be a reason for detainment and in extreme cases, termination. IDs can be 'read' from a distance. IDs possess biodata and other details such as physical and personal data, etc., cross referenced with central records held at Columbus.

INTERHEARANCE
Electronic eavesdropping. Rather than general surveillance to which all devices are subject, INTERHEARANCE is targeted. Usually the practice of corp competitors, or agents, seeking specific information not otherwise available. This can be to discredit, frame, or blackmail individuals, or to acquire industrial data, policies, etc.

INTER-FEAR-ANCE
A method of instilling paranoia by randomly giving the impression that communications are being intercepted and analysed. Clicks, hums, and echoes during transmissions give this impression although actual eavesdropping or 'bugging' may not present.

LAUNCHER
Hand held device longer and heavier than a pistol used for projecting a variety of 'grenades' which might be explosive, traceable stain, lethal or debilitating gases, etc.

LEO
Law Enforcement Officer. Officers intended to support or enforce legislation enacted by the state or corps. There are no LEOs employed directly by the state. The responsibility for policing and security is handled by the 'corps'.

MECHANICALS
A term used to describe purely robotic 'bots' that do not have segments.

METAMAGNETIC PULSE
All the electrical energy within a system is diverted to initiate a very brief metamagnetic pulse within its own system creating a field strong enough to destroy its memory/data storage. Millions of components containing varying amounts of energy in operation are given release time codes depending on their accumulation rate and storage capabilities. When triggered simultaneously, the result is a pulse of enough magnitude to initiate a metamagnetic environment within the system for a period of between 1.6 and 1.8 nano seconds. This is proven to be enough to sufficiently degrade data storage devices within a predictable radius. 'Built in' MMP transmitters can obliterate local data with an irretrievability factor of one hundred. Drives are essentially wiped and need to be formatted prior to accepting new data, software, etc.

OVERSPEAK
(References all unwanted noise) Interference usually caused by crowded frequencies or mismanaged interhearance, tapping, etc.

PEEPS
Short for 'people' and particularly those wearing hoods who 'peep' out from them.

PERMISSIONS
Allowances specific to particular events or practices, usually applied for.

PISTOL
Any hand held device capable of projecting a charge with the intention of stunning [amber indicator] or killing [red

indicator] a target. Stun setting will immobilise both bots and humans, bots do not recover without re-programming. Compare 'Launcher'

PODS

A lightweight airborne vehicle able to hover, rise and fly usually piloted by two bots. They are considered too unsafe for humans. Like the bots who fly them, they are subject to environmental corrosion and degradation. They suffer malfunctions caused by electrical storms, static and other sources of interference. They hang on gantries where they recharge and where their bot pilots wait for instructions. They are notoriously unsteady and dangerous to anyone or anything beneath.

POLICE [LEO]

Retrained civilians working as law enforcement officers.

PORTAFILES

Computer data in a super compressed format usually carried on a data cartridge. Computers do not carry any data, only the operating systems and drives for ancillary equipment however they can retain 'shadows' q.v.

PRIVILEGES

Anything bestowed upon the individual by the state or corp in the form of allowances, permissions, etc.

READER

Hand held device for 'reading' a chip implant, ID card, etc. All persons must have on them at all times their ID so it can be 'read' by officers and those who are permitted to do so.

REHAB

Facility for corrective training and punishment. Theoretically inmates are allocated sentences during which they undergo corrective training after which they are released into community care programmes. In practice inmates are released, if at all, when they have been retrained for specific state or corporate sponsored duties. These are likely to be androbots, wardens, and other menial state operatives particularly in the state and corporate cleansing departments. Most inmates are detained indefinitely as cheap labour on the Rehab farms and industries.

RIGHTS

What people feel they should be allowed to do, have, or make use of by the nature of them being, and stemming from natural justice.

SEGMENT

Harvested brain parts used to enhance and control bot functions. Segments are primarily functional and do not have intelligence but can self-correct anomalies and some malfunctions. Interface technology currently limits the scope of brain segment and limits their usefulness.[See also 'Bot']

SENTRY BOTS

A surveillance Robot usually operating a Sentry pod.

SHADOWS

When used in connection with computers - compressed copies of file data which are stored to enable fast retrieval. These files are not normally accessible independently [without owner's portafiles] but have been known to be accessed by expert data miners or hackers.

SP

Sentry Pods - containing one or two BOTS. Pods are unreliable airborne vehicles susceptible to corrosion. Used on surveillance duties stationed on gantries and other elevated structures. Used by bots for menial policing duties include investigating misdemeanours, crowd and traffic control, etc. often first on the scene. See PODS and BOTS.

TEJAM

The End Justifies All Means'. First initiated by the CUpal surveillance corporation. No longer in use, now taken as normal practice. Pronounced Teh-jamm

TRESPASS

In computer speak - to enter prohibited areas within a system without permission, whether or not the system is HACKED [q.v.], for instance by using a stolen pass code, duplicate bioprint, etc.

WARDENS

Ground based uniformed officers originally responsible for traffic and vehicle policing. Close proximity to the public enables them to report anti state behaviour, and to carry out undercover work for agencies, spying, eavesdropping , etc. Original function mostly obsolete particularly where traffic has been reduced by deregulation etc.

NOTES

Printed in Poland
by Amazon Fulfillment
Poland Sp. z o.o., Wrocław